B.J. Daniels is a *New York Times* and *USA TODAY* bestselling author. She wrote her first book after a career as an award-winning newspaper journalist and author of thirty-seven published short stories. She lives in Montana with her husband, Parker, and three springer spaniels. When not writing, she quilts, boats and plays tennis. Contact her at bjdaniels.com, on Facebook or on Twitter, @bjdanielsauthor

Cindi Myers is the author of more than fifty novels. When she's not crafting new romance plots, she enjoys skiing, gardening, cooking, crafting and daydreaming. A lover of small-town life, she lives with her husband and two spoiled dogs in the Colorado mountains.

Also by B.J. Daniels

Also by Cindi Myers

Discover more at millsandboon.co.uk

DOUBLE ACTION DEPUTY

B.J. DANIELS

RUNNING OUT OF TIME

CINDI MYERS

MILLS & BOON

First Published in Great Britain 2020
by Mills & Boon, an imprint of HarperCollins*Publishers*
1 London Bridge Street, London, SE1 9GF

Double Action Deputy © 2020 B.J. Daniels
Running Out of Time © 2020 Harlequin Books S.A.

Special thanks and acknowledgement are given to Cindi Myers for her contribution to the *Tactical Crime Division* series.

ISBN: 978-0-263-28037-1

0720

MIX
Paper from
responsible sources
FSC C007454

This book is produced from independently certified FSC™ paper to ensure responsible forest management.

For more information visit: www.harpercollins.co.uk/green

Printed and bound in Spain
by CPI, Barcelona

DOUBLE ACTION DEPUTY

B.J. DANIELS

This book is for Kay Hould for all her loving support and encouragement. She is definitely not the gray-haired historical society woman in my Whitehorse, Montana series. But that is how we first met because of it.

Chapter One

Ghostlike, the woman stumbled out of the dark night and into the glare of his headlights. The tattered bed-sheet wrapped around her fluttered in the breeze along with the duct tape that dangled from her wrists and one ankle.

He saw her look up as if she hadn't heard his pickup bearing down on her until the last moment. The night breeze lifted wisps of her dark hair from an ashen face as she turned her vacant gaze on him an instant before he slammed on his brakes.

The air filled with the smell and squeal of tires burning on the dark pavement as the pickup came to a shuddering halt. He sat for a moment, gripping the wheel and staring in horror into the glow of his headlights and seeing…nothing. Nothing but the empty street ahead just blocks from his apartment.

He threw the truck into Park and jumped out, convinced, even though he hadn't felt or heard a thud, that he'd hit her and that he'd find her lying bleeding on the pavement. How could he have missed her?

If there'd been a woman at all.

In those few seconds, leaving the driver's side door gaping open, the engine running, he was terrified of what he would find—and even more terrified of what he wouldn't.

Could he have just imagined the woman in his headlights? It wouldn't be the first time he'd had a waking nightmare since he'd come home to recuperate. He felt the cold breeze in his face even though it was June in Montana. The temperature at night dropped this time of year, the mountains still snowcapped. He shivered as he rounded the front of the truck and stopped dead.

His heart dropped to his boots.

The pavement was empty.

His pulse thundered in his ears.

I am losing my mind. I hallucinated the woman.

For months, he'd assured himself he was fine. Except for the nightmares that plagued him, something he'd done his best to keep from his family since returning to Cardwell Ranch.

Doubt sent a stab of alarm through him that made him weak with worry. He leaned against the front of the pickup. Why would he imagine such an image? What was wrong with him? He'd *seen* her. He'd seen every detail.

He really *was* losing his mind.

As he glanced around the empty street, he suddenly felt frighteningly all alone as if he was the last person left alive on the earth. This late at night, the new businesses were dark in this neighborhood, some still under construction. The ones that were opened closed early, making the area a ghost town at night. It was one reason he'd taken the apartment over one of the new shops. He'd told his folks that he moved off the ranch for the peace and quiet. He didn't want them knowing that his nightmares hadn't stopped. They were getting worse.

A groan from the darkness made him jump. His

heart pounded in his throat as he turned to stare into the blackness beyond the edge of the street. The sound definitely hadn't been his imagination. The night was so dark he couldn't see anything after the pavement ended. The sidewalks hadn't been poured yet, some of the streets not yet paved. He heard another sound that appeared to be coming from down the narrow alley between two buildings under construction.

He quickly stepped back to the driver's side of his pickup and grabbed his flashlight. Walking through the glow of his headlights, he headed into the darkness beyond the street. The narrow beam of light skittered to the edge of the pavement and froze on a spot of blood.

Deeper into the dirt alley, the beam came to rest on the woman as she tried to crawl away. She clawed at the ground, clearly exhausted, clearly terrified, before collapsing halfway down the alley.

She wasn't an apparition. And she was alive! He rushed to her. Her forehead was bleeding from a small cut, and her hands and knees were scraped from crawling across the rough pavement and then the dirt to escape. In the flashlight's glow, he saw that her face was bruised from injuries she'd suffered before tonight. From what he could tell, his pickup hadn't hit her.

But there was no doubt that she was terrified. Her eyes widened in horror at the sight of him. A high-pitched keening sound filled the air and she kicked at him and stumbled to her feet. He could see that she was exhausted because she hadn't taken more than few steps when she dropped to her knees and tried to crawl away again.

She was shivering uncontrollably in the tattered sheet wrapped around her. He caught up to her, took off his jacket and put it over her, fearing she was suffering from hypothermia. He could see that her wrists and ankles were chafed where she'd been bound with the duct tape. She was barefoot and naked except for the soiled white sheet she was wrapped in.

"It's all right," he said as he pulled out his cell phone to call for help. "You're all right now. I'm going to get help." She lay breathing hard, collapsed in the dirt. "Can you tell me who did this to you? Miss, can you hear me?" he asked, leaning closer to make sure she was still breathing. Her pale eyes flew open, startling him as much as the high-pitched scream that erupted from her.

As the 911 operator came on the line, he had to yell to be heard over the woman's shrieks. "This is Deputy Marshal Brick Savage," he said as he gave the address, asking for assistance and an ambulance ASAP.

Chapter Two

After very little sleep and an early call from his father the next morning, Brick dressed in his uniform and drove down to the law enforcement building. He was hoping that this would be the day that his father, Marshal Hud Savage, told him he would finally be on active duty. He couldn't wait to get his teeth into something, a real investigation. After finding that woman last night, he wanted more than anything to be the one to get her justice.

"Come in and close the door," his father said before motioning him into a chair across from his desk.

"Is this about the woman I encountered last night?" he asked as he removed his Stetson and dropped into a chair across from him. He'd stayed at the hospital until the doctor had sent him home. When he called this morning, he'd been told that the woman appeared to be in a catatonic state and was unresponsive.

"We have a name on your Jane Doe," his father said now. "Natalie Berkshire."

Brick frowned. The name sounded vaguely familiar. But that wasn't what surprised him. "Already? Her fingerprints?"

Hud nodded and slid a copy of the *Billings Gazette* toward him. He picked it up and saw the headline sprawled across the front page, *Alleged Infant Killer Released for Lack of Evidence*. The newspaper was two weeks old.

Brick felt a jolt rock him back in his chair. "She's *that* woman?" He couldn't help his shock. He thought of the terrified woman who'd crossed in front of his truck last night. Nothing like the woman he remembered seeing on television coming out of the law enforcement building in Billings after being released.

"I don't know what to say." Nor did he know what to think. The woman he'd found had definitely been victimized. He thought he'd saved her. He'd been hell-bent on getting her justice. With his Stetson balanced on his knee, he raked his fingers through his hair.

"I'm trying to make sense of this, as well," his father said. "Since her release, more evidence had come out in former cases. She's now wanted for questioning in more deaths of patients who'd been under her care from not just Montana. Apparently, the moment she was released, she disappeared. Billings PD checked her apartment. It appeared that she'd left in a hurry and hasn't been seen since."

"Until last night when she stumbled in front of my pickup," Brick said. "You think she's been held captive all this time?"

"Looks that way," Hud said. "We found her older model sedan parked behind the convenience store down on Highway 191. We're assuming she'd stopped for gas. The attendant who was on duty recognized her from a photo. She remembered seeing Natalie at the gas pumps and thinking she looked familiar but couldn't place her at the time. The attendant said a large motor home pulled in and she lost sight of her and didn't see her again."

"When was this?" Brick asked.

"Two weeks ago. Both the back seat and the trunk of her car were full of her belongings."

"So she was running away when she was abducted." Brick couldn't really blame her. "After all the bad publicity, I can see why she couldn't stay in Billings. But taking off like that makes her either look guilty—or scared."

"Or both. This case got a lot of national coverage for months. Unfortunately, her case was tried in the press and she was found guilty. When there wasn't sufficient evidence in the Billings case to prosecute, they had no choice but to let her go. My guess is that someone who didn't like the outcome took the law into his own hands."

Brick nodded. "It would be some coincidence if she was abducted and held by someone who had no idea who she was." He shook his head, remembering the terror he'd seen in her eyes. "What if she's innocent of these crimes?"

"It seems that all of her nursing care positions involved patients with severe health issues," Hud said. "It's no surprise that a lot of the old cases are being reopened now. All of her patients died before she moved on to her next nursing job."

"So foul play was never considered in most of the other deaths?" Brick said. "But it is now even though she was released. No wonder she ran."

His father nodded. "Several of the Billings homicide detectives are on their way. I get the impression they might have discovered more evidence against her. It's possible they plan to arrest her—or at the least, take her into custody for questioning."

Brick rubbed the back of his neck as he tried to imagine the woman he'd found last night as a cold-blooded killer. "And if they don't?"

"Unless one of the other investigations across the country wants her detained, then, when she's well, she'll be released from the hospital and free to go."

"To be on her own knowing there is someone out there who means her harm?" Brick couldn't help being shocked by that. "Someone abducted her, held her captive for apparently weeks and if not tortured her, definitely did a number on her." He couldn't help his warring emotions. The woman might be guilty as sin. Or not. Clearly, she wasn't safe. He'd seen how terrified she'd been last night. *Someone* had found her. He didn't doubt they would again.

"Once the press finds out who the woman is in our hospital, it will be a media circus," his father was saying. "I know you found her, but I'd prefer you stay out of this. However, I'm sure Billings homicide will want to talk to you. This will have to be handled delicately, to say the least."

"You don't think I can do *delicate*?"

The marshal smiled as he leaned back in his chair. "I think you're going to make a damned good deputy marshal, maybe even marshal, in time." In time. Time had suddenly become Brick's enemy. "You've gotten the training," his father continued, "and once you get the last medical release…"

Brick didn't need the reminder of what had happened to him. The fact that he'd almost died wasn't something he'd forgotten. He had the scars to remind him. Those and the nightmares. But he hadn't just been wounded in the mountains of Wyoming and almost died. He'd killed the man who shot him. He wasn't sure which haunted him the most.

He also didn't need another pep talk on being patient until he got a mental health physician to release him for active duty. Until then, he was sentenced to doing menial desk job work.

"I should get going." No matter what his father said, he had to see the woman again. He wasn't scheduled to work until later. He had plenty of time to stop by the hospital before his appointment with the shrink and his desk job shift. But as he started to get to his feet, his father waved him back down.

"Brick, if you're thinking of going by the hospital, you should know that she can't tell you what happened to her or who is responsible. She's in what the doctor called a catatonic or unresponsive state, something often associated with trauma."

"I know, I already called, but I have to see her." He couldn't forget that moment when she'd appeared in front of his headlights. It haunted him—just as the woman did. "I found her. I almost hit her with my pickup. I feel...connected to her."

Brick knew it was a lot more than that. He was going crazy sitting behind a desk, cooling his heels until the shrink said he was ready to get to work. It left him too much time to think.

Not that he would tell his father or the psychiatrist he was required to see later today, but finding that woman last night *had* brought back his ordeal in Wyoming. That was another reason he wanted—needed—to see this through.

MARSHAL HUD SAVAGE leaned forward to study his son. "How are the nightmares?"

Brick shook his head, not meeting his gaze. "No longer a problem."

He watched his son shift on his feet, anxious to get out the door. "Son, you know how happy I was when you wanted the deputy marshal job that was coming open."

"I can do the job, if that's what you're worried about."

"I believe you can, but not yet."

"I'm healed. Doc cleared me weeks ago."

"I'm not talking about your physical injuries. You need clearance from a mental health professional as well, and I heard you missed your last appointment."

Brick swore. "I'm fine. I had a conflict... Besides, is it really necessary after all this time?"

"It is." He was more convinced of that after seeing how personally involved Brick had become with the woman he'd found last night. Although Brick and Angus were identical twins, they were so different it amazed him. Brick had always been the carefree one, hardly ever serious, ready with a joke when he got in trouble. He was also the one who made his mother laugh the most and that meant a lot to Hud.

Dana was delighted to have her son come home six months ago to recuperate. Hud knew she hoped that he'd be staying once he was well. Brick had always taken wrangling jobs with his brother. That was how he'd ended up down in Wyoming. She'd thought maybe she could convince him, like she had Angus, to stay on the ranch and work it with his twin.

So Dana wasn't as pleased that he wanted to follow his father's footsteps into law enforcement. She blamed Hud for making the profession look too glamorous, which had made him laugh. Her dream was that their children would embrace the ranch lifestyle and return to Cardwell Ranch to run it.

But Brick had always stubbornly gone his own way even as a child.

"It wasn't just your body that went through the trauma," Hud said now to his son. "You need to heal. I suspect one of the reasons you're so interested in this case is that finding that woman in the condition she was in brought back what happened to you in Wyoming."

Brick scoffed. "I was *shot*. I wasn't tied up in some basement and abused."

"I don't think you've dealt with how close you came to dying or the fact that you were forced to take another man's life. It's standard procedure, son. Don't miss today's appointment."

BRICK GLANCED AT the time as he drove to the hospital. There would be hell to pay if he missed his doctor appointment. But he had to at least see the woman again. He felt confused. Not that seeing her lying in the hospital bed would probably help with that confusion.

He still couldn't believe that the woman he'd rescued was the notorious nurse who'd worked as a nanny for a young couple in Billings. The couple's newborn son had multiple life-threatening medical problems. They'd opted to take their son home and be with him for as long as they had.

Natalie Berkshire had sworn that when she came into the nursery she found the baby blue. She'd tried to resuscitate him, screaming for the mother to call 911. But he was gone. An autopsy revealed that the baby had died from lack of oxygen. It wasn't until fibers from the baby's blanket were found in his lungs that Natalie was arrested, and then released when the case against her wasn't strong enough for a conviction.

Now as Brick took the stairs to her floor, he told

himself that he was invested in this case whether his father liked it or not. True, he was restless and ached to get back to actively working, but he also wanted to prove to his father that he could do this job.

He knew his dad had had his reservations. All Brick had known growing up on Cardwell Ranch in the Gallatin Canyon was wrangling horses and cattle. He'd never shown an interest in law enforcement before, so he couldn't blame him for being skeptical at first.

After coming home to recuperate after his ordeal in Wyoming, he'd realized it was time to settle down. When he'd heard about the deputy marshal position coming open, he'd jumped at it. He told himself that he wasn't grabbing up the first thing that came along, as his father feared. Somehow, it felt right.

At least he hoped so as he came out of the stairwell on Natalie Berkshire's floor. He was only a little winded by the hike up the stairs, but he was getting stronger every day. Physically, he was recovering nicely, his doctor had said. If it wasn't for the nightmares...

Walking down the hall, he was glad to see the deputy stationed outside her door. He'd been relieved last night when his father had assigned a deputy to guard her after the lab techs had taken what evidence they could gather—including her fingerprints, which ID'd her.

Brick had feared she was still in danger from whoever had held her captive. At the time, he hadn't known just how much danger this woman was in—or what she was running from.

After being raised in a house with his marshal father, he believed in innocence until proven guilty. If this woman was guilty, she deserved a trial. But even as Brick thought it, he wondered if she could get one anywhere in this country after all the publicity.

As he approached her room, he hoped his father hadn't told the guard not to let him in.

"Hey, Jason," Brick said as he approached the deputy sitting outside her door. The marshal department in Big Sky was small, so he knew most everyone by name even though he was new. And everyone knew him. Being the marshal's son was good and bad. He wouldn't get any special treatment—not from his father. If anything, Hud Savage would be tougher on him. But he couldn't have anyone thinking he was special because of his last name.

"That must have been something, finding her like you did," Jason said.

Brick nodded as he looked toward her closed door. "Any trouble?"

"Not a peep out of her."

"No one's come by looking for her?" Brick knew how news traveled in this small canyon town. He feared that whoever had held the woman captive would hear that she'd been taken to the hospital. The hospital was small and busy during the summer season. If someone were determined to get in, they would find a way.

"Nope."

Brick heard a sound inside the room and looked quizzically to the guard.

"Nurse." The deputy grinned. "Good-looking one too. I'd let her take my vitals."

Brick smiled, shaking his head at the man, and pushed open the door. As he did, the nurse beside the bed who'd been leaning over the patient now looked up in alarm.

He took in the scene in that split second as the door closed behind him. The guard was right. The nurse was a stunner, blonde with big blue eyes.

"I didn't mean to startle you," he said as he stepped deeper into the room, sensing that something was wrong.

"You didn't." The nurse began to nervously straighten the patient's sheet before she turned toward him to leave. He realized with a start that the patient had been saying something as he walked in. He'd seen Natalie's lips moving. Her eyes had been open, but were now closed. Had he only imagined that she'd spoken? How was that possible if the woman was catatonic and nonresponsive?

Also, when he'd come in and the nurse had been leaning over the patient, she'd clearly been intent on what Natalie was saying. She'd straightened so quickly as he'd come in. But before that, he'd seen something in the nurse's face...

The hair rose on the back of his neck.

"I heard the patient was catatonic. Any change?" he asked.

"No, I'm afraid not," the nurse said and started toward him on her way out of the room.

"Please don't let me stop you from what you were doing."

"I'm finished." She had to walk right past him to get out the door. As she approached, he looked at her more closely. If he was right and had heard Natalie speak, then the nurse had lied about there being no change. But why would she lie?

Looking past her, he noticed a pillow on the floor where she'd been standing. It had apparently fallen off the bed. It seemed strange that she hadn't taken the time to pick it up and put it back on the patient's bed. But that wasn't half as odd as her apparent need to get out of this room as quickly as possible.

His gaze shot to her uniform. No name tag.

Even as he raised his arm to stop her, he still couldn't be sure of what he'd thought he'd seen—and heard. But he couldn't shake the feeling that something was very wrong here. That he'd walked into something… "Hold up just a minute."

The moment he reached for the woman, she jerked back her arm and spun to face him. Before he could react, she jammed her forearm into his throat. As he gasped for air, she kicked him in the groin.

Even as the pain doubled him over, he grabbed for her, but she slipped through his fingers. He tried to call to the deputy stationed outside the door, but he had no breath, no air, no voice. All he could do for a few moments was watch her push out of the hospital room door.

Limping to the door after her, he found the deputy out in the hall talking to the doctor. The hallway was empty. He tried to speak but nothing came out as he bent over, hands on his knees, and sucked in painful breaths.

The woman in the nurse's uniform was long gone.

Chapter Three

The marshal sat back in his chair and listened as his son told him again what had happened at the hospital. Brick had called it in on his way to his psychiatrist's office. Hud had been glad to see that his son hadn't used what happened to him at the hospital as an excuse to get out of his doctor's appointment.

Hud had been having trouble believing this story. The doctor had insisted that Natalie Berkshire was still catatonic and questioned if the deputy had actually heard her speak. But the description of the nurse Brick had seen didn't match that of any woman who worked at the hospital. Five-foot-five, blonde, big blue eyes, a knockout.

"So you didn't actually witness her doing anything to the patient," Hud said now. He could see how upset his son was. Finding the woman last night had clearly shaken him and now this. As Brick had said, he felt responsible for her, something he admired in his son. But Brick couldn't take on this kind of responsibility every time he helped someone as a deputy marshal. He wondered again if this job was right for him. Or if his son was ready for any of this after what had happened to him.

"No, I didn't actually see her threaten the patient,

but there was a pillow on the floor and she was act-ing...suspicious. Also, I swear, I heard the patient say something to her. If you'd seen the nurse's reaction to whatever Natalie was saying..."

"But you didn't hear the actual words?" Hud asked.

Brick shook his head. "She was whispering and the nurse was leaning over her. My attention was on the nurse and her expression. I'm telling you, the nurse was looking down at the patient as if she wanted to kill her. But whatever Natalie was saying appeared to have... shocked her."

"You got all of this in an instant when you walked into the room?"

His son shrugged. "It was just a feeling I got when I walked in that something was wrong. So maybe I was paying more attention. I know what I saw *and* what I heard. If I hadn't gone in when I did, who knows what the woman would have done."

Hud groaned inwardly. If they arrested every per-son who acted suspicious there would be no room in the jails for the true criminals. He said as much to his son.

"She was pretending to be a nurse. Not to mention the fact that she attacked me, an officer of the law. Isn't that enough?"

"You said you grabbed her arm as she was starting to leave. Did you announce yourself as a deputy marshal?"

Brick sighed. "No, but I was wearing my uniform, and if you'd seen the way she was looking down at the patient..."

Hud admitted it sounded more than a little suspi-cious. "Okay, the hospital staff will be watching for her should she try to get into the woman's hospital room again. She could just be a reporter looking for a story. Brick?" He could see how rattled his son was. All the talk in the marshal's department would be about this case. "I want you to take the rest of the week off. I'll talk to your doctor at the beginning of next week. If he gives the all clear…"

His son chuckled and shook his head. "By then, Natalie Berkshire will either be arrested and hauled off for questioning, or gone."

"It's for the best."

BRICK SWORE UNDER his breath. "I know what I saw and what I heard. That woman posing as a nurse was in that room to kill Natalie. But whatever Natalie said to her made her hesitate. Then I walked in… What if this nurse is the one who's been holding Natalie captive?"

"I'll find out the truth," his father said. "I wasn't just suggesting that you take the rest of the week off. It's an order. Go camping. You're too involved in this case. Take advantage of this time off. Hike up into the mountains to a nice lake and camp for a few days. I brought you on too soon and I'm sorry about that."

He was about to argue when his father's phone rang. He wasn't leaving. Not until he convinced the marshal that he couldn't get rid of him that easily.

Then he saw his father's expression as he finished his phone conversation and hung up. What had happened? *Something.* "I'm meeting with a psychiatrist. I'm doing everything you asked. So stop trying to get rid of me. Tell me what's happened. You know I'll find out one way or another anyway. And if you don't want me trying to find out on my own—"

With a sigh, Hud said, "From your description and surveillance cameras at the hospital, they've been able to make a possible ID of the woman pretending to be a nurse. Her name is Maureen 'Mo' Mortensen."

"She must have some connection to the case," Brick said.

His father nodded. "The baby in Natalie Berkshire's care when he was allegedly murdered was her sister's."

Brick swore. "That would explain why she was standing over Natalie staring down at her as if she wanted to kill her."

"What makes this case more tragic is that Maureen Mortensen's sister committed suicide just days after Natalie was released."

"Tricia Colton," he said. "I remember seeing the husband on the news. He blamed Natalie for destroying his family. His wife had hung herself in the family garage. So Maureen Mortensen is her sister? Is she in the military or something? She attacked me as if she was trained in combat."

"She was a homicide detective in Billings."

"Was?"

"She's been temporarily suspended."

"Why?" Brick asked.

"I suspect it has something to do with her conflict of interest in the case. Apparently, she had been doing some investigating on her own before Natalie was released. She was ordered off the case, but refused to listen." He gave Brick a meaningful look.

Brick ignored it as he thought of what he'd seen at the hospital. "She wasn't the one who abducted and held Natalie Berkshire captive."

"What makes you say that?"

"Just a feeling I got that she hadn't seen Natalie for a while." He felt his father's gaze on him. "What?"

"Always trust your instincts."

He smiled. It was the most affirmation his father had given him since he'd signed on as a new deputy. "Thanks."

"But that doesn't mean that you aren't wrong."

He thought about it for a moment. "This woman, Mo, wants her dead—not tied up and tortured."

"You have no evidence that Mortensen was trying to kill the woman," his father pointed out. "Also, the doctor said that Natalie Berkshire couldn't have spoken to the woman. She's still nonresponsive."

Brick shook his head. "I swear I heard her. What's more, the fake nurse-slash-cop heard her."

"I've put a BOLO out on Mortensen to have her picked up for questioning."

"How about for assaulting a lawman?"

"It's enough to at least hold her for a while. I'm sure Billings PD will want to talk to her once they get here. But I do wonder how it was that she found out Natalie Berkshire was in the Big Sky hospital," his father said. "Unless she's been looking for her since her suspension—and Natalie's disappearance."

"Well, now she's found her," Brick said. "I wouldn't be surprised if she tries to get to her again."

Brick was still trying to process everything his father had told him. He'd been so sure that Natalie Berkshire had been the victim and that Maureen Mortensen was the criminal. Even if his father picked up the blonde cop, his instincts told him that she wouldn't be behind bars long. When she got out, he put his money on her going after Natalie Berkshire.

Maybe his father was right, and Maureen "Mo" Mortensen wouldn't have killed the woman lying in the hospital bed if he hadn't walked in. But from her expression, she'd darn sure wanted to.

"I bet the cop hasn't gone far," he said, wondering where she'd been staying. Probably at one of the local motels. He said as much to his father.

"I know she hurt your ego and you might want to go after her yourself because of it, but you're staying out of this. I shouldn't have put you on the schedule until we had the release from the mental health doctor. Don't argue with me about this. And come to dinner tonight. Your mother would love to see you."

Brick rose and started for the door.

"One more thing," his father said behind him. "I'm going to need your badge, star and weapon."

Brick turned to look at him as he slowly took off his star, pulled his badge and unsnapped his holster and laid all three on his father's desk.

"You can order me to take a few days off, but you can't make me go camping. Just as you can't order me to come to dinner." He turned and walked out, telling himself that becoming a deputy and working under his father was a huge mistake.

MAUREEN "MO" MORTENSEN wiped the steam off the cracked mirror and locked eyes with the woman in the glass, but only for an instant. She didn't like what she saw in her blue eyes. It scared her. Sometimes she didn't recognize herself and the woman she'd become.

Splashing cold water on her face, she thought of what had happened at the hospital. She'd come close to getting caught. But that wasn't all she'd come close to. If that deputy marshal hadn't walked in when he had…

She was still shaken, not just by Natalie's condition. She felt sick to her stomach at the memory. She'd looked down at the woman's bruised face. It had been true, what she'd heard. Natalie had been abducted and held prisoner. She'd thought she couldn't feel sympathy for what the woman must have gone through, but she'd been wrong. She didn't wish that sort of treatment on anyone, even a murderer.

For a long moment, she'd stood next to Natalie's bed, staring down at her. Had she been trying to see the monster behind the skin and bone? When the woman had opened her eyes, it had startled her. She'd read on her chart that she was catatonic. But looking into the Natalie's eyes, she'd seen fear, surprise and then something even more shocking—resignation.

Natalie had known why Mo had sneaked into the hospital dressed as a nurse. Would Mo have gone through with it? She might never know because the woman's words had stopped her cold.

Mo still felt stunned. By the time the words had registered, the deputy had come into the hospital room. She'd wanted to scream because she'd known that her chance to question Natalie had passed. All she could do was clear out of there with the hope that she could get another chance to question Natalie alone.

It surprised her that now she wanted the truth more than she wanted vengeance.

Unfortunately, she also now had the law looking for her. Getting free of the deputy had been instinctive. How could she reach Natalie again, though, with even more people looking for her? That cocky deputy marshal would be after her.

She pushed the thought away. She had more problems than some deputy marshal. Her body ached. Even when she could find the haven of sleep, she often woke bone-weary, more tired than she'd ever been. In her dreams, she'd been chasing Natalie Berkshire for months. In real life, it had only been since the woman had been released from custody—two weeks ago.

Today was the closest she'd come to finishing this. That moment of hesitation had cost her. She remembered looking into those pale hazel eyes. Natalie had known exactly who she was. The words she'd spoken weren't those of a mad woman. Nor of a liar. That was what had made them so shocking.

Natalie had known why Mo was there. She'd been ready to die. Because she knew she deserved it? Or because she knew she couldn't keep running?

In all the time she'd been a cop, Mo had never hesitated when everything was on the line, and yet earlier... If Natalie really had been catatonic... If she hadn't opened her eyes. If she hadn't spoken... The thought chilled her. Would she have gone through with what she'd planned?

Shaking her head at her disappointment in not being able to question Natalie after the woman had dropped that bombshell, she threw what little she'd brought into her suitcase. She didn't have time for introspection or recriminations. Or to try to analyze what the woman said or what it could mean.

She would get another chance to talk to Natalie—hopefully alone. She had to. Natalie had evaded almost everyone—except whoever had abducted her. Mo thought about the woman's bruises. Whoever had found her didn't want her dead. They wanted to punish her and had.

The thought pained her. It wasn't as if the woman was a stranger. She'd known Natalie. Or at least she thought she'd known her. Mo had spent time at that house with her sister and brother-in-law and their live-in nanny. She'd watched the woman not just with little Joey, but with her sister. Tricia had bonded with Natalie. The three women had become friends. Mo had liked the quiet, pleasant Natalie Berkshire. What's more, she'd seen that her sister had liked the woman as well and vice versa. Natalie, during those months, had become part of the family.

That thought hurt more than she wanted to admit. They'd all trusted the woman—even Mo. She *had* to talk to Natalie again. If there was even a chance that what she'd said might be true...

It surprised her how just a few words from the woman could change everything. When a friend at the police department had called her to say that something had come up on the scanner, she'd driven to Big Sky as fast as she could. The marshal in Big Sky said he'd called Billings PD to let them know that he had Natalie Berkshire after she'd apparently escaped after being abducted. Mo had arrived late last night. When she'd stopped on the edge of Big Sky to get something to eat at an all-night convenience store and deli, she'd overheard a table of nurses talking. One night shift nurse had described the woman who'd been brought in.

Mo had felt a chill ripple through her. From the description, she'd known it was true. The patient was Natalie, no matter how bizarre the circumstances that had landed her in the Big Sky hospital.

She'd listened to the night nurse talking in a low, confidential tone and caught enough to know that the woman brought in had been held captive for an unknown amount of time. She heard the words *duct tape, bruises, a torn and filthy sheet*.

She'd also heard that a deputy marshal by the name of Brick Savage had found her and gotten her to the hospital—the closest hospital in the area—where she had originally been listed as a Jane Doe. Until her prints had come back.

This morning, Mo had picked up scrubs and Crocs at the discount store. She'd walked into the hospital as if she knew what she was doing. The older woman at the information desk only smiled as she went by.

Upstairs, she'd found Natalie's room by looking for the deputy she'd heard had been parked outside it. All she'd had to do was give him a smile and walk right into the room.

One glance toward the bed and she'd known she was about to get her chance for justice. It was Natalie, and given the shape she was in, Mo knew that someone else had caught up to her first. She'd suspected for some time that she wasn't the only one looking for the woman.

She'd thought she'd known exactly what she would do when she found her. She owed it to her sister and to Thomas, her sister's still grieving husband, and to little Joey, their infant son. She'd kept what she was doing from Thomas. He'd been so devastated by the loss of his son and wife that he'd begged Mo to let it go.

"I can't take anymore," he'd cried when she'd argued that she had to find evidence to stop Natalie.

"But she'll kill again," she'd argued.

"For the love of God, Mo. I never want to hear that woman's name again. For months Tricia and I thought we'd get justice. When Natalie was released…" Tricia had killed herself. "I need to make peace with this. I hope you can, too."

She had known that she wouldn't find peace until Natalie was either dead or behind bars. She had been determined that Natalie would not destroy another family.

But then Natalie had opened her eyes and said

the only words that could have changed her mind—
even temporarily.

Mo moved to the motel room door, suitcase in hand.
She looked back to make sure she hadn't left anything
behind. She figured that it wouldn't take long, between
the deputy who'd gotten a good look at her and the surveillance cameras, before they knew her name. That
would definitely make finding her easier since she'd
used her real name when she'd checked into the motel.

She wouldn't make that mistake again, she thought.
Nor would it be a good idea to stay in any one place
too long. Not that she was planning on this taking any
longer than necessary. She would get back into the hospital. Security would be tighter. They would be watching for her.

Mo knew that the best thing she could do was wait
until Natalie was released, but she had no idea when
that would be. Also, she knew that Billings homicide
were on their way—because some old cases were now
being reopened and other departments were anxious to
talk to Natalie. If they didn't arrest her and Natalie was
released from the hospital, she would run like a scared
rabbit and be all that much harder to catch.

She picked up her purse on the table by the door,
swung the strap over her shoulder and, shifting the suitcase in her hand, reached with the other one to open the
door. She already had a plan simmering at the back of
her mind, a way to get into the hospital again.

She'd go to the store, get some supplies to change her
appearance. This time she'd go in not as a nurse, but as
a male workman instead. She would bluff her way in
and no matter what she had to do, she'd get into Natalie's room. She would get the truth out of the woman
and then…

Mo refused to think beyond that point. What she had in mind had never sat easy with her. But she felt she had no choice. She was convinced of what would happen if Natalie was as guilty as she believed and she didn't stop her.

With purse and suitcase in hand, she opened the door and stepped out of the motel room—right into a pair of deputies…and handcuffs.

Chapter Four

Angry and frustrated, Brick was even more determined to find out the truth about Natalie Berkshire. He knew he was taking one hell of a chance, but he drove through town to Highway 191 to the convenience store where Natalie Berkshire had allegedly been abducted. Inside, he bought an ice cream cone and asked the clerk if she'd been on duty that day when the woman had been abducted. She hadn't, but she told him everything the other clerk had told her.

Behind the wheel of his pickup again, he sat and ate his ice cream cone. The appointment with the psychiatrist had gone better than he'd hoped. He liked the man and thought his father was right. Talking about what had happened up on the mountain might get rid of the nightmares. He would gladly see the last of them. They were too vivid and bizarre, a jumble of confusing, frightening images that finally woke him in a cold sweat.

He knew he shouldn't have been surprised, but after talking about it and everything else that had happened in the past twenty-four hours, he felt drained. He had gotten hardly any sleep last night after Natalie Berkshire stumbled into his headlights. He'd been coming from the late shift. Finding her had added even more dark images to his sleep.

Now he couldn't help thinking about her or the blonde cop, Mo. Was Natalie a killer? Or was she innocent? Was Mo a vigilante cop with a need for vengeance? Or was she like a lot of people who feared Natalie had gotten away with murder and would kill again if not stopped?

Two women. One set on escape. The other on closure. But someone else, who was set on dispensing his own brand of justice, had already abducted Natalie Berkshire. Would they have eventually killed her if she hadn't escaped?

And what would the rogue cop do now if she wasn't found and stopped?

Brick knew the answers were out there and he desperately wanted to find them. He still swore that Natalie had spoken to the cop. Said something that had stopped her. Something in addition to continuing to swear she was innocent. The more he thought about it, he realized that the two had known each other before the murder. Natalie had been her sister's nanny. Who knows how close they might have been.

What a complicated, intriguing case. It did make him wonder who was innocent. It also made him want to help solve it more than he'd ever wanted anything.

He sat in his truck for a few minutes after eating his ice cream, trying to decide what to do—if anything. He was exhausted from everything that had happened, not just in the past twenty-four hours. As he shifted in the seat, he felt his harmonica in his pocket and pulled it out. He'd carried the musical instrument from the day his grandfather Angus had given it to him. It had taken him a lot longer than he'd hoped to learn how to play it. But he'd stayed with it until he'd finally mastered a few of his favorite tunes. As was his character, he wasn't one to give up.

That was why it hurt so much to realize that he hadn't played the harmonica since the events up on the mountain in Wyoming. Nor did he want to. He put it back in his pocket and had to swallow the lump in his throat. Maybe he wasn't as well as he thought he was. Not yet. But he would be.

He needed to solve this puzzle for his own sake. It seemed to him that at least two people were after Natalie Berkshire. One was a suspended cop. The other was the person who'd caught up to her, abducted her and abused her. The clerk at the convenience store had said that all the other clerk had seen was a large motor home driven by an elderly man.

Starting his pickup's engine, he realized a place to begin would be finding where Natalie had been held. He'd discovered her on his street, but he knew she could have come from anywhere. All he knew for certain was the first spot she'd appeared.

He drove to his neighborhood. The businesses were all open now, the streets busy since it was June in Montana and the beginning of tourist season. He circled the block, extending his circles further out with each lap.

If he were going to abduct someone he would need a safe place to keep the person. Somewhere away from other people. In a way this could be the perfect neighborhood—at least at night. But during the day, there were too many construction workers around as well as tourists and shop owners and workers. Also, most of the new structures didn't have basements, so where had Natalie been held?

Brick had just turned down another street when he saw that he was running out of town. The landscape around Big Sky was sagebrush before the terrain went up into towering pine-covered mountains. The Gallatin River cut through it, forming the deep, often dark canyon. A sign caught his eye. Campground.

He felt as if he'd been touched with a cattle prod. The clerk at the convenience store had seen a motor home pull in when she'd lost sight of Natalie. He'd at first assumed that the motor home had blocked her view of whoever had taken the woman. But what if whoever had taken the woman had been driving the motor home?

He pointed his truck down the road to the south, but he hadn't gone far when he heard the bleep of a siren. Glancing in his rearview mirror, he saw the quick flash of the light bar on the patrol SUV that was now behind him.

With a curse, he pulled over and got out to walk back to talk to his father.

"I know what you're doing," Hud said with a sigh.

Brick wasn't going to deny it. "I think I know where she was held. That motor home that pulled in. I think she was being held at the campground up the road."

His father shook his head in exasperation before saying, "Get in. I was just headed there. How did I know you'd be going my way?"

Brick grinned at him as he slid in. "You're psychic. I remember when Angus and I were boys. You were always one step ahead of us."

"And you were always the ringleader and the one that never did what you were told, let alone listened to any advice I gave you."

"Her feet were covered in dirt from walking through soil before she reached my neighborhood."

His father didn't respond, but he saw a small smile curve the man's lips as he drove and Brick buckled up.

The campground was just off Highway 191 in stands of pines that offered privacy for campers. It also allowed self-contained rigs to stay for several weeks for free because there were no outhouses or water. Just as there was no campground host. The isolated campsites were large enough to accommodate a motor home.

Even this time of day with the sun high in the sky, the canyon was cold and dark. Brick had been away from home for so long he'd forgotten just how tight the Gallatin Canyon was in places. Highway 191 was a narrow strip of pavement hemmed in on one side by the river and mountain cliffs on the other. It was often filled with deep shadows and stayed cool even in the summer because of a lack of sunshine. During the last widening of the highway, small pullouts had been added for slower vehicles to pull over to let others pass when there was room.

June weather was often unpredictable. It wasn't uncommon for it to snow and end up closing some roads. That was why July and August were the big travel months in this part of Montana. Because of that, the campground would have been relatively empty the past few weeks.

Only two rigs were still parked among the trees. One was a pickup and camper. The other an SUV pulling a small travel trailer.

The marshal pulled in, turned off the engine and said, "Stay here and try to remember that you're just along for the ride."

Brick watched his father unsnap the weapon on his hip as he climbed out and walked toward to the small trailer. If Marshal Hud Savage was anything, he was cautious, and with reason. They had no idea who had taken Natalie Berkshire prisoner or how many people might be in on it.

Over the patrol SUV radio came a call. Brick picked it up. "Deputy Brick Savage."

The dispatcher said, "Just wanted to let the marshal know that a couple of deputies just brought in Maureen Mortensen."

They'd found the blonde cop already? "I'll let him know." As he got off the radio, he saw his father standing at the trailer door. Sometimes he forgot how large a man Hud Savage was. He had always been broad-shouldered and strong as an ox. Even at almost retirement age, he was still a big man, still impressive in not just his size. He'd always been good at what he did as well, Brick thought with a flood of emotion. He wanted so badly to follow in this man's footsteps, but worried he could never fill his boots.

He watched as a rather rotund man answered the marshal's knock.

Popping open his door so he could hear, Brick listened to his father questioning the man before moving on to the next rig.

Brick couldn't hear as well this time, but he saw the man who answered the marshal's knock point to a space at the back of the campground. His father nodded, then headed in that direction.

Brick got out of the patrol SUV and followed him into a stand of dense pines. If the motor home had been parked here, it wouldn't have been visible from the highway. Nor was it near any other campsite. Even if Natalie had screamed bloody murder, she might not have been heard. But he doubted that whomever had taken her had allowed her to scream at all.

He stopped short when he saw what his father was

doing—snapping photographs with his phone of the tire tracks left in the soft earth. This was where the motor home had been. But had Natalie been inside it?

"A call just came in on the radio," he told the marshal. "A couple of deputies picked up Maureen Mortensen." He wasn't sure what response he was expecting, but his father only nodded.

Without a word, they walked back to the patrol SUV and climbed inside before his father said, "You need to learn how to take orders." Hud started the engine. "You always were the stubborn one."

Brick chuckled at that. "Just like my father and grandfather, I'm told."

"Well, at least your namesake grandfather." Brick had heard stories about his grandfather Brick Savage, the former marshal. If half of the stories were true, then his father and the former marshal had butted heads regularly.

"Any update on Natalie?" he asked him now.

"Still catatonic." His father sighed, picked up his radio and called in a description of the motor home that the man in the camper had given him. It sounded like one of those rental motor homes. Older driver. Only description was elderly and gray.

If Natalie had been held in the motor home, the driver could be miles from here by now—or parked at the hospital. His father obviously thought the same thing as he asked that a deputy watch for a motor home at the hospital parking lot and ordered that another deputy go to work calling motor home rentals in the area.

They drove in silence back to where Brick had left his pickup. As he started to climb out, his father said, "Deputy, you want this job? Take a week. I don't want to see you again unless it's at your mother's dining room table. And stay clear of Billings PD's case. Got that?"

"Got it."

As he closed the door, Brick heard a call come in over the radio that all law enforcement available were needed for a three-vehicle pileup in the canyon twenty miles south of Big Sky. His father sped off, leaving him standing next to his pickup.

Brick knew he should go camping. Go back into the mountains and not come out until his next doctor's appointment. But as he watched his father's patrol SUV disappear over the rise, he realized this was his chance to go to the hospital and see Natalie. Maybe she was catatonic. Maybe she wasn't. He knew that he'd heard her say something. There was only one way to prove it.

His father was closing in on the theory that she was abducted by a person driving a motor home. It wouldn't be long before the marshal made an arrest. Meanwhile, the Billings homicide detectives should be arriving at any time—if they hadn't already been to the hospital.

And down at the jail there was a blonde cop with a nasty kick locked up behind bars. He wondered what she'd have to say for herself. His groin still hurt, not to mention his bruised ego. He realized that there was nothing he would enjoy more than seeing her behind bars.

Chapter Five

Mo couldn't believe her luck. She'd been arrested on a charge she could wiggle out of the moment she went before a judge, and these backwoods lawmen had to know that. But how long would that take?

She could feel the clock ticking. Once Natalie was released from the hospital, she would be gone again, only this time, she wouldn't make the same mistakes. She could disappear down a rat hole and might not surface for months, even years. By then she would have had numerous jobs. Which meant numerous victims. Mo couldn't let that happen any more than she could let Natalie get away without having the chance to talk to her one more time.

As it stood now, there was no proof that she'd been at the hospital with any felonious intentions. All they had her on was pretending to be a nurse. Given her connection to Natalie Berkshire, the law could try to make something out of that. But ultimately, they wouldn't be able to hold her on any of it—except for her attack on the deputy marshal, Brick Savage—the man who'd found Natalie after her escape from whoever had abducted her.

Mo paced in her cell. She kept thinking about standing over the woman's bed, hearing the hoarse whisper, feeling the woman's words hit her like a hollow-point slug to her chest. She'd had her right where she wanted her. The truth had been within her reach.

Natalie would run the moment she was released from the hospital. But what was she running from? The law? Her own guilt? Fear? Or this thing she'd kept secret?

At the sound of the door into the cell area opening, she turned to see Deputy Marshal Brick Savage come in and head toward her. She groaned inwardly. Of course he would come to gloat.

When he stopped at her cell door, she warned herself to be cool even as she wanted to wipe that grin off his face. He was enjoying how the tables had turned a little too much. Earlier, she'd felt guilty for attacking him. Right now, not so much.

"Enjoying your stay here?" he asked, shoving back his Stetson to expose a pair of very blue eyes fringed in dark lashes.

"Not really." He was more handsome than she'd taken the time to notice at the hospital. Handsome, well-built and physically fit. And he was clearly looking for a fight. She could tell she'd banged up his ego more than his body.

"You go by Mo?" he asked.

She waited, fairly sure she already knew what had brought him here. She just wondered how long it would take him to get to the point.

Fortunately, it wasn't long. "Look, I know you were planning to kill her earlier in the hospital—just as I know she told you something," he said.

She wanted to say, "Prove it!" but thought better of it. Antagonizing a deputy, let alone the son of the marshal, was probably not in her best interests—even out here in the sticks. Maybe especially out here in the sticks.

"I'm sorry if there was a misunderstanding at the hospital," she said with cavity-inducing sweetness.

He laughed, a beguiling sound. "Oh, I understood you just fine. I saw the way you were looking at Natalie Berkshire. Like you wanted to kill her."

"Fortunately, that's not against the law."

"Attacking an officer of the law is."

She tried not to smile. "I didn't realize you were a lawman."

"The uniform probably threw you," he said sarcastically.

She shrugged. "I thought you were a lecherous security guard."

His blue eyes narrowed, but he smiled.

"You did grab me, and you didn't announce who you were. It was a innocent mistake."

"I doubt there is anything innocent about you," he said.

Mo chuckled at that, thinking how true that was. She was no longer the naive woman who'd believed in the law. That had changed everything about her. She was more daring in every aspect, she realized, as if she had nothing left to lose. In the past, she would have been more careful around a deputy who had her locked up behind bars. Heck, she would have been maybe even a little tongue-tied around a cowboy as handsome as this one. But right now she didn't feel shy or cowed in the least.

She met his Montana-sky-blue gaze, so much deeper and darker than her own. "You're new at this, aren't you? Green as springtime in the Rockies."

His brows furrowed. "Seasoned or not, I'm still a deputy—"

"On medical leave. I also heard that you're the one

who found her last night," Mo said. She didn't want to argue semantics. She didn't have time for it.

He eyed her sharply. "Sorry it wasn't you who found her?"

She was, but she wasn't about to admit it to him. "You haven't asked if I was the one who abducted her."

"I don't believe you are. Not your style."

Mo raised a brow and couldn't help but chuckle. "You think you know my style after one…confrontation? I must have made quite an impact on you."

To her surprise, he chuckled, as well. "You could say that. It's why I was anxious to see you—behind bars."

She liked that he could joke. She also liked that he was smart. He'd spotted her quickly for the fraud she was at the hospital. Too quickly. She was curious, though, why he was really here. Just to taunt her? Or did he want something, as she suspected? It was clear that he thought he knew her. That was almost laughable. He had no idea.

"What did she say to you?" he asked.

She felt his gaze on her, a welding torch of heat and intensity.

"She said something to you," he continued. "I heard her."

"I'm not sure what you thought you heard, but the patient, I'm told, is in a catatonic state, unable to speak." She was still dealing with Natalie's words. They'd been private, disarming, horrifying if true. She wasn't about to share them with anyone, especially this half deputy.

"What she said got one hell of a reaction from you," he said as if he hadn't heard her denial. "It stopped you from killing her."

She said nothing, surprised to be hearing the truth in his words. She had gone to the hospital to get an answer to one question and then, well, then, she planned to make sure Natalie never destroyed another family again.

"Sorry, but I don't believe you," the deputy said. "You were leaning over her. I saw her lips moving. I heard her whispering something to you. I want to know why her words made you change your mind."

She started to argue that he had no idea what was in her mind—and even if he did, he couldn't prove it, but he cut her off.

"You want out of this cell? Tell me the truth."

"The truth?" she mocked. "The truth is that Natalie Berkshire is guilty as sin."

"You can prove that?"

"It will get proved, but unfortunately, not before someone else dies because our judicial system takes so long."

"I'm still waiting to hear what she said to you," he said, cocking his head to study her with those intense blue eyes of his.

Mo pulled her gaze away first. She didn't want to tell this cocky cowboy deputy anything. She'd overheard the nurses talking about him last night at the deli. The cowboy had reputation with the women and yet women still seemed to be attracted to him, knowing that he might break their hearts. Good thing he wasn't her type.

"I'm guessing that what Natalie said had something to do with your sister." When she said nothing, he added, "Tricia, isn't that right?"

Her pulse pounded in her ears. Had he heard Natalie say Tricia's name? She groaned inwardly. Natalie Berkshire wasn't just a killer. She was a psychopath who manipulated people. Look how she'd deceived Tricia and her husband, Thomas, and especially Mo herself. Wasn't that the part that kept her up at night?

Trust didn't come easy for her and yet Natalie had gained her trust, and in a very short time. Natalie had walked into their family and become a part of it. Mo had felt as if she'd always known the woman—that was how comfortable she'd been in her presence. Mo didn't make friends easily, but she did make them for life.

When she'd first heard that homicide was being called in, that little Joey was believed to have been smothered, that Natalie was their number one suspect, she hadn't believed it. She'd seen Natalie with Joey. Seen how careful she was with him since his health was so precarious.

But there had been only one other person in that house that afternoon and it was Tricia. According to her sister, she'd been upstairs asleep and had only come down when she'd heard Natalie screaming. It was no wonder the woman had been arrested. Who else could have killed Joey?

That was why Mo had come here to end this nightmare. For weeks she'd rationalized what she had planned, no matter how crazy it seemed most days. Now, she looked the deputy in the eye and told the truth based on what she knew at this moment. "She'll kill again. Unless she's stopped."

"You just know that, right?" he asked, his gaze intent on her. "You have no idea if that is true or not or even if she is the killer." She didn't bother to answer. "Okay, let's say you're right. How exactly do you plan to stop her?"

"That is the question, isn't it?"

"It seems pretty simple. You're no longer a cop—"

"I'm only suspended," she said in her defense, but wondered how long before they found out what she was up to and fired her.

"My point is," he continued, "you have no authority to take her in, and I understand there are no charges pending against her at this point—only suspicions. So why do this? As a homicide detective you know what will happen if you kill her in cold blood."

"You and I wouldn't have been having this discussion only a few months ago. Since then, things have gotten…complicated."

"You're a vigilante cop upset with the system. Doesn't seem all that complicated. Why take it on yourself? I understand that since Natalie was released, other law enforcement departments are reviewing deaths where the woman might have been involved. If she's guilty, it will be just a matter of time before she's under arrest again and a jury will decide," he said.

Mo let out a snort. "What you say may be true, but there isn't time to prove you wrong." She flipped her hair back and met his gaze, narrowing those tropical-sea-blue eyes on him. "When Natalie gets out of that hospital she'll run. She'll be looking for her next job. Her next victim. Someone has to stop her."

"If she's guilty." He was studying her. She felt the burn of his gaze on her skin. "Admit it. You're having your doubts, especially after what she said to you. I saw your reaction. Tell me and I'll get out of here."

She snorted at that. "You're wrong. Nothing Natalie could ever say would convince me that she isn't a killer. So I guess you and I have nothing more to say to each other." She turned her back on the cowboy deputy.

"You change your mind, you let me know."

Brick studied the woman a few moments longer. She had her slim back to him now, her head held high, radiating self-confidence and righteousness. He remembered what the deputy outside Natalie's hospital room door had said about the blonde. At the hospital, he hadn't had the time to get a really good look at her. She was definitely attractive from her thick blond hair that fell over one sea-blue eye before dropping in an asymmetrical cut to her shoulders to her slim, clearly physically fit body. He hadn't known what to expect on actually meeting her, but it was clear to him that she was sharp. She didn't come across as some crackpot on a mission.

Yet while her original intention seemed perfectly clear to him, something had changed when Natalie Berkshire had spoken to her. That intrigued him. Mo hadn't made any bones about her belief that Natalie was guilty. What could the nanny have said to her that would keep her from doing something that she said she was still committed to finishing?

He thought of the pillow on the floor, convinced that his walking into the room wasn't what had stopped her. But he also couldn't imagine what Natalie could have said.

He'd seen the conviction still in Mo's eyes. She wouldn't stop until she found the woman and ended this—one way or another. And like Natalie, soon this woman, too, would be free to do just that.

And that was what had him worried as he left and drove toward the hospital. Mo Mortensen's certainty that Natalie would kill again had him rattled. He was even more anxious to see Natalie Berkshire after talking to the cop. He needed to decide for himself if she was a monster or a victim.

Also, he wanted know exactly what Natalie had said to her, because he no longer believed the woman was catatonic. He could even understand why she was fak-

ing it. She was running scared. It was why she'd bailed
out of Billings—only to get caught by someone he suspected had been seeking his own kind of justice. Natalie
had to know the person would come after her again—or
someone like him—not to mention the law now looking for her.

The woman had to know that her house of cards was
about to come crashing down on her at any moment—
whether she was guilty or not. Wasn't there still the
chance, though, that she wasn't?

As he walked down the hall toward Natalie's room,
he noticed the deputy leaning back in his chair outside
her door, legs outstretched. The deputy appeared to be
asleep. As he got closer, he saw that the man's hat was
pulled down low over his eyes. His heart began to race.
Things might be dull on the floor, but there was no way
a deputy would fall asleep on the job.

He rushed to him, touched his shoulder. The deputy
keeled over onto the floor. Brick felt his chest constrict
as the man's hat fell away and he saw the blood and the
large goose egg on the deputy's forehead. He quickly
checked the man's pulse in his neck—strong—before
rushing into Natalie Berkshire's room.

Just as he'd known, the bed was empty. He swore.
Hadn't he known she wasn't catatonic? Just as he'd
known that she'd spoken to Mo. He quickly looked
around. The bathroom door was closed. "Natalie?" He
stepped to the door and grabbed the knob. "Natalie?"
No answer.

He opened the door. Of course the room was empty.
Because Natalie Berkshire was gone.

He started to pull out his phone when he heard a
moan coming from somewhere in the room. The sound
froze his blood. He wasn't alone in here after all?

Brick spun around. The room was still empty. Another moan. He caught movement under the bed and rushed to push the bed aside. The nurse lay on the floor, gagged and bound with IV tubing. She was attired in nothing but panties and a hospital gown.

As he pulled off the gag and began to untie her, she said, "She jumped me. She took my uniform, my bra, my socks and shoes. She…" The nurse began to cry. "She threatened me. Said if I made a sound…"

"How long ago did she leave?" Brick asked as he freed her.

"Five minutes, maybe more."

At the sound of the deputy regaining consciousness out in the hall, Brick rushed out. "Take care of the nurse and call this in."

"The nurse?" The deputy touched the bump on his head gingerly. His eyes widened as if he realized at last what had happened. "The patient. Is she…?"

"Gone."

"I don't know what happened."

"Say that to my father," Brick called as he ran down the hall.

He told himself that the woman might not have gotten out of the building yet. She was wearing scrubs—just like every other nurse.

Brick took the stairs three at a time and burst out on the lower floor to race for the front door. After pushing out through it, he stopped to glance around the parking lot. He didn't see her.

At the growl of a motorcycle, he spun around and saw a woman in scrubs roar past. Her hair was a dark wave behind her as Natalie Berkshire sailed away.

Brick ran to his pickup and went after her. But he hadn't gone two blocks when he realized he'd lost her.

He called it in, but didn't hold out any hope that she would be caught. The dispatcher told him that a young man who'd been in the hospital parking lot was calling to say that a nurse had shoved him off his motorcycle and taken it.

Brick pulled over, slamming his fist down on the wheel. Natalie was in the wind. What were their chances that they could find her? At the moment, she wasn't wanted by the law for anything but questioning. Her life was in danger, though, and she had to know that. Without money or transportation other than a stolen motorcycle, where would she go? Her car had been impounded. And considering what was found in her car, she'd already been running scared before she was abducted. What would she do now?

His cell phone rang.

"I get only one call so don't make me waste it." He recognized the voice at once, a little sultry, definitely direct. "I just heard the news here at the jail," Mo said. "Natalie has taken off. I suspected she'd pull something like this. But I can help you find her if we hurry."

He scoffed. "Too bad you're behind bars."

"Listen," Mo said. "I *know* this woman. I knew she would run when she was released from jail. I knew she'd take off the way she has. You'll never find her without my help. You want the blood of her next victim on your hands? Give it some thought. Then get me out of here." She hung up.

Brick shook his head as he disconnected. He was on a forced medical leave and she was suspended. Neither of them had any authority to go after Natalie. Mo really thought he would spring her?

He knew she'd be out by morning, once she went before a judge. But at least for the moment she was locked up. Unfortunately, that didn't make Natalie safe. Who knew who all was after the woman?

He sat in his pickup for a moment, his mind a rabbit warren of thoughts. What if Mo was right? What if the real person in danger was Natalie's next client?

Starting the pickup, he drove to his apartment. On the way, he half expected to see Natalie in his neighborhood. He knew it wasn't logical. Just as he knew he would always be expecting to see her somewhere until she turned up again. If she ever did. He still hadn't decided if she was a victim or a possible serial killer.

Mo Mortensen thought she knew, but she was too personally involved. He couldn't trust her judgment any more than his own.

At his apartment, he walked in, closing the door behind him. He stood just inside looking around the studio apartment as if seeing it for the first time. Nothing about the space reflected him in any way. It was as if no one lived here. Clearly, it was a hiding place, not a home.

He sighed as he pulled off his Stetson and raked a hand through his hair. His father was right. He wasn't healed. Nor did he have any idea how to put himself back together again. He felt unsure of everything—except the steady beat of his heart. He was alive. He'd survived a bullet. Maybe he could survive the rest. Maybe. But not here in this colorless, empty apartment.

Brick walked over to the wardrobe, pulled it open and began to dump what he might need into a backpack. Swinging it over his shoulder, he took one last look around before he walked out.

Chapter Six

"Took you long enough," Mo said as she held on to the bars of her cell as if trying to bend them. "We've lost valuable time."

Brick shook his head. "You were that sure I was coming for you?" he asked as he held up the keys that would free her.

She smiled in answer, and if he hadn't realized that this woman might be trouble, he was beginning to. "Well?" she demanded. "Did you come to taunt me or get me out where we can find Natalie before it's too late?"

"I'm not unlocking your cell until you tell me what she said to you and why you reacted the way you did." He could see the internal battle going on inside her. For a moment, he thought she would simply move away from the bars, go sit on her bunk, tell him to go to hell. He wouldn't have been surprised.

Except for one thing. She was desperate to find Natalie. He had to know why. He no longer thought it was to harm her. But then again, he could be wrong about that, too. He could be letting another kind of monster free.

"Tell me why her words hit you so hard," he said, and when she didn't answer, he said, "Fine, then stay where you are. I'll find Natalie on my own."

"You won't," she snapped as he started to turn away. "I know how she thinks. You, on the other hand, are convinced that she is some innocent, helpless creature who needs you." She reminded him that Natalie had played him after he'd tried to help her.

"Okay," he conceded, keeping his back to her. "Maybe she wasn't as traumatized as she appeared."

"*You think?* You'd better hope we find her before whoever held her captive does. I'm betting he's also looking for her and will try to abduct her again. You need me."

He smiled to himself as he turned back to her. "And you need me. So…"

"She said Tricia didn't kill herself."

He felt the weight of words fall on him. *What the—?* "What does that mean?"

"Natalie was probably lying. Trying to save her own skin. But if there is a chance she was telling the truth…"

Brick shook his head. "That explains why you looked so shocked. You must have thought there was more than a chance she was telling the truth. But if so—"

"Then someone killed her."

"Why would someone kill your sister?"

"That's what I have to find out. So, are you going to help me or not?" Mo let go of the bars and met his gaze. "I'll tell you everything. Just get me out of here so I can find her—before someone else gets to her."

Her last words shook him more than he wanted to admit. Natalie had already been abducted and held captive. He didn't doubt that there were others who were determined to see that the woman paid for what they believed she'd done. Mo had been one of them, he knew. Had a few words from Natalie really changed that?

"*We* find her." He waited for her to agree. "We do

this together or you stay where you are. I posted your bond. I keep my investment safe by not letting you out of my sight."

"Fine." She motioned impatiently for him to unlock the cell.

He hoped he wasn't making a huge mistake as he inserted the key. "I already picked up your belongings."

"My car?"

"You won't be needing it. My truck's outside," he said as he turned the cell door key.

"My car would be more comfortable, not to mention, I'm an ace driver."

"I'm sure you are. That's why I can just see you leaving me high and dry."

"Have you always been so suspicious?" she asked as they headed out of the building.

"Apparently, since I spotted you for the fake you were quickly enough at the hospital."

She rolled her eyes as they walked together toward the parking lot. "I thought I made a pretty believable nurse." Her gaze locked with his for a moment. "Until I had to kick your butt."

He laughed. "Yes, there is that score to settle yet."

"Until next time."

"Only next time I'll see you coming."

She chuckled. "Just keep telling yourself that," she said over her shoulder as she continued down the sidewalk.

"Maureen?"

They were almost to the parking lot when she turned to see the man who'd called her name coming down the sidewalk toward her. She was as shocked to see her brother-in-law here as he sounded to see her.

"It *is* you," Thomas said as he reached her and Brick. "I saw you coming out of the jail…" His gaze sharpened. "What are you doing in Big Sky?"

"I could ask you the same thing," Mo said, taken off guard by seeing him here of all places. Since her sister's funeral, she'd been avoiding him and felt guilty about it. But Thomas reminded her of all Tricia's hopes and dreams now gone forever. He'd also made it clear that he wanted to put Natalie and the rest behind him, something she couldn't do. "What are you doing here?"

He raised an eyebrow. "I'm here on business. Life does go on, Maureen. But it seems you know that. You're back at work?" He shot a glance at the law enforcement building. He thought she was here also working—certainly not just being released from jail.

She didn't answer as she looked past him to the cute brunette with him. Her eyes narrowed.

Following her gaze, he turned and drew the young woman into the conversation. "This is Quinn Pierson. We work together." He sounded defensive.

Mo instantly regretted making him feel that way. Thomas had been through enough with the loss of his son and wife. Surely she didn't resent that he was here on business with a colleague, probably attending some seminar since she knew that many of them were held here at the resort each year. But she did resent that he'd gone on with his life when she couldn't.

"I'm sorry," she said, meaning it. She saw that he was staring at Brick with the same questioning look she'd given the brunette. "This is Brick Savage. A…friend."

Thomas seemed to turn the name over in his mouth as if trying to place it. Brick's name was unusual enough that she knew he was bound to eventually tie it to Natalie since the deputy's name had been in all the news as the man who'd rescued the distraught woman in the middle of the night. Once Thomas did figure out who Brick was, he'd know what she was up to. Unless he'd already heard about Natalie being in the hospital here before making her daring escape.

But now he merely lifted a brow at her before he stuck out his hand to shake Brick's. "I'm also a friend of Mo's," he said, making her feel worse, if that was possible. He'd made his position clear after the funeral, the last time they'd talked.

"I really don't care what happens to Natalie Berkshire," he'd said. "I never want to hear her name again."

"You don't want justice?" Mo had demanded.

"Justice? My son is dead, my wife is dead. Tracking down Natalie won't bring either of them back."

"But she'll kill again, she'll destroy other families, she'll—"

"I can't do anything about that."

"Well, I can," Mo had snapped. "And I will."

Thomas had begun to cry. "Please, for my sake, if not your own, let it go, Maureen. I can't bear anymore. I'm begging you. Let your sister and the rest of us find some peace."

Had he found that peace? She sure hadn't.

"We really should get going," Quinn said, dragging Mo back from the past. "We're already running late for the seminar." She gave Mo an apologetic shrug and held out a flyer. "I don't know if you're familiar with Palmer's seminars. They're enlightening."

Mo took the sheet of paper without looking at it.

"It was nice to meet you," Quinn said. She really was pretty. And young. The word *fresh* came to mind.

"You, too," Mo said automatically as she wished she hadn't run into them now of all times. As the two walked away, she saw Thomas turn to Quinn and say something. The brunette's soft laugh filtered back, making Mo uncomfortable. She thought about Tricia. Something had been wrong in that house. Natalie had tried to tell her, but Mo hadn't wanted to hear. Now she regretted it.

"You going to tell me what that was about?" Brick said once the two were out of earshot.

"That was my brother-in-law." She realized she hadn't introduced Thomas by his last name. "Thomas Colton. Tricia's husband."

Brick had to catch up to her since she'd turned and taken off, wanting to put that entire scene behind her. Sometimes she spoke before she thought. Change that to *often*. It got her into trouble. She wouldn't be suspended right now if she were capable of keeping her mouth shut.

"He knew Natalie well, I'm assuming?" Brick said as he caught up to her and motioned to where his pickup was parked. She nodded and slowed, no longer cringing, but glad to have put distance between her and Thomas and his…associate.

Once in his pickup, he reminded her that she hadn't finished her story.

She realized she was still holding the flyer the woman had given her. Wadding it up, she tossed it on the floor. "Drive and I'll tell you everything. Natalie already has a huge head start."

He hesitated, but only a moment before he started the truck. "We need to establish some ground rules," he said as he pulled away from the jail. "We do this together. You take off, you go back behind bars. You help me find her, but then she's going to be returned for questioning about her abduction and any other deaths under her employ. Is that understood?"

"Whatever you say."

"I'm out on a limb here. Don't saw it off, because I don't want to be hunting you next."

"We don't have time to argue," she said, dismissing his concerns. "Tell me how she got out of the hospital."

He told her about Natalie taking the nurse's clothing and leaving her gagged and bound half-naked under the bed before stealing a motorcycle and escaping. "She probably got the idea from you."

Mo seemed to ignore that. "She'll be looking for different clothing first. Which way did she go when she left the hospital?" He told her. "Then take that street."

"There are no stores that way."

"She has no money. She'll be looking for clothing she can steal."

BRICK WONDERED IF she was talking about what she would do under the same circumstances—or about Natalie. But he didn't argue. He drove through the residential area as Mo craned her neck down each side street they passed.

"So," he said. "Tell me."

She sighed. Clearly, it was a story she'd condensed, having lived with it for so long. "I stopped by Tricia's that day. She was sleeping so I didn't want to disturb her. She'd been struggling with everything—postpartum depression, the baby's health issues, who knows what else? Anyway, I decided to just look in on Joey. I was worried about him because of all his medical problems and even more worried for Tricia. She'd had trouble conceiving. It looked like she and Thomas weren't going to be able to have children, something Tricia had wanted desperately. Then, out of the blue, she'd gotten pregnant. I'd expected her to be over-the-moon happy, but she seemed anxious all the time. Then, when Joey was born with all the medical problems and the doctors said he probably wouldn't make a year..." Her voice trailed off for a moment.

"That day I sensed something being...off. Joey was fine. He was such a beautiful baby. If you didn't know about his health problems... As I started to leave, Natalie stopped me by the front door. She was trying to tell me something when Tricia came down the stairs. I could tell Natalie was upset. I knew she was worried about Tricia. I was, too."

Brick thought about this for a moment, seeing how upset Mo had become just retelling it. "Natalie never told you what she had to talk to you about?"

Mo shook her head. "We never spoke after that. Natalie was arrested, and evidence was coming out about her. Even if she told me what might have been going on in that house."

"What do you mean, about what was going on in that house?"

Mo looked away for a moment.

"I realize this is hard for you—"

"Thomas and Tricia were my family. I hate talking about personal details of their lives. I hate that because of what happened, their personal lives have become media fodder."

"They were having problems," he guessed. "I would imagine the stress..."

She nodded, some of her anger visibly evaporating. "I think it might have been more than the pregnancy and even Joey's health."

"You don't think Thomas and the nanny were—"

"Having an affair?" She shook her head adamantly. "But something was wrong. Tricia wouldn't talk about it and neither would Thomas—not that I tried very hard. I was so intent on proving Natalie guilty and getting justice that I wasn't there for my sister when she needed me the most."

"That's why you want to believe that she didn't kill herself," he said. "Could there have been another man?"

Mo hesitated a little too long. "She and Thomas had been together since college. They were the perfect couple." As if sensing his skepticism, she said, "He idolized her. He was so excited about the baby. He was a wonderful father."

Brick kept driving, wondering what he'd gotten himself into, when she cried, "Stop! Down there."

Backing up, he drove down the side street until she told him to stop again. By then she was out of the truck. He swore, threw the pickup into Park and went after her, thinking she was already breaking their deal.

Instead, she rushed over to an older house with a long three-wire clothesline behind it. The day's wash flapped noisily on the line except for the spaces where it appeared someone had removed items randomly.

A woman came out of the house brandishing a broom. "Don't even think about it. What is this, some kind of scavenger hunt?" she demanded. "You're not taking any more of my clothing."

Brick quickly introduced himself. "We're looking for the woman who stole the clothes off your line. Was she dressed like a nurse?"

The woman nodded. "I couldn't imagine why a nurse would be stealing my clothes."

"Can you tell me what she took?" Mo asked. "And describe the items?"

The woman lowered her broom and thought about it for a moment. "A pair of my black active pants, my favorite flowered shirt, a pair of jeans and my husband's hooded sweatshirt. It's navy. The flowered shirt is mostly red."

"Thank you. Did you see her leave? What she was driving? Which way did she go?"

The homeowner shook her head. "I saw her taking the clothes and ran outside but she disappeared around the side of the house. Wait. I did hear what sounded like a motorcycle engine. Does that help?"

Brick nodded. "It does, thanks. How long ago was that?"

"Thirty minutes ago, maybe longer."

"We'll do our best to get your clothes back for you," he said and turned toward the pickup.

They were back in the pickup when Mo said, "She'll ditch those clothes as soon as she gets some money. I hope that woman doesn't hold her breath about getting them back. She'll dump the motorcycle first—if she hasn't already. She'll be looking for a vehicle. One that won't be missed for a while."

Brick shot a look at Mo as he started the truck. "You make her sound like a hardened criminal. What if she's innocent and now has people chasing her who want to do more than hurt her? Maybe she's just trying to stay alive as best she can."

"That's exactly what she's trying to do. She's running for her life."

Brick's cell phone rang. He thought it would be his father. He'd already ignored three calls from him. Instead, it was the deputy from the hospital.

"I heard you're looking for the patient that got away," the deputy said. "I hope you find her. The marshal wants to have my head over this." He explained that while he was getting examined for the wound on his head, he heard that an attendant's purse had gone missing about the same time that Natalie took off. "She thinks the patient who escaped took it."

Brick told Mo.

"Ask how much money was in the purse," she said.

He did and hung up. "Just over a hundred and fifty dollars."

"So Natalie has some money. Now all she needs are wheels," Mo said. "If I were her, I'd be looking around bars, cafés, places where everyday people work and don't worry about their vehicles being stolen."

"Anyone ever mention that you think like a criminal?"

Mo smiled. "Thanks. There's a bar up ahead. Pull in."

As Brick did, his cell phone rang again. This time it was his father.

HUD STARTED TO leave another voice mail on his son's phone when, to his surprise, Brick answered. He'd come back to the office to find out that not only had Natalie Berkshire taken off before the Billings homicide detectives arrived, but his son had broken suspended homicide detective Mo Mortensen out of jail.

"What the hell are you doing?" he demanded the moment his son answered the call. "You spring a woman you don't know from Adam. A woman who is in our jail because she attacked you? Are you trying to end your career before it even starts?"

"I'm on leave, remember."

The marshal swore. "What is that noise in the background?"

"I'm standing outside a bar waiting for Mo."

Hud wanted to scream. "Mo, is it now? Brick…" He

let out an angry breath. "I hope the bar doesn't have a back door. Why did you bust her out of jail?"

"She's going to help me find Natalie."

"Are you crazy? You said this woman wants to kill Natalie."

"Maybe she wants to, but she won't. And even if she still did, I won't let her."

He swore under his breath. "Do I have to tell you again that Natalie Berkshire isn't wanted for anything other than questioning at this point? Or that you don't have the authority to go after her, let alone arrest her, even if there was a warrant out for her? Worse, Natalie might not be the woman you have to fear. You could be with the real criminal right now. How do you know she wasn't involved with Natalie Berkshire's abduction?"

"She wasn't. Which means that she isn't the only one on this woman's trail. We need to find her first. I was right about what happened at the hospital. Natalie did say something to her, just as I thought I heard. She said that Tricia, Mo's sister, didn't kill herself."

"What?"

"Apparently there was more going on with that family than anyone—other than Natalie, who lived in the house—knew. If Tricia didn't kill herself, if Natalie didn't take that baby's life, then who did?"

"Brick," his father snapped. "What are you going to do with her if you find Natalie? Maybe more to the point, what is Mo going to do? Even if you find Natalie, you can't restrain her in any way or you'll find yourself behind bars for kidnapping. Clearly the woman was well enough to escape the hospital. Letting the cop who's chasing her out of jail is just asking for trouble."

"Maybe Natalie lied about all of it. But what if she didn't?" Hud heard the music in the background change.

Then his son said, "I think I see the motorcycle she stole. I have to go."

He swore as Brick disconnected. He tried to call him back, but the phone went straight to voice mail. He debated putting a BOLO out on both his son and Mo. Natalie already had one out on her. Along with being wanted for questioning, she was wanted for tying up a nurse and stealing a motorcycle and a purse at the hospital. Also at this point, Hud had no doubt that the woman would be safer behind bars.

The marshal looked up to find a deputy standing in his doorway. "Anything more on the motor home?"

"So far I haven't found any that have been returned in the past twenty-four hours that might have been damaged as if someone had broken out of it," the deputy said, clearly unhappy with this assignment.

Hud waved him away, saying, "Keep trying." As the deputy left, he wondered if it wasn't a waste of manpower. Maybe whoever had rented the motor home would be smart enough not to turn it in anywhere nearby. That was if he was right and there'd been damage to it when Natalie had escaped.

HERBERT LEE REINER could feel sweat running down the middle of his back. He watched the two men in the glassed-in vacation rental vehicle office. Whatever they were discussing, it looked serious.

He thought about walking out. The car rental agency was just down the road. He could get there quickly enough. But it would mean leaving behind his reimbursement check. His deposit was a hefty amount—even after the repair bill had come out of it.

He glanced toward the motor home sitting where he'd parked it, then back at the men in the RV rental office. It was hot in here. He wanted to push back the sleeves on his shirt, but then the scratches would show. The clerk, a young man named Gil, had been suspicious enough when he'd seen the damage done to the door in the motor home's one bedroom. Now Gil was in the office talking to his older boss.

His throat dry as dust, Herb spotted the drinking fountain off to the side and walked over nonchalantly, hoping he looked like a man without a care in the world. He turned it on and took a long drink even though the water wasn't quite cold enough. It also had a funny taste. But at his age, everything was either tasteless or strange. Aging taste buds, though, were the least of his worries right now.

Glancing at his watch, he felt time running out. As he took another drink and straightened, Gil came out of the glass enclosure holding his paperwork. Herb felt his heart drop as he saw that the man's boss was now on the phone.

"I really need to get going," Herb said. "Is there a problem?"

"No," the clerk said a little too quickly. "I'm just new at this and I want to do it right."

He tried not to be impatient as he watched the clerk tap at his computer keys. Had Gil been told to stall Herb until the police arrived?

Glancing toward the outside door, he considered making a run for it. But his legs felt as if they'd turned to blocks of wood. He hadn't run anywhere in years and there was his bad knee to consider. He shifted on his feet, looked down and frowned. There was a spot of blood on his right sneaker. The sight elevated his heart rate. He felt his chest tighten.

"I think I have it now," Gil said. The printer began to

grind out more paperwork. How much paperwork did it take to un-rent a motor home anyway?

Gil moved to the printer, pulled out the papers and began sorting through them. Through the glass window into the office, Herb saw that the boss was off the phone and looking in his direction.

But the man's gaze dropped the moment it connected with Herb's. His heart was pounding now, making breathing more difficult. If he didn't get out of here—

Gil handed him a stack of papers. On the top was a check for both his deposit and his refund since he was turning the motor home in earlier than he planned. He signed where Gil pointed and picked everything up with trembling fingers.

"Thank you," he said automatically and turned toward the door, trying not to rush.

"I thought you needed a ride?" Gil called after him. "If you can wait just a few minutes—"

He couldn't wait. He burst out the door, expecting to hear sirens in the distance. Breathing in the fresh, cool air, he turned left and began walking toward the car rental agency.

All of the rental places were along a frontage road not far from the airport. He kept walking, checking behind him every few minutes. He was limping a little, the bad knee, as he listened for the crunch of gravel behind him. He was that sure that a patrol car would be pulling up any minute.

He'd thought he was being so smart renting the motor home. But he'd seen Gil's expression when he'd seen evidence of the violence that had destroyed the bedroom door. Fortunately, Gil hadn't noticed where the duct tape had taken the paint off the bed frame.

At the car rental agency, Herb stopped and looked

behind him. Cars whizzed past. No cop cars. He hurriedly stepped inside, closing the door, and took a deep breath, trying to quiet his pounding pulse. At this place at least the air conditioning was working, he thought as he moved to the counter.

Had he cleaned up any evidence he might have left in the motor home? That was the question that nagged at him as he again filled out paperwork and produced a credit card and Arizona driver's license.

It wasn't that he worried about being caught. He knew that was going to happen soon enough. He just couldn't get caught until he'd fulfilled his promise to his wife of fifty-two years.

The paperwork took just enough time that he was sweating profusely even in the air-conditioned building. But eventually, he walked out with the keys to a white panel van. The clerk had asked him if he was moving.

"Getting rid of a few things," he'd said.

Once behind the wheel, he drove down the highway to the small coffee shop where he'd left his wife. Dorie was sitting by the window, staring down into her coffee cup as he pulled up. He hit the horn twice. For a moment he thought she hadn't heard.

Then slowly, she raised her head. He figured the sun was glinting off the windshield because it took her a minute to recognize him before she smiled. He was used to her slack-jawed empty stare. Just as he was her confused frowns. Often it was hard to get her attention.

While those times felt like a knife to his chest after all these years together, it was her gentle, sweet smile that was his undoing. In that smile he saw the accumulation of both her pain and his. Their loss was so great they no longer cared what happened to either of them.

Dorie rose slowly from the table inside the coffee

shop. As she lifted her head, she changed before his eyes. He saw the young woman she'd been the first time he'd seen her. She didn't look frail. She didn't look like a woman who was dying. He knew all that was keeping her alive was the promise he'd made her.

A part of him had thought Dorie might not be strong enough to go on. He'd told her he would go alone, but she'd insisted that like him, she would see this through. Dorie climbed into the van without looking at him. Instead, she noticed something on her sleeve. As if sleepwalking, she picked a long, dark hair off her sweater and held it up to study it for a moment, her face grim, before she whirred down her window and threw it away.

Finally, she turned to him. "Can you find her again?"

He nodded, knowing that he would go to the ends of the earth for this woman he'd spent the better part of his life with. "I'll find her."

Dorie reached over and placed her small, age-spotted hand on his arm for a moment before she looked toward the mountains, that distant stare returning to her beautiful eyes as she absently ran her fingers down the sleeve of her sweater as if looking for another strand of Natalie Berkshire's dark hair.

Chapter Seven

The light was dim inside the bar. At this hour, the place was packed. Mo stood just inside the door, letting her eyes adjust as she did a quick scan for Natalie. She didn't see her. Behind her, Brick came into the bar, closing the door and the afternoon out. "There's a motorcycle beside the bar. It looks like the one she stole from the hospital parking lot."

Mo nodded. "I'll check the restroom. If you see her—"

"Don't worry, I won't let her get away."

Mo headed for the ladies' room, the smell of beer and nachos seeming to follow her. Her stomach growled and she realized she couldn't remember the last time she'd had something to eat. Brick had broken her out of jail before she'd been fed.

Pushing open the bathroom door, she saw two women at the sinks. One was putting on lipstick, the other drying her hands and talking a mile a minute about some guy she'd met at the bar. Three of the stalls' doors stood open. Two were closed.

As Mo started toward the closed doors, one came open and a dark-haired woman stepped out in a red shirt. For a split second, Mo thought it was Natalie, but then the woman turned. She moved past and took the stall next to the one with the closed door.

Bending down, she glanced under the neighboring stall. No nurse's Crocs, but that didn't mean that Natalie hadn't changed into the fairly new-looking sneakers in the stall next door. She'd had plenty of time to find a change of footwear.

Mo sat down on the toilet fully clothed and waited. The talkative woman at the sink left with her friend. She could hear water running, then the grind of the paper towel machine. The bathroom door made a whooshing sound and the room fell silent.

Next to her, the woman in the stall hadn't moved. Hadn't reached for toilet paper, hadn't flushed. Mo knew she could be wasting valuable time. Natalie could have already stolen a car from the bar lot and was now miles from here.

She cleared her voice. "I'm sorry, but could you hand me some paper?" she asked the woman in the next stall. "I'm all out over here."

Without a word, the woman pulled off some paper and handed it under the side of the stall. Mo saw the freshly painted fingernails as she took the rolled up paper. Nothing like the chipped ones she'd seen on Natalie's hands in the hospital.

"Thanks," she said, dropped it into the toilet and flushed before she pushed open her door. She was washing her hands when the woman came out of the stall and swore.

Mo saw her looking around. "Lose something?"

"My purse. I left it right there." She shook her head, exasperated. "I hope my friend picked it up for me."

"Any chance you had your car keys in it?" Mo asked. The woman's eyes widened in answer.

As they walked out of the bathroom, she told Brick what had happened. He stepped outside with the woman who'd lost her purse—and her car, as it turned out. He called it in to the marshal's department.

Mo was considering getting a drink while she waited for Brick to return when a male voice said, "Bartender, give that woman a beer on me." She turned in surprise as she recognized the voice.

"Shane, what are you doing here?"

Shane Danby laughed. "Same thing you are, I would imagine. Thought we had come to take Natalie Berkshire back to Billings. But got here too late. The nurse nanny got away. You wouldn't know anything about that, would you? Maybe it had something to do with you being on the wrong side of the law?"

His laugh told her that he knew about her being arrested. "Sorry, but I'm not interested in discussing it with you."

"Not interested in discussing it with me?" he mocked, his voice rough with anger. "You always thought you were better than the rest of us, didn't you, Mo? Well, you aren't the only one looking for Natalie. There's a bounty on her head. That's right, some father of a kid she killed is offering a reward to anyone who brings her in—dead or alive. Everyone in four states is looking to collect. If I find her first I'm going to shoot and ask questions later."

Mo feared it might be true. "And what if she's innocent?" she demanded. She realized that she was starting to sound like Brick. But she couldn't bear the thought that some trigger-happy lawman killed Natalie before she could get to the truth when it hadn't been that long ago that she'd thought that was exactly what she'd wanted. "She deserves a trial."

Shane scoffed. "The crazy psycho deserves the same treatment she gave those patients under her care."

"No wonder you didn't make Homicide." She started past him, but he grabbed her arm and dragged her into an alcove away from the people at the bar. When she started to fight back, he grabbed her by the throat and shoved her against the wall, holding her there with his body.

"Assault, Shane?" she asked around the pain in her throat. "I'm still a homicide cop."

"Are you? That's not what I hear. I heard you went after Berkshire to put her down like a mad dog. Now I'm wondering if you're trying to help her slip the noose."

Just the reminder of how her sister had died brought up a low growl from her throat. "I suggest you let me go."

"Oh, really? Is that what you would suggest?" he said with a laugh. "I can tell you'd like to kick my ass right now." He was so close she could see the dark spots among the brown in his eyes and smell the onions he'd had on his burger for lunch. "The only reason you got Homicide over me is because you're a woman. Gotta meet their quotas." He turned his head to spit on the floor. His hand on her throat tightened. "It's all bullsh—"

The rest of his words were lost as he was grabbed from behind and slammed into the wall next to her. Brick had several inches in height on Shane and was in better shape. He grabbed him by the throat—just as Shane had held her.

"I'm the law, you idiot!" Shane cried and swore.

"You're not the only one," Brick said. "Deputy Marshal Brick Savage. You think you're tough, being rough with a woman?"

As much as she wouldn't mind seeing Brick kick

his butt, she stepped in. "Let him go. Trust me, he isn't worth it."

Brick let go of him so quickly, Shane stumbled and almost fell. As Brick started to turn away, Shane picked up an empty bottle someone had left in the alcove and went for him—just as Mo knew he would. She put her foot out, and the lowlife cop went sprawling. The bottle shattered in his hand. As he started to get up, Brick stepped on his hand, pressing it to the glass-strewn floor and making him cry out.

"We done here?" Brick said, lifting his boot to free the cop's bleeding hand.

"Need a man to fight your battles, Mo?" Shane yelled as he sat back to cradle his cut hand.

She stepped around the corner to grab a rag off the bar and tossed it to him. "Shane, you just don't learn." As she started to turn, he kicked out, catching her in the shin. She spun on him and kicked back, catching him in the thigh. He doubled over, writhing on the floor. "Don't ever grab me by the throat again or next time, it won't be my boot toe. It will be a bullet."

"That man is dangerous," Brick said as they walked away. "From what I heard, he has a grudge against you."

"Shane has a grudge against the world. You can't take him seriously."

"Mo, you need to watch your back around him."

She couldn't help being touched by his concern. "While I appreciate you coming to my rescue, now you have to watch your back as well when it comes to him."

"You could have taken him." He was studying her as they walked.

Mo nodded. "I could have that time because I saw him coming. That's the problem with men like Shane Danby. When he's most dangerous is when you don't

see him coming. But he told me something disturbing."
Mo told him about the bounty. "It might be a lie. But it
also might be true, in which case we have to find Natalie before anyone else does."

"WELL, AT LEAST WE know what Natalie is driving,"
Brick said as they left the bar. A deputy from the department was taking down the information on the stolen car. He and Mo hadn't needed to hang around to
listen to the description of the thief the woman from
the car was giving the deputy. "There's a BOLO out
on the car. I wouldn't be surprised if she's picked up
within the hour."

Mo snorted as she and Brick left. "Have you ever
noticed how large Montana is?" She shook her head.
"There isn't enough law enforcement to cover it all. But
more important, Natalie grew up here. She knows the
state. She'll know where to go."

He glanced over at her. "You really have no faith at
all in the law, do you?"

Mo was busy calling up a map on her phone. "If
you wanted to go to the closest small town, which one
would you chose?"

"West Yellowstone. Or cut across to Ennis. They're
both small. She'd be harder to find in Bozeman, though."

"Ennis," she said emphatically. "Let's go."

Ennis wouldn't have been his choice, but he didn't
argue. Mo said she knew Natalie. He headed south down
the canyon toward the cut-across to Madison Valley and
Ennis. "I'm curious. How did your sister find Natalie?"

"Through the hospital. Natalie had left her information there. She had a great résumé. She seemed perfect
since she specialized in patients with special needs and
she'd worked as a nurse nanny."

"Did your sister get references on her?"

Mo nodded. "She made a few calls, but once she met Natalie, she liked her so much she didn't bother checking the rest of the references."

Brick thought of the woman he'd seen on television and photographed in the newspaper. Slightly built, Natalie was a plain, nonthreatening young woman with what he would have thought of as an honest face.

"It was for such a short time since Tricia planned to stay home full-time, but had to tie up loose ends at her job. Also, Natalie didn't mind the short-term employment. Mostly, Tricia was just so grateful to find someone so experienced. But I know a lot of it was that she liked Natalie right away. I did too when I met her. She had this way of making you feel at ease around her. It's no wonder that she's fooled so many people."

"If she's guilty," he said, and she grunted.

As he drove past the turnoff to his family ranch, he glanced in that direction. A cold chill ran up his spine to lift the hair on the nape of his neck. He had the worst feeling that he might not ever see it again. It was a crazy premonition that something bad would happen and he'd never make it home again. He didn't believe in premonitions. He wondered what the shrink he saw would make of it. But it still shook him.

"You know anything about her background?" he asked to clear his own thoughts.

"Trying to profile her? Good luck with that. It's pretty boring. She was raised on a ranch in eastern Montana, two hardworking parents, an only child. She was valedictorian and president of her senior class. Got top grades in nursing school and excelled at the two hospitals where she worked before going into in-home care."

"Was she ever arrested before?" he asked as he drove

down the canyon. The sun dropped behind the mountains and twilight began to cast long shadows in the canyon.

"No. Not even for a parking ticket. But who knows about her other nursing jobs? Apparently the patients all had life-threatening medical problems. Most of them weren't expected to live, so when they died…"

"But she was never a suspect before, right?"

"That doesn't mean that she's not guilty," Mo said defensively. "Maybe this time she wasn't as careful. Or the medical examiner was more qualified."

He glanced over at her. "But now any deaths where she was the nurse are in question." He drove in silence as he thought about the woman he'd seen in his headlights not even twenty-four hours before. "I'm sorry, but I keep thinking, what if she really is innocent? We hear about babies dying of SIDS or doctors being unable to pinpoint what caused a death. Maybe she wasn't responsible for any of them. Maybe it's just bad luck on her part. And if what she told you is true…"

"If it's true, why didn't she tell the police?"

"Maybe she did. I doubt they were apt to believe her. You're still not sure you do."

She shot him a look before she said, "Let me know when we reach Ennis or if you need me to drive." Then she turned away from him and a few minutes later, he heard her slow, rhythmic breathing and realized she'd fallen asleep.

Mo CAME OUT of the nightmare fighting.

"Whoa! Take it easy," Brick cried as he held up a hand to ward off her blows while keeping the pickup on the road with the other.

She sat up blinking as she fought off the remnants

of her bad dream. She could feel Brick's questioning gaze on her. She ignored him. No doubt he'd seen and heard enough as she was coming awake to know it had been a nightmare. She didn't want to talk about it and hoped he wouldn't ask.

Through the pickup's windshield she could see lights ahead illuminating the small Montana town on the horizon. "Ennis?" she asked, sitting up straighter, still trying to shake off the dream. It was a familiar one. Some things changed, but the feeling was always the same. She was trapped in a small, dark space all alone and yet there was someone nearby. She could hear them breathing. Then she heard something rattle. Whoever was out there wasn't content to leave her to die. They were coming in for her.

"Ennis," he said, stealing glances at her. Fortunately, he didn't ask, but she knew he was wondering about her—as he should be. "What now?" he asked as he drove into the tiny Western burg.

"Food and then somewhere to sleep."

That surprised him. "I thought we were in a hurry to catch her."

"We are. If I'm right, she's already here. She won't leave until she is forced to."

He seemed surprised, but only said, "Well, I could definitely eat something," as he pulled into a space in front of a log cabin café.

But neither of them moved for a moment as if happy not to be in motion after hours on the road.

HERB LICKED HIS praline ice cream before it melted down the cone and watched the couple that had just driven up in the pickup. He recognized the man behind the wheel.

Deputy Marshal Brick Savage had been pointed out to him as the man who'd discovered the abducted woman.

"Enjoying your cone, Dorie?"

She smiled over at him, chocolate ice cream on her lips.

They'd gotten ice cream on their very first date fifty-three years ago. He'd known then that he was going to marry her. Their future had been so bright. There'd been a few bumps in the road over the years, but nothing they hadn't been able to overcome together.

Until the death of their youngest grandchild, the first boy out of six. Their daughter had named him Herbert after his grandfather, an honor that had brought tears to Herb's eyes. He'd been so happy and had gladly offered to pay for a full-time nanny to live in the house and help their youngest daughter with her first child, since the baby had some special medical needs.

He wiped at an errant tear and noticed that his ice cream was melting. He quickly turned his attention back to his cone—and the pickup. The occupants hadn't gotten out. He could see the woman sitting on the passenger side. Another cop? The hospital had been in pandemonium over what had turned out to be a suspended homicide detective pretending to be a nurse, he'd heard when he'd stopped by. The woman had gotten into Natalie Berkshire's room—right past the deputy stationed outside the door.

Herb wondered what the cop had been planning to do. Or if she was merely trying to find out who had taken Natalie captive. That was when he'd decided it was time to get rid of the motor home.

Seeing the two law officers here in Ennis, he knew he'd been right about where he could find Natalie again. He realized that they might be able to help him. He glanced over at Dorie. She'd almost finished her cone. She looked content for the moment and that alone made him happy.

Unlike him, he thought she had moments when she didn't remember what had happened to their only grandson. What a blessing for her and one that he just assumed he wouldn't have until he died, which wasn't that far off given the way he'd been feeling lately.

But first, he intended to take the woman who'd killed his grandson with him as soon as he found her again. It was time.

HUD WALKED INTO the old two-story house on Cardwell Ranch, hung his Stetson on the hook by the door and dropped onto the bench to take off his boots.

"You look exhausted," Dana said as she hurried to help him with his boots, an offer she'd given him most nights since they'd married. Tonight, though, he seemed glad for her help as if he needed it badly. For months, she'd been encouraging him to retire. Their children were raised, and she suspected it wouldn't be that long before they had grandchildren.

"It was one of those days," the marshal admitted as he gave her a wan smile. "You're going to hear about it soon enough anyway…" He seemed to brace himself. "Brick…" He raked his fingers through his graying hair.

Sometimes it hit her how much they'd both aged. Like now. Normally when she looked at her husband, she saw the young, big strong man he'd been when she'd fallen in love with him. She was still desperately in love with this man, looking past the gray and the wrinkles and the slight stoop of his broad shoulders.

"Brick has gotten himself involved in a case that could blow up in all of our faces," Hud said finally.

"I thought he was technically still on medical leave?"

"Tell that to him. I told him until I got the release from the head doctor…" He met her gaze. "He's still having the nightmares, I know he is. He thinks he's fine. You know him."

"Is this about the woman he found?"

Hud nodded. "She escaped from the hospital after taking a nurse's clothing and leaving the woman tied up under the bed."

Dana gasped. "This is the same woman that someone had abducted and held?" He nodded. "Why would she do something like that?"

"I suppose she's scared. Or she heard Billings homicide was on its way to question her. But what complicates it is this cop who's after her…"

"The one who attacked our son?"

For a moment, he looked surprised that she'd heard that detail through the grapevine. He shouldn't have been. He had to know how talk moved down this canyon.

Hud sighed. "We had her behind bars, but Brick broke her out. Now the two of them have gone after the woman who escaped the hospital. Brick to save her and…who knows what Mo has planned."

"Mo?"

"Maureen 'Mo' Mortensen, the suspended cop who your son is now mixed up with."

Dana had to bite her tongue. She'd been against Brick going into law enforcement from the beginning. For years she'd worried about Hud's safety every time he left the house to go to work. She didn't want to have to worry about one of her sons, as well.

"He was born to do this," her husband said as if seeing her expression. She met his gaze, too upset to speak.

"I didn't encourage him. And I certainly didn't approve of this. But you know how he is."

"He wants to please you," she said, her voice breaking. "He idolizes you, so of course he wants to follow in your footsteps." Hud said nothing. Clearly he had to know there wasn't much he could say. She saw how difficult this was for him. He was worried and upset. She felt her anger vanish as quickly as it had appeared.

Stepping to him, she wrapped her arms around him. He pulled her down on his lap and buried his face into her neck. "Brick will be fine," she whispered. "He's enough like you, he'll be fine."

Hud nodded against her shoulder, and she tightened her arms around him as she hoped it was true. His cell phone rang, making her groan. That was another reason she was anxious for him to retire. They deserved peace and quiet at this age—not the constant sound of a phone ringing at all hours and Hud having to go take care of marshal business.

She stepped from his arms so he could take the call. But she didn't go far. If this was about Brick... She listened to her husband's side of it, something about a motor home being found. So *not* about Brick.

Turning away, she headed toward the kitchen to bake something, anything. That was what she did when she was upset—bake. She didn't want to know about the dark things her husband dealt with daily. She didn't want to think about what Brick had involved himself in or how dangerous it might be.

She turned on the oven, anxious to smell something sweet filling up the old ranch house kitchen.

"I CAN'T BELIEVE Natalie would stop this soon," Brick said as he looked around at the busy main street as people were enjoying the warm summer night. Everywhere there were tourists with their campers and sunburned kids, fishermen wearing fly vests, an older couple sitting outside eating ice cream cones and watching all the activity. "But I can see where she could blend in here since the locals seem to be outnumbered."

His comment rated him one of Mo's smiles. This one actually reached her blue eyes. He felt himself grow warm under the glow of it and warned himself to be careful. If she turned it on him too much, he might find himself feeling close to her and that would be a mistake, especially given his reputation—and hers.

"Natalie knows this area. She went to college in Bozeman so she's floated the Madison River on tubes, drunk beer in Bogert Park's old band shell and sledded Pete's Hill. There are just some things you do when you attend Montana State University. Or at least we did back in the day."

He turned toward her. "You went to MSU?" She nodded. "Did you know—"

"Natalie?" She shook her head. "But we were there about the same time. I wouldn't be surprised if we crossed paths and didn't know it." She seemed to be studying the activity on the main street.

He followed her gaze to all the people dressed in shorts and sandals. It made him think of a summer when his parents took them to Yellowstone Park. Growing up on the ranch, there was no such thing as a lazy summer. There was always work to do. It was why he used to sneak away and find a place in the shade to take a nap, but his mother always found him. She would scold him and before she was through, she'd suggest they all go down to the creek for a swim.

That summer in Yellowstone he'd felt like one of

the tourists. It had been a great summer with his twin, Angus, brother Hank, sister Mary and cousins Ella and Ford. He realized Mo was staring at him.

"Nice memory?" she asked. "Let me guess. There's a girl involved."

He laughed. "As a matter of fact, there is. My mother." He told her what he'd been thinking about and the picnic lunch they'd had in Yellowstone, swimming in the Firehole, watching Old Faithful go off at sunset before pitching tents at Lake Campground and sitting around a campfire roasting marshmallows. Ranch kids often didn't get those kinds of trips. Too many animals that needed tending to. "The whole trip was my mother's idea."

She didn't say anything for a moment. "She sounds like a great lady."

He smiled. "She is. Not that Dana Cardwell Savage isn't tough when she has to be. She's one strong, determined woman." He met Mo's gaze. "A lot like you."

"She doesn't want you doing this, does she."

Brick leaned back behind the wheel, watching tourists stream past for a moment. "She doesn't want me doing a lot of things, including becoming a deputy marshal."

He could feel Mo openly studying him. "Maybe you should listen to her."

He turned so he was facing her. "You don't think I have what it takes?"

"I didn't say that."

"But it's what you were thinking."

She shook her head. "Don't assume you know what I'm thinking." They both grew quiet. "I just don't want to be responsible for your mother having to attend your funeral."

"Then you'd better make sure nothing happens to me," he said and laughed. "Look, it's nice to know you care, but I'm not your responsibility. This is my choice and I can take care of myself."

He followed her gaze. Mo was watching the older couple down the street. They were taking all day to eat their ice cream cones. "And you aren't responsible for me. If the only reason you're here is to stop me, well, I just hate to see you risking your life for nothing."

"What was your nightmare about?" he asked.

"I don't remember." She opened her door. "I thought you said you were hungry?"

Brick knew a nightmare when he saw one. He found himself watching Mo out of the corner of his eye as they took a booth inside the café.

After the waitress brought them menus and water, he opened his, but found himself distracted by what had happened in the pickup earlier. Mo had been sleeping soundly when she began whimpering. He'd asked if she was all right, but hadn't gotten an answer. Her whimpering had become louder and stronger and she began to quiver until he'd reached over and touched her arm.

She'd come unglued, swinging her fists at him, her blank blue eyes filled with terror. Did this have something to do with Natalie and her fears that the woman was telling the truth and Tricia didn't take her own life? Or was there more about Maureen Mortensen that he had to worry about?

"I'll take the special, the chicken-fried steak," Mo was saying. "Mashed, white gravy and the salad with blue cheese."

He hadn't realized that the waitress had come back until Mo spoke. He closed his menu. "I'll take the same." He could feel her staring at him.

"I wish you wouldn't," she said, when the waitress had picked up the menus and moved away.

"Wouldn't order what you did?"

She mugged a face. "Wouldn't ask."

He nodded sagely. "Wouldn't ask about your nightmare. I'm guessing it isn't your first. I say that because I've had a few of my own lately."

Mo seemed surprised to hear that.

Brick looked away. "Supposedly I almost died after being shot. But I don't think that's what's causing the nightmares. I killed a man after he shot me."

"Your first." It wasn't a question. She picked up her fork and her napkin and began to polish the tines.

"What about you? Have you had to kill someone as a cop?"

She put down the fork and picked up the knife and began polishing it. "Why did you order the same thing I did?"

The woman was anything but subtle when it came to changing the subject. "I wasn't paying any attention to what was on the menu. I was more concerned about you."

"Having doubts about coming with me now because I had a bad dream?"

He shook his head. "I had doubts about going anywhere with you long before that." Their gazes met across the expanse of the table and held for a long moment. He felt heat race along his veins.

The waitress put down their salads, breaking their connection. Mo laid her knife down and picked up her fork again. He watched her eat her salad, wondering if she'd felt that flutter at heart level that he had just moments ago. The waitress brought the rest of their food and Mo dug in, avoiding his gaze. He was hungry too and happy to just eat in the companionable silence that fell between them.

"You're a cowboy, right?" she asked halfway through the meal. "So why follow your dad into law enforcement?"

"I grew up on Cardwell Ranch, yes. But I never wanted to just be a rancher." He shrugged. "When I heard that a deputy marshal position was opening up, I thought, why not? I found out that I could do a lot of my year at the police academy online. The rest I'll do once I get my medical release." He looked up and met her blue eyes and again felt as if he was falling down a deep well before she shifted her gaze back to her plate. "When Natalie stumbled out into the street in front of my pickup that night..." He shook his head. "The more I learned about this case, the more I wanted to know what happened."

"You want to solve it."

"Don't you?"

She shrugged and continued eating for a moment. "Law enforcement isn't for everyone. It can be dangerous and soul-stealing. It can take you to places you never wanted to go and can never forget." She looked up, locking eyes with him. "It can change you into a person you no longer recognize."

"Was it law enforcement that did that? Or Natalie Berkshire?"

Mo said nothing as she finished her meal. But her words were still haunting him as they left the café. As they climbed into the pickup to drive to the closest motel, he saw her freeze for a moment.

"What's wrong?" He followed her gaze up the street.

"Nothing. I thought I saw... Never mind. I just imagined it. Let's go."

But he noticed how quiet she was as they checked

into a room with two beds. Had she thought she'd seen Natalie? Or someone else?

"And yes, I got us just one room *because* I don't trust you, in case you're wondering," he said as she looked at the two queen beds that took up most of the space.

"If I wanted to get away from you, I could."

"So why haven't you?"

She seemed to study him. "I either like your company or I think you might come in handy."

He raised a brow. "Let's be clear. I'm here to keep you from doing anything stupid when we find Natalie."

Mo smiled as she closed the distance between them. "I asked around the jail about you. I know about your reputation with women. You're a heartbreaker."

He started to object, but she placed a finger against his lips to silence him.

"You won't be breaking my heart, and please don't take that as a challenge." She had a great smile. Her lips turned up at one corner a little more than the other. It was cute. She was more than cute. She was adorable, but also dangerous if the pounding of his heart was any indication.

He pulled her finger from his lips. "Like I said—"

"Right, you're just here to protect Natalie and me from myself." She moved within a breath of her lips touching his lips. "Then I should be able to rest peacefully tonight knowing you will keep me from doing anything…stupid."

As she stepped away, he let out the breath he hadn't realized he'd been holding.

EARLY THE NEXT MORNING, Hud looked up from his desk to see his deputy standing in front of him, grinning. "You found the motor home we're looking for."

"Well," he said, his grin shrinking some. "I think so. It was returned yesterday, and it did have damage to one of the bedroom doors."

The marshal got to his feet. "Tell me it hasn't been cleaned or the damage repaired."

"It hasn't. It was rented by a man named Herbert Lee Reiner out of Sun Daisy, Arizona."

Arizona? Hud recalled one of the inquiries he'd gotten about Natalie Berkshire was from Arizona. "Send a forensic team." He frowned. If the man had used his real name to rent the motor home, then maybe this wasn't the right one.

As the deputy left his office to notify the team, the marshal returned to his computer to gather what information he could about Herbert Lee Reiner. Married to Doris Sue Thompson for fifty-two years. Herbert had been a postman until his retirement. That meant his fingerprints would be on file.

It didn't take long before their names began coming up in newspaper articles. The articles read much like the ones that had run in the Billings newspaper. The older couple were the grandparents of an infant with health problems born to their youngest child. The other name that came up in the baby's death was Natalie Berkshire.

BRICK WOKE TO the sound of the shower. He looked around the motel room, then at the queen-sized bed he lay in. The covers weren't overly disturbed. He hadn't had a nightmare. That alone surprised him.

He stretched, feeling better than he had in weeks. That too surprised him. Maybe what he'd told his father was true. Maybe this was exactly what he'd needed, something he could sink his teeth into, he thought as Mo came out of the bathroom in nothing but a towel.

"Oh, good you're awake." She dug in her suitcase, pulled out jeans, a T-shirt and white panties and bra. "I thought you might want a shower," she said pointedly when he hadn't moved.

He'd been doing his best not to look at her since the towel was pretty skimpy. "You think I need one?"

"I just don't want to have to try to dress in that dinky bathroom." She cocked her head toward the open bathroom door. "Do you mind?"

He threw back the covers and swung his legs over the side. Last night he'd slept in his boxers and nothing else. He hesitated.

"I've seen men in a lot less," Mo said, shaking her head with obvious amusement.

As he strutted past her into the bathroom, he heard her chuckle. He stepped into the bathroom and opened his palm to remove the keys to the pickup he'd grabbed before coming in here. He tucked them under a towel and turned on the shower, smiling to himself. If Mo was planning to leave in his pickup this morning, she was in for a surprise.

He recalled last night when she'd told him he wasn't going to break her heart. It had sounded way too much like a challenge, he thought. But that was the old Brick. He hadn't been serious about any woman—at least not for long. That apparently was how he'd gotten the reputation—news to him.

When he thought about Mo, about the look they'd shared at the café, about how his body had reacted with her standing so close last night and again this morning in that towel... The woman had been taunting him. Well, if she thought for a moment that he was going to make a move on her...

Brick turned the shower to cold for a few moments

before climbing out. He wasn't going to let this woman distract him. In the mirror, he ran his fingers through his dark hair. It was a lot longer than he usually wore it, he thought. Also, he had a day's stubble. He rubbed his jaw, but decided to leave it, not wanting to take the time to shave. Grabbing a towel, he dried off, then pulled on his boxers. He stepped back out of the bathroom.

Mo was gone.

Chapter Eight

Mo looked up as she came out of the local grocery store. From the expression on Brick's handsome face, he'd thought she'd left him for good. She could see that he was upset and trying to hide it—now that he'd found her. She felt almost guilty for giving him a scare. Also for giving him a hard time last night. She had seen first-hand that the man definitely had a way with women. But then, she'd known that the moment she'd laid eyes on him.

He was too good-looking, too cocky, too full of himself, she'd told herself. And yet since they'd hooked up, so to speak, she'd seen another, more vulnerable side of him. Not that she was going to let that fact weaken her resolve to keep everything between them professional.

"You could have left a note," he said, walking up to her.

She laughed. "You sound like we're a thing. If you must know, I went out to get us some doughnuts and coffee," she said, indicating the bag she was holding in one hand and the to-go tray with two coffees in the other. She handed him the bag, then took one of the coffee cups from the tray and handed it to him. "Also, I looked for an apartment." He blinked. "Not for us, sweetie. For Natalie."

The morning was sunny and just starting to warm up. She could smell pine and river scents drifting on the breeze. There was a picnic table on the lawn in front of the small motel. She walked to it and sat down. To anyone watching, they might look like a married couple on vacation.

She opened the bag of doughnuts and offered one to Brick as he joined her.

He took a glazed one and said, "An apartment for Natalie?"

"If you were her, what would you do? She can't keep running. We know she has limited funds. She has to look for a job. Why not a small tourist town where people with money have built huge summer homes and would love a nanny? Most are probably from out of state and have never heard of Natalie Berkshire—not that she will use her real name, I would imagine. It would only be for the summer or maybe just a few weeks. Exactly what she's looking for."

He shook his head. "I'm still surprised she'd stop so close to where she was caught."

"Because she knows that we expect her to run farther," Mo said and took a sip of her coffee. "She needs to find a job, and if I'm right, disappear into a family with her next victim. She's getting desperate. I believe that's why she made the mistake she did."

"What mistake was that?" he asked and took a bite of his doughnut, chasing it with a sip of coffee. He frowned at the cup in his hand.

"You do take your coffee with sugar and cream, right?" she asked.

He looked up in surprise. "How did you—"

"It's no mystery. You had an old cup in your pickup.

It was written on the side along with your name and the logo of your favorite coffee shop." She grinned.

"Okay, you're observant. I'll give you that. What mistake did Natalie make?"

"She let her guard down and got caught. She'll want to do what comes naturally to her, which isn't running. She's here in this town. I feel it." Mo saw his skepticism and reached into her pocket to take out a scrap of paper. She handed it to him. "The apartment comes with a garage where she can hide the stolen car—if she hasn't had a chance to get rid of it already."

"Where did you get this?" he asked as he turned the strip of paper over in his fingers. He had nice hands, she noticed. Long fingers. Strong, tanned hands. A man's hands. She felt a shiver at even the thought of those hands exploring her body.

"You want my jacket?" Brick asked, thinking she was chilly. He was already starting to take off his jean jacket.

She shook her head. "It was on a bulletin board in the only grocery store in town advertising a studio apartment cheap with the telephone number on the slips of paper on the bottom. Only one other slip of paper had been pulled off so I figured the ad hasn't been posted for long."

"That doesn't mean Natalie took the other one."

She nodded in agreement. "But there is one way to find out." She pulled out her phone and called the number. No answer. She left a message saying that she was looking for a long-term rental and hoped the apartment was still available.

When she looked up at Brick, she expected to see disapproval in his expression because of how easily the lie had come to her lips. Instead, he was rising to his feet, his eyes fixed on his pickup parked in front of their motel unit. She watched him walk over to the truck and pull what appeared to be a folded sheet of paper from under the passenger-side windshield wiper.

As he unfolded the paper and read what was written there, his gaze shot to her. Mo felt her heart begin to pound.

BRICK HANDED Mo the note he'd found on his pickup's windshield. He watched her quickly unfolded it and read the words neatly printed there.

Chasing me won't give you the answers you want. You should be looking for the man Tricia had been seeing. I don't know his name. I only saw him once. Blond with blue eyes, about six-two or six-three. I swear I didn't hurt the baby. But if Joey was her lover's baby… By the way, someone is following you.

He watched her refold the note and put it into her pocket without a word. He could tell that she was upset, but what was written on the note didn't seem to come as a shock compared to what Natalie had already told her at the hospital. Was it why she hadn't let Natalie tell her that day at the house before Joey died? She hadn't wanted to hear it, still didn't want to believe it.

"We going to discuss this?" he asked when she still said nothing.

Mo opened her mouth, but closed it as her cell phone rang. She checked the phone and then took the call, listening for a few moments before she said, "That's too bad. I'm one of the new teacher aides at the elementary school." Brick's eyebrows shot up. The woman was a born liar. "Do you have any other units?" If Mo were right, Natalie would have only taken the apartment short-term, apparently now making the landlord regret renting it. "I'm moving here soon and anxious to get settled into a place." Again she listened before she smiled. "I'd love to see it." If Natalie had rented the apartment, she would have already been moved in, he thought.

Mo gave the man her number again and disconnected. "He's going to call the new renter to see if she's home and he can show the apartment. She only rented it for a few weeks." When the phone rang, he started and saw Mo take a breath before she picked up. "Hello? Yes? Oh, that's too bad. But could you at least tell me where it is? I could drive by. If I like the area, I'll get something temporary until it opens up."

He saw her nod before she disconnected. "Let's go," she said and started for her side of the pickup. "She's at the apartment. But the call from her landlord will probably spook her."

"You're that sure the woman who rented the apartment is Natalie?" he said, wondering if Mo was ever wrong about anything. She didn't bother to answer, her gaze on the street ahead as she repeated the directions to the apartment that the landlord had given her.

Brick felt his pulse jump. This could be it. They could be about to confront Natalie. Ennis was already busy, the traffic slow and congested until they got away from the main street in town. He tried to remain calm, uncertain how this would go down. He could see Mo tapping the edge of her side window with her fingertips, clearly impatient. Clearly anxious. He was glad he was driving instead of her. She wore an expression that told him she would have plowed through the cars and pedestrians, horn blaring.

The apartment was in an older area of town. He drove down the street slowly, looking for the stolen silver SUV in a state that had hundreds of silver SUVs.

"The apartment is on the third floor, a small one-bedroom with stairs off the back," Mo said. "That's it." She pointed at a tall white building with navy trim that had clearly once been a single dwelling, now made into three apartments. Two bikes were chained to the front porch. A small pickup was parked out front along with a smaller compact car next to the two-car garage.

He pulled over. "I don't see a silver SUV, but I suppose it could be in the garage."

"She probably ditched it and picked up something else." Mo opened her door, climbed out and started across the street.

"We're taking her back to Big Sky for questioning," he reminded Mo.

"You wouldn't have found her if it hadn't been for me," she said under her breath as they approached the apartment house. "You'd be looking as far away as Spokane."

"Mo—"

"I just need to talk to her, so let's find her before we debate what to do with her."

He knew she was right. It felt as if they were chasing a ghost. He glanced behind them, thinking about the note. Was someone really following them? Look how easily Natalie had found them. He remembered Mo thinking she saw someone last night. Natalie? If so, the woman had seen them and could have followed them to the motel.

"I'll take the back stairs," Mo said now. "You go in

the front door. Bleeding heart or not, try to remember that this woman is dangerous." She took off at a run around the back.

He headed for the front door, determined to get to the woman before Mo did—if Natalie was in this building. Brick tried the front door, not surprised when it opened into a small foyer. There were two doors and stairs.

He took the stairs two at a time, no longer worrying about making too much noise. If Natalie had rented this apartment, if she was still up there…he had to get to her and fast.

At the top of the stairs, he found a door and quickly stepped to it to knock. He thought he heard a sound on the other side of the door and for a moment, he thought about drawing his weapon. Mo had warned him that Natalie was dangerous. But he remembered the terrified woman he'd seen in his headlights. The woman lying in the hospital bed. He still wanted to believe that she was a victim, an innocent victim. He left his gun holstered and tried the door.

It opened, startling him.

"Come in," Mo said on the other side of the doorstep. "She's gone."

"Natalie?" Mo didn't answer as she turned back into the apartment. He followed, a little stunned. Had she been right about Natalie renting this place? "How do you know for certain it was her?"

She shoved a copy of a local shopper at him. It was folded so that the want ads were on top. Several positions had been circled. His heart slammed against his ribs as he saw they were for nanny positions. One of them for an infant that needed special care.

Mo had moved into the bedroom, where she was standing at the end of the unmade bed.

"Are you all right?" he asked her. She wasn't moving, hardly appeared to be breathing. He realized that his heart was still thundering in his chest. Mo hadn't just been right about the apartment. She'd been right about Natalie looking for another job. A possible new victim.

"Maybe she'll come back," he said.

Mo shook her head. "She's gone. I found something interesting in her trash in the bathroom. She's changed her appearance, cut her hair and colored it red." He could hear regret in her voice. They'd come so close. They couldn't have missed her by more than a few minutes.

Her gaze met his, but only for an instant as she pushed past him and left.

He stood for a moment looking at the room. From what he could see, it appeared that the renter had left in a hurry. One of the drawers in the bureau stood open and empty. The door to the small closet was open, the metal hangers bare. That was if Natalie had even had time to pick up more clothing. He suspected she was traveling light.

They'd gotten close. Just not close enough.

He found Mo outside, leaning against the side of his pickup. She appeared to be looking up at the snow-capped mountains. But as he drew closer, he saw that her eyes were closed, her chest heaving as if she was having trouble breathing.

As he approached her, her eyes opened. A lock of blond hair fell over one blue eye as she turned to him abruptly. "You still think she's innocent?" She sounded angry and upset and disappointed, he realized. Disappointed not just because they hadn't caught up to Natalie. He had a feeling she was even more disappointed in herself for not wanting to hear what Natalie had tried to tell her that day at the house.

"You can't second-guess yourself," he said quietly. "You can't change what happened."

She shook her head and looked away. "No, but I can find out what happened to my sister. I can make sure Natalie doesn't hurt anyone else."

Did he still think Natalie was innocent? Did he think the circled job openings were about her needing to get back to work because she needed money? Or as Mo said, a woman looking for her next victim?

He squinted toward the mountains. "I want to find her as much as you do."

Mo shook her head. "You don't. Which is why you need to go back to Big Sky and your job before you lose it. Don't throw your career away like I did. This isn't about you."

"It's about justice. Without it, we're nothing but outlaws. And if I went back, I'd have to take you with me. I'm not sure I can trust you to appear at your hearing."

She met his gaze and held it. "Fine, stay. Just remember, I warned you."

Her cell phone rang. She pulled it out of her pocket and looked at the screen before she stepped away to take the call.

Mo HEARD THE anger in Thomas's voice and groaned inwardly. "That man you were with the other day," her brother-in-law said without preamble. "Deputy Marshal Brick Savage? He's the one who found Natalie—and lost her again. Maureen, what are you doing?"

She realized it always bothered her that he'd never called her by her nickname. It had always been Maureen. "Thomas, why have you never called me Mo?"

"What?"

"I just realized that you've never called me by my nickname."

"Are you drunk? Or have you just completely lost your mind?"

"Thomas—"

"What are you doing, *Mo*?" He sounded more pained than angry now. "I begged you at the funeral to let it go. Joey is gone. Tricia is gone. Why are you destroying your life, too? I called the police station. They said you've been suspended. Please, Maureen, Mo, whatever. *Stop.*" His voice broke.

She felt a painful tug at her heart. She'd met Thomas at college when her only eighteen months older sister had started dating him. They'd hung out with the same crowd. He was like a brother to her. She'd been maid of honor at their wedding.

"I can't talk to you about this," she said. "It doesn't have anything to do with you."

"How can you say that?" he asked, raising his voice. "Joey was my son, Tricia was my wife. Natalie was like a member of our family. This has been a nightmare. One I just want to put behind me."

"I wish I could, but I can't."

"So, what are you going to do?" he demanded.

She looked back at Brick leaning against his pickup, waiting for her. They needed go after Natalie. She was getting away. Again. She thought about telling Thomas about the note, about Natalie saying that Tricia hadn't taken her own life, but didn't. Like he said, he was trying to put it all behind him. Until she had even a shred of proof that it was true, she needed to keep it to herself. She didn't want to hurt him any more than she already had. "I don't know what I'm doing." She could almost see him shaking his head.

"The cops let her go, Maureen."

"That doesn't mean she was innocent."

"But it could, couldn't it?" He sounded as if he was pleading. "Isn't it possible Joey just died? The doctor had said he might die. If he'd lived, he was going to have to have all those surgeries and even then, the doctor said he might never..." His voice broke again. She could hear him crying.

She'd done this. "I'm so sorry. This is why I didn't want to tell you."

"Then don't do this. Go back to work. It's the only thing I've found that helps. I'm sure you can get back on at your old job if you leave all of this behind. You know you being obsessed over this is the last thing Tricia would want."

She didn't know what to say because she knew it was true. But then again, she questioned if she'd ever known her sister at all. Tricia was having an affair? It seemed impossible. She still didn't believe it, but knew she had to find out the truth no matter where it led her.

"You and I shouldn't have any secrets, Maureen. We're..." His voice broke again. "Family."

Her heart clinched. The worst thing about this was lying to Thomas. His losses were so much greater than hers. And now she had him worrying about her.

"I need you to be all right," he'd told her at Tricia's funeral. "I can't bear losing anyone else."

The anguish in his voice now broke her heart all over again. "I'll be okay," she said, wondering if it would ever be true. She'd told herself that she would be fine as soon as she got the justice her sister and Thomas deserved. But she wasn't even sure of that anymore.

"I know I can't stop you, but promise me this. That you'll call every few days, Maureen. I need to hear your voice. I need to know that you're okay."

"I'll call," she said. "Thomas?" She searched for something to say that would help them both. "It's going to get better." At least she hoped so.

Chapter Nine

"Your brother-in-law?" Brick asked as Mo pocketed her phone and walked toward him and his pickup. She nodded without looking at him. "You all right?"

He watched her look away to hide her raw emotions. "You don't have to worry about me."

"I wish that were true." When she met his gaze, he reached over to brush a lock of her hair back from her face. "You're having second thoughts."

She shook her head. "You have no idea what I'm thinking."

"I see more than you think. You're conflicted about all of this."

"Of course I am," she snapped and tried to step past him, but he blocked her way. She sighed. "What is it you want me to say? That maybe you're right and I'm wrong? Don't you think I wish that were true?"

"What if it is?"

She glared at him, clearly losing her patience. "Here is the problem. When we find her, and we will, you'll still be debating it all in your mind. She will use that against you and you'll end up dead."

"You've made her into a monster with powers that don't exist."

She scoffed at that. "This woman's greatest advantage is that she doesn't look or act the part. It's her strongest defense and most dangerous attribute." She pulled out the folded note he'd found on his pickup's windshield. "You think I don't want to find out if this is true? You think I don't want to believe that my sister didn't take her own life?"

"Why would Natalie lie?" Brick asked.

"It's nothing but a distraction. So instead of going after Natalie, I chase my sister's death only to find out it was all a lie. But by then, Natalie is long gone. She's living in someone else's house, taking care of a patient for a family who has no idea what horror has walked through their door." She pushed past him. "We need to get moving."

Mo FELT CLOSE to tears. She couldn't help being upset. She hated hurting Thomas more than he was already suffering. Add that to her disappointment. They'd come so close to catching Natalie. She could feel the note in her pocket, the words burned into her brain. Tricia was having an affair. She didn't want to believe it. Just as she didn't want to believe any of this was happening.

And yet, it was happening. It had happened. What if Tricia really did have another man in her life? Did that really change anything? Unless it was true and Tricia hadn't taken her own life. All Mo could think was, why hadn't she known? She and Tricia used to be so close. How had she not known what was going on with her own sister?

"Where to now?" Brick asked as they climbed into the pickup cab again and he started the engine.

She pulled out her phone to call up a map and tried to get her emotions under control. Thomas's phone call had gutted her. She kept thinking of the wedding. Her sister had been so happy. The two had been in love since college. Everyone said they made the perfect couple. But after trying so many times to have a child and failing… Is that when everything changed?

"Take 287 north," she said to Brick and pocketed her phone. "We'll watch the truck stops, the convenience stores." In truth, she had no idea what Natalie would do now. "She'll be wanting to get rid of the vehicle she's driving."

"While you were on the phone, I spoke to one of the neighbors. He said she left in a hurry, driving a tan older model two-wheel-drive pickup, so she's already dumped the car she stole in Big Sky," Brick said.

She looked over at him. "Nice work."

"This one sounds like it might have been cheap enough that she bought it with the money she's stolen so far."

Mo nodded. "I suspect Natalie's been living on the run for a long time, afraid to stay anywhere for too long. She's at the point now that she'll do whatever she has to do to survive." A part of Mo felt that way, as well. She'd given up everything—her job, the life she'd made for herself, her savings—to find this woman.

What am I doing? Chasing a possible killer and if so, when and how would it end? She feared the answer.

FROM DOWN THE STREET, private investigator Jim Cameron slid down behind the wheel as he watched the two climb into the pickup. He held the phone tighter to his ear.

"I'm looking at them as we speak," he said into the phone. "The female cop and the deputy marshal."

"Did they find Natalie?"

"No. Apparently she went out the back before I got here."

"Stay on it. This has to end."

He thought about the elderly couple that had cruised by in a sedan earlier—before the cop and the deputy had arrived. He'd noticed the way they'd stared at the three-story house.

"There's this old couple," Jim said. "I've seen them too many times and they drove by, both of them staring at the house."

"I'm not worried about some old couple. Stay on the cop and the deputy. Make sure they don't find Natalie first."

Jim shook his head. As many people as there appeared to be after this woman, himself included, none of them had gotten their hands on her except for whoever had abducted her in Big Sky. And the woman in question had managed to escape.

"Keep me informed." The line went dead.

Jim disconnected and sat up a little. The cop and the deputy had been sitting in his pickup unmoving so far. This had seemed like a simple enough job when he'd taken it on. If he wasn't getting paid so well…

He tried not to question what exactly was going on. It seemed to him that Natalie Berkshire was doing her best to crawl into a hole and stay there. Why roust her out? Why keep forcing her to run? Why not let her land somewhere and then throw a net over her?

The pickup with the cop and deputy was moving again. He waited a few moments before he fell in behind it.

BRICK DROVE THROUGH the residential area toward the center of town. Mo was lost in her own thoughts. What would Natalie do now? Run! What choice did she have? This time, she might run farther and be harder to find.

They were almost to the main drag in town when Mo saw the lights of police cars and what appeared to be a wreck in the middle of the intersection. As they drew closer, an officer waved him around the two-vehicle accident. She saw that a sedan had been involved—and a tan older model two-wheel-drive pickup.

"Isn't that the couple we saw eating the ice cream cones last evening?" Mo asked as he started to drive past the couple the police were talking with.

"Maybe, but that definitely looks like the description of the pickup Natalie was driving," Brick said.

"Stop." Mo threw her door open and she was out, slamming it behind her. She heard the cop order Brick to keep moving as she disappeared into the crowd gathered at the scene.

"Did you see what happened?" she asked several people on the street.

"That older couple T-boned that pickup with the woman inside," a man told her. "I swear that elderly driver sped up just before they collided."

"What happened to the woman in the pickup?" Mo asked. From where she stood, she could see that the driver's side of the pickup was caved in—and the passenger door was hanging open.

"She got out of the passenger side and limped off before the cops arrived," a woman said. "She was hurt, bleeding, but she took off down that way. The police are looking for her. Maybe she thought the accident was her fault and she wanted to get away. Or she was so shaken up that she didn't even know what she was doing."

"How badly hurt was she?" Mo asked.

"She was limping," one of the bystanders told her. "And bleeding."

"I bet she doesn't get far," someone said.

Mo wouldn't have taken that bet.

She continued down the street until she spotted Brick. He'd pulled over into the first parking space he'd found and now stood next to his truck, waiting. That he knew she'd find him made her realize how much their relationship had changed. Only this morning he'd thought she had taken off. She didn't know what had changed or when—just that it had. Smiling to herself, she realized she was actually glad to see him and had to swallow the lump in her throat as she joined him and told him what she'd learned.

As Brick climbed behind the wheel, he pulled out his phone. "There's something I want to check." He called his father's cell. The marshal answered on the first ring. "Brick—"

"Before you start in, didn't you tell me that the woman at the convenience store said the man in the motor home was elderly?" He knew he'd hit on something when all he heard for a moment was silence.

"We found the motor home," his father said. "A forensic team found evidence that it was the one where Natalie Berkshire was held captive."

"And the elderly driver?"

"Herbert Lee Reiner and his wife, Doris Sue, out of Sun Daisy, Arizona. They're grandparents of a woman whose baby died. Natalie was the nanny. I have a BOLO out on them."

Brick felt his stomach drop as his father described the two. "They just tried to kill Natalie in Ennis. She's on the run again, although injured after her vehicle was

rammed by their car. I just thought you'd want to know."
He disconnected before his father could lecture him and
turned to Mo to tell her what he'd learned.

"So we head up Highway 287 north?" he asked as he
started the pickup and glanced in his rearview mirror.
He'd seen a dark SUV earlier. But now he saw nothing suspicious.

"Change of plans," Mo said. "What would you do if
you'd just lost everything again and were now injured?"

"Go to the hospital?"

"Not just any hospital. You'd go to where your ex-
husband the doctor worked. He's a surgeon at the hospital in the state capital—and not that far from here."

Chapter Ten

On the drive to Helena, Mo seemed to relax. He respected how she seemed to bounce back from disappointment quickly.

"Tell me about Brick Savage," she said out of the blue.

He glanced over at her for a moment before turning back to his driving. "Not much to tell," he said, wondering if she was just bored or if she were really interested.

"I doubt that's true since your reputation with women precedes you. Apparently you like to lasso them, but you always set them free."

"I wouldn't believe everything you hear." He cleared his throat. "You want to hear my life story or just the raunchy parts?"

She laughed. "I want to hear it all," she said, settling into her seat for the drive.

"Okay. I was born and raised in the Gallatin Canyon, grew up on a ranch with a mother who ran day-to-day operations and a father who was the local marshal. My whole family lives in that canyon. Ranching and wrangling is all I've ever known."

"And yet you're a deputy marshal," she said. "Or will be if I don't get you fired before you even start."

He ignored that. "I guess in the back of my mind I always thought I would follow in my father's footsteps."

"Will working with me ruin that for you?" she asked, sounding actually concerned.

"Don't worry about me." Brick had to admit, he'd always been impulsive, going with what felt right at the moment. He'd never felt rooted to the ranch the way his siblings had. He'd always been a free spirit.

Then again, he'd always had his twin brother, Angus, the solid, steady one, to help steer him out of trouble—until recently. Not to mention, he'd also had his very wise cousin Ella. But now he was on his own since both of them had moved on with their lives.

And now here he was. On his own. Two rogue lawmen. He couldn't depend on Mo to steer him into anything but trouble.

"So you said you were shot. An angry husband?"

"I've made a habit of steering clear of married women. My brother and I and my cousin Ella were helping a rancher in Wyoming on a cattle drive. Her husband, who she was divorcing, was giving her a hard time. I just got in the way of a bullet."

"That explains a lot. It was all about rescuing a woman in distress. You just can't help yourself, can you?"

He shook his head and sighed as they reached the Helena hospital where they would find Natalie's ex. "You just like giving me a hard time, don't you?"

Mo grinned. "Now that you mention it…"

THE TALL, DARK-HAIRED doctor came into the room on a gust of air-conditioned breeze. He closed the door and went straight to his desk, sitting down behind it before he considered the two of them. Clearing his voice, he glanced at his watch and asked, "I don't have a lot of time before my next surgery. What is this about?"

"We're here about your ex-wife Natalie," Mo said, trying to see the woman she'd known with this man. In the time she'd spent time around the woman, Natalie had never mentioned her ex.

"Natalie and I are no longer married."

"We are hoping you'd seen her today," Brick said.

Dr. Philip Berkshire shook his head. "Why would I? I haven't even seen her in years." He started to rise.

"She contacted you for bail money when she was arrested," Mo said.

He slowly lowered himself into the chair. "I said I hadn't seen her. I didn't say I hadn't heard from her."

"She didn't call you today?" Brick asked.

"No. She called when she needed bail money, and I turned her down."

"Why?" Brick asked.

"Why?" the doctor seemed shocked by the question. "Because I don't owe her anything."

"Or because you believe she's guilty?" Mo asked. "The two of you worked together. That's how you met and married, right?"

"That was a long time ago. I know nothing of the kind of woman she is now."

"What kind of nurse was she?" Mo asked.

"She was a fine nurse, a devoted, compassionate nurse."

"Why did she quit nursing to become a nanny?"

"You would have to ask her that."

Brick shifted in his chair. "I would love to, but since she's not here and you are…"

"We divorced."

"Why?"

Berkshire shot Brick a narrowed look. "That's personal."

"Look, we're trying to find her. Her life is in danger," he said. "Also, she might have information that we need in another death."

The doctor closed his eyes and slowly shook his head. "She had this thing about babies, sick babies. I'm sure you already know this," he said, opening his eyes and turning his attention on them again. "She had a younger sister who was born very sick. The doctor had given the infant only weeks to live. Natalie told me that she couldn't bear the child's suffering and was relieved when the baby passed. That is what you're looking for, isn't it? A reason?"

"You think she put her sister out of her pain and suffering?" Mo asked, feeling sick to her stomach. What if it had begun when Natalie was only a child herself?

"I think she wanted to. Whether or not she did… I believe it's why she became a nurse and why when we divorced, she left the hospital to become a nanny for fatally ill children."

"Is she capable of killing a suffering infant?" Brick asked.

Berkshire steepled his fingers in front of him, studying them for a moment before he spoke. "Not without causing herself great harm. If Natalie is anything, it is too caring. She was incapable of keeping any distance between herself and her patients. I could see how it was eroding her objectivity. She was too involved, too compassionate."

"Does she have a close friend that she might turn

to?" Mo asked, hoping for some clue where the woman might be headed now that she was injured.

He shook his head and then shrugged. "I have no idea."

Brick leaned forward in his chair. "She was injured in a car accident in Ennis. I thought maybe she might have come to you for help."

"No. Natalie wouldn't come to me. Not after I wouldn't give her the bail money. Her pride wouldn't allow that."

"What about her family?" Mo asked. "Would she go to them?"

"Her mother's dead and she had a falling out years ago with her father when her mother got sick. Look, I'm sorry, but I'm scheduled for a surgery," he said as he rose to leave.

Mo asked for directions to Natalie's father's house and the doctor told her. "What kind of falling out?" she asked as he headed for the door.

The doctor stopped but didn't turn around. "Her mother asked Natalie to help her die." With that, he was gone.

BRICK FOLLOWED A long dirt road that cut across arid country bare of little more than sagebrush. They'd been driving all day across Montana, from Ennis to Helena and now to the eastern portion of the huge state. He was wondering if they'd taken a wrong road when they came over a rise and he saw an old farmhouse in the distance.

As they grew closer, he could see that the two-story stick-built house was once white. Over the years, the paint had faded and peeled until now it was a windswept gray. The yard resembled other ranch and farmyards he'd seen across Montana. Ancient vehicles rusted in the sun along with every kind of farm implement. An old once-red barn leaned into the breeze. A variety of outbuildings were scattered like seeds over the property.

As they pulled down the driveway, an equally weathered looking man came out the screen door. Shading his eyes, he watched the pickup approach as if he hadn't seen anyone this far out in a very long time.

Brick parked, killed the engine and got out. He heard Mo exit the pickup and wondered what she was thinking as she took in this place. This was where Natalie had grown up?

"You lost?" the man asked. His voice and on closer inspection, his face, though weathered, was closer to fifty than eighty. Brick realized he was probably looking at Natalie's father.

"We're looking for Natalie Berkshire," Mo said.

Before she could get the words out of her mouth, the man was shaking his head. "Never heard of her," he said, already turning back toward the house.

"She's your daughter," Mo snapped.

The man stopped, his back to them. "Not anymore."

"She's on the run from people who want to hurt her," Brick said quickly. "She's injured and scared and probably has no one else to go to. Why wouldn't she come here?"

The man let out a deep-rooted bitter sound and slowly turned to face him. "Because she knows better than to come here."

"You wouldn't help her?" Brick asked, finding it hard to believe that blood wouldn't help blood.

"I wouldn't throw water on her if she was on fire."

"I don't believe that," Mo said.

"What do you know about anything?" the man demanded.

"I know she's your only child and if there is something wrong with her, then you have to share in that blame."

The man narrowed his eyes, anger making his nose flare. "Leave my property before I get my gun and run you off. That girl was a bad seed from birth." His voice broke. "Her mother tried to save her with love and look where that got the woman. Dead and buried." There were tears in his eyes as he went back inside, slamming the screen door behind him.

MO WATCHED THE arid landscape sweep past as they drove back to the two-lane highway. Neither of them had spoken as if they didn't know what to say. As Brick pulled up to the stop sign, he glanced over at her.

"Which way?" he asked.

For a moment, she didn't know how to answer. They could drive to the closest town, where Natalie would have gone to school, find someone who knew her when she was young, maybe even find out why the woman's father hated her so much.

But Mo realized that none of that would help. For all she knew, the car crash could have caused internal bleeding and Natalie could be lying in a ditch somewhere, dying or already dead. Or she could have appropriated another vehicle and stolen some cash, and was on her way to her next job in another city, even in another state.

Mo had to make a choice. She felt as if she was at a crossroads. Maybe Natalie had nowhere to go, no one to help her. If she wasn't badly injured, she would keep going. Maybe Brick was right and it wasn't Mo's job to stop the woman—even if she could.

So what did that leave? Keep chasing Natalie or face a possible truth about her sister? If she wanted answers, she was going to have to find them herself without

Natalie's help. A part of her still believed that Natalie was lying. But if she wasn't… It was a chance she couldn't take.

Brick was still waiting. "South to Billings," she said. "If it was true and Tricia was seeing another man, I need to find out who he is and what part he might have contributed to all of this." She kept having nightmares about that day and what role she may have played herself. Maybe if she'd listened to what Natalie had to tell her then…

He turned onto the highway headed south. Mo leaned back in the seat and closed her eyes for a moment. She feared sleep, especially after meeting Natalie's father. If that didn't bring on more nightmares, she didn't know what would.

She could tell that man had shaken Brick, as well. When Natalie told her that she grew up on a ranch, Mo had pictured rail fencing, horses running around a green pasture, a large house with a mother baking in the kitchen. She realized that Natalie had let her picture that, wanting Mo to believe that she was a born and bred Montana girl as open and honest as the big sky.

Victim or monster? Mo still couldn't say. Brick wanted to believe the best. But even if Natalie was the murderer Mo believed she was, it didn't mean that she'd killed Joey. Who was this woman and how much of what she'd told her was true?

"I believe that Natalie knows more than she told the police," she said. "More than she's told me. She was trying to warn me that day. She seemed worried about Joey. Worried…" She looked over at him and felt tears fill her eyes. She was fighting to make sense of all of this.

She looked away as he voiced her worst fear.

"Worried that Tricia might have harmed her own baby?"

Mo quickly wanted to argue that Tricia wouldn't, couldn't. But in truth, given the condition her sister had been in the last time she'd seen her, she didn't have an argument in response. Fortunately, Brick didn't give her a chance.

"Natalie was living in that house, right? Of course she would have seen things, overheard things… If she didn't kill Joey, then someone else with access to that house did. If there was another man…"

Mo felt the weight of his words and hated that he was right. "It's time to find out if anything the woman has told me is the truth." Whether she wanted to hear it or not.

Chapter Eleven

Brick couldn't help but question how far he would go to see this finished as he drove toward Billings. He'd been hell-bent on saving Natalie Berkshire, convinced that she was a victim. He still was determined to see that she got a trial. With all the evidence he feared was coming out against her, a trial, it seemed, would only land her in prison for the rest of her life.

And yet not even Mo was now convinced that she'd hurt Joey. Unless Natalie was lying. Was she lying about everything else, as well?

As he glanced over at Mo, he knew that no matter what, he would see this through. Mo needed him, even if she didn't think so. He smiled to himself at the thought as he listened to the sound of the tires on the highway as the miles swept past. And he had needed her. He felt himself getting stronger. Not just physically but emotionally, as well.

Whatever happened now, he and Mo were in this together. As they crossed high prairie, the sun setting behind the Little Rockies, he kept thinking about Natalie's ex and her father. Was the young woman a bad seed?

He thought of that old couple that had rammed her pickup and injured her. Guilty or not, she deserved better. He hoped that old couple got the book thrown at them, then remembered what his father had told him. The couple had lost their grandchild and believed Natalie was responsible. Not that it gave them the right to take the law into their own hands.

"So if Natalie is the person you suspect she is, how long do you think she's been doing this?" he asked, realizing that his greatest fear was that Mo was right and Natalie would kill again.

"I wouldn't be surprised to find out that this started a lot longer ago than we know. I'm sure there has always been a lack of evidence. Maybe she wasn't even a suspect in most of the cases. Natalie seems to have the ability to be whatever she thinks other people need. Her father aside, I do believe there is something very wrong with her and that her childhood played a part in making her the woman she is now." Mo looked over at him. "Or maybe she is completely innocent of not just Joey's death but the others that are now being reinvestigated."

"Maybe," he said, though no longer sure of that. He realized that he was tired of thinking about it. Right now he was more interested in the woman sitting in the pickup cab next to him. "What about you?"

"What about me?" she asked, sounding surprised by the question.

"I've told you my life story—"

"Hardly."

"And you haven't told me anything about you."

She shook her head. "You know everything that is of any interest."

He scoffed at that. "So, where did you grow up?"

"Really?" She sighed. "Southern California."

He waited, but of course she wasn't forthcoming with more. "A surfer girl."

She scowled. "What is it you're looking for?"

"Maybe just polite conversation."

She gave him a look that said he'd come to the wrong place for that. But after a moment, she said, "My aunt raised me after my parents divorced and couldn't hold it together long enough to raise a child."

He hadn't been expecting that and he was sure his expression showed it. "What about your sister?"

"She was eighteen months older, so she went to live with our grandmother who said she could use the help." Mo shrugged. "Gram was a sour old woman but Tricia got along with her fine, I guess."

"So how was it living with your aunt?"

"I loved my aunt and uncle. They were wonderful to me. My uncle was from Mexico and they owned an authentic Mexican restaurant. I worked there from the time I was nine. I loved it. In fact, my happiest memories are of hanging out in the kitchen as they cooked. There was always music playing and laughter. My uncle cooked the best mole sauce you have ever tasted." She kissed her fingers. There were tears in her eyes.

"Are they still—"

"They were both killed in a drive-by shooting when I was weeks away from eighteen. Before you ask, yes, it is probably why I studied criminology in college and became a cop. I'd already gotten a scholarship so I headed to the same college where my sister was enrolled, Montana State University. Enough?"

"I'd ask about your love life—"

"But you're way too smart for that," she said. "Stop up here. I need something to eat."

As he pulled into a convenience store on the edge of a very small town, his cell phone rang.

"Want me to get you something?" she asked.

"Surprise me." As she climbed out of the cab, he took the call.

"Where are you?" his father asked without preamble.

He felt his pulse jump. "What's happened?" he asked, hearing something in his father's marshal voice.

"Natalie Berkshire has been found. She's dead. She died of her injuries from the car accident."

The breath he'd been holding came in a whoosh as he watched Mo moving around inside the convenience store. He wondered how this would impact her. He felt shaken.

"Herbert Lee Reiner and his wife Doris have been arrested in Ennis for her abduction and her death."

Brick didn't know what to say. "Maybe if we hadn't gone after her—"

"Son, there have been more investigations being reopened. It appears there were a lot of suspicious injuries and deaths at her past jobs."

"You're telling me that she was guilty."

"She might have seen them as mercy killings."

Brick shook his head. He'd wanted to believe she was a victim. He'd wanted to believe he could save her. Or at least keep her safe until she could have a proper trial. His father was right. He'd gotten too involved. Maybe he wasn't cut out for law enforcement after all.

"It's over. You need to come home."

Brick couldn't speak for a moment as he thought of the night Natalie had stumbled into his headlights and how that had led to this moment and the blonde homicide cop standing at the register inside the convenience store.

"It's not over. Not yet. If Natalie was telling the truth then she wasn't responsible for the baby's death and Mo's sister was murdered."

His father swore. "You have no idea what you're getting yourself into. Even if you don't get killed, you could end up in jail."

"That's a chance I have to take. Mo needs my help."

The marshal swore. "You've always led with your heart instead of your head."

"And that's a bad thing?" he joked as he watched Mo finish paying inside the store.

"Not according to your mother," his father said with a sigh. "I wish you'd come home."

"Pretend I'm up in the mountains camping until you see me again." Mo headed out of the store. "Thanks for letting me know."

"Brick? Promise me you'll be careful. Maybe especially with your heart."

As he disconnected, Mo looked up at him, stopping in midstride as if seeing the news etched on his face.

He got out of the truck and went to her. "That was my father. They found Natalie. She died of her injuries from the car crash. The older couple has been arrested."

Her expression didn't change as she nodded. And then she was in his arms, sobbing against his shoulder. He held her, unsure if her tears were of relief or of grief. Like she'd said, she'd known the woman, she'd liked her. But she'd been terrified that Natalie would kill again if not stopped. Now, though, there was no chance of finding out anything more from Natalie. They were on their own.

As quickly as she'd thrown herself into his arms, Mo stepped out of them and wiped her tears before climbing into the cab of his pickup.

"I'm sorry," he said as he slid behind the wheel, not sure of his own feelings. It wasn't what he wanted for Natalie. He wanted justice, but that might have been years of waiting for numerous trials where she was found guilty. She might have ended up on death row in one of the states or merely spent the rest of her life behind bars. If truly guilty, she might have been saved from all that by dying from her injuries.

"I'll understand if you want to stop this," he said to Mo, realizing that this might change everything.

She'd been sitting, holding a convenience store bag on her lap, and staring out the truck windshield. But now she turned to look at him in surprise. "I can't stop now. I have to know the truth. All of it. But you don't have to—"

"I'm in this with you. All the way."

She smiled through fresh tears for a moment before opening the bag in her lap. "I brought you doughnuts. If you're going to be a cop…"

"So… Billings?" She nodded and handed him a doughnut. He took a bite and shifted into gear.

Several hours later, they were on the outskirts of the largest city in Montana. They approached from the north, giving Brick a different view than he normally had approaching the city. He could see the bands of rock rims that ran on each side of the Yellowstone River— and the city. From this vantage point, higher than the city itself, it appeared to be lush green. The bowl between the rims was a canopy of treetops and a green ribbon of Yellowstone River.

And somewhere in Montana's largest city hopefully were the answers Mo so desperately needed.

EARLIER, MO HAD insisted on driving part of the way, letting Brick sleep. They'd stopped in Roundup at the convenience store to use the restroom and get something more to drink, and Brick had taken the wheel again.

"Where do we start?" he asked now as he drove through what were known as The Heights before dropping down into Billings proper.

"Tricia had a friend from high school and college who she still saw. If anyone knows what might have been going on with my sister it will be Hope."

He shot her a look, hearing something in her tone. "A friend you don't like."

She looked over at him in surprise. "It isn't that I don't like her—not exactly." She mugged a face. "Fine, I don't like her. I never trusted her. I always thought Tricia felt sorry for her. Hope is one of those people who demands a lot of sympathy. I swear she makes her own bad luck just for the attention."

"You were jealous of her relationship with your sister."

Mo rolled her eyes but didn't argue the point since he was right. She gave him directions to the woman's house. The house was small and located in an older neighborhood that had seen better times. Weeds grew tall in the yard and the siding could have used a coat of paint years ago.

"You think she's back from work?" he asked as he pulled up out front and checked the time.

Mo snorted. "If she had a job," and opened her door to get out, but stopped.

BRICK COULD TELL she was about to tell him he didn't have to come with her. But apparently changed her mind, adding, "On second thought, she'll take to you right off."

He wasn't sure he liked that, but followed her up the walk nonetheless.

The thin, dark-haired woman who answered the door

wore a tank top and shorts. Her feet were bare. She had a plain face made plainer by her straight shoulder-length hair.

She frowned at Mo, clearly questioning what she was doing on her doorstep. But when her gaze took him in, she smiled and gave him a more welcoming look.

"I didn't expect to see you," Hope said as she jammed her hands on her hips and glared at Mo. "You weren't exactly friendly at the funeral."

"It was a *funeral*, not a party you were invited to." Brick could tell Mo was wishing she didn't need this woman's help. He thought Mo might want to try sugar rather than vinegar in this instance, but kept his mouth shut.

"Look, Hope, I didn't come here to argue with you about some past slight or misunderstanding," Mo said.

"What? You didn't come by to apologize?"

As if seeing that her tactics weren't working, Mo said, "Hope, could we please come in? I need to ask you something about Tricia."

The woman in the doorway hesitated, her gaze going back and forth from one to the other of them before she stepped back with obvious reluctance.

Once inside, Hope didn't offer them a chair. Instead, she stood just inside the door, arms crossed waiting.

"Thanks, we'd love to sit down," Mo said and walked into the living room to perch on the edge of the couch. She looked at Hope and snapped, "Could you drop the drama queen act? I need to know if Tricia had a lover."

Brick had moved to the fireplace and stood waiting to see how all of this was going to shake out. Hope looked pointedly at him without moving.

"This is Deputy Marshal Brick Savage. He's helping me investigate Joey's death," Mo said.

"Wait, *you're* investigating? I heard you got kicked off the force and aren't a cop anymore."

"I was suspended, not fired. Are you going to answer my question or just give me a hard time?" Mo sounded tired and weary. Brick knew the feeling. It had been another long day.

Hope must have decided to cut Mo some slack because she dropped her belligerent stance and moved away from the door to take a chair at the edge of the living room.

"If Tricia had wanted you to know what was going on in her life, she would have told you," Hope said haughtily.

Mo swore. "Tell me who the man was."

"Tell me why I should? Tricia's dead. I promised her I wouldn't tell anyone ever, especially *you*."

"How long had she been seeing him?"

Hope looked away for a moment. "Over a year."

Brick heard Mo emit a painful sound that made Hope smile. But he knew what Mo had to be thinking. There was the possibility that the baby had been her sister's lover's and not Tricia's husband's—just as Natalie had questioned.

"Was she in love with him?" Mo asked.

Hope shrugged. "At first it was just a fling. She didn't think it would last. I think she realized that she'd gotten married too young and she wanted to see if she'd missed out on something. Apparently she had. It was thrilling, she said. I think it was fun because it was a secret. No one knew but me. Your sister knew what you'd say if she told *you*."

Mo seemed to ignore that. "Did you meet him?" Brick saw the answer. "So you never met him."

"They had to keep it secret. Billings may be the largest city in Montana, but it isn't so large that you can have an affair and people don't find out," Hope said.

"So you don't know his name," Brick said, making the woman look over at him. He got the feeling she'd forgotten all about him until then.

"I didn't need to know his name," Hope said irritably. "But why should I tell you even if I did know?" she demanded of Mo.

"Because I have reason to believe Tricia didn't kill herself."

The woman's eyes widened. *"Seriously?"*

"Seriously."

"So…" Hope was frowning again. "You think someone killed her?" Mo said nothing. "You can't think it was Andy."

"Andy?"

Brick saw that Mo's eyes had widened in surprise. "Who is Andy?" he asked.

"A friend of Thomas's."

MO COULDN'T BELIEVE THIS. "Andy? It's Andy?"

"She never told me it was Andy," Hope said quickly, backpedaling. "Just that it was someone from college, someone she'd had a crush on."

With relief, she realized that if Natalie had been telling the truth, the man Tricia had been having the affair with was blond and more than six feet tall. Andy was short and dark-haired.

She looked at Hope, wanting to throttle the woman. "So you never saw him, never met him. I'm beginning to wonder if Tricia even confided in you."

"She did!" the woman cried. "She was in love and heartbroken because she didn't want to hurt Thomas."

"She was in *love*?" This wasn't adding up. "I thought it was just a fling?"

"At first. She thought it was just for fun, but then it turned into something else and then…" Hope looked away.

"And then she got pregnant," Mo guessed. All those months of trying to get pregnant with Thomas's child and suddenly she had an affair with another man and got pregnant. "Whose baby was Joey?"

Hope shook her head. "She didn't know. She was in a panic. I tried to get her to take a DNA test before the baby was born."

"Did she?"

The woman shook her head. "She was determined that it was Thomas's. She broke off the affair. She told me her boyfriend was really upset."

Mo thought about the emotional roller coaster Tricia had been on during her pregnancy. No wonder she'd been all over the place. "Did her boyfriend not want the baby?"

"Oh, no, he wanted it. He wanted her to leave Thomas and marry him, but she was having second thoughts, regrets, you know. Thomas had found out that she was pregnant and was so happy that she convinced herself that it was his and lied to her boyfriend about taking the test. She said the baby was her husband's and that the affair was over."

"But she didn't know who Joey's father was?"

Hope shook her head. "Then when he was born with so many medical problems and the doctor said he probably wouldn't live…"

Mo knew her sister. "She blamed herself."

"I told her it was stupid. That it was just bad luck."

Mo sat back on the couch. This explained so much.

Natalie must have seen how out of control Tricia had been. Once she saw Tricia with the other man... "If you think of anything she might have said about the man that might give me a clue who he was..."

"Like I said, she didn't tell me that much about him. Mostly she talked about the way he made her feel. He was like her. He loved animals." Mo thought about her sister's disappointment that she couldn't have a dog because Thomas was allergic. "And he was romantic," Hope was saying. "One time he carved their initials into a tree."

Mo pulled out of her thoughts to look at the woman. "Where was this?"

"On a camping trip they took some weekend when Thomas was at one of his seminars. Their inside joke was how taken Thomas was with the Jeffrey Palmer seminars." She looked over at Brick. "Jeffrey Palmer is a self-made millionaire. He gives leadership seminars that he charges a fortune for so others can believe they might one day be rich, too. Thomas idolizes him and never misses one of his seminars, especially since his company sends him along with his associates so they can become leaders."

"The carving on the tree," Mo said pointedly. "Where was it exactly?"

Hope seemed to give it some thought. "I think it was near Red Lodge by a creek." She shrugged. "I just remember how happy Tricia was."

"Until she wasn't."

"I hope you find him. I do remember that when Tricia told me about breaking up with him over the pregnancy, she didn't come out and say it, but I could tell that she'd been worried about how he was going to take it. She said he was so angry, she'd never seen him like that, and she was sure that she'd done the right thing by breaking it off, but then later he called. She sat right here and cried her heart out. I think she really loved him."

Mo felt her heart ache for her sister. "She kept seeing him, didn't she?" Hope looked away, answer enough. Mo got to her feet, thanked her and started for the door.

Brick asked behind her, "Where was this photo taken?" She turned to see that he was pointing at a snapshot that had been stuck into the edge of a framed photograph on the mantle.

It appeared to be one of Tricia. In the photo, her sister was smiling at the person taking the photo. She did look happy. Behind her was a stream and pines.

"Oh, I forgot all about that photo," Hope cried. "Tricia left it here since she couldn't take it home. It was her favorite from their camping trip. He said it was his favorite photo of her and gave her a copy of it. I'm sure there were others of the two of them but she never showed them to me. That reminds me." Hope got to her feet. "She left some stuff here. I thought you might—"

"I'd like it, please," Mo said and they waited as the woman disappeared through a door and returned moments later with a large manila envelope.

"I don't know what's in it. I never looked." She handed it to Mo. "Tricia said I should give it to you if anything happened to her."

"Are you serious?" Mo demanded. "When were you going to tell me about this?" She clutched the envelope to her chest and glared at the woman.

"If you hadn't been such a bitch at the funeral—"

"I'm curious. Why the secrecy?" Brick interrupted. "Why wouldn't Tricia tell you the man's name since she told you everything else?"

Hope shrugged again. "I wondered about that, too.

I think he was somebody, you know? A name that either I would know or would have heard of. She was so worried that Thomas would find out and maybe do something to him."

"Or she thought you wouldn't have been able to keep her secret," Mo said, still clearly angry.

Hope glared back at her. "At least I knew what was going on." She raised a brow as if to say, *and she was your sister.*

Brick surreptitiously pocketed the photo he'd taken from the mantel and quickly got them both out of there.

Once in the pickup and driving again, Brick said, "This makes me wonder if Natalie wasn't telling the truth about all of it. You knew her. You liked her. She was worried about your sister, worried about Joey. She tried to warn you about what was going on. She was even convinced that Tricia didn't commit suicide and swears that she didn't harm Joey."

"What is the point of debating it now? She's dead." All she could think was that caught in this heartbreaking triangle and filled with guilt over Joey's paternity and health, her sister could have been in such an emotional state that she had killed herself.

"She wasn't lying about Tricia having an affair," he pointed out. "I don't think she was lying about your sister not killing herself."

"I don't know," Mo said, the manila envelope resting unopened in her lap. She saw him check his rearview mirror and not for the first time. "What is it?"

"We're being followed and have been since we left Hope's house."

Chapter Twelve

"You were right," the PI said into his hands-free device. "She went by the house. She was in there a good half hour. I'm following her and the deputy now."

He swore as he realized that he'd been spotted. "I'm going to have to let them get ahead of me." He turned at the next street. He was pretty sure where he could catch up to them again.

"How did they seem when they came out of the house?"

"Hard to say." He got paid to spy on people, photograph them, follow them. He didn't get paid to analyze their feelings, but he was smart enough not to say that. "Subdued." He could hear that the answer didn't make his client happy.

Ahead, he saw the pickup, but this time he stayed back. "They've pulled into a motel and are going inside the office." He told his employer the name of the downtown Billings motel as he pulled over to wait. "What would you like me to do? It appears they have booked a room and are now carrying their bags there."

"One room?"

"Yes, they both went into the same room." Jim listened for a moment. "Right, I can do that. I'll put the tracking device on the pickup tonight." Now that they knew they were being followed, he couldn't let them see him again.

"Once I can track them myself, I think it would be best if I took it from here."

"You're the boss."

"I'll stop by your office and pay you in cash when I pick up any file you might have made on this."

The man was worried that hiring a private detective to follow a homicide cop and a deputy marshal might come back on him?

"I understand." He hung up, telling himself he was glad to be done with this one. But just to cover his own behind, he'd keep a digital copy of his work and the man's requests. Hopefully, he would never have to use it, he thought as he waited for it to get dark enough to go back to the motel and attach the tracking device to Deputy Marshal Brick Savage's pickup.

"I'M NOT SURE I'm up to understanding any of this," Mo said once they were settled into the motel room and she'd taken a peek inside the envelope. She was exhausted—and still upset. Her sister had told Hope to give it to her in case anything happened to her. What had Hope been thinking? Clearly the woman didn't have a brain the size of a pea.

But what scared her was the realization that Tricia had known there was a chance that something *would* happen to her. So she'd left whatever was in this envelope for Mo. If only Hope had given it to her right away.

"What is it?" Brick asked as he pulled back the curtain to look out into the street.

"A stack of photocopied financial reports," she said. "I can't make heads or tails of them, not tonight." She wasn't sure what she'd hoped to find in the envelope.

A diary. Photos. A suicide note. Something personal to Mo to explain what it was that she'd left for her. It made her question if Tricia had been in her right mind. Wasn't that her fear? That Natalie hadn't killed the baby? The only other person in the house that day was Tricia.

"I'm tired, too," Brick said as he checked outside again.

"Have you seen the vehicle that you thought was following us?" she asked, putting the manila envelope into her suitcase.

"No, maybe I was just being paranoid."

"Or letting Natalie get to you," Mo said with a sigh. "I'll wash up and go to bed."

Brick moved away from the window and stretched out on top of his bed.

By the time she came out of the bathroom, he was sound asleep. She crawled between the sheets in the matching queen bed. She couldn't quit thinking about her sister. Had Tricia fallen in love with the mystery man? That she would even have an affair was so unlike her, it was hard to believe. Tricia had always been the good one. It was one of the reasons she had gone to their grandmother's instead of Mo.

She closed her eyes, desperately wanting to put the day behind her. Natalie was dead. Whatever secrets the woman had refused to give up would go to the grave with her. She felt sleep tugging at her. Her last thought was that she hadn't gotten a chance to tell her sister goodbye.

Mo came out of the dream screaming. She felt hands on her and fought to shove them off, but the fingers were like steel.

"Mo. *Mo?*" The hands gave her a shake, and she

opened her eyes, startled and instantly embarrassed because she knew she'd had another one of her dreams.

Brick released her and she sat up, backing against the headboard as she chased away the last of the darkness. They'd hardly spoken after renting the motel room. Mo didn't remember falling asleep but it must have been quickly.

She gulped air and tried to still her pounding heart. A chill in the room dried the perspiration on her skin, but her nightshirt still felt damp. As the light on in the room chased away the dark shadows that followed her sleep, she began to breathe easier.

"Better?" Brick asked now. He was sitting on the edge of the bed, but no longer touching her.

She nodded, unable to look at him. The nightmares were terrifying and embarrassing. They made her feel weak. Worse, vulnerable.

"A bad one, huh? I've had a few that followed me into daylight," he said quietly. "The worst ones don't go away easily. They always make me afraid to close my eyes again because I know the terror is waiting for me."

She glanced in his direction and saw that he was looking at the hideous mountain painting on the opposite wall instead of at her. Her heart seemed to fill. He understood what she was going through because he'd not only had the bad dreams, but also he'd felt the weakness, the vulnerability, the embarrassment of them.

"If it helps, I can leave the light on," he said when he finally did look at her.

Mo shook her head. As he started to get up from her bed to turn off the lamp next to them, she touched his hand. She hadn't meant to reach for him. It was as if an inner need was stronger than she was. She hated needing anyone and yet she did.

"I can turn out the light and stay here, if you want me to," he said quietly.

She nodded, tears filling her eyes. She wiped at her the wetness on her face, heard him turn off the light, then felt his weight settle in next to her on the bed. She took a few calming breaths before she slid down in the bed to lie next to him.

Staring at the ceiling in the ambient light coming through the motel room's curtains, she felt him take her hand in his large warm one. Until that moment, she hadn't realized that she was trembling. But as he held her hand, she felt his warmth move through her until she quit shaking, until she was no longer afraid to close her eyes.

BRICK WOKE WITH Mo snuggled against him and his arm around her. He didn't dare move, not wanting to wake. Not wanting to let her go just yet. He wondered about her bad dreams and was glad she hadn't had another one later last night.

With a shock he realized that he hadn't had one since the two of them had joined forces. Maybe he really was getting better. He smiled to himself and felt her shift in his arms. He held his breath.

"I know you're awake," she whispered.

"How can you tell?" he asked.

"Because your hand isn't on my breast anymore."

Brick withdrew his arms as she turned to face him. "I'm sorry, if I did anything—"

"I was joking," she said smiling. "You were a perfect gentleman." She eyed him as if surprised by that. And maybe…disappointed? "Should I be insulted?"

He chuckled. "Trust me, it's not because I haven't wanted to."

She laughed and turned to get up on the opposite side of the bed. "Trust you?" she said, her back to him. "Won't that be the day. I'm going to get a shower." She stopped and turned. "Have you ever carved your initials into a tree along with the name of one of your... women?"

"No."

Mo nodded and smiled. "I'm anxious to find that tree. I'm assuming you'll want to go along?" She said it over her shoulder as she headed for the bathroom.

"I'm stuck to you like glue," he said before she closed the door.

They spent the morning canvassing the neighborhood around Tricia and Thomas's house. Brick knew Mo was hoping that one of the neighbors might have seen a man going into the house who wasn't Thomas over the weeks that Tricia had been having the affair—or on the day she'd died.

When they came up empty, they stopped for lunch and then headed toward Red Lodge in hopes of finding the campsite where Tricia's lover had left their initials carved in a tree.

THEY ARRIVED AT the forest service campground mid-morning. Most of the sites were open. A few occupants in tents and small trailers were packing up to leave as he drove slowly through the pines higher up the mountain.

He had the photograph that Tricia's alleged lover had taken on their camping trip.

On the way to the campground, Mo had been looking through the envelope her sister had left for her. Now she put it away, apparently still not understanding why Tricia wanted her to have it.

"I'm still shocked that we are looking for the identity of my sister's lover," Mo confided. "Tricia was always the rule follower, the voice of reason. For her to do this…"

"People fall in love," he said. "At least that's what I've heard."

She swung her gaze on him. "You've never been in love?"

He seemed as surprised by the question as she was shocked that he hadn't been in love. He slowly drove through another loop of the campground. "Why? Have you?"

"Middle school, my science teacher. High school, this sweet boy who wrote me these awful poems. A couple of times in college. Several since then."

He laughed. "That's your love life?"

"Apparently, it's better than yours. You've really never been in love?"

He could feel her gaze on him as he pulled over and cut the engine in an empty campsite. "There's a tree down," he said in explanation for stopping. "We're going to have to walk to see the upper end of the campground, where we should have a view of the creek that's in the photo."

"You didn't answer my question," she said, keeping him from exiting the truck cab. "You weren't in love with even one of the women you dated?"

"I cared about all of them. Maybe you and I have a different definition of love. When I tell a woman that I love her it will be right before I propose marriage." With that, he climbed out of the pickup and closed the door.

Mo exited the truck as well, still looking surprised by his answer. They started up the mountain road, climbing over downed trees and limbs. "Looks like they had a storm up this way," he said. This high up the mountain, there were only the sounds of birds, the breeze high in the tops of the pines and the whisper of the stream. As they climbed higher, though, the sound of a roaring creek grew louder.

"Seriously, you've never felt...love?" she asked.

"The head over heels kind?" He shook his head and glanced at her. "I'm assuming you haven't, either. It's probably why you can't understand what happened to your sister."

She seemed to consider that. "You're probably right. It seems...reckless, something Tricia never was. At least I thought that was true. Let me see the photo." He handed it to her. "I think that's it up there," she said excitedly. "See that mountain in the distance?" She held up the snapshot.

"Lead the way," he agreed as they quickened their pace. Now all they had to do was find a tree up here with Tricia and her lover's initials carved in it.

As THEY REACHED the campsite, Mo stopped to check the photo again. "This is the campsite." She turned to see Brick already checking trees.

For a moment, she merely stood looking at this beautiful sight. The creek cut a green swath through the rocks and pines to fall away down the mountainside below them. She breathed in the rich, sweet scent of pine and caught a hint of someone's campfire smoke trailing up from a site below.

She thought of her sister, the last person she could imagine enjoying camping. That Tricia might have slept up here in the blue tent in the photo... It boggled the mind. She tried to imagine the man who could sweep her sister off her feet.

"Mo? I think you'd better come over here," Brick said.

She turned to find him standing next to a large pine tree at the edge of the mountainside, overlooking the roaring of the creek. As she approached, she saw the crude heart carved into the bark of the pine.

There were two sets of initials at the center of the heart. TM, a plus sign, and JP. Tricia's lover had used her maiden name initial. Wishful thinking on his part? Or was that the last name she'd given him? This man had understood from the beginning that Tricia was married, hadn't he?

"Know anyone with those initials?" Brick asked.

Mo shook her head. "I have no idea who JP is."

The gunshot echoed through the trees, splintering the bark on the tree next to her. Several nearby birds took flight, wings flapping wildly as Brick lunged for her, taking them both to the ground.

The second shot ricocheted off the tree where they had been standing, sending bark flying again. And then there was nothing but the sound of the breeze in the pines and seemingly hushed roar of the creek. Not even the birds sang for a moment as Mo tried to catch her breath.

Chapter Thirteen

In the distance, Brick heard an automobile engine start up. Through the trees he caught a flash of silver as the vehicle sped off, the sound dying as whoever had taken the potshots at them drove away.

Mo was on her feet as quickly as he was, the two of them running back down the road to where they'd left the truck. They had to slow down to climb over the downed trees and limbs, but finally reached the pickup.

Brick started it and drove as fast as he could out of the campground. By the time they reached the highway, there was no sign of the vehicle they'd glimpsed through the pines.

"Whoever that was, wasn't driving the black SUV that had been following us yesterday," Brick said. "What I want to know is how they knew we were going to the campsite?"

"Hope? You think she lied about knowing the man's name. She could have called him to tell him what she'd told us? That would be pretty stupid of her, wouldn't it? Especially if Tricia's lover is the one who just shot at us."

Brick pulled off his Stetson and raked a hand through his hair. "Then how did anyone know where to find us?"

"She must have told someone, unless…" Mo met

Brick's gaze across the cab of the pickup. "You don't think…"

"I do think." He pulled the pickup to the side of the road and they both got out to search the undercarriage. They found the tracking device quickly enough. Brick was about to destroy it when Mo stopped him.

"Let's give whoever did this something to follow," she said, pointing to the freight train moving slowly along the tracks on the other side of the road.

Brick smiled and spotted a dirt road that ran beside the train track. Back in the truck, he drove along a narrow road along the tracks. Heading off the slow-moving freight train, he jumped out of the truck and waited for it to catch up to him. He was back to the pickup within minutes.

"All done." His gaze locked with hers. He was still shaken by the close call on the mountain. "Any idea what is going on?"

"I think we're getting close to the truth." She shook her head. "But I'm nowhere near figuring out who JP might be or what these documents are that Tricia left me."

"I need to go back up the mountain to get that one slug that lodged in the tree," he said. "That is, if we're going to take this to the police."

Mo shook her head. "It's a long shot we could ever track it to the gun, but at least we will have the evidence."

He drove back up the mountain. "Why don't you wait here? I won't be long." He pulled his spare pistol out from under the seat of his truck and handed it to her. "Fire a shot if you need me."

She smiled. "You just handed me a loaded gun. I think I'll be able to take care of myself."

He wasn't gone long before he returned with the slug he'd dug out of the tree with his pocketknife.

"Do you think the person who shot at us was trying to kill us or just scare us?" she asked.

Brick smiled. "If he was trying to kill us, then he was a piss-poor shot. I think he was trying to send us a message."

"To quit looking for the man Tricia was involved with? Or stop looking for her killer?"

"Could be one and the same," Brick said.

Mo made a disgruntled sound. "All he did was make me more determined—and more convinced that what Natalie told me was true. Tricia didn't kill herself."

"He? The shooter could be a woman."

"My money is on her boyfriend. Who else would be worried about us finding out his identity?"

He could tell that Mo had been racking her brain, trying to figure out who JP could be while he was up on the mountain getting the slug.

"I can't even imagine how Tricia crossed paths with him between taking care of her house and her day job, though," she said.

"What is it?" Brick asked as he saw her freeze and then hurriedly pull out her phone.

"Something Hope said." She scrolled on her phone for a moment before she looked up. "My sister volunteered every other Saturday at a nonprofit dog shelter. I remember Thomas complaining that she spent more time there than at home and had to shower before he could get near her."

"Any luck?" he asked as he watched her thumb through the shelter site.

She shook her head. "No one on the board with those initials. I'm going to call Hope. Maybe the initials mean something to her." When Hope answered, she put the cell on speakerphone.

"We found the campsite and the carving on the tree of the heart with their initials in it. Do you remember anyone from college with the initials JP?"

"*JP?* No. Honestly, I've always thought it was Andy. He's such a sweetie and he's always liked her."

"Think. Do you know anyone by those initials?"

Hope was quiet for a moment. "Sorry, I don't. Tricia always referred to him as her special friend."

Mo HUNG UP and put her phone away, irritated with Hope and even more irritated with herself. If she'd let Natalie tell her what was going on that day, she could have talked to Tricia. At least she would have tried to help her rather than hiding her head in the sand, not wanting to hear that anything was wrong.

"I'll call my partner at homicide when we get back to Billings," she said. "We can give him the slug you dug out of the tree—although I doubt it will lead us to the shooter. But I want to get everything I can on my sister's death."

An hour later, Mo introduced Brick to her partner, Lou Landry, outside the diner around the corner from Billings PD. A little gray around the edges and highly seasoned after thirty-five years at this, Lou was more like a father figure than a partner. Mo knew she'd been placed with him so he could keep her out of trouble. It had worked—until the Natalie Berkshire case.

"You are opening up a can of worms," Lou said after she told him what she needed. "Are you sure you want to do this?"

"I have to know if what Natalie Berkshire told me was true."

"Mo, I probably shouldn't be telling you this, but we are getting inquiries from all over the state and even the country about Natalie. It's much worse than we first thought. People are demanding the cases be reopened. They want answers and quite frankly it appears there is only one answer. Natalie Berkshire was a serial murderer."

"She swore she didn't kill Joey." She saw his pitying look.

"Just as she swore that your sister didn't kill herself?"

"At least I know that Natalie didn't have anything to do with Tricia's death. She was behind bars when Tricia hung herself."

Lou shook his head. "I'll get you the autopsy report, but I don't think you're going to find any answers in it. The coroner ruled it a suicide. If there had been anything suspicious—"

"I want to see the photos taken at the scene, as well."

He sighed. "Why put yourself through that?"

"Because I can't close that door until I'm sure."

"All right. I'll meet you back here in thirty minutes."

"Lou…thank you."

"What are partners for?" His expression saddened. "You're not coming back to the force, are you?"

"I don't know."

He nodded. "Thirty minutes." And he was gone.

She looked at Brick.

"He seems like a nice guy."

"He is."

"Are you really never going back?"

She shrugged. "Buy me a cup of coffee?" As they entered the diner, she saw Shane Danby and several of his friends leaving. Her stomach dropped, half expecting him to make a scene. To her surprise, he merely nodded and left.

Thirty minutes later, Lou entered the coffee shop and handed her a paper sack. "I hope you know what you're doing," he said and left.

Mo glanced into the sack and saw a copy of the autopsy report and the photos taken at the scene. She closed the bag and turned to Brick. "I thought we could take these back to the motel. But first I need to use the ladies' room."

"I'll be waiting for you outside," he said, looking worried. Like Lou. Both knew that seeing the report and the photos was going to hit her hard. But she had to know. Since her sister's death and Joey's, she'd been having the nightmares. She had to believe that the reason for them was that justice hadn't been meted out. Not yet anyway.

BRICK STEPPED OUTSIDE the coffee shop into the summer sun. He was worried about Mo with good reason, he thought as he started down the street to where he'd parked his pickup. The threat against her was real. Someone had taken potshots at them. And now she was looking into her sister's death. Had they been followed to the campsite outside of Red Lodge?

He'd watched for a tail and hadn't spotted one. Who else knew about Tricia having been there? Who else knew about the carving on the tree with the initials on it? Tricia's lover.

"Well, look who it is?" said a male voice as he walked past an alley near where he'd left his truck. He'd been so lost in thought that he hadn't seen the man. Turning, he saw cop Shane Danby and two other men. Clearly, the three had been waiting for him. "Guess we meet again."

"What a coincidence," Brick said. "And you're looking for trouble just like last time, only this time you brought your friends to help you."

Shane's jaw muscles bunched along with his fists as he took a step closer. "You should have stayed out of it with me and Mo. You messed with the wrong man." He took a swing, but Brick easily sidestepped it.

"Get him!" Shane cried and charged, head down. Brick caught him in an uppercut that knocked the man to his knees, but then Shane's buddies were on him. One slammed a fist into his lower back, knocking the wind out of him, as the other grabbed him in a headlock from behind.

He tried to fight them off as Shane got to his feet again and attacked with both fists before the cop's friends threw Brick to the ground. As he tried to get to his feet, Shane kicked him in the side, then the stomach, then in the head.

Brick heard the sound of sirens as he fought not to black out.

"He's a cop, man," one of his friends said as he pulled Shane away to keep him from kicking Brick again.

"I didn't know he was a cop," Shane said as he stumbled over to him and pulled his wallet out. "I was just walking by and the bastard attacked me. The two of you saw it. I didn't know he was some deputy marshal until I pulled his ID and by then, I had arrested him."

"That's your story?" one of Shane's friends demanded.

"That's *our* story," Shane snapped.

"You are going to get us into so much trouble," his friend complained.

"I already called in the attack," Shane said with a

laugh. "A disturbance in an alley near Henry's Bar. Might need medical attention. Cops attacked."

As the cop car came roaring up, siren blaring and lights flashing, Shane said, "Just stick to the story." Walking past Brick, the cop got in one more kick.

Just before he passed out, Brick heard Mo's angry voice and then she was taking his truck keys as he was being carried to the cop car. The last thing he heard was her saying, "Don't worry, I'll get you out."

Mo HAD WANTED TO attack Shane herself. Instead, she demanded that Brick be given medical attention, promising to bail him out as quickly as she could.

"Shane, you best watch your back," she warned him quietly as Brick was loaded into the back of the ambulance behind the police cruiser.

"You aren't threatening an officer of the law, are you, Mo?" He smirked at her. "Careful, or you'll end up behind bars, as well."

She'd already been behind bars, so she kept her mouth shut. This was all her fault. If she hadn't involved Brick in this… If he hadn't come to her rescue at the bar… Through her anger, she told herself that there was nothing else she could do for Brick. He wouldn't be arraigned until tomorrow at the earliest. All she could do was wait and then get him out on bail—just as he'd done for her.

In the meantime, she had the autopsy report and the photos, and she knew the initials of Tricia's lover. It wasn't much, but there had be something in them to prove that Tricia hadn't taken her own life. Once she did that, she wouldn't let it go until her sister's murderer was caught.

Storming over to Brick's pickup, she climbed in and

tossed the paper sack Lou had given her onto the seat. It toppled over, spilling some of the contents onto the floor.

Mo saw one photo of her sister, the noose around her neck, and burst into tears. She leaned over the steering wheel, letting it all out. For weeks, she'd used her anger keep her from releasing the pain inside her. Now it overflowed with chest-aching sobs, the dam breaking.

After a few minutes, she gulped and wiped furiously at her face. Finally under control, she leaned down to pick up everything that had fallen. She was shoving it all back into the paper sack when she realized the paper in her hand hadn't come out of the bag Lou had given her.

She stared down at the sheet of paper. It took her a moment to realize what she was looking at—the flyer Thomas's associate Quinn had handed her outside the jail. Something caught her eye. She smoothed out the sheet of paper.

Jeffrey Palmer, the self-made man and seminar speaker. JP. She remembered Thomas talking about the wonderful speakers his company always managed to book. Hadn't Tricia gone to one of these with her husband?

The multimillionaire's list of accomplishments was a mile long. She stared at his photograph. He had to be pushing seventy with thick gray hair and bushy gray eyebrows. This man couldn't have been Tricia's lover, could he?

Jeffrey Palmer was hosting a cocktail party the last night of the conference at his home in Big Sky. She was telling herself that it was just a coincidence that the man had the same initials as Tricia's lover when she turned the flyer over and froze.

In this photograph, Jeffrey Palmer Sr. stood next to his son, Jeffrey "JP" Palmer Jr. Her gaze dropped to the cutline under the photograph. Palmer and his son had received the governor's award for a nonprofit corporation they'd started called My Son's Dream, an animal sanctuary.

Her heart began to pound harder. My Son's Dream. MSD, Inc. The animal shelter where Tricia had volunteered. Mo remembered a baseball cap with MSD, Inc., on it that her sister had worn to a picnic last summer.

She looked closer at the photo of JP. According to his bio, he was just a year older than Mo. The closer she looked at him, she realized she recognized him. He'd changed considerably since college. He'd filled out, no longer wore thick dark-rimmed glasses, and his dull brown hair was now blond. In college, he'd gone by Junior.

Like Hope, Jeffrey junior had always been at the periphery of the group that she and Tricia had hung out with. So Hope would have known Jeffrey junior, but probably wouldn't have remembered him by JP any more than Mo had.

Was it possible this was Tricia's lover? It had to be. It was his animal shelter that Tricia had worked at. She recalled Thomas complaining about how much time she spent down there. That had to be where they'd met, and hadn't Hope said that Tricia and her lover had shared a soft spot for animals?

Her heart was a drum in her chest. She recalled Hope saying that Tricia and her lover had joked about how much Thomas loved Jeffrey Palmer's seminars. The pieces of the puzzle fit.

"I've got you, JP," she said as she started the pickup. Now all she had to do was find out why her sister had wanted her to have the papers she'd left for her. They must have meant something to Tricia. Mo had a friend, Elroy, in finance.

Thirty minutes later, she dropped off the papers. Elroy promised to get back to her. She thought about waiting until she got Brick out on bail before she confronted JP, but that would be so not like her, she thought as she drove out to the animal shelter.

Chapter Fourteen

Brick sat on the cot in the cell, worrying about Mo. He knew she could take care of herself. But he also knew how emotionally involved she was in finding out the truth about her sister's death. That alone could put her off her usual guard. Not to mention, they'd already been shot at. He no longer doubted that they had been on the trail of a killer. A killer who now knew that Mo was after him.

At the rattle of his cell door, he looked up to find a guard standing there. "Phone call," the man said, not sounding happy about it as he unlocked the door. "Come on."

In a small office off the cell block, he took the phone that was handed to him. "Hello?" He was hoping to hear Mo's voice. But his gut told him there could be only one person calling. He closed his eyes at the sound of his father's voice.

"What the hell, Brick?"

He turned his back to the guard, keeping his voice down. "I was jumped in the alley by three cops. Believe me, I didn't start this."

Marshal Hud Savage sighed. "Maybe it's the best place for you right now."

"It's not." He glanced at the cop standing by the door.

"Mo is out there trying to find her sister's murderer. I'm worried about her."

"I'm worried about *you*."

"Mo will get me out once I see a judge."

"Brick, if you're serious about keeping your job—"

"I'll take care of this." There were witnesses at the bar when Shane attacked Mo and he had hopes that the other two cops would tell the truth when push came to shove. But this wouldn't look good on his record if he couldn't convince a judge of his innocence.

Mo REALIZED THAT she would have never connected JP with the young man she remembered from college. Seeing this version of the man, she could understand how Tricia might have fallen for him. He had broad, well-developed shoulders and had apparently traded the glasses for contacts, and his face was ruggedly handsome, all sign of his bouts of acne long gone under his tan.

But the shyness was still there. Mo could see where Tricia would have found it charming. She watched him move through the crowd, greeting people as he went. Apparently the shelter was having a fund-raiser this evening. Mo thought of all the organizations father and son were involved in, including MSD, Inc. But it was the shelter that would have helped steal Tricia's heart.

When he reached her, she saw the sparkle of surprise in his blue eyes. She hadn't expected him to remember her. But then again, if he'd been having an affair with her sister…

"Maureen," he said and reached for her hand, cupping it in both of his large ones. "It is so good to see you. I didn't realize you were an animal lover."

"Not as much as my sister, Tricia, I'm sure."

His eyes narrowed slightly, but his smile remained

in place. "Let's step into my office." She followed him down a thick-carpeted hallway lined with framed professional photographs of adorable animals.

Everything about this part of the shelter felt lavishly done so she wasn't surprised when he opened the door to his office. It had the same polished, rich look to it from the shine of the huge mahogany desk to the well-appointed other furnishings.

"We're having a little thank-you party for some of our donors, so I don't have much time to spare." He closed the door behind him. "Please have a seat," he said as he motioned to one of the chairs in front of the desk. He took his seat behind the desk. "Can I get you some coffee, water, champagne?"

"I'm good, thanks," she said as she sank into the soft leather. "It's been a long time." She considered him. "You've changed."

He chuckled. "Just on the outside. I'm still that shy, tongue-tied awkward guy I was in college."

She highly doubted that and said as much.

Leaning back, he seemed to study her. "I didn't think you ever knew who I was at college."

She knew that Tricia would have been impressed by these surroundings. JP, like his father, had made something out of himself and he was saving animals. It would have been a deadly combination.

"But my sister would have remembered you," she said. "When the two of you ran into each other here at the shelter."

His eyes lost some of the blue twinkle. "She told you about us?"

"No, *you* did. The heart you carved in the tree at the campground above Red Lodge. You used her maiden name initial. TM plus JP. Instead of *C* for her married name, Colton. You did know she was married, right?" She saw the answer in his expression. "Mortensen was the name you'd known her by in college, but I guess I don't have to tell you that."

"She didn't pay any more attention to me in college than you did, but we realized we knew some of the same people."

Was that bitterness she heard in his voice? "Is that why you decided to ruin her marriage and ultimately her life?"

He sat forward so abruptly it startled her. "I *loved* her. I still love her." His voice broke and tears flooded his eyes. "It just happened. Working here together, we fell in love. We didn't mean for it to happen."

She looked around his posh office for a moment. "Did your father know about you and Tricia?"

He sat back again. "Why would you ask that?"

She said nothing and waited, her gaze coming back to him.

Finally, he said, "My father wasn't happy about my falling in love with a married woman, no. But I didn't care and I told him as much. I was going to marry her and we were going to raise our son together."

"*Your* son?" She stared at him. "Joey was your son?"

"I don't know that he was mine biologically. It didn't matter. As far as I was concerned, he was ours no matter what."

"That's very noble," she said, unable to keep the sarcasm out of her voice.

"I told you. I loved her. I would have done anything for her. *Anything.*"

"Where did the two of you get together besides here?" she asked, having seen the inviting leather couch off to one side of the room.

He sighed. "Does it really matter?"

She narrowed her gaze on him. "It does to me."

"My father has a cabin outside of Red Lodge." She could just imagine what Jeffrey Palmer Sr.'s *cabin* was like. "Are these questions really necessary? Your sister is—"

"Dead. Yes, I know. When did Tricia break it off?" She waited and when he didn't answer, she said, "She did break it off, right? You must have been upset."

"Of course I was upset. She told me she was pregnant with Thomas's son. I knew she couldn't know that for sure. But it was clear she wanted Joey to be his. She was determined to make her marriage work as if she had to pay penitence for falling in love with me."

"But even after she broke it off, the two of you were still seeing each other," Mo said.

He looked away for a moment. "We couldn't stay away from each other. I wanted her to tell Thomas. I was sick of lying and hiding in the shadows. I wanted everyone to know how much I loved her."

"You must have been angry when she wouldn't."

JP groaned. "What are you getting at? You think me putting pressure on her drove her to suicide?"

"Do you think she killed herself?"

He went stone cold still, his eyes widening. "I… I was told that she did. Are you telling me she didn't?"

She didn't take her gaze from his face. "I think there's a chance someone murdered her."

JP looked as if he was in shock. He stood up, but then sat back down. His gaze ricocheted around the room before falling on her again. "She was *murdered*?" He seemed genuinely shocked.

"I don't have any proof. Yet."

He stared at her. "Then why would you say something like that?"

"Natalie. She told me it wasn't suicide."

"How would Natalie know?" When she said nothing, he continued as if trying to work it out himself. "Tricia didn't accidentally hang herself. Though Natalie certainly isn't the most reliable source." Mo realized that JP hadn't heard about Natalie's death. He'd just referred to her in the present. "But if Natalie is telling the truth…" His gaze locked with hers. "I always feared what Thomas would do when he found out."

"But he wasn't going to find out—not unless you told him," Mo said. She thought of what Natalie had written in the note. "After Joey was born, she refused to see you again, didn't she? Natalie witnessed your argument."

Mo watched his expression sour. She could see the answer in the hard glint of his blue eyes. He tapped his freshly manicured nails on the edge of the desk for a moment before balling his hands into fists. She could see him fighting to get control again.

"Tricia was a mess. She blamed herself for Joey's medical problems. She thought it was karma, payback. I tried to reason with her… We were so right for each other. We loved each other. We belonged together." He looked down, saw his tightly fisted hands and quickly relaxed them.

Mo thought of how stubborn her sister could be. "I take it she wouldn't listen to reason?"

He scoffed. "She didn't want to break Thomas's heart. My heart was another story." His hands had fisted again and his blue eyes had gone dark. He met her gaze, and in that moment she saw a man capable of murder.

Chapter Fifteen

Back in downtown Billings, Mo went to work to free Brick. She canvassed the neighborhood near the coffee shop until she found what she was looking for—a surveillance camera that had caught everything that happened in the alley.

"I'd prefer to handle this in-house," the chief of police told her after he'd watched the surveillance video she'd copied to her phone. He'd watched it twice before swearing and handing her phone back. She knew this wasn't the first time there had been complaints against Shane Danby. "Email me that," he said gruffly. "We should talk about you coming back to work."

Mo got to her feet. "I appreciate everything you've done for me—"

"I'm not accepting your resignation if that's what you're about to say. Mo, I know how hard all this has been on you. You need time, so take as much as you want. Please, don't make a hasty decision."

She nodded. "Thank you. Can you release Deputy Marshal Brick Savage for me?"

He groaned. "What the hell was Shane thinking? A deputy marshal whose father is the marshal at Big Sky?" Shaking his head, he picked up the phone and called down. Hanging up, he turned to her again. "He's all yours."

She smiled at that.

"By the way, I'm not sure what the two of you are up to…" He waited as if he'd hoped she would fill in the blanks.

"We're just friends enjoying a Montana summer together."

Her boss groused. "Have it your way."

Downstairs, Mo was waiting as Brick was brought out. She grimaced at his swollen black eye, the bandaged cut on his temple, a split lip and the bruise on his cheek. She could tell from the way he was moving that his ribs were bruised. She hoped she didn't run into Shane in a dark alley because she knew it would take a half-dozen men to pull her off him.

Not wanting Brick to see how shocked she was by his injuries or how furious it made her, she joked, "We really have to quit meeting like this."

He smiled even with his cut lip. "Good to see you, too."

"This is all my fault," she said. "If I hadn't got into it with Shane—"

"Nothing about this is your fault. He's a bad cop. You already knew he was dangerous and he's worse when he has two friends with him."

"Well, all charges against you have been dropped. A surveillance camera on one of the businesses across from the alley caught it all. Shane will be lucky to keep his job, and the other two…" She shook her head. "Fools that they are, hopefully they'll wise up and put some distance between themselves and Shane. But I have good news."

"Sounds like you already gave me the good news," he said as she handed him his keys.

"I found JP," she said.

"YOU FOUND HIM?" Brick grinned at her as they walked out of the police station. She just kept amazing him. He couldn't believe how glad he was to see her—and not just because she'd gotten him out of jail. The moment he'd spotted her coming toward him, he'd felt his pulse kick up. When she smiled at him… What was it about this woman? She was often prickly as a cactus, annoyingly stubborn and impossible to reason with much of the time. But just the thought of this being over and never seeing her again…

He tried to concentrate on what she was telling him.

As she finished filling him in on her meeting with JP at the animal shelter, he felt sick. While he was behind bars, she'd risked her life. "You shouldn't have gone there alone. If there is even a chance that he's responsible for your sister's death—"

She laughed at that as they exited the building. "You keep forgetting that I'm a cop. I can take care of myself. Protecting me, well, that's not why I need you."

He felt heat rush to his veins and smiled as he stopped to face her. "You need me?" He locked eyes with her for a few breathless moments.

She laughed. "You're growing on me, okay?"

He'd been fighting the urge to take her in his arms and kiss her for too long. He pulled her to him, his mouth dropping to hers. She melted into him as if she'd been made to fit there. Her lips parted as he pulled her closer, deepening the kiss and completely forgetting where they were until he heard cheering and clapping.

They pulled apart as a group of cops came out of the police station and headed for his pickup.

He opened her passenger-side door for her before he walked stiffly around to climb behind the wheel. When he looked over at Mo, he saw that her cheeks were flushed. "About the kiss—"

She cut him off. "I liked it, okay? Let's leave it at that for now."

He couldn't help his grin as he punched the key into the ignition. "So," he said, clearing his throat. "Do you think JP might be responsible for your sister's death?" Brick heard her settle into her side of the pickup cab. He wondered if her heart was pounding as hard as his was.

"I don't know. I think JP's life of privilege and his unrequited love for my sister makes him capable of murder. I want to talk to his father. The elder Jeffrey Palmer was not happy about the situation. I'm wondering what he might have done about it."

Her cell phone rang. She checked to see who it was and quickly picked up. "Elroy, tell me you made sense of those papers I gave you." She listened, nodding, then smiling over at Brick. "If you're sure that's what needs to be done. Just keep a copy of them for…insurance." She chuckled. "No, I don't trust anyone. And thanks again." As she disconnected, she looked like the cat who'd eaten the canary. "We definitely should talk to Jeffrey Palmer Sr."

"You aren't going to tell me?"

She merely smiled. "Let's see what Jeffrey says first."

He liked that there was no question about them not working together anymore. They were in it to the end. He just didn't like thinking about it ending.

"Jeffrey Palmer Sr. has a lodge near Lone Peak

Mountain outside of Big Sky. I thought we could pay him a surprise visit."

Brick smiled over at her as he started the pickup. "Lucky me, I know the way."

THE TRACKING DEVICE isn't working."

The PI sat up in bed, blinking as he tried to wake up. He'd been on an all-night surveillance trying to get the goods on a cheating husband and had just gotten to sleep when his cell phone had rung.

He started to ask, "Who is this?" but then he knew. He'd thought it was the last he'd be hearing from this client. "I put it on the deputy's truck."

"Well, you must have not gotten it right because I show the truck is on its way to the Midwest."

Jim groaned. "He must have discovered it." That could mean only one thing. "He must have caught you following him." Silence. He closed his eyes, cursing silently. This is why he hated to have clients take over the surveillance. They thought they could do this, but often learned the hard way that it wasn't that easy. Now his client had blown it.

"What can we do now?"

He opened his eyes, having been here before. "I might be able to find them but it will take time and money."

"Find them. I don't care what it costs."

The PI smiled. This was why he always put a second tracking device on the vehicle that only he could access on his phone. He knew it wouldn't be found because the first device was where it couldn't be missed. Once they found the first one, they never looked for a second.

"I'll do what I can." He hung up and reached for his phone to check the device. It appeared the deputy was headed home to Big Sky. Turning off the phone, Jim lay back down and closed his eyes. He would let the client stew for at least a few hours before he called to inform him of the cost before he told him where he could find the deputy.

A THUNDERSTORM MOVED across the tops of the mountains, smothering the sunlight and throwing the canyon in deep shadow as they neared Big Sky.

"I don't know about you, but I'm hungry," Brick said. He'd had breakfast in jail, but hadn't eaten since.

"I'm starved," Mo said and glanced around, surprised they were almost back to Big Sky. She realized she must have fallen asleep—and not had a nightmare. That alone surprised her almost as much as the earlier kiss. Oh, she'd known that Brick was going to kiss her. She'd been expecting it for some time.

What had come as a shock were the emotions the kiss had evoked. Not just desire. The deputy was drop-dead sexy. But the close feeling she'd felt. The safe, protected...loving feeling that had filled her. Was that why she hadn't had the nightmare?

That she'd even come close to thinking the *L* word scared her. She knew his reputation and she wasn't about to fall for him. Maybe she hadn't had the nightmare because she knew she was close to getting justice for her sister—if not for Joey.

"I know a great place to eat," Brick said and pulled out his phone. "I'll get us a reservation."

"Reservation?" She looked down at what she was wearing. "I'm not dressed for somewhere fancy."

"Trust me, you're dressed perfectly for this place." He grinned at her and even the approaching thunderstorm couldn't dampen the moment.

She smiled back at him, enjoying his enthusiasm. How easy it would be to fall for this man. She shook her head at that stray thought and realized the time. It was almost five in the afternoon. Whatever restaurant he called must have just opened for the evening.

"Great, we'll be there in about twenty minutes," he said into the phone and disconnected. "The special tonight is roast beef with mashed potatoes, freshly picked carrots in a butter sauce and chocolate cake for dessert."

She groaned. "You are making my mouth water."

"And what a mouth it is."

She felt heat rush to her cheeks and looked away, telling herself not to get caught up in his flirting. At the same time, she was glad to have Brick distracting her. For so long her mind had been dominated by getting justice. She was looking forward to a meal with this man. She'd actually missed him while he was locked up in jail—not that she'd admit it to him, she thought with a smile.

As he passed the exit to Big Sky, she wondered where this restaurant was that he was taking her to. A few miles later, he turned off the highway. The pickup bounced along the dirt road, over a bridge spanning the Gallatin River, and came to a stop in front of a large two-story ranch house. She saw barns and outbuildings, corrals and horses. Up on the mountain was a series of small cabins.

"Brick?" she asked as she took in the house again. This didn't look like a restaurant. As the front door opened and an older woman stepped out wearing an apron, Mo saw the resemblance immediately. "Is that your mother?"

"Best cook in four counties," he said, smiling as he got out of the pickup and came around to her side to open the door for her as if this was a date. She realized that to Brick, it was. Worse, he'd taken her home to meet his mother? And if that patrol car parked on the other side of the ranch pickup was any indication, it wasn't just his mother.

Mo cursed him under her breath. She was having dinner with the marshal and his wife? What had Brick been thinking?

Chapter Sixteen

"Mom, this is Mo," Brick said and quickly added, "Maureen Mortensen."

Dana smiled and reached for Mo's hand. "When my son called and asked about bringing a guest for dinner, I was delighted. I don't see enough of him and it is always wonderful to meet a friend of his."

Mo started to correct her about their relationship, but Brick cut her off as he put his arm around her and said, "I was just telling Mo that my mother is the best cook in four counties."

"Oh, you quit that," Dana said, letting go of Mo's hand to swat playfully at him. She frowned as she took in his injuries, but didn't say anything. No doubt she'd already heard he'd been in jail. "In case you haven't noticed, my son tends to exaggerate."

"I've noticed," Mo said and turned to gaze up at him, her blue eyes hot as a laser. "He's just full of surprises."

His mother cocked her head at him as if wondering about his relationship with this woman, but she was smiling as she ushered them both inside. "Your father should be here shortly. He's checking the new foal. I thought it would be nice to just have dinner with the four of us."

"Where's Angus and Jinx?" he asked as they entered

the farmhouse with its wood floors, Native American rugs and antlers on the walls. The place never changed and that was what he loved about it. Coming here always felt like home. The house was cool even on the hot summer evening and rich with the scent of roast beef cooking in the kitchen.

"Your brother has Jinx up on the mountain, helping him at the house," Dana said and turned to Mo. "Angus and his wife are building a home on the ranch. I assume you haven't met either of them yet?" She looked to her son.

He shook his head. "We've been busy."

"So I've heard."

"Angus is my twin brother. I'm the charming one," Brick said. "I'm also the handsome one."

"Don't believe anything Brick says," his mother chided. "He just can't help himself." At the sound of the front door opening, she insisted they have a seat in the dining room while she saw to his father.

Brick knew what that meant. The marshal was unaware of their dinner guests.

"This was a very bad idea," Mo said under her breath as he steered her toward the huge table that took up most of the equally huge dining room.

"It's fine, trust me."

"There you go again thinking I'm going to trust you." She stopped short of the table and turned to face him. "And why are you letting your mother think that we're…"

"Lovers?"

Her eyes flared even hotter. "Involved."

"We *are* involved. And last night we slept together." He grinned to show that he was joking. "What does it matter what she thinks about our relationship?"

"It's not honest. And I like her. I don't want to lie to her."

He cocked an eyebrow at her. "I had no idea you were so straight-laced," he said, leaning close to whisper the words. "I'm beginning to wonder just about your relationships with those men you said you thought you had fallen in love with before."

"If you're asking what I think you are…" She gave him a shove. Brick chuckled, seeing her face redden charmingly before he realized they were no longer alone.

"Marshal," Mo said.

Brick turned to face his frowning father. "I guess Mom warned you that you have dinner guests."

"Everyone, please sit," his mother said, rushing into the room. "Brick's been bragging up my cooking, so I'd better get that roast out before it's overdone."

"Let me help you," Mo said and left Brick alone with his father, which he realized was her plan.

"I hate to even ask," Hud said.

"Then don't. I promised Mo a good meal with lively conversation."

His father harrumphed at that. "Not from me."

"Never from you," Brick said and laughed.

As the marshal moved toward his seat at the head of the table, he placed a hand on his son's shoulder and gave it a squeeze. "Glad to see you're still alive and not in jail."

"Me, too," he admitted as he hurried to help his mother with the huge platter of roast beef. She always cooked as if for an army so he'd known there would be plenty. Mo brought out bowls of towering fluffy mashed potatoes and freshly snapped and cooked green beans from his mother's garden as well as the buttered carrots.

As Brick pulled out a chair for Mo to sit, his mother ran back into the kitchen for the homemade rolls still warm from the oven, along with butter and honey.

"Brick, if you would pour the iced tea," she said as she took her seat on her husband's right. She always sat close to the kitchen in case anyone needed anything. He knew that one of the reasons she stayed in such good shape was that she kept so busy taking care of all of them.

And yet as the food was passed around and his mother kept the conversation going, he was reminded that both of his parents were at the age where they had started to slow down. He was glad that he'd come home to stay and could help out more.

"Interesting how you two met," his mother was saying.

"I sprung her from jail," Brick said. "Will make a fun story to tell our children."

Mo KICKED HIM under the table and said, "He is such a kidder, isn't he?"

"Isn't he though?" the marshal agreed, joining the conversation for the first time. "Are you about done with your…investigation?"

"We're getting it narrowed down," Brick said. "Tonight we're going to a cocktail party up on the mountain. Jeffrey Palmer Sr. is putting it on. Are you familiar with him?" he asked his father.

"Only by reputation."

Mo noticed that this part of the conversation had definitely piqued the marshal's interest, though.

"He's a very powerful man," the marshal said. "I hope—"

"That we'll be well behaved?" Brick said and laughed. "Always."

"Brick," Dana began, but was cut off.

"I've had the charges against Mo dropped," Hud to his son. "I believe the charges against you in Billings have also been dropped? I was hoping that would be the last of your combined jail times."

"Our hope, as well," Brick agreed.

Mo saw that the marshal's gaze was on her. "You still believe that your sister was murdered?"

She nodded, sorry that the conversation had taken this turn. She was enjoying the wonderful meal and pleasant conversation with Dana. She had liked her at once. What a warm, loving woman. No wonder Brick was the man he was.

"And where does Jeffrey Palmer fit into this?" the marshal asked.

"His son, JP, was having an affair with my sister," Mo said.

Hud sighed. "He's a suspect, but his father…?"

"His father knew about the relationship and disapproved," Mo said. "If he wanted my sister out of his son's life badly enough…" She didn't add what Elroy suspected about the financial papers Tricia had left for her. He was having a friend look at them and would get back to her.

The marshal leaned back in his chair, pushing his nearly empty plate away. "You two are scaring me. If you really believe either of these men is capable of murder…"

"We'll be careful," Brick said.

His mother rose to take their plates, announcing that there was chocolate cake for desert. Mo could see how nervous she was with this kind of talk. After all the years her husband had been in law enforcement, Mo would have thought that she'd gotten use to it. She got up to help with the cake.

"It's a cocktail party," Mo said, trying to relieve her concerns as she came into the kitchen. "There will be lots of people there. I'm sure there won't be any trouble."

Dana turned to look at her. "You know that I'm not delighted with Brick joining the marshal's department."

Mo nodded, seeing that she also wouldn't be delighted with having another cop in the family. "Brick and I aren't...in a romantic relationship."

The ranch woman smiled at her, the skin around her eyes crinkling with humor. "I was going to say that I've accepted that Brick wants to follow the path his father took. I'll never get used to the discussions we've had around my dining room table, but I've also never seen Brick happier. Thank you." Dana reached for her hand and squeezed it. "We'd better get this cake out there and save my son from his father's interrogation."

Mo wanted to tell her that she wasn't responsible for Brick's happiness, but before she could, the woman pushed four dessert plates into her hands. Dana picked up the most beautiful chocolate layer cake Mo thought she'd ever seen before leading the way back into the dining room.

It wasn't until after dessert that Mo found herself alone with the marshal. She felt she had to say something into the heavy silence that had fallen over the room in Brick's and his mother's absence.

"I'm sure you're angry at me for getting your son involved in this," she said and waited.

Hud studied her openly for a moment, then shook his head. "Brick is his own man. He's always been determined to finish what he started. What worries me is that he's never brought a woman home. That he brought you home for one of his mother's meals… He's falling for you." He must have seen her surprise. "He jokes around, yes, but I know my son. All I ask is that you not break his heart since this is a first for him."

Their conversation ended abruptly as Brick and his mother returned from helping his mother with the dishes, something he'd insisted on. Clearly the two had been in silent alliance.

Mo had trouble following the rest of the conversation before she and Brick left for the cocktail party at Jeffrey Palmer Sr.'s. She kept thinking about what the marshal had said and wanting to deny—even to herself—how close she and Brick had gotten.

THE PI MADE the call earlier than he'd planned when another case took precedence. After the client wired him the extra fee, he said, "She returned to Big Sky." He held the phone away from his ear as his client let out a thunderbolt of curses.

"Why would she do that?"

Jim had to assume it was a rhetorical question since he didn't know the woman.

"Is she still with that deputy?"

"I can only suppose so. I just know that they returned to Big Sky. If you want more information—"

"I'll get it myself," the client snapped and disconnected.

The PI also disconnected and checked to see where the pickup was now. It appeared to be on the opposite side of the river from the town of Big Sky. He looked closer. It appeared to be at a ranch of some sort.

As he put away his cell phone, he realized that he knew where the deputy's pickup was, but he couldn't be sure that the female was still with him.

He shook his head as if to clear his thoughts. The client was determined to take it from here. He considered what he'd been hired to do over the past few days and tried to make sense of it before he stopped himself.

He often didn't understand why people did what they did. In all the years he'd been a private investigator, he'd found they often did the one thing they shouldn't because it was going to get them into trouble. But they still did it.

He had a feeling his client was about to do something that he would regret.

Jim was just glad he'd gotten his final payment before the fool either ended up dead or in jail. But he had to wonder why the man was so obsessed with the woman cop.

Chapter Seventeen

Jeffrey Sr. ushered them into his den, closing the door behind him before striding around to sit behind his desk. "I was surprised to hear that the two cops who crashed my cocktail party now want to speak to me in my office. Deputy Marshal Brick Savage and Homicide Detective Mo Mortensen?" He pretended to tip his hat to them each. "To what do I owe this honor since one of you is suspended and the other is on inactive duty, as I understand it?" Mo thought it interesting that the man had taken the time to check on both of them first. "So can I assume this isn't a professional visit?"

"Assume whatever you like," she said as she took a seat even though he hadn't offered her one. Brick remained standing next to her chair. "Your son was having an affair with my married sister."

The senior Jeffrey showed no reaction to her statement. She reached out and stroked the wings on the large sculpture of an eagle that graced his desk.

"I'm sure you were aware they were using your residence outside of Red Lodge for their…clandestine rendezvous." To her surprise, she saw that he hadn't been aware of that. His face clouded, eyes darkening, but he quickly recovered.

"If you're asking if I sanctioned such a…relationship, I did not."

"I believe it was at your Red Lodge home that Tricia learned something she shouldn't have. Something about one of your nonprofits that you didn't want the public to know." Still no response. "Knowing Tricia, she would have taken her concerns directly to you. I would imagine you alleviated her fears, but you couldn't trust that she might say something, so you went to her house that day. You knew Thomas wasn't there because he was at work. You're a big strong man. It wouldn't have taken much to see that she never talked. Although Tricia would have fought you. I suspect you drugged her, but that will come out once toxicology tests are run."

"Wasn't her body cremated?"

That this man knew that chilled her to the bone. "I guess you haven't heard. A scientist found a way to get evidence from a cremated body. I've turned Tricia's remains over to Forensics."

Did Jeffrey look paler? He wiped a spot on his upper lip that had turned shiny.

"The police had no reason not to believe it was a suicide after Tricia lost her baby—and maybe a hint that her marriage was on the rocks," Mo said. "How am I doing so far?"

"It's your tale," the man said, looking bored.

"Basically, you killed two birds with one stone. You weren't happy about your son and Tricia's relationship, especially with a baby involved. So that took care of that as well as making sure your secret never came out."

Jeffrey chuckled. "I'm much smarter than I thought since apparently I also got away with it because all of this is simply conjecture. If you had any proof, the *real* police would be here, right?"

"I can't prove that you killed her, but you definitely had motive."

Jeffrey sighed. "I really have no idea what you're talking about. What is it you want from me? I'm a busy man and my guests are waiting."

Mo pushed to her feet. "Nothing. I believe I'll have what I've come for soon. Justice for my sister."

She started to turn to leave but stopped. "By the way, those incriminating papers Tricia found in your study at the Red Lodge cabin? She made copies. She loved dogs and when she realized what you were using the nonprofit facility to do, she planned to stop you. But she must have told you that." She hesitated for a couple of beats. "Or maybe she only told your son. That kind of information could destroy you and JP if he knew about it. But I'm sure he denied everything to her—unless she didn't believe him. Oh, and the evidence? I put it somewhere safe with instructions that if anything should happen to me or anyone around me, it would be released to the FBI and the media—and not just locally."

With that she headed for the door. Behind her, she heard Jeffrey pick up the eagle sculpture from his desk. It shattered just feet from them as she and Brick walked out.

ONCE OUT IN the hallway, Brick swore as he spotted his father moving through the crowd. "My father is here. I need to see why—other than worrying about us."

"I could use some fresh air," Mo said. "I'm going to step out on the patio. Holler if you need me."

He chuckled at that. He would always need her, he thought, and quickly stepped away before he was fool enough to say it.

"Tell me you didn't follow us," Brick said as he stepped up behind his father.

The marshal turned, pretending surprise to see his son there. "I just came for the champagne."

Brick laughed. "Sure you did. Seriously," he said, lowering his voice. "What are you doing here?"

"It has nothing to do with you."

"Right."

"But I do wish that you and Mo would get out of here soon," his father said, glancing around.

Brick felt the hair prickle on the back of his neck. "You're here for a bust? *And arrest?* Is it—"

The marshal shot him a look that made him swallow back the words. He thought about what Mo had said to Jeffrey Sr. Did she really have some kind of evidence on him that would be worth killing to keep secret? Or had she been bluffing? The woman could craft a lie faster than anyone he'd ever met and yet…

He met his father's gaze. "I'll find Mo and we'll go."

AFTER BRICK LEFT to talk to his father, Mo had started for the doors out to the patio when she'd heard a voice directly behind her. She'd instantly tensed as she'd recognized it.

"We should step out on the patio." JP had placed his hand in the center of her back, his touch gentle but insistent.

Mo didn't put up a fight as he'd pushed open the patio doors and they exited the cocktail party. The patio was large, hanging over the side of the mountain, and the view was spectacular. The patio was also empty since the breeze was a reminder that the mountains around them were still snowcapped. Or maybe she felt the chill because she suddenly found herself alone on the edge of a precipice with a man who very possibly was a killer.

Jeffrey steered her to the edge, as far from the party as possible. "What are you doing here?" he demanded. He was dressed in formal attire and couldn't have been more handsome and distinguished. Her heart ached at the thought that if Tricia had seen him like this, she would have fallen instantly in love with him. He would have been everything she didn't have in her life with Thomas, everything she'd apparently yearned for and maybe hadn't even realized it.

Unlike Mo, her sister wouldn't have seen beyond the veneer and the money and prestige. "I wanted to talk to your father."

He frowned. "Why?"

"To tell him that I knew what was going on at your nonprofit animal shelter and probably all you and your father's other businesses—and so did Tricia."

"What are you talking about?"

Did he really not know? No, Tricia would have told him, wouldn't she? She would have given him a chance to explain.

"I'm talking about the reason the woman you say you loved is dead."

He shook his head, looking confused. "You think it has something to do with the shelter?" He raked a hand through his blond hair. "You can't possibly think that I... I loved her," he said with both conviction and what sounded like pain. "I would have done anything for her. Anything."

"You said that before. What *did* you do for her?" Mo asked as she hugged herself against the night chill and the knowledge that she was taking a chance with her life being here with him. She glanced toward the house. She doubted anyone but Brick knew she was coming out here.

"What are you trying to accuse me of?" he demanded, some of that anger she'd seen before surfacing.

"You said she wouldn't leave Thomas, or was it the baby that was the problem?"

He stared at her as if in disbelief.

"What happened between you and Tricia at the end?"

He shook his head. "I told you. She broke it off."

"And you never saw her again. You never tried to change her mind. You never went by her house."

His gaze narrowed as he settled it on her again. "The nanny saw us, didn't she?" He let out a bitter chuckle. "I thought at least she would have told you or Thomas what she'd overheard, but I guess she was busy with her own…problems."

"I know you were angry, much as you are right now."

He seemed to catch himself and draw back, pulling in his ire as he dropped his voice again. "She did break it off, but then she changed her mind. We were going to raise Joey together. She was going to tell Thomas but then Joey was killed, Natalie was arrested…"

"She never told Thomas."

Jeffrey shook his head. "You know Tricia. She was devastated by all of it, but Thomas was inconsolable. She couldn't do it. She begged me to give her time."

"And when you didn't—"

"Why are you so determined to make me the villain?" he demanded. "I told her she could have all the time she needed. I was a mess, too. I'd been looking forward to us being a family. With Joey gone…" He looked away. "She wasn't sure she wanted to risk having another child. I told her we could adopt. We were planning a future together. Why would I kill her?"

Mo studied him in the faint light coming from the house and realized that he at least believed every word of it. And she believed that he'd loved Tricia as she saw his eyes fill. He hastily wiped at them as the glass doors into the house opened and his father called his name.

"I have to go," he said and cleared his throat. His watery gaze met hers. "I loved her. If I'd had any idea that she might…" He shook his head, reached for her hand and squeezed it. "I miss her so much."

With that, he walked back toward the house and his waiting father.

Mo stood at the edge of the patio, looking out across the mountaintops into the darkness beyond. Lost in her thoughts, she started when she felt a hand on her arm and spun around to find Brick.

"We need to get out of here."

ON THE WAY off the mountain, Mo told Brick what Elroy had told her.

"Money laundering?" He shook his head. "And your sister knew?"

"Apparently. Why else would she copy the financial records? Tricia was a whiz at math and loved all that stuff, while just the thought makes my head hurt. She either recognized what was going on or at least suspected."

"Your theory is that she told JP?" He heard Mo hesitate.

"She was in love with JP. I believe she found the papers at his father's home outside of Red Lodge. I think she went to the old man."

He shot her a look. "Then he killed her to keep her from coming forward?"

"Also from telling his son. According to the lecture

series flyer that Quinn gave me that day, the animal shelter was something he did for his son. If JP knew how it was really being used…"

Brick shook his head. "JP has to know. Whoever came by Tricia's house that day was someone she knew and trusted. Otherwise she wouldn't have opened the door to him." He saw that Mo hadn't wanted to believe it.

She put her face in her hands for a moment. "How could a man who professed his undying love for her kill her?"

"You're a homicide detective. You know. She'd hurt him. He could have lied about this rosy future the two of them had planned. It could be a case of *if I can't have her, neither will Thomas.*"

"That isn't love," she said, removing her hands to look over at him.

"No. But love and hate can be two sides of the same coin…"

"I guess I've never been in love."

He considered her for a moment as he drove down from the mountain into Meadow Village. "Never, huh? Maybe we have that in common."

She didn't look at him and asked, "Where are we going?"

He hadn't really known where he was headed. After everything she'd told him, he had to assume that Tricia wasn't the only one who'd suspected something was going on with Jeffrey Palmer's nonprofit businesses. The self-made man could be in handcuffs by now—and so could his son. "I hadn't thought—"

"Let's go to your apartment."

"To my apartment?" He must have misheard her.

"Are you sure about that?" She shot him a look. He held up one hand in surrender. "My apartment it is."

He could feel her gaze on him. As he pulled into the parking spot behind his apartment, he asked, "Are you sure about this?"

She chuckled. "It's the only thing I've been sure about for a very long time."

Brick met her gaze in the glow of a streetlamp up the block. "You know my reputation. I don't want to hurt you."

Mo smiled. "You won't because whether you know it or not, you're as crazy about me as I am about you."

He laughed. "You think?"

"I *know*." Her words came out a whisper, as light as a caress.

He studied her in the dim light, realizing that he was a captive to everything about her—and had been since the moment he broke her out of jail. "Are you ever unsure about anything?"

"*Everything*, but this." She leaned toward him, cupping his face in her hands, and kissed him gently on the lips.

He drew her to him, buried his face in her hair and whispered, "Do you know how badly I want you?"

"As much as I want you," she whispered as she leaned her head back to let him trail kisses down her throat. He felt her shudder, his desire spiking, as his kisses reached the rise of her breasts. He could see her hard nipples through her bra and the fabric of her blouse.

"You are so dang sexy. I want to take you right here."

"What's stopping you?" she asked, her voice cracking with emotion.

He chuckled. "Bucket seats," he said and drew back to look into those blue eyes of hers. He took a breath, suddenly terrified. He didn't just want this woman. He *wanted* this woman, all of her, for keeps. He'd never felt like this and it scared the hell out of him.

"You ready to see my apartment?" he asked. "It's not much to look at."

"I doubt we'll be looking at the decor." She reached to open her door.

He caught her before she could get out, and opened his mouth to say what? He'd never know because she put a finger over his lips and shook her head.

A low, seductive chuckle rose from her lips. "We're acting as if this is the scariest thing we'll ever do. It just might be because I suspect there's no coming back from it." With that, she exited the pickup.

Brick sat for just a moment before he opened his door and followed her. He actually fumbled opening the door. He felt tongue-tied and uncertain as if this was his first time. In so many ways, it was.

He held the apartment door open and Mo stepped through. The moment he entered and closed the door behind him, she turned to him and, stepping forward, she began to slowly unbutton his shirt. She looked up at him with those big blue eyes and he was overcome with a longing for something he'd never experienced before. He lowered his mouth to hers and knew he was lost.

Mo LAY IN Brick's arms. They'd finally made it to the bed. Earlier, the moment the door had closed, they were tearing at each other's clothing. They had been headed here for some time, she knew, but she hadn't expected the kind of passion they'd inspired—and neither had Brick, it seemed from the dazed look on his face.

After their crazed lovemaking, they'd lain on the floor, unable not to laugh as they stared up at the ceiling and tried to catch their breaths. After a few minutes, they looked over at each other. She remembered looking into those deep blue eyes of his and feeling… love and desire, hotter than a Fourth of July firecracker.

They'd made love again, slower this time, but with no less passion.

It was crazy, no doubt about it. They hadn't known each other but for a few days. Mo thought of her sister. Tricia would have said that they didn't know each other, that they needed to take some time, that they didn't even know where this was headed.

But then again, Mo thought, maybe her sister wouldn't have said any of those things. Tricia had fallen in love with a man who wasn't her husband. That she could do something like that given how straight-laced she was… Well, Mo smiled to herself. Maybe Tricia would have understood, maybe even approved since the only two people who could get hurt were Mo and Brick.

Mo started at the pounding on the door. She shot a look at Brick. "Your father?"

He shrugged and got up from the bed to pull on his jeans. She grabbed what she could find of her clothing and hurried into the bathroom and closed the door. She could hear voices. The marshal?

She was dressed pretty much by the time Brick tapped on the door.

"There's someone who needs to see you," he said.

She opened the door and looked out. Her brother-in-law, Thomas, stood just inside the door—which was almost in the middle of the tiny studio apartment.

"Thomas?" she asked, stepping from the bathroom. Out of the corner of her eye, she saw Brick pull on a shirt. They were both barefoot and she hadn't been able to find her bra. Her body still tingled from their lovemaking and she knew her cheeks had to be flushed. "What are you doing here?" she asked, catching the tumble of covers on the unmade bed out of the corner of her eye.

"I have to talk to you," he said, a muscle jumping in his jaw as he looked from her to Brick. "I had a feeling you'd be here." He didn't sound approving, which instantly got her hackles up.

"We should step outside." She moved toward him even as he glanced pointedly at her bare feet. "This won't take long," she said to both him and Brick. Once out on the outdoor second-story landing, she demanded to know what he wanted.

As if seeing her ire, he said, "I'm sorry, but I had to talk to you. I came up after Jeffrey called me, but when I got there, he and JP were being arrested. Do you have any idea what is going on? Does it have something to do with Tricia's death?"

His words stopped her cold. Did he know about Tricia and JP? "Why would you ask that?"

"Because she worked at that animal shelter they owned."

"Remember, I was suspended. I don't know what charges are being brought against them," she said truthfully.

"It's not just that," Thomas said. "I found something in Tricia's closet, hidden in the back."

"Why were you digging in—"

"It's a box with a note on top that says I am to give it to you."

She took a breath and let it out slowly. "Did you look inside?" Of course he would look. Any normal person would.

"There were some papers in a manila envelope. I couldn't make heads or tails out of them."

Mo nodded. "She left some other ones for me, as well. You don't need to worry about it. I'm taking care of it." She started to turn back to the door inside. The night air was chilly. Brick's warm arms called to her. She hadn't let herself admit it, but she felt safe with him. Safe and protected in a way that didn't take away her own strength, her own ability to take care of herself.

"It wasn't just paper," Thomas said. "There was also a key to what appears to be bank security box in the bottom of the envelope. I wasn't able to open the box at the bank, but I thought with your police connection…"

She stopped midstep. A safety deposit key? Maybe Tricia had left something even more important. Mo still wanted a letter or a note from her sister. She knew Thomas did, as well.

"Give it to me and I'll see what I can do," she said, holding out her hand.

"I don't have it. I locked it up in my desk at work until I saw you. I didn't expect to find you here in Big Sky or I would have brought it."

She studied him in the faint starlight. "Why are you here if you hadn't known I was?"

"Jeffrey. He called to say he needed to see me."

"About what?"

"He wouldn't say. I just assumed it had something to do with one of his seminars. He had approached me about working for him if I ever thought about leaving my pharmaceutical job."

This surprised her. "Were you thinking of leaving it to work for him?"

Thomas let out a laugh. "Not now that he's been arrested. Listen, I'll let you get back to…" He waved a hand toward the apartment door. "I'm helping lock up Jeffrey's house after the FBI are finished."

"I didn't realize you and Jeffrey were that close." She could tell the question irritated him.

"It's not just me. There's a group of us who have volunteered to help. I'm sure he'll be out within hours once he calls his lawyer." Mo wasn't so sure about that, but she kept her thoughts to herself. "I plan to drive back to Billings tomorrow afternoon," he was saying. "If you're back by then, why don't you stop by my office?"

"Tomorrow's a Sunday. You normally don't work—"

"I like working on the weekends. It gives me something to keep my mind off everything." He must have seen her hesitation. "Or you can wait until Monday or whenever to get the key. Up to you."

He had to know how anxious she was to find out what Tricia had left for them. "I'll drive over tomorrow. I'll call when I get to town." In the meantime, she wanted to spend the rest of this night with Brick.

BRICK'S CELL PHONE brought him swimming up from the wonder of deep, nightmare-less sleep. For a moment, he couldn't find his phone, he was so wrapped up in Mo's warm body. His hand snaked out. He felt around on the table beside the bed and finally found it by the fourth ring. "Hello?" His voice was rough with sleep and the remnants of a night of lovemaking.

"Brick?"

His mother's voice brought him fully awake. "Mom?" Through a crack in the curtains he could see daylight just breaking behind the mountains. He untangled himself from Mo to sit up. She sat up as well, concern in her expression as she turned on the nightlight. "What's wrong?"

"It's your father," his mother's voice broke. "He's had a heart attack. I'm at the hospital with him." The words hit him like thrown stones. "Your uncle Jordan is here with me. We're waiting to hear word on his condition. The rest of the family is on the way."

"Mom, is he…" Brick realized he couldn't say the words. But she wasn't listening. He could hear voices in the background. He felt his heart drop. What was happening? "Mom? Mom?"

"The doctor says they're flying him down to Bozeman to the ICU. I have to go. You can meet us there."

Brick disconnected and looked at Mo.

"I HEARD," MO SAID quickly, squeezing his arm. "Go."

He turned to pull her into a hug for a long moment before he released her and swung his legs over the side of the bed. "Come with me?"

"Brick, I'm the last person your father would want to see—let alone right after a heart attack."

"You know that's not true," he said as he pulled on his jeans and looked around for his boots.

"I'll follow you to the hospital for an update. Then I have to go to Billings. Until I have those papers and that key in my hand…" When she'd come back into the apartment last night, she'd told him everything Thomas had said. He'd insisted that the two of them would go to Billings first thing this morning.

"I know," he said, turning to look at her. "I just don't like you going alone. Even with the Jeffrey Palmers under arrest, they can still get word out to their…associates. You're in danger if they fear the evidence your sister found is more damning than what the feds already have."

She shuddered, well aware of how powerful the men

were—and what kind of friends they must have made in the money laundering business. Also, she didn't want Thomas figuring out a way to get into the box without her. She had a bad feeling that she needed to be there when the box was opened.

"Once I have the papers and whatever was in that safety deposit box…"

"I know. Just be careful and call me as soon as you have everything and are safe," he said.

"I will." She climbed out of bed to kiss him, pressing her body against his as if to memorize the feel of him. He groaned and kissed her hard, bunching the fabric of the sheet she had wrapped around her as he held her to him. She didn't want him to let her go and that told her how afraid she was that something would keep them apart. "I'll call you later to find out how your father is," she said.

He gave her another kiss and released her, though with obvious reluctance.

"What are you doing?" she asked as he pulled out his phone and called the marshal's office to inquire about her car. "You don't have to do that."

He smiled at her and mouthed, "Yes I do," as he asked that one of the deputies bring her vehicle to his apartment. "Just leave the keys under the mat. Thanks." He disconnected. "I'm not leaving you high and dry without your car."

"Stop worrying about me and go. I know how anxious you are to get to your father."

Brick nodded as he pulled on his boots. "Be careful and hurry back to me." His voice sounded rough with emotion.

She swallowed the lump in her throat. "I will." She touched the tip of her tongue to her lower lip, remembering their night of shared intimacy as he recovered his shirt.

As he started for the door, he stopped to look back at her as if hating to leave her. She knew the feeling. Being in his arms, she'd felt free of pain, her heart lifting, her blood a welcoming hammer in her veins. She would have given anything to never leave this bed, never leave this man.

What surprised her even more were the tender feelings she felt for Brick. She'd gotten close to him in a matter of days, something completely unheard of for her, especially with a man. Now he didn't want to leave her any more than she wanted him to.

"Don't worry," she quickly assured him. "I can handle this on my own. You just worry about your dad. I'll call later to see how he's doing. Once I have whatever Tricia left, I'll be back. My prayers are with your dad and the rest of your family. Call me if you need me."

His gaze softened in the early-morning light as he opened the door. "I suspect I am always going to need you." He looked as if he wanted to say more.

"Don't worry. We're not done. Whatever it is you want to say to me, there'll be time."

Brick picked up his Stetson. "I forget that you're always right. Hope you are about this."

"I am." And he was gone.

She stared at the closed door until she could no longer hear the sound of his pickup engine. Even then, she didn't want to move. She still felt wrapped in last night's lovemaking. Brick had been a generous, thoughtful lover. He'd made her feel things she'd never felt before. Afterwards, they'd lain in each other's arms, needing no words.

They'd been spooned together when he whispered next to her ear, "You were right. I'm crazy about you."

She'd smiled and reached back to touch his stubbled cheek. "You're going to get tired of saying that." He'd chuckled and pulled her closer and she'd closed her eyes, drifting off into a sleep free of nightmares.

Still warm with the memory, she headed for the shower.

SITTING NEXT TO the hospital bed in ICU, Brick held his father's large, sun-browned hand in his two hands. He studied the scars and brown spots as if all the man's secrets were hidden there. The doctor said Hud was out of the woods. He'd been lucky that it had only been a mild heart attack.

There would have to be some changes, the doctor had said. Less stress, more dietary restrictions. Brick had seen the relieved look on his mother's face, the tears in her eyes at the good news.

"He has to retire," she'd said. "But will that kill him?"

Brick had shaken his head and hugged her. "He can live vicariously through me, if he lets me back on the force."

"It won't be easy," his mother had said, worry etched on her still pretty face.

"Dad's tough. There isn't anything he can't handle. He'll handle retirement. Maybe there'll be a few grandkids for him to chase around."

She'd smiled. "He would love that and so would I. Thinking of anyone in particular?"

"Angus and Jinx," he'd joked. He would imagine his twin would be all for a passel of kids.

"What about you?" Dana had asked.

"If I found the right woman…"

She'd swatted playfully at him. "You can't fool your mother."

Now he thought about the future for not just his father and mother and the rest of his family. He was worried about Mo and what she would find in that safety deposit box at the bank. He knew how anxious she was to get the key. Maybe, now that his father was out of the woods, he'd drive down to Billings and—

"Brick."

His head jerked up and he looked into his father's eyes.

"You're awake." He let go of his father's hand. "I need to get Mom. She made me promise—"

"Just a moment. I need to say something to you."

"Dad—"

"I'm proud of you."

Brick chuckled. "I know that."

"Do you? Of all my children I've given you the hardest time. It's because you are so much like me and yet also like your mother. What a deadly combination of our free spirits. I realized that I've never told you…" He coughed.

"You really don't have to do this now."

"I do. When I felt that pain in my chest…" His father's eyes filled with tears. "I thought I might not get a chance…" His dad coughed before he added, "I like her."

Brick frowned at him, not sure who he was referring to.

"Mo. She suits you. Don't let her get away."

He laughed and patted his father's hand on the bed. "I don't intend to. But if I don't let Mom know that you're awake she will never forgive me." And yet he didn't want to leave his father. "Thanks, Dad."

His father's eyes closed again. He stepped out into the hall to see his mother headed in his direction. She looked alarmed at first until she saw him smiling. She handed him the cup of coffee she'd brought him and hurried to her husband's side.

Brick thought he'd give them a minute and walked down the hallway away from his dad's room. As he did, his cell phone rang. He stepped into the stairwell to take the call. He'd thought it would be Mo and he really needed to hear her voice.

"Deputy Savage?" The voice was that of an elderly woman. "This is Ruth Anne Hager." The name meant nothing to him at first. The elderly woman had to remind him that he was the one who had approached her.

"I live kitty-corner from the woman who died."

"Oh, yes, Mrs. Hager, I'm sorry."

"It's Miss, but you can call me Ruth Anne."

"All right, Ruth Anne." He waited.

"You said to call if I thought of anything. The other day I was busy with my grandson when you stopped by and didn't have time to even think, let alone recall what happened weeks ago. But since then, I got to thinking. I did see someone go into the back of the house that day. I recall because I was waiting for my trash to be picked up. I'd made some cookies for the men and didn't want to miss them. They're partial to my toffee cookies and they do such a good job, I like to make treats for them."

"You saw someone go into the back of Tricia's house," he gently prodded.

"I was surprised to see the husband return," the woman said. "He never came home at this time of the day, let alone park behind the house. I thought he must be ill."

Brick held his breath for a moment. "You're sure it was her husband?"

"Yes. He was always so punctual on when he came and went. Same time every morning, home same time every night all week long. I liked that about him. Seeing him in the middle of the afternoon on a workday, I was worried."

"What did he do?"

"He went into the house. I'd seen the nanny come out not thirty minutes before that as if headed for the store. That nice-looking young woman. I can't believe what they are saying on the news."

"How long was her husband inside?"

"Well, the two men who pick up my trash came by. I went out to take them their cookies. They always comment on how nice my backyard looks and how neat I keep the area around my trash containers."

"So you visited for a while. Did you hear any noise coming from the house?"

"Their truck was still running so I wouldn't have heard anything but maybe the other neighbors might have. Did you talk to them?"

He and Mo had. "They didn't hear anything."

"I'm sure everything was all right because I saw him when he left. He did seem a little upset, but he wouldn't have just gone back to work if he'd found her. He wouldn't have left her, now, would he?"

The moment Brick got off the phone, he called Mo. Her cell went straight to voice mail. "I need to talk to you before you see Thomas. It's urgent." He left the message, then thought it more likely she would see a text.

T went home day Tricia died.

He sent it and then hurried into his father's room, where his mother was sitting next to the bed. He quickly told them his suspicions.

"I'm afraid she might not get the message before she sees Thomas," he said.

"Call the Billings police," his father said.

Brick shook his head. "I can't trust them after what happened with me."

"Then go," Hud said and reached for the phone beside the bed. "I'll get you a patrol car so you can use the lights and siren. It will get you there much faster."

Mo THOUGHT ABOUT her sister, missing her, as she rode up the elevator to the top floor of the office building. As she stepped out, she had to wipe her tears. Looking around, she caught a glimpse of the Billings skyline through the floor-to-ceiling windows. The rim of rocks the city was famous for gleamed golden in the lights from the city.

She'd never been to Thomas's office. She walked to the wall of glass and tried the door. Then she heard a click and the door opened into a room full of tiny cubicles. Mo realized that she'd never asked Thomas if he enjoyed his work. When he and Tricia had gotten engaged, Thomas had been on his way to medical school. So how had he ended up working for a pharmaceutical company in one of these small cubicles?

The office, she noticed, was empty, most of the overhead lights dark. She started toward the area where there was light when her phone lit up and a notification pinged from her shoulder bag, indicating an incoming text. She started to check it when Thomas called out, "Over here."

She wound her way toward him, thinking of her sister. Had Tricia been unhappy with her choice in a husband? Had nothing turned out the way she thought? Or had she just fallen in love with JP, something she hadn't seen coming? Something that had turned her life upside down and ended in her death?

Mo still had so many questions and feared she might never get all the answers. But at least the paperwork from the animal shelter had helped bring down Jeffrey and JP. She knew the feds had been building a case for a long time. But after Elroy had taken the papers to the FBI, they had moved quickly.

"Hey," Thomas said as he turned in his chair to look at her.

She took in his cubicle, the small desk, the stacks of paperwork, a few sticky notes on his bulletin board to remind him of meetings. A framed photograph of Tricia sat in the corner. She stared at her sister's smiling face and remembered the day the photo was taken. They'd all been at a family picnic not long after Thomas and Tricia were engaged. Her sister looked happy.

"Are you all right?" Thomas asked, bringing her out of her thoughts.

She nodded distractedly. "Were you happy?"

He blinked. "You mean married to Tricia?" She waited for his reply, not sure why she'd asked. "She was the only woman I ever loved."

"But were you happy?" She motioned to their surroundings.

Thomas looked around as if seeing his office space for the first time.

"I remember when you wanted to be a doctor."

He swallowed and looked away. "Dreams change. We were going to start a family. Medical school would have taken so long and been too expensive and Tricia wanted a home and…" His voice died off. "Why are we talking about this now?"

She knew he was right. She cleared the lump in her throat. "You said you found more papers and a safety deposit box key?"

He nodded and rose. She could see that her earlier questions had upset him. "I need a cigarette."

"I didn't know you smoked."

"I hadn't for years until… It's a terrible habit, but right now I need one. Do you mind?"

She did. The drive had been long. She was tired and wanted to get this over with. Tomorrow her partner had said he would go with her to the bank to get the safety deposit box opened.

"If you could just give me the key and papers…"

"Maureen, can't we just step outside for a few minutes? Please?"

The empty office felt eerie and the last thing she wanted to do was breathe in secondhand smoke. But what was one cigarette? "Sure. But after that, I need to go." She wanted to get back to Brick. Once she got the safety deposit key, she would drive back to be with him and his family.

Thomas was rummaging around on his desk for his pack and lighter. "This will just take a minute. I hardly ever see you anymore. I've missed you." She watched him dig around nervously in the drawer.

Something shiny caught her eye on his desk. A lethal-looking silver letter opener. She tried to make out the design, moving the stack of papers until she could see the logo: MSD, Inc. The name of the corporation that ran the nonprofit animal shelter when Tricia met JP? Her heart bounced in her chest.

"Got it." Thomas said as he pocketed his cigarettes and lighter. "We can go outside."

Mo heard her phone ping with another text. She started to check it when Thomas took her phone out of hand.

"You can do without this for a few minutes. I'd like your undivided attention for once," he said, putting the phone down on his desk next to his computer.

As he turned out of the cubicle, she impulsively picked up the letter opener, tucking it into the back waistband of her jeans and covering it with her shirt and jean jacket.

"Coming?" he asked, looking back at her.

She saw something in his gaze. Suspicion? She was sure he hadn't seen her pick up the letter opener. But he did glance at the desk as if he couldn't remember what was on it. Important papers he hadn't wanted her to see? Or something else?

She felt foolish for taking the letter opener. Did she really think taking it would be any less of a reminder of Tricia's betrayal once her affair with JP came out? And she feared it would come out now that he'd been arrested. Tricia had known something was wrong. Would she have blown the whistle had she lived?

Nor was it necessarily strange that Thomas had the letter opener. Tricia could have picked it up at the animal shelter and given it to him before the affair.

Or maybe he'd gotten it from Jeffrey Palmer Sr. The man probably gave them away at his seminars. Thomas having it didn't mean anything. And yet her heart was pounding like a war drum in her chest. She was so sick of all the secrets and lies and worse, the suspicions. Thomas was making her nervous.

"I just need a quick cigarette," he said as he unlocked a door at the end of the long, dimly lit room. It opened onto a set of stairs that rose to another door. He motioned for her to lead the way.

The stairs were even more dimly lit. Their footfalls echoed as they climbed up to the next door. Thomas opened it.

Mo stepped out onto the dark rooftop, Thomas right behind her, and felt a chill that had nothing to do with the summer night air.

Chapter Eighteen

Mo hesitated on the rooftop. She'd never been that fond of heights.

"Come on, you have to see the city from over here." Thomas moved past her, leading the way to a corner of the roof where there were a couple of benches and a planter. She could smell stale cigarettes and see a can filled with butts.

Thomas lit a cigarette and stepped to the edge. "Quite the view, don't you think?" He took a drag. From where she stood, she could see that his hand was shaking as he put the cigarette to his lips again.

Mo moved closer to look out over the city. The view really was breathtaking. But she felt anxious and more nervous than she wanted to admit.

Thomas exhaled and squinted through the smoke as he looked over at her.

Mo felt a frisson of apprehension move through her. From the look in his eyes, he'd brought her up here for more than a cigarette.

"There's something I've been meaning to ask you," he said quietly. "How long have you known Tricia was cheating on me?"

She felt as if the air had been knocked out of her. Any doubt she had about whether or not Thomas knew was answered in that heartbeat. There was also an alarming sharp edge to his question, accusation as jagged as a hunting knife's blade.

"I didn't know. Until a few days ago." She met his gaze. "Tricia didn't tell me. I never would have suspected. I didn't believe it at first."

He let out a hoarse laugh. "I know what you mean." His eyes narrowed again. "You and Tricia were always so close. I thought if anyone knew what was going on with her, it would be you." He waited a beat, then added, "So you know about JP."

"I figured it out."

Thomas nodded. "Have you narrowed it down to which one of them killed her? She must have confronted JP and his father and they had to stop her from going to the cops."

It still hurt that her sister hadn't come to her. Mo felt her aching heart break a little more. Tricia hadn't trusted her. Not until it was too late. She pressed her hands to the top of the short parapet wall and stared out at the city, the lights blurring through her tears.

"It had to be someone Tricia trusted, otherwise she wouldn't have let him into her house—let alone accepted a drink from him." Still she didn't look at Thomas.

"A drink?" he asked, sounding confused.

"Her ashes. I took some to the lab. It's amazing how far forensics has come. There was a time when a person could have a body cremated to cover a crime. Not anymore." At least that much was true. "She was drugged." It amazed her sometimes how easily she could lie.

Thomas angrily snuffed out his cigarette and lit another, his hands shaking so violently that it took several tries. "Drugged?"

"How else would the killer have been able to put a noose around her neck without her fighting back?" The image turned her stomach along with the acrid scent of Thomas's cigarette smoke.

"How did you find out about Tricia's affair?" she asked.

He made a guttural sound. "Jeffrey called me."

Mo closed her eyes, imagining the pain Thomas had felt to have the man he idolized be the one to tell him that his wife was having an affair with the man's son. She turned to look at him. "I'm so sorry."

"Tricia and Thomas, the perfect couple, isn't that what everyone said?" His gaze hardened before he broke eye contact to look out over the city. "And after everything we went through, Tricia finally getting pregnant. We were going to be a little family. Only something was wrong with our baby. *Our baby.* What a laugh."

She could hear the pain and anger in his voice, the night growing colder as a breeze moved like a specter across the rooftop.

Thomas let out a stream of smoke and looked over at her. "Guess how I felt when the doctor told me that they wouldn't be needing my blood for my son's first operation because it wasn't a match?" He nodded, smiling a monster's twisted smile. "I knew Joey wasn't mine. What I didn't know was that Tricia was no longer mine, either. Everything I'd believed was a lie."

"I didn't know about Joey," Mo said quietly.

"No one did." He let out a laugh that sounded more like a sob. "I kept it to myself, still hoping that however Joey had come into existence, it wouldn't destroy our lives. Do you have any idea what it is like to carry a burden like that?"

She couldn't imagine the kind of hell he'd gone

through learning of Tricia's deception, her betrayal, and said as much. But it was her sister who made her heart ache. She tried not to think of her last minutes on earth, balancing on a chair with a noose around her neck, knowing that her husband was going to kill her.

Mo tried not to glance past Thomas for the exit. She didn't want to estimate about how far she might get before he caught her. She could feel the letter opener digging into the flesh at her back. All her excuses as to why she'd picked it up, she knew it hadn't been impulsive. It had been instinct. She was a born cop. She calculated how many seconds it would take to reach for it under her jacket and shirt, get her fingers around the handle and pull it. Too long.

She told herself that she had a better chance reasoning with Thomas. But when she met her brother-in-law's gaze, all hope of talking him down fled. He planned to end this up here on this roof tonight.

Chapter Nineteen

Brick sped into downtown Billings, the rim rocks around it glowing in the lights from the city. He turned off the lights and siren a few blocks before the building where Thomas worked. He didn't want him to know he was coming. Mo had told him that it was where Thomas had said he had the papers and key locked in his desk drawer. She was meeting him there to pick them up.

He told himself that there was no cause for alarm. That Mo would have gotten the papers and already left. But he'd tried her phone a half-dozen times. Each time it had gone straight to voice mail. Each time, he'd left a more urgent message. Each time, she hadn't called back.

In his gut, he knew. Mo had realized that her brother-in-law was the killer. As he pulled up in front of the building, he saw Mo's car parked on the almost empty street and felt his heart drop. Mo was in there with a killer.

The front door opened onto a small entry. He ran to the elevator and the information sign next to it. The pharmaceutical company was on the top floor. In the elevator he pushed the button again and again until the doors finally closed and he felt the lift begin to climb.

His heart was pounding. He tried to tell himself that she could take care of herself. If she saw it coming. But the fact that she was still here, that she hadn't called, that she wasn't taking any calls told him she was in trouble.

The elevator finally came to a stop, the door sliding open. Brick rushed off only to find a deserted office full of cubicles behind a wall of glass. He tried the door. Locked. He looked around, frantic to get inside. He could see a light on deep inside but saw no one.

Spying a fire extinguisher at the end of the hall, he pulled his weapon and using the butt end, smashed the cover and lifted the fire extinguisher out. Moving to the glass door into the office, he swung the heavy fire extinguisher and let it go, shielding his eyes as the glass shattered.

He shoved his way through the shattered glass, felt a shard bite into his arm and catch on his long-sleeved shirt. But he ignored the pain as he rushed in toward the only area that was lit.

"Mo!" he called as he ran, his pistol he'd taken from the patrol car drawn. "Mo!" His voice echoed through the emptiness, sounding hollow. He knew before he reached the last set of cubicles that Thomas and Mo weren't here.

But a suit jacket lay over the back of a chair nearest the exit. Brick stepped to the desk and saw Mo's cell phone sitting beside the computer. She was here and hadn't gone far. Where was Thomas? Brick picked up the scent of cigarette smoke from the jacket and looked toward the exit. A hardcore smoker couldn't go long without one, which meant there was no way he went all the way down to the ground floor every time he took a break.

He ran toward the exit door and shoved it open to a

set of stairs that led up. Taking them, he followed the scent of cigarette smoke as if it were a bread crumb trail.

As he burst out the door onto the roof, he didn't see anyone. But he heard the murmur of voices. His instincts had him closing the door quietly behind him as he moved toward the sound, his weapon drawn.

Mo never thought she'd find herself on a rooftop fourteen floors above the city with a killer. What made it more surreal was that she *knew* this man. She'd loved Thomas like a brother.

"I knew you would figure it out if you kept at it long enough," Thomas said, his gaze locked on her. "Tricia used to say that you were like a dog with a bone when you got something into your head. How could I forget that you're a cop, through and through? Her ashes, huh?"

"When did you realize that I knew?" Mo asked as Thomas lit another cigarette, never taking his eyes off her.

"You forget. You and I go way back, Maureen. I met you even before I met your sister. I know you. What I don't understand is why you would come here alone tonight to meet me, knowing what I'm capable of doing." He started as if it finally hit him. *"You didn't know."*

She felt the fine hairs stand up on the back of her neck. "You're not a killer."

His laugh sounded full of glass shards. "I wouldn't have thought so not all that long ago, but now…" His expression soured. "But maybe you haven't noticed, I've changed."

She shook her head. "You killed Tricia in a fit of passion, I would imagine. Killing me would be in cold blood."

"It's not all that much different, I don't believe. It's about survival. I don't want to go to prison. I want to live."

She knew in that instant. "Quinn."

He smiled, his teeth looking sharp in the glow of the city below them. "You picked up on that right away, didn't you?"

"So you and Quinn—"

"I wasn't having an affair at the same time my wife was, if that's what you're asking. I got to know Quinn after Tricia died—"

Mo felt a stab of anger at how blasé he was about her sister's death. "She didn't *die*. She was *murdered*."

His gaze narrowed. "You want to hear this or not?"

She didn't really want to. Was she that sure that he wouldn't hurt her? Or that sure that she could take care of herself?

Right now both seemed foolish. Thomas had fallen in love again. He had even more reason to want to be free of the past and that meant being free of his sister-in-law, as well.

"I got to know Quinn. She's sweet."

"You thought Tricia was sweet."

His eyes narrowed dangerously again. "But I never thought of you that way, Maureen."

His words actually hurt. "You're confusing sweet with vulnerable." Mo had forgotten that her sister had been in love with another boy at college before she'd met Thomas. The boy had broken it off. Had she not realized how vulnerable Tricia had been when she'd met Thomas? Had he recognized it, though, and preyed on her?

She'd thought she had such a clear picture of the past, but now it wavered as if for years she'd remembered only what she wanted to. Thomas and Tricia, the not-so-perfect couple.

Even in the beginning, hadn't she seen tiny flaws in their relationship? Red flags that her sister had ignored. She suspected that Thomas had never let Tricia forget that he'd given up medical school for her. Add to that Tricia's problems getting pregnant—until she met JP.

She told herself she could talk him off this roof. Talk them both off. "I was surprised when you had her cremated."

He finished his cigarette, brutally stubbing it out with the others. "You think she deserved a nice burial?" He snorted. "When I confronted her, she told me that she had planned to tell me. Leave me, is what she meant, but then she realized she was pregnant. Apparently her lover wasn't interested in fatherhood so she broke it off. Or so she said. But often I smelled him on her skin." His eyes swam with tears. "That's right, your precious sister wasn't just an adulteress, she was going to pass off another man's son as mine." He made a swipe at his tears with the back of his sleeve. "It was just one betrayal after another."

She considered her options. He was standing only inches away. If she made any kind of sudden move, he could grab her before she took a step. He was a good foot taller and sixty pounds heavier. He worked out almost every day. She didn't stand a chance against him even with her training.

"If you turn yourself in—"

He laughed. "And go to prison for the rest of my life? I don't think so. Just tell me this. Does your deputy friend know?"

"No," she said quickly. Maybe too quickly because Thomas smiled.

"When I caught you at his apartment, I couldn't believe it was like that between the two of you. I never thought you'd find a man who you felt was your equal."

"Who said I think Brick is?"

Thomas laughed. "Sorry, *sister*, I don't believe you. I know how distraught you've been over your sister's death. But I never expected you to jump off the roof of my office building."

"I'm not jumping, Thomas." She didn't move even when he pulled the pistol from under his shirt behind him and pointed it at her. She wasn't the only one who had a weapon tucked in her waistband, it seemed.

She met his gaze and saw both desperation and determination. One way or another, she was going off the roof of this fourteen-story building.

BRICK MOVED ACROSS the dark rooftop. The glow of the city illuminated a portion of the roof at the corner. He spotted the two figures silhouetted against the city lights—the radiance bouncing off the weapon in Thomas's hand. The barrel of the gun was pointed at Mo's chest. She was talking quietly, cajoling, but the figure opposite her was tense and on alert.

Brick worked his way closer, staying to the shadows. The sound of traffic fourteen floors below drowned out his footfalls. He wanted to rush Thomas, but didn't dare. He couldn't take the chance that the man would get a shot off before he tackled him to the rooftop.

He was within a half-dozen yards now. He could see that Thomas's hand holding the gun was shaking. The man was about to do something stupid, but then he'd already done that when he'd killed his wife.

Unfortunately, Brick couldn't get a shot from where

he was without jeopardizing Mo's life. He had to get closer because he could feel time was running out.

Mo saw Brick out of the corner of her eye. She wanted to call to him, to warn him, but as he stealthily approached, she knew he must have seen the gun Thomas was holding on her. She didn't dare look straight at him for fear Thomas would see and turn and fire.

"You don't want to do this."

"No, I don't. But you've given me no choice, Maureen. I begged you to let it go." His voice broke. The gun in his hand wavered just enough to tempt her.

Taking it away from him was dangerous, but he was getting more anxious by the minute. She had to do something. She could still feel the letter opener digging into her back. "We can both walk away from this."

He shook his head. "Even if Tricia hadn't been your sister, you couldn't forget this. It's that cop in you. You just couldn't leave it alone. That damn Natalie had to open her mouth…" He shook his head. "Did she say how she knew that Tricia hadn't killed herself?"

"No. I never got to talk to her before she died. Maybe she was just suspicious."

Thomas made a sound like a wounded animal. "That would be just like her. She was always watching us, couldn't keep her nose out of our business. I hated having her living in our house. I could see how close Tricia was getting to her. I would see them with their heads together. I'd walk into a room and they'd both shut up as if they'd been talking about me. I'm sure they were. I'd failed Tricia over and over. I couldn't even give her a child."

She had to keep him talking. Brick was edging closer.

Once he was close enough... "Tricia loved you. That's why she broke off the affair. She wasn't leaving you."

"Is that supposed to make me feel better?" he scoffed. "Do you really think I wanted anything to do with her after she'd been with him? After she'd had *his* baby? That was supposed to be *our* family. *Our family*. Not his."

Mo felt a shock race like fire through her veins. Joey. "Thomas, the baby, you didn't..." She couldn't breathe as she saw the answer in his eyes. "You killed him."

"He was going to die anyway."

She felt bile rise to the back of her throat. She was going to throw up. "You let Natalie take the blame."

"She would have done it if I hadn't. Don't you think I watch the news? She's under investigation for other murders. You know how badly I wanted a family. I gave up my dreams. I gave up everything." His gaze hardened. "Why haven't you tried to get away or take the gun away from me, Mo?"

"And give you an excuse to coldcock me with the gun and throw me over this wall?"

Thomas took a step toward her. She stepped back and he advanced again, this time pinning her in the corner of the rooftop.

She reached back, supporting herself with one hand, pulling out the letter opener with the other. "Thomas, don't do this."

"You've left me no choice. I begged you..." His voice broke. "Climb up on the ledge, Maureen. I don't want to hit you. Make this easy on yourself."

"On you, you mean."

BRICK SAW THAT time had run out. He was close now. But not close enough. Thomas had Mo trapped in the corner at the edge of the roof.

"Thomas!" he called out, making the man jump and begin to turn. He'd seen Mo reach behind her as if to steady herself on the short wall an instant before he caught the glint of something long and lethal in her hand.

As Thomas saw Brick, he must have also seen Mo's movement out of the corner of his eye. He swung the gun toward her. The weapon in his hand arced in a circle as she ducked the blow aimed at her head.

The gun caught her in the back, doubling her over on the narrow short roof wall. Turning, Thomas got off a couple of wild shots before he grabbed Mo, lifting her to push her over the wall.

Brick charged, watching in horror as she was lifted up. He saw the flash of the object in her hand as she drove the weapon into Thomas's side. He let out a scream of pain. She struck him again as Brick grabbed him from behind and brought him down to the rooftop. But Thomas didn't release Mo, taking her down with him at the edge of the roof.

Belatedly, Brick saw that Thomas hadn't lost his grip on his gun. The man grabbed Mo and put the barrel against her temple.

"You both should have stayed out of it," Thomas spat and pulled the trigger. As he did, Mo stabbed the man in the throat with what appeared to be a letter opener at the same time Brick fired his own weapon. Thomas's shot was so close, it had to be deafening for Mo. But fortunately, the bullet missed. Brick's, though, had found its mark. Thomas crumpled to the ground next to her.

Brick quickly pulled Mo up into his arms. He held her, refusing to let her go as he called 911.

Chapter Twenty

There was nothing more wonderful than a summer day in the Gallatin Canyon of Montana. Unless of course it was a warm summer night on the Fourth of July with everyone on the Cardwell Ranch gathered to celebrate.

Brick found Mo down by the creek. She'd spent most of the morning in the kitchen with his mother and aunts, preparing the picnic feast they'd had earlier. He'd loved watching Mo with the other people he loved. His mother had taken to her, and his father seemed pleased that Brick hadn't let her get away. It made his heart swell to see how easily she had fit into the Cardwell-Savage clan. The two of them had moved into a larger apartment in Big Sky. Though anxious, Brick had known to give Mo time.

So much had happened, maybe not even the worst of it on that rooftop in Billings. Mo had lost so much. But if the woman was anything, she was resilient. He'd never met anyone stronger or more determined. In the weeks since, everything had come out about Tricia's and Joey's murders. Jeffrey and JP Palmer were still behind bars, both denied bail because they were flight risks. Jeffrey had money stashed all over the world. Passports with new identities had been found for both of them, although JP swore he had no idea what his father had been doing.

Thomas's body had been cremated, his ashes dumped in the Yellowstone River. Brick had stood beside Mo as they watched the last of him wash away. Once the slug from the campground tree was compared to the bullets in Thomas's gun, they'd known who'd taken the potshots at them outside of Red Lodge. Nor had it taken much to find out that Thomas had hired a private investigator to track Mo. He had known that Mo wouldn't stop until she got justice.

Once the dust had settled, Brick had gotten his mental health clearance and gone back to work as a deputy marshal. With his father retiring, there was going to be an opening for marshal. Hud had suggested Mo might be interested. Brick had encouraged her to apply for the position.

"You really wouldn't mind me being your boss?" Mo had asked, sounding surprised.

"Of course not. You have the experience. I think you would make a good marshal. I'd be honored to work with you. Or for you," he added with a grin. "Just so long as when we walked through our apartment door, you remember who is really boss." He'd laughed just in case she hadn't realized he was joking, and she'd stepped to him and kissed him.

"Are you all right?" he asked now as he joined her. Moonlight played in the water's ripples, the sky overhead a canopy of stars.

Mo nodded and turned to smile at him. "I was just making a wish on that star." She pointed at a bright one sitting just over the top of Lone Peak Mountain.

"I know that star. I've made a few wishes on it myself." He met her gaze. "Your sister?"

"I wish none of that had happened, but I can't change any of it. That wasn't what I wished for."

"No?" he asked, eyeing her more closely. "What did you wish for?"

"If I tell, it won't come true."

He looked at the star and made a wish before he turned to her. "I'm glad I found you down here. There's something I need to tell you."

She turned her face up to him and waited as if not sure what to expect.

"I love you."

Mo laughed. "I gathered that."

"I don't just love you. I've never told a woman that I love her because, as I once told you, if I did, it would be only if I then asked her to marry me."

She smiled. "You were serious about that?"

He pulled her to him. "I've never been more serious about anything. I want to marry you. I want you to be my wife."

Mo LOOKED AT this handsome cowboy and felt her heart swell. Tricia used to tease her, saying she was too picky when it came to men, and no wonder she hadn't gotten married. It was true.

But she'd never thought she'd ever meet a man like Brick Savage. She doubted the Lord had made more than one. She laughed in delight as she looked at him, wondering how she could have gotten so lucky.

"I love you, Brick Savage, and I would be honored to be your wife."

He grinned and kissed her as the fireworks show at the ranch began with a boom that exploded over their heads. Twinkling lights showered down to expire before hitting the ground around them. The summer breeze stirred nearby pines as the creek next to them was bathed in moonlight.

For so long, she'd been looking back. But as Brick pulled her close, she looked to the future. She'd already fallen for his family and this amazing ranch life here in the canyon. Cardwell Ranch felt like home.

The other night, she'd found Brick sitting on the porch after dinner with his parents. He'd been playing a song on a harmonica and she hadn't wanted for him to stop. But he must have heard her approach, because he'd finished the song and turned to her.

"I didn't know you played," she'd said, realizing she had so much to learn about this man and how much she was looking forward to it.

"I didn't play for a long time," he'd said. "For a while, I wondered if I ever would again. But then you came along. You filled my heart with music again."

She'd smiled and whispered, "If that's a line to get me into your bed—"

He'd grabbed her and pulled her onto his lap. "If that's all it takes…"

She'd known long before that moment, sitting out there on his family's porch swing, that she was in love with this man.

"Come on," she said now. "Let's go celebrate with your family."

As they headed arm in arm back to the festivities, more fireworks exploded over their heads. Mo felt as if he were leading her out of the darkness. Ahead was a bright future that she couldn't wait to share with the man she loved.

* * * * *

RUNNING OUT
OF TIME

CINDI MYERS

Prologue

Who knew death could be so satisfying?

Half the people in town had gathered, watching police—every cop in the county from the looks of it—mill about while the paramedics wheeled out the gurney, the body on it covered by a sheet. Whispering, like the rush of wind through catalpa trees, rose from the crowd as people speculated on the identity of the person under the sheet. Mayville, West Virginia, population 2,000, was small enough that almost everyone knew everyone else.

But they didn't know each other. Not really. They didn't know what people were really capable of doing.

This was the third death in as many days. No one felt safe anymore. Things they had taken for granted—something they had trusted—had turned deadly. Eat too much chili at lunch? Pop a Stroud's Stomach Soother. Stress have your guts in a knot? Stroud's Stomach Soothers to the rescue. Safe and Natural—Our Promise to You. It said so right on the label.

Not so safe now.

A woman broke into sobs. Tammy somebody, who worked on the factory floor. "How can this be happening?" she wailed. "This used to be such a safe place."

Two other women moved in to comfort Tammy. The men around them shuffled their feet and stared at the ground, their expressions grim. Fear hung in the air like diesel exhaust, a choking poison that threatened to kill the town.

The killer had done that. One person had brought a town—a whole region, even—to its knees.

What a rush to have that kind of power. Seeing the body on the gurney sparked an idea. The perfect way to solve problems.

Chapter One

"We've got another tough case on our hands." Jill Pembroke, director of the FBI's tactical crime division, surveyed her team from the head of the conference table in the Bureau's Knoxville headquarters. "One that requires a great deal of discretion."

Something in the director's tone made Agent Laura Smith sharpen her focus. Pembroke, with her well-cut silver hair and feminine suit, might be mistaken for a high society grandmother, but she was as hard-nosed as they came, and not prone to exaggeration. That she reminded her team of the need for discretion pointed to something out of the ordinary.

The door to the conference room opened and a man slipped in. Tall and rangy, Agent Jace Cantrell moved with the grace of an athlete. He nodded to the director and eased into the empty seat next to Laura. No apology for being late. Typical. Laura slid her chair over a couple of inches. Cantrell was one of those men who always seemed to take up more than his share of the available space.

"We're going to be investigating product tampering at Stroud Pharmaceuticals in Mayville, West Virginia." Director Pembroke stepped aside to reveal a slide showing a squat factory building set well back on landscaped grounds.

"The antacid poisonings." Agent Ana Ramirez spoke from her seat directly across from Laura. She tucked a strand of dark hair into the twist at the nape of her neck, polished nails glinting in the overhead light. "That story has been all over the news."

"Do the locals not want the FBI horning in?" Agent Davis Rogers—the only member of the team not wearing the regulation suit—sat back in his chair beside Ramirez, looking every bit the army ranger he had once been. "Is that why the extra discretion?"

"No, the local police are happy to turn this over to us," Pembroke said. She advanced to the next slide, a listing of the deaths—six so far, with two additional people hospitalized—attributed to Stroud's Stomach Soothers, a natural, organic remedy that claimed a significant share of the market as an alternative to traditional antacids. "This hasn't been released to the public, but the poison in the contaminated tablets was ricin."

Laura would have sworn the temperature in the air-conditioned room dropped five degrees. "Any suggestion of a link to terrorism?" Hostage negotiator Evan Duran, bearded and brooding, spoke from the end of the table. "Anybody claiming credit for the deaths?"

Pembroke shook her head. "At this point, we aren't assuming anything. Obviously, we want to avoid panicking the public."

"The public is already panicked," Rowan Cooper, the team's local liaison, said. "People have been organizing boycotts of all Stroud products." She absently twisted a lock of her jet-black hair, brow furrowed. "We'll need a strategy for managing the public's response."

"The facility where the Stomach Soothers were manufactured has been closed for the time being and the product is being pulled from store shelves," Pembroke said. "But another facility in town, which manufactures other items, remains open, and the company has reduced hours and reassigned as many employees as possible to the single plant. The company, the town, even the state officials, are very anxious to downplay this tragedy and get Stroud up and running full-speed as soon as possible."

"Why do that?" Kane Bradshaw, Agent-at-Large, said. Laura hadn't noticed him until now, seated as he was behind her and apart from the rest, almost in the shadows. Kane always looked as if he'd just rushed in from an overnight surveillance, all wind-blown hair and shadowed eyes. The fact that he was here spoke to the gravity of this case. While always on hand when the team needed him, he wasn't much on office decorum.

"Jobs." Cantrell's voice, deep and a little rough, like a man who smoked two packs a day, sent a shiver through Laura. He didn't smoke, but maybe he once had. "Stroud Pharmaceuticals is one of the biggest employers in Boone County," he continued. "The coal mines are shutting down, and there isn't a lot of other industry. Stroud has been a savior to the community. They—and the officials they elected—are going to do everything in their power to keep the company running and redeem its reputation."

"Even covering up murder?" Laura asked.

Cantrell turned to her, his gaze cool. "I doubt they want to cover it up, but they'll definitely downplay it and keep it quiet."

"They want us to help, but they don't want us to be obvious." The youngest member of the team, computer specialist Hendrick Maynard, jiggled his knee as he spoke. A genius who looked younger than his twenty-six years, Maynard never sat still.

"Precisely." Director Pembroke advanced to another slide of a small town—tree-shaded streets lined with modest homes, some worse for wear. A water tower in the distance displayed the word *Mayville* in faded green paint. "Agents Smith and Cantrell, you are to pose as a married couple and take jobs at the Stroud factory. Investigations so far point to the poisonings having originated from within the plant itself, so your job is to identify possible suspects and investigate. Agent Rogers, you'll be in town as well…"

Laura didn't hear the rest of the director's assignments. She was focused on trying to breathe and holding back her cry of protest. She and Cantrell? As a couple? The idea was ridiculous. He was rough, undisciplined, arrogant, scornful…

"You look like you just ate a bug." Cantrell leaned toward her, bringing with him the disconcerting aroma of cinnamon. His gravelly voice abraded her nerves. "Don't think I'm any more excited about this than you are."

"Do you have a comment, Agent Cantrell?" Pembroke asked.

He straightened. "I think Agent Smith is going to stick out like a sore thumb in Mayville. Everything about her screams blue blood as well as law enforcement."

"I've worked undercover before." Laura bristled. She didn't care what Cantrell thought of her, but to imply she wasn't capable of doing her job—

"I'm sure Agent Smith will adapt," Pembroke said. "Smitty, you'll be working as assistant to the plant director, Parker Stroud, son of company owners Steve and Donna Stroud. This should give you access to personnel files, as well as financial records and other information you might find useful. Agent Cantrell, you'll be on the manufacturing floor."

Where he'd fit right in, Laura thought. Cantrell had the Southern drawl and casual attitude of the classic regular-guy down pat.

"Our profiler, Dr. Melinda Larsen, will assist with evaluating suspects," Pembroke continued. "She'll be available to travel to Mayville if necessary. Agent Maynard is on call for research and anything else you need. Agent Rogers and

Agent Ramirez will be the FBI's official representatives in the area and will be on location as backup."

Davis Rogers cracked his knuckles. "Happy to help."

"Smitty, you and Cantrell will need to report immediately to the support center for your background documents and everything you'll need to start your assignment. You'll depart for Mayville tomorrow. Rogers and Ramirez will be a few hours ahead of you." She surveyed the team again, then nodded, as if satisfied with what she saw. "Any questions?"

There were none. The team knew how to launch a new op and hit the ground running. "Then get to work." Pembroke dismissed them.

Laura pushed back her chair and started to stand. "Agent Smith, a word, please," Pembroke said.

Self-conscious over being singled out, Laura kept her eyes on the table as the others left. Cantrell stood and slid a stick of gum into his mouth, then leaned over her chair. "Later," he said, with a cinnamon-scented grin.

When she and the director were alone, Pembroke sat beside her. "I know you're not happy about this assignment," the director said.

"I never said—" Laura began.

"You didn't have to say it." Pembroke smiled. "Your dislike of Agent Cantrell is clear, but he's very good at his job, and he has a connection to this region that makes him ideal for this assignment."

"Is he from Mayville?" Laura asked.

"He's from a small town in Tennessee. A town very similar in many ways to Mayville. He has an insight into the culture of the area that could prove very useful. I'm counting on you to rein in some of his more unorthodox tendencies."

Great. She was on this job to babysit.

"I also think this assignment will be good for you,"

Pembroke said. "You're very dedicated and skilled. You pay attention to details. Those are the skills this assignment requires. But you'll also need to make friends among the locals and attune yourself to the overall atmosphere. I know you prefer to work alone, so this assignment will help you build your skills at relying on others for help and information."

"I work with this team every day," Laura protested.

Pembroke nodded. "You do, but you also can be a bit… aloof. I believe it's this tendency to hold yourself a bit apart that's behind Agent Cantrell's belief that you'll have trouble fitting in at the factory. I'm counting on you to prove him wrong."

Laura did her best to hide any response to this criticism, though the director's words stung. So what if she wasn't one to hang out with her fellow agents after work or discuss her private life with them? She preferred to keep her personal and business lives separate, but that didn't mean she was as cold as Pembroke made her sound. "I'll do my best," she said.

"You always do." Pembroke rose, signaling an end to the meeting.

Laura rose also and was gathering her coffee cup and notebook when the door opened and a slim young man entered. "Sorry to interrupt, Director," he said. "But there's a call for you. It's urgent."

Pembroke nodded and walked to the phone in the corner of the room. Laura moved toward the door. She had just opened it when the director called to her. "Smitty, wait."

Laura turned. As the director continued to listen to whoever was on the other end of the line, some of the color drained from her face. "Yes," Pembroke said. "We'll get right on it." She hung up the phone, her expression grave.

"What is it?" Laura asked. "What's wrong?"

"That was West Virginia State Police Office. They've

just learned that at least a dozen bottles of potentially tainted Stomach Soothers are unaccounted for."

"You mean consumers didn't turn them in?"

Pembroke shook her head. "According to the company's records, these bottles were never sent to stores. They're missing from the factory. They might have been stolen."

"Or the person who planted the ricin in the product originally has stashed them, maybe waiting until things calm down to release them again," Laura said. Like a deadly bomb the killer could set off to wreak havoc whenever he wanted.

Chapter Two

Driving down Main Street in Mayville, West Virginia, on Sunday afternoon gave Jace an itchy feeling between his shoulder blades, as if someone had slapped a target back there and he was bracing for the first shot. He had never been here before, but he already knew what he'd find: a mix of aching beauty in blooming azaleas and stately homes side-by-side with the despair of lost glory and opportunities passed by. Closed storefronts, weedy lots, and idle men and women paired with groups of laughing children, flourishing gardens and rolling fields.

He'd grown up in a place like this. His family—his parents and sister—still lived there. Whenever he visited, he couldn't wait to leave, smothered by all the problems he couldn't fix.

"It's not like I thought it would be," Smitty said.

He glanced at her strapped into the passenger seat of the ten-year-old mustard-colored Chevy pickup. Her blond hair, normally twisted back in a bun, hung loose around her shoulders, the no-name jeans and peasant top making her look younger and softer. More accessible.

He focused on the street once more. A man would be a fool to think there was anything soft or vulnerable about Agent Smith, especially where Jace was concerned. She didn't exactly curl her lip in disgust when he approached, but the expression was implied.

"What do you mean?" he asked, slowing the truck to allow an elderly couple—her with a walker, him with a cane—to cross the street.

"It's so quiet," she said. "It doesn't look like a place where violence has made national headlines. I expected more press, and people milling around."

He slid a fresh stick of cinnamon gum into his mouth from the pack that rested on the dash and then gave the truck some gas. "I imagine the powers that be are tamping down any hint of panic," he said. "From the media reports, the politicians are downplaying the poisonings as an attempted terrorist attack that has already been stopped."

"What about the dozen potentially poisoned bottles that are unaccounted for?"

"They haven't released that information to the press and they're counting on us to find them before anyone else dies."

She shuddered. "If someone else does die, the politicians will be pointing their fingers at us."

"If that bothers you, you should be in another line of work."

She stiffened, just as he had known she would. "I take a great deal of pride in the work the Bureau does," she said. "As should you."

"But I don't waste time worrying about what a bunch of pencil pushers and pontificators think of me," he said.

"Except those are the people who sign the bills that ultimately pay your salary," she said.

"They need people like me more than I need people like them." He glanced at her. "If you remember that, it makes the job a lot easier."

"Easier to cut corners and ignore the regulations, you mean."

He grinned. "That, too."

She made a noise in her throat almost like a growl. Kind

of sexy, but if he told her that, she would rightly blow a gasket. Smitty was the poster child for "wound too tight."

"We need to figure out who has it in for the Strouds," he said.

"You think that's what's behind this?" she asked. "Destroy their reputation by sabotaging their most popular product?"

"Don't you?"

She didn't answer right away, staring out at the passing scenery—a park with a bronze statue of a coal miner in overalls and hard hat, lunch bucket in one hand, a pick over his shoulder. Jace's father could have been the model for that statue, before he got sick.

"Maybe the goal isn't to destroy the Strouds," Smitty said. "You said yourself the town depends on the company for jobs. Maybe someone has a grudge against Mayville. And there's always the possibility that the target was one of the people who died, and everyone else is just a way to muddy the waters."

"Maybe," he said. "Whoever it is isn't being subtle. Ricin isn't like putting a little rat poison in someone's soup and hoping you used enough to do the job. It only takes a few grains of ricin to kill."

"Maybe we'll know more after we visit the factory."

"Rogers is supposed to brief us later today, after he and Ramirez meet with the local cops. Meanwhile, we have to move in." The back of the truck held everything a down-on-their-luck young couple might deem worth transporting to a new home—clothes, kitchen items, a television, and an antique chest of drawers that was someone's idea of a family heirloom. The Bureau's support center was known for its attention to detail. They had also supplied identification for Jason and Laura Lovejoy—a surname Jace was certain was someone's idea of a joke. The rental they were moving into was supposed to be furnished with everything else they'd need.

He turned the truck onto an unpaved side street identified by a leaning green sign as Lover's Lane.

"You have got to be kidding me." Smitty sneered at the sign.

"It's probably just the first suitable place they found to rent," Jace said. He watched the addresses on the mailboxes at the end of each drive and turned into the rutted lane at the very end of the street. The trailer was a rectangular white metal box with faded blue metal shutters, set well back from the road in the shade of a catalpa tree, the large heart-shaped leaves a brilliant green, the faded orchid-like blossoms littering the ground around the tree.

"Not what I was expecting." Smitty ground out the words through clenched teeth.

"It fits the profile," Jace said, shutting off the truck's engine. "We're broke newlyweds, remember? Besides, it's at the end of the road, with no close neighbors to spy on us."

Smitty got out of the truck, and he followed her up a two-foot-wide crushed gravel path to a porch, apparently made of old pallets, at the front of the trailer. She climbed the steps, inserted the key in the lock and shoved open the door.

They stood frozen for a moment, taking in the dark wood paneling, avocado-green carpet, and faux-leather sofa and matching recliner, complete with duct tape patches. The room smelled faintly of stale cigarette smoke. Smitty made a strangled sound, took a step forward and did a slow turn. "At least it looks clean." Her eyes met his. "I've never lived in a trailer before."

He had, but he wasn't going to share that with her. "Let's unload the truck," he said, and moved back outside.

She didn't immediately follow. He lowered the tailgate of the truck and pulled out a square cardboard box labeled

KITCHEN. By the time he'd made it up the walkway with this burden, Smitty was waiting for him on the porch. "We have a problem," she said.

"What is it?" Jace moved past her and carried the box to the kitchen table, a metal and Formica relic from the 1960s. A hipster might have deemed it charmingly vintage, while his parents had discarded theirs years ago as a piece of junk.

"There's only one bed," Smitty said.

"The rental agreement said two bedrooms." The document, complete with their own expertly forged signatures, had been included with all their other paperwork.

"There are two bedrooms, but only one bed," she said. The faint worry lines on her high forehead deepened.

He shrugged. "So we'll get another bed tomorrow."

"What are we going to do tonight?"

"I guess you can either share the bed with me or sleep on the couch." He gave her a wolfish grin—primarily because he knew it would get a rise out of her.

Sure enough, her cheeks turned rosy and sparks all but snapped from her blue eyes. "Why should you get the bed?" she demanded.

Because we're equal colleagues and any other time you'd be insulted at being treated with deference because you're a woman. "Because I'm bigger and taller. You fit the couch better. Of course, I'm always willing to share."

She twisted the plain gold band on the ring finger of her left hand. He wondered if she would take it off and throw it at him. "That is no way to speak to a fellow agent," she said.

"No. But it's how I might speak to my wife."

She was saved from having to think of a retort by the crunch of tires on gravel. They both turned to watch a silver Honda creep up the drive and stop behind the truck. Agent Davis Rogers unfolded his tall frame from the driver's seat and stood, hands on hips, studying the trailer. Sun burnished the dark brown skin of his bare arms and glinted on the steel frames of his Wayfarers.

Smitty moved ahead of Jace to greet Rogers at the door. "This looks like a cozy little love nest," Rogers said.

"Where are you staying?" Smitty asked.

He tucked the sunglasses into the neck of his pale blue polo shirt. "The Magnolia Inn on the other side of town."

Jace was pretty sure the Magnolia Inn was a few stars down from wherever Smitty was used to staying, but he'd have bet she would have traded places with Rogers in a heartbeat.

"I'll help you unload the rest of your stuff and we'll talk," Rogers said.

It didn't take long for the three of them to move the assorted boxes and bags into the trailer. While Smitty opened windows, Jace made coffee, then they gathered around the kitchen table. "Ramirez and I met with the local police department," Rogers said. "They seem pretty competent and did a good initial investigation, given their limited resources. As we already know, they think the Stomach Soother poisoning was done prior to the safety seals being applied. There was no sign of tampering with the packaging in the bottles they've been able to recover."

One of Jace's goals working on the factory floor was to determine who might have tampered with the product, and how. "What about the missing bottles?" he asked.

"Stroud's computer system assigns a bar code to every bottle at the plant," Rogers said. "Those bar codes are matched to shipments that go to each store. If someone uses a store loyalty card when they make a purchase, they can even tie a specific bottle to a specific customer. They were able to recall most of the suspect medication that way. These twelve bottles, however, never went to a store or made it to a consumer. They disappeared shortly after they were filled."

"What do you mean, disappeared?" Smitty asked.

"They show up on the records as having been manufactured," Rogers said. "There's no trace of them after that."

"Does that happen often?" she asked. "Maybe employees help themselves?"

"The potential has to be there," Jace said. "But with these jobs, if you're even suspected of stealing, you're out on the street. And I'll bet they have cameras on the factory floor."

Rogers nodded. "The local cops say if the Strouds have ever had trouble with employees lifting product, they've handled it themselves."

"What do the Strouds say?" Smitty asked.

"Ramirez is talking to Donna Stroud right now. She's also making sure everything is set for you two to show up tomorrow as the newest employees of Stroud Pharmaceuticals." He grinned. "Better you than me."

BALLOONS, FLOWERS AND a couple of stuffed animals decorated a section of chain link fence in front of the headquarters of Stroud Pharmaceuticals. A stiff breeze rattled the ends of a ribbon bow tied to a vase of wilting daisies as Agent Ana Sofia Ramirez walked past. She stopped to study the display. The flowers lay in front of a hand-lettered sign on white poster board. "We'll never forget you, Gini," it read.

Virginia Elgin, chief financial officer of Stroud Pharmaceuticals, had been the third person to die after using the contaminated Stomach Soothers. The bottle, found in her desk, had been traced to a local grocery store, as had the bottles that contained the tablets that had killed Herbert Baker and Gail Benito, the first two victims. The other five victims, three of whom had died, had purchased their

Stomach Soothers from two different stores in a county directly east of Mayville.

Would the missing bottles turn up on yet another store's shelves, or in the medicine cabinet of the next victim? Were they merely lost in the system, or stashed on a shelf in the killer's closet, waiting to stir up a new panic?

Donna Stroud was a middle-aged woman with dyed black hair in a sensible cut, dressed for business even on a Sunday afternoon in flat shoes and the type of pantsuit that had never been in or out of fashion. She greeted Ana with a firm handshake. "Thank you for coming, Agent Ramirez. My husband and I are anxious to do anything we can to get to the bottom of this tragedy. I appreciate you meeting with me on a Sunday. I hate to upset the staff any more than I have to."

"We appreciate your cooperation," Ana said.

"I've reviewed all the information you gave local and state law enforcement," she continued when she was seated in front of Donna's desk, a scarred oak model whose surface was obscured by towers of precariously leaning paperwork. "When did you discover that some of the product in the batch in question was unaccounted for?"

"My son brought it to my attention yesterday afternoon. I notified the state police right away."

"That would be Parker Stroud, the plant manager?"

"Yes. He was in charge of verifying the inventory reports and noticed the discrepancy. Everyone is putting in overtime, trying to determine how this could have happened."

"Has anything like this ever happened before—inventory going missing?"

"No!"

Ana didn't hide her skepticism. "You've never had an employee decide to, say, help herself to a box of something?"

"No." Donna leaned across the desk toward Ana. "We

have a zero-tolerance policy for that sort of thing. Employees and their belongings are subject to search at any time, and we have closed-circuit TV monitoring all parts of the factory. Beyond that, we're very careful about who we hire. We screen potential employees thoroughly, train them well, and I'm proud to say we have an industry-high retention rate. We have employees who have worked for Stroud for twenty years."

"So you don't have anyone you suspect might be responsible for contaminating the Stomach Soother tablets?"

"No one."

Donna Stroud looked Ana in the eye when she spoke. She was clearly weary, and frightened. But Ana didn't think she was lying. "We're hoping our agents here at the facility will be able to spot irregularities you may not have noticed," Ana said. "We appreciate your willingness to allow us access."

Donna sat back. "It's not as if I have much choice, is it? But I'd like to be allowed to inform Parker about what's going on. After all, one of the agents will be working under him, and the other will be right in his office."

"No." Ana spoke as firmly as she could. "It's imperative that as few people know about this operation as possible. If you'll remember, that was part of the agreement we reached that allows you to keep the rest of your facility still operating. If you don't feel you can uphold that agreement…" She let the words hang, an implied threat.

The lines around Donna's mouth tightened. "I understand."

Ana stood. "The Lovejoys will be here for orientation at 8:00 a.m. tomorrow." She handed over a business card. "If you think of anything that might be helpful to the investigation, or spot anything suspicious, don't hesitate to call me. That's my direct number and I'll answer anytime, day or night."

Donna stood also, weariness bowing her shoulders. "Thank you, Agent Ramirez," she said. "I hope you can get to the bottom of this quickly. Then we can at least begin to get back to normal."

She escorted Ana out of her office. They passed a side door marked V. Elgin, CFO. Ana stopped. Donna followed her gaze to the door. "As horrible as all of this is, it's even more horrible, losing Gini," she said, her voice tight with emotion.

"I understand she died here, at the office?" Ana asked.

Donna nodded. "She came back from lunch and was working in there, with the door closed. One of the admins went in to discuss the agenda for an upcoming meeting and found her." She put a hand to her mouth. "We thought at first it might have been a heart attack. She suffered from chronic heartburn and we thought maybe it was something more serious after all." She cleared her throat. "When they told us it was the Stomach Soothers, we couldn't believe it."

"What do you know about ricin, Mrs. Stroud?" Ana asked.

"They—well, the local police chief—told us that was what was in the Stomach Soother tablets. I know it's deadly… Maybe something terrorists have used elsewhere? Do you think this was done by terrorists?"

"We haven't reached any conclusions at this point. I won't take up any more of your time." She left the office, aware of Donna and several other women watching her walk away. She felt sorry for them, ordinary people caught in such a nightmare. But she wouldn't let her pity get in the way of doing her job. The most likely scenario involved someone inside the factory contaminating those tablets, which meant the Strouds and everyone who worked for them were potential suspects.

As she turned onto the sidewalk, she noticed a man standing in front of the makeshift memorial. He was young, early-to midtwenties, wearing new-looking jeans and a blue dress shirt unbuttoned and untucked over a gray T-shirt. She stopped and studied him. He looked out of place. Lost.

A trio of women, possibly factory workers on the weekend shift returning from a lunch break, approached. Ana caught their eye. "Who is that man?" she asked.

The oldest of the trio, an African American woman in her forties, glanced toward the memorial, and her expression changed to one of sorrow. "That's Miss Gini's boy, Leo."

"Gini Elgin?" Ana clarified.

A very pale woman with hair the color of carrots nodded. "He's real tore up about his mama's passing."

The third woman, brown-haired and freckled, made a face. "It's terrible about Miss Gini, but that Leo always was a little odd."

"What do you mean, odd?" Ana asked. Leo had moved closer to the memorial now, actually standing on some of the flowers, head bowed, hands shoved in the front pockets of his jeans.

"Just, odd," the woman said.

"Not friendly," the older woman said. "Real quiet. Now, Miss Gini was as friendly as could be, and not what you'd call quiet."

The others nodded. Then, as a group, they moved on. Ana continued down the sidewalk. When she was about ten feet from the memorial, Leo Elgin leaned down and snatched up the vase of flowers and hurled it over the fence. It smashed on the concrete on the other side, sending glass and petals flying. Then he turned and ran away, with the awkward gait of someone who doesn't run often. He didn't look at Ana as he passed, but she had a clear view of his face, his expression one of agony, tears streaming down his cheeks.

Chapter Three

Laura spent most of her first night in Mayville tossing and turning and deeply resenting Jace for sleeping so soundly. She could hear him snoring in the next room. After she finally managed to doze off she overslept, awoke in a panic and charged into the trailer's single bathroom to find a shirtless Cantrell, face half-covered in shaving cream, a straight razor in one hand.

Even half-asleep, she was impressed, both with the way he wielded the razor over his cheekbones and the impressive abs and pecs revealed in the anemic bathroom light. Stammering, she backed out of the room, his laughter trailing her all the way to the kitchen.

By the time he emerged from the bathroom, she was halfway through her first mug of coffee and had managed to rein in her racing heart. She ignored him and went to take her turn in the steamy shower, unsettled by the knowledge that he had been in here only moments before—naked. Then she was even more disturbed by the idea that he could hear her in here and might at this very moment be imagining *her* naked.

Clearly, she hadn't had nearly enough sleep. She and Cantrell were both professionals. She did not fantasize about her coworkers as a rule, so why should she assume he did? Then she remembered his wolfish grin when they had argued over the bed and bit back a groan.

When she returned to the kitchen, he shoved something wrapped in a paper towel in her hand. "We have to go now or we'll be late for our first day," he said.

"What is this?" She stared at the warm bundle in her hand.

"Fried egg sandwich."

"I don't eat fried foods." Her usual breakfast was a cup of yogurt or a piece of toast.

"Today you do." He handed her her purse. "Let's go. I'll drive and you can eat in the truck."

The sandwich was delicious, though she was aware of him watching her eat, which made her feel self-conscious and awkward. Then again, everything about this assignment was awkward.

The next hour passed in a blur. Laura suffered through an orientation that consisted of a ten-minute film about the history of Stroud Pharmaceuticals, a fifteen-minute drill on safety procedures and thirty minutes signing paperwork with her new fake name. Finally, she was directed to her new office, where she was greeted by a slender young man with thinning hair, oversized ears and a sour expression.

"Are you the new admin?" Parker Stroud, her new boss, asked.

"Yes, Laura Lovejoy." Laura offered her hand. He stared at it until she put it back down at her side.

"Great. Can you start by getting me some coffee?" He moved past her toward his office. "Two sugars," he called over his shoulder.

She retrieved the coffee from the machine in the adjacent break room and carried it in to him. Stroud was seated behind his desk, staring at a computer screen. He accepted the coffee and looked her up and down. "My mother said she hired you for this position," he announced. "What happened to Cheryl, the girl who was here before?"

The "girl" was fifty-five years old and had been temporarily relocated to work in the accounting department. "I'm not sure," Laura responded.

"No offense to you, but I'm thirty-four years old. I don't need my mother to pick out my secretary—excuse me, administrative assistant." He sipped the coffee, gaze lingering on her chest in a way that made her bristle. "Though I have to say, you're a lot better looking than Cheryl. And you know how to make a decent cup of coffee. So we'll see how it goes."

"Yes, sir." She tried to appear neutral in front of him, though inside, she seethed.

"Well, don't just stand there. Go back to your desk." He waved her away. "If I need you, I'll call you."

She returned to her desk and studied the row of old-fashioned filing cabinets along one wall. She'd investigate their contents under the pretense of organizing her workspace or something. Later, she'd attempt to hack into the firm's personnel and financial records. She could contact Maynard for help if she needed it.

She tucked a strand of hair behind her ear. She wasn't used to wearing it down at work, and it felt in the way. But the support office had deemed her usual chignon too sophisticated for the role she was playing.

She opened the top drawer of the first cabinet and stared at a row of files, each labeled with a month and a year. A quick flip through the first file revealed production records for the two manufacturing plants—one of which had produced all of the Stomach Soothers sold by Stroud's, the other responsible for herbal throat lozenges, a sleep aid and a preparation for teething infants.

"It's a little early in the day to be looking for an insomnia cure."

She hadn't heard the door to Parker's office open, and his voice right behind her startled her. She choked off a gasp, returned the file and shut the drawer, then turned to him with a smile firmly in place. "Did you need some-thing, Mr. Stroud?"

"Call me Parker. Mr. Stroud is my father." He nodded toward the filing cabinets. "Every bit of this data is in our computer system, but my father insists on hard copy re-cords. Just one of the many examples of how my parents are keeping this company from realizing its full potential."

"Surely you'll be in charge of the company one day," she said.

"Thinking you'll be moving up in the world if you stick with me?" he asked. "Don't hold your breath. My folks have made it clear they don't intend to let go of the reins for years to come. Though why they'd even want it now, I don't know."

"You mean, because of what happened with the Stom-ach Soothers?"

"Yeah, what else do you think I mean?"

She widened her eyes, feigning ignorance, hoping she wasn't overacting.

Apparently, Parker bought it. He rolled his eyes. "Go down to accounting and tell them I need last month's fi-nancials ASAP. And don't let them give you any nonsense about this whole business with the Stomach Soothers dis-rupting workflow. That isn't the only product we make and people have wallowed enough."

"Yes, sir." The way he said the words sounded re-hearsed, as if he'd been practicing a tough-guy act in front of a mirror. Maybe that was how he thought a hard-nosed CEO should behave.

She hurried out of the office, but slowed as soon as she turned the corner. Now was as good a time as any to famil-iarize herself with the layout of the building. She strolled the halls, opening and closing doors, locating the men's and women's restrooms, an empty classroom, a larger meeting room and the janitor's supply closet.

"Can I help you with something?" A round-faced young woman with a halo of brown curls, a sheaf of papers clutched to her chest, approached as Laura shut the door to the supply closet.

"I'm looking for the accounting department," Laura said.

"I'll show you." The woman motioned for Laura to follow, then set off down the hall, high heels clicking like castanets on the polished tile floor. "Ask for Angela," she said, indicating a frosted glass door, then turned and tap-tapped away.

Angela proved to be a middle-aged woman with flawless brown skin whose desktop was dominated by an oversized computer monitor. "Mr. Stroud needs the April financial reports," Laura said. "Parker Stroud," she clarified.

Angela frowned. "Today is the third. Those reports aren't compiled until the tenth. He knows that. And now you know it, so don't bother me again."

"Did he send me here to bother you to give me a hard time because I'm new, or does he do this every month?" Laura asked.

Angela's frown eased some. "Probably a little of both. Don't let him get to you. He's really okay, just a little tightly wound, I guess. A lot different from his mom and dad, that's for sure."

"I'd think everyone would be a little extra tense right now," Laura said.

"You got that right." She held out her hand. "Let's start over. My name is Angela Dupree. Welcome to Stroud Pharmaceuticals."

Laura took the hand, which was warm, smooth and beautifully manicured. "I'm Laura Lovejoy. I'm the new administrative assistant to Parker Stroud."

"This is a good place to work, despite the recent troubles," Angela said.

"Scary to think about the poisoning." Laura leaned toward Angela and lowered her voice. "I heard a reporter say the police think someone who worked at the plant must have put the poison in those bottles. Who would do such a horrible thing?"

"Nobody I know," Angela said. "And I think the reporters are wrong. I know it's a cliché to say a workplace is like a family, but we really are here at Stroud. No one has any reason to want to hurt people like that."

"That does make me feel a little better," Laura said. "Thanks."

"It was nice meeting you, but we both need to get back to work."

"Yes, ma'am."

Laura started to turn away, but Angela stopped her. "Laura?"

"Yes?"

"It would probably be a good idea if you didn't go around talking about the poisonings and such," she said. "People are pretty upset and it's not the best way to make a good impression."

"Gotcha. Thanks."

Laura wasn't worried about the kind of impression she made, except that getting people to like her might help her do her job. Had Angela warned her off because she was really trying to be helpful, or because she knew people here had things they wanted to hide?

"Who is that woman in with Angela?" Merry Winger craned her head around the edge of her computer screen to look toward the office. She had a view of a woman's slim back, long blond hair in graceful curls, slim-fit khaki trousers, low beige heels and a light blue shirt.

"That's Parker's new admin." Jerri Dunn followed Merry's gaze toward the office door. "She's a cutie, isn't she?"

"I didn't know they'd filled that position." Merry tried to hide her disappointment.

"Yeah, I think the job was only posted a week ago, but I guess they wanted to fill the spot quick."

Merry had put in for that position. It would have been ideal—she and Parker working together, seeing each other every day, not just a few times a month. He had an office with a locking door and a big desk—the fun they could have had in there. "You'd think they would choose someone from inside the company," she said.

"I gave up second-guessing decisions around here a long time ago," Jerri said.

Merry waited until the blonde left, then stood. "I'm going to the ladies'," she said.

She bypassed the ladies' room and headed for Parker's office. The blonde looked up from her desk when Merry entered. She was pretty enough, though kind of skinny and flat-chested. "Hello. May I help you?" she asked.

"I need to see Parker."

Merry started to walk past the desk, but the blonde stood. "Let me see if Mr. Stroud is available. What is your name?"

"Merry Winger. That's Merry, with two *r*'s and an *e*. Like *merry* Christmas." She wanted to make sure this woman knew exactly who she was. "And I'm sure Parker will want to see me."

"I'll let him know you're here." She knocked on Parker's door and, when he said "Enter," she slipped inside, leaving Merry to cool her heels in the outer office. He had better not refuse to see her. Not after all she'd done for him. Done with him.

The door opened and Parker followed the blonde out. "Merry, come in." He gestured toward the office. No smile of welcome, but then, Parker wasn't much for gestures of affection.

Parker shut the door behind them, but didn't move toward his desk. "What do you want?" he asked, keeping his voice low.

She pressed her palm against his chest and gave him a warm smile. "Maybe I just wanted to see you."

She stood on tiptoe and tried to kiss him, but he turned away. "I told you, not at work," he said.

She pouted. "Why not at work? Are you ashamed of me?"

"Of course not." He patted her shoulder. "But there are rules about executives dating workers. If anyone found out, we'd have to quit seeing each other and I don't want that, do you?"

If he married her, she wouldn't have to be an employee here anymore and that would solve the whole problem, but she knew better than to bring that up. Parker was the type of man who liked to think of things himself. "You're so considerate of me and my reputation," she said instead. "It's one of the things I love about you."

"Thanks for being so understanding. Now you'd better get back to work."

He urged her toward the door, but she resisted. She nodded toward the outer office. "Who is she?"

"The new girl?" He frowned. "I don't know. Someone my mom hired."

"You don't even get to pick out your own admin?"

"She's just a body behind a desk. I don't really care."

"I was hoping to get that job," she said. "Did you know I applied?"

"No, but it's just as well you didn't get it."

"Why not? Wouldn't you like having me around all the time?"

"I think it would be too distracting—for both of us." There was definite heat in his eyes now. A thrill shot through her. Whenever she started to worry he was getting tired of her, he always did something to quell her doubts. He really did care, he just had to be careful, given his position and all. She needed to be patient. When the time was right, they'd be together forever.

She left the office, even smiling at the new admin as she passed her desk. The blonde might look down her nose at Merry now, but she'd be singing a different tune when Merry was Mrs. Parker Stroud. By then, Parker would be running the whole business. And Merry would be running Parker.

LAURA WAITED UNTIL Merry and Parker were in Parker's office, then she moved to the door and pressed her ear to the gap between the door and the frame. A few moments later, she moved away. So Parker was fooling around with one of the office staff. That didn't strike her as a motive for mass poisoning. But she filed the information away as one more facet of the picture she was assembling of the company and its inner workings.

Promptly at five o'clock, Parker Stroud exited his office. "Go home," he told Laura. "No hanging around hoping for overtime."

"Good evening to you, too," she said.

He frowned and moved on.

She was searching Parker's desk a few minutes later when Cantrell strolled in. Jace. She needed to get used to thinking of him as Jace, so she wouldn't slip and address him as Cantrell, blowing their cover. Dressed in gray coveralls with his name in red script on the pocket, he still carried himself with a swagger. He was chewing gum—not smacking, but the muscles of his jaw bunched in a way she found distracting. He leaned on the doorjamb and watched her rifle through the desk drawers and peer under the blotter. "Find anything interesting?" he asked.

"Nothing." She shut the last drawer and moved toward him. "What about you?"

"I'm getting a feel for how this place operates. I can tell you, things aren't as watertight as the Strouds think. I'll fill you in at home. Let's get out of here."

They crossed the parking lot in a crowd of other workers leaving for the day. Heat billowed out of the cab of the truck when she opened the door, and she slid in carefully to avoid burning the back of her legs. Jace climbed into the driver's seat. "I'm starved," he said as he cranked the engine. "What's for dinner?"

"Why are you asking me?"

"I made breakfast. And lunch. It's your turn to cook."

Lunch had been a ham-and-cheese sandwich. With mayonnaise, which she hated. She had pulled out the cheese and eaten it with the apple and fig cookies, which had been surprisingly good. Her stomach grumbled at the memory. "Let's get takeout."

"Then your choices are pizza or barbecue."

They opted for barbecue, which was moist, smoky, spicy and some of the best food she had ever eaten.

"Director Pembroke says you grew up in a place like this," she said, wiping sauce from her fingers with a paper napkin.

"Yeah."

"What was that like?"

"What do you want me to say? It was okay, until it wasn't."

"I'm just asking. Trying to be friendly."

Some of the tension went out of his shoulders. "Sorry. I grew up in Hatcher, Tennessee, which is a whole lot like Mayville. My mom and dad and sister still live there. My dad has had some health problems, so transferring to the Knoxville office means I can be around to help out more."

"I'm sorry to hear about your dad." She set aside the

wadded-up napkin. "What's wrong with him? If you don't mind my asking."

"He has mesothelioma. A lung disease coal miners get from inhaling asbestos underground." He spoke very matter-of-factly, but his eyes wouldn't meet hers, as if he was afraid of revealing too much emotion.

"That must be rough," she said.

He shrugged. "What about you? Where did you grow up?"

"All over. My dad was in the military."

"That explains a lot."

"What do you mean by that?"

"Your 'don't color outside the lines' attitude. No offense. The military just ingrains that in you. I know. I was in the army for six years."

"You saw action?"

"Too much action. Fallujah. Baghdad, Kamdesh. It's how I ended up with the Bureau. They were recruiting military types."

She never would have described him as a "military type." "Davis Rogers came out of the military," she said.

"Yeah. He and I have compared notes. How did you end up with the feds?"

"I have a degree in forensic accounting from George Washington University, so it seemed like a good fit."

"Of course."

He spoke as if he had her all figured out. "What does that mean?" she demanded.

"You're a number cruncher. The whole coloring in the lines thing again. Don't get your back up. It's a useful skill. It'll probably be a big help with this case."

She forced herself to relax. They were never going to be able to work together if she took offense at everything he said. "You think money is behind the poisonings?"

"I think money has a lot to do with everything. And Stroud Pharmaceuticals is a multimillion-dollar concern."

"You said things in the factory aren't as secure as the Strouds like to portray. What did you find out?"

"I'll want to verify this, but apparently, the facility where the Stomach Soothers were manufactured is identical to this one. The surveillance cameras are focused on the production area, but not the break rooms or hallways or restrooms. I think it would have been possible for someone working with their back to the camera to slip the poison into a batch of the tablets before the bottles were sealed."

"What about the missing bottles of Stomach Soothers?"

"I haven't figured that out yet, but it's early days. Anything suspicious in the front offices?"

She shook her head. "Parker Stroud is apparently involved with one of the women who works in the offices, Merry Winger."

"What's Stroud like?"

She made a face. "Full of himself. Disdainful. Kind of a jerk, but as far as I can tell, competent. I got the impression he resents that his parents don't want to retire and turn the whole business over to him, but he was very clear that he stands to inherit one day, so I can't see a motive for him to destroy the company's reputation by poisoning their most popular product."

"We should dig into the personnel files, see if anyone has a grudge, maybe because they were passed over for a promotion or something."

She nodded and was about to ask him more about how the factory was set up when an ear-piercing siren shrieked. All over the restaurant, chairs were shoved back and people stood. "Fire alarm," a man said as he hurried past.

Another man pressed his cell phone to his ear. "It's at the plant," he said.

"Stroud's?" Laura asked.

The man nodded, then broke into a jog toward the parking lot. Jace threw some money on the table, and he and Laura joined the others leaving the restaurant. As he started the truck, both their cell phones rang.

"It's not a fire," he said, phone pressed to his ear.

"No." Ana Ramirez had just informed Laura of the reason for the alarm. "Someone planted a bomb at Stroud Pharmaceuticals."

Pharmaceuticals...

Chapter Four

Yellow crime-scene tape flapped in a hot wind that carried the acrid scents of burning plastic and ash. Ana stood
with Rogers just outside the tape, surveying what had once
been a side entrance to Stroud Pharmaceutical Headquarters. The steel door, now grotesquely twisted, lay on the
buckled sidewalk in front of a scorched hole rimmed by
jagged brick. The windows on either side of the door had
shattered and buckled. The area swarmed with fire and
law enforcement personnel while farther back, dozens of
Stroud employees and townspeople crowded against police barriers.

Rowan Cooper, the team's liaison officer, stepped
through the wreckage of the doorway. A tall, slender
woman with long black hair, Rowan was skilled at soothing ruffled feathers and persuading even the most reluctant law enforcement officers to cooperate with the FBI.
She spotted Ana and Rogers and started toward them, followed by a stocky man with a gray buzz cut and heavy
jowls. "This is Special Agent Terry Armand, ATF," Rowan
said. "Terry, this is Special Agents Ana Sofia Ramirez and
Davis Rogers."

They shook hands with the Alcohol, Tobacco, Firearms
and Explosives agent. "What can you tell us about the explosion?" Rogers asked.

"Everything I can tell you is preliminary, but it looks

like the explosive was wired to the door lock. Inserting a key in the lock set the trigger, and a few seconds later—enough time for someone to step inside—it went off. The bomb itself was a fairly simple pipe bomb. The damage is pretty typical." He glanced back toward the doorway.

"Would whoever planted that bomb need access to the interior of the area?" Rogers asked.

Armand nodded. "Oh yes. As best as we can determine at this preliminary stage, the bomb itself was located just inside the door."

"Whose key set off the explosion?" Ana asked.

"Lydia Green, forty-four," Rowan said. "She'd worked at Stroud for three years as an independent commercial cleaning service."

"I talked to a few people who said that door is kept locked and generally only used after hours," Armand said. "The plant is only running one shift right now, and that ended at five. Otherwise, many more people might have been injured."

"Was that intentional or coincidental?" Rogers wondered. "We need to find out who had keys to that door."

"Here's the person who can tell us," Ana said.

They turned to watch Donna Stroud make her way through the crowd. She was still dressed in a boxy pantsuit and low heels. Only her red-rimmed eyes and pale face betrayed her distress. She hurried to join Ana, Rogers and the others on the sidewalk. "What is going on here?" she asked. "I thought you were here to help, and now this happens."

"Mrs. Stroud, have you or your husband or son received any threats?" Rogers asked. "Anyone trying to intimidate or coerce you?"

"If there was anything like that, I would have told you," she said. "We've been as cooperative as we know how to be." She looked back toward the ravaged doorway, her face a mask of pain. "Did the same person do this who poisoned the Stomach Soother tablets?"

"We don't know," Ana said. "Do you think there's a connection?"

"I don't know what to think." She shook her head. "They told me Lydia was killed. She has three children. What is going to happen to them now? What is going to happen to all of us?"

"Mrs. Stroud, where is your husband?" Ana asked. "Is he still out of town?"

The haunted look in her eyes increased. "My husband isn't well," she said.

Before Ana could ascertain the nature of his illness, a young man in jeans and a golf shirt elbowed his way through the crowd and jogged up to them. "I just heard the news," he said, putting his arm around the woman.

"My son, Parker Stroud," Donna said. "These are Agents Ramirez and Rogers, from the FBI." She frowned at Rowan and Terry. "I'm sorry, I don't know these people."

"It doesn't matter." Parker waved away the introductions and scowled at Rogers. "If you're the FBI, what are you doing to put a stop to this persecution of my family?"

"So you feel these attacks are personal?" Rogers asked. "Aimed directly at your family?"

"What else am I supposed to think?" Parker asked. "The Stroud family is Stroud Pharmaceuticals. This is clearly an attempt to destroy our reputation and our livelihood."

"Who has a key to that door?" Ana asked.

Donna took in a deep breath and moved out of her son's embrace. "I do, of course. Parker. Angela Dupree in accounting. Merry Winger, the accounting admin. Gini Elgin before she died. And of course, Lydia had a key so she could come in and clean." She pressed her lips tightly together.

"Was this Mrs. Green's usual time to enter the building to clean?" Ana asked.

"No." Donna paused and took a deep breath. "Most of the time, Lydia came in the morning, before the other employees reported for work. I like to get an early start myself, so I often saw her then. But this morning she reminded me that she was due to leave on vacation tomorrow, and would I mind if she cleaned tonight, so she could get an early start."

"How many people knew about this change of schedule?" Rogers asked.

"I'm not sure," Donna said. "I didn't mention it to anyone, but Lydia might have."

"What about Mr. Stroud?" Ana asked. "Does he have a key to that door?"

Donna exchanged a telling look with her son. "My father isn't well," he said.

"How exactly is he unwell?" Rogers asked.

"My husband suffers from early-onset dementia," Donna said.

"He's not able to participate fully in the business anymore," Parker said. "I do what I can to help my mother, though I could do more if she'd let me."

"I'm still capable of running this company," Donna said.

"What happened to Gini's key after she died?" Ana asked.

Donna's face clouded. "I don't know. I've been meaning to ask her son for it, but with so much else going on…" Her voice trailed away.

"Whoever set up that bomb knew only certain people had the key to that entrance," Ana said. "It's possible one of those people was the target."

"That's too big a coincidence," Parker said. "This has to be related to the tampering with the Stomach Soothers."

"Then who do you think is targeting the company?" Ana asked. "Do you have a rival who would wish you harm? A disgruntled former employee? Or perhaps a personal enemy?"

"We don't have any of those things," Donna said. "This has to be random. Some kind of terrorist."

"Whoever did this, it's your job to find out and put a stop to it," Parker said.

"We fully intend to do so," Ana said. "And if you have any suspicions about anyone, be sure to share them with us."

"You might start by interviewing the Lovejoys. They just started work today and now this happens. That's a pretty odd coincidence, don't you think?"

Ana followed his gaze across the parking lot, to where Jace and Laura stood with a group of other employees. "I really don't think the Lovejoys had anything to do with this," Donna said.

"No, that's a good idea," Rogers said. "We'll be sure to talk to them. Is there anyone else you can think of who might be angry with you personally, or with the company in general?"

Donna stared at the ground but said nothing.

"There isn't anyone," Parker said.

"Gini Elgin's son was very upset when I spoke with him yesterday," Donna said. "He blames us for his mother's death. But he certainly didn't poison Gini. I think it was mostly grief talking. I remember him from when he and Parker went to school together, and he was always such a nice young man. Gini was very proud of him and I know her death has devastated him."

"What is his name?" Rogers took out his phone to make a note.

"Leo Elgin," Parker said. "But he didn't have anything to do with this. You're wasting your time with him."

"Have you spoken to him since he came back to town?" Donna asked her son.

"I haven't had time," Parker said. "I've been too busy trying to keep this company going."

"I think it would mean a lot to him if you touched base," Donna said.

Parker shook his head but made no reply.

"Is there a location near here we can use to interview people?" Ana asked.

"Can't you do that at the police station?" Parker asked.

"It would be easier if we had someplace closer." Ana said. "Since we'll need to talk to all your employees. It's possible one of them saw or heard something unusual."

"There's a conference room at the back of the production plant across the parking lot," Donna said. "We use it sometimes for training. If there's anything else you need, let us know."

"Thank you," Rogers said. "We'll start with the Lovejoys. Agent Cooper, would you bring them to us, please?"

Rowan left to fetch Cantrell and Smitty. Donna turned away. Instead of following her, Parker moved closer to Ana. "If you learn anything, come to me first," he said. "My mother doesn't need any more stress right now. My father is a lot worse off than she wants to admit. That, along with everything else that has happened with the business, has her at her breaking point. I've been trying to persuade her to turn everything over to me, but she just can't give up that control."

"We'll share information with you as we are able," Ana said. But Donna Stroud was still president of Stroud Pharmaceuticals, and would be informed as well.

LAURA AND JACE kept up the pretense of not knowing Rogers, Ramirez and Rowan Cooper until they were all in the back conference room, which, as a precaution, the ATF had swept with bomb-sniffing dogs, and Rogers had checked for listening devices. Jace dropped into the chair across from Ramirez. "Before you ask, we haven't found out anything so far."

"Parker Stroud thinks you two are suspicious," Ramirez said.

"Both of us?" Laura glanced at Jace. "I'm surprised he even knows we're a couple."

"You said he didn't strike you as incompetent," Jace said.

"Did you know Steve Stroud is suffering from dementia?" Rogers asked.

"No." It annoyed Laura that that information had escaped her. "Though it explains why Parker thinks his parents should turn the business over to him now."

"Does he resent his mother's stubbornness enough to try to sabotage the business?" Jace asked.

"Why undermine his own inheritance?" Laura asked. "I think we'd be better off focusing on anyone who has a grudge against the company or the Strouds personally."

"It's possible the bombings and the medication tampering are the work of two different entities," Ramirez said.

"That makes the most sense to me," Jace said. "Poison and bombing are two very different modes of attack. For one thing, the poisoning took out a number of random individuals. The bombing seems more focused."

"Only a handful of people had a key to that door," Rogers said. "The bomb was set to go off when someone inserted their key into the lock."

"But the bomb was planted inside the building," Ramirez said. "Someone would need access to the area on the other side of the door—and time to plant the bomb, probably after everyone left for the day."

"There was only an hour between end of shift and the time of the explosion," Jace said. "They'd need fifteen or twenty minutes at least to be sure the office was empty. We should find out who stayed late that day."

"Or who came back after everyone left," Laura said. "Is there a security camera at that entrance?"

"There was," Rowan said. "It was destroyed in the blast, but maybe the tech guys can pull something off of it."

"Donna mentioned that Gini Elgin's son, Leo, is blaming Stroud Pharmaceuticals for his mother's death," Rogers said. "He could have used Gini's key to let himself into the building after everyone left."

"I saw him here at the factory yesterday," Ramirez said. "At that makeshift memorial on the corner of the property. He smashed a vase full of flowers and looked pretty upset."

"We'll definitely be talking to him." Rogers braced his hands on the back of a chair and leaned toward them. "Ramirez, Cooper and I are going to be talking to every employee over the next few days. But we're counting on you two to figure out what they aren't telling us. Somebody associated with this place has secrets. We learn those, we'll be closer to finding our killer or killers."

THE DAY AFTER the bombing, the factory operated as usual. Jace's job was to monitor a machine that boxed up herbal throat lozenges—twelve bottles of lozenges to each box. He pulled out any boxes that unfolded crookedly or didn't contain twelve bottles. Mistakes didn't happen often, and he had plenty of time to observe the workers around him who monitored various other aspects of the packaging process. Since all the poisoned Stomach Soothers, as well as the missing bottles, were from a single lot, manufactured on a single day, he suspected someone had intercepted the bottles before they were sealed, introduced the ricin in the form of a fine powder that had clung to the tablets, then put the bottles back into the assembly line to proceed to packaging.

How to do that, though, without being noticed?

The woman who was training him, Barb Falk, stopped

by two hours into his shift. A stocky middle-aged woman with bleached hair pulled back in a ponytail and sharp blue eyes that didn't appear to miss anything, she was affable and talkative. "How's it going?" she asked.

"No problems so far," he said.

"Yeah, things run pretty smoothly around here," she said. "It can make the job boring at times but be thankful for the boredom. I worked at a place before this where the machinery was always breaking down. We were constantly playing catch-up. Better to sit back and have nothing to do than to constantly be scrambling to do the impossible."

"I can't help thinking about that tragedy with the Stomach Soothers," Jace said. "I heard on a news report that the FBI thinks someone tampered with the tablets before they even left the factory, but I don't see any way that's even possible."

"I guess anything is possible if you try hard enough," she said.

"Being a trainer, you probably know every part of the manufacturing process," Jace said. "How do you think it was done?"

She shook her head. "I don't even go there," she said. "Even if it could be done, why would anyone do it? These are good jobs, hard to come by. Most people who get them really appreciate them." Her eyes met his, her expression daring him to disagree.

"I hear you," he said. "My wife and I feel lucky, getting hired on here. I just hate to think of anyone trying to do something like that, messing everything up for the rest of us."

"If anyone had, they'd be out of here before they knew what hit them," she said.

"Has anyone been fired recently?" he asked.

Her eyes narrowed. "I don't see how that concerns you.

Now come on, let's head over to the box sealer. You'll like that one—you actually have to operate the cutter."

He spent the next two hours pressing down on a lever to cut the tape that sealed the top of each box. Not any more exciting than his previous position, but it did require the use of one hand.

He thought about heading upstairs and seeing if Laura wanted to have lunch with him, then thought better of it. Lunch was his best opportunity to interact with his fellow factory workers. While Laura played the role of his wife well enough in public, he didn't sense she relished acting the part more often than necessary.

Still, she wasn't as bad as he had feared she would be. After the first day, she made no complaints about living in a house trailer or giving up her designer clothing. He hadn't been surprised to learn she was a military brat with an accounting degree, but when she had talked about her background he had glimpsed the geeky girl who never lived in one place long enough to make fast friends.

She was an intriguing combination of prickly and soft. It was like she couldn't allow herself to enjoy life. He'd seen that in the military—people so scared of losing control, they clung to the regulations like a lifeline. Do what you're told and you'll be safe.

Except you were never safe. Not really. Obey all the rules and an IED could still take you out when you were crossing the street. Eat all the right things, do all the right things, and cancer could still show up one day when you least expected it. People like Laura clung to the illusion of control instead of surrendering to the reality that they had none.

She would no doubt be horrified to know he had thought of her that way for even one moment. Smiling to himself at her imagined reaction, he collected his lunch from his locker and made his way to the break room. He sat at a table with some coworkers he recognized, opened the lunch bag and studied the contents. Laura had insisted on making lunch this morning. He had another ham sandwich but with mustard, not mayonnaise, and lettuce, tomato, onion—and was that *cucumber* on top? Instead of chips, he had carrots and celery sticks.

"You don't look too happy with your lunch." The man to his left, whose coveralls identified him as Ed, said.

"My wife's trying to get me to eat healthier." He picked the cucumber slices off the sandwich and set them aside. At least Laura had packed Oreos. For all her love of vegetables, she had a sweet tooth.

"She's the new admin in the office, right?" Phyllis, across from him, asked. "The pretty blonde."

Jace nodded. "Yeah, we were really lucky to both get jobs here. I heard these jobs were hard to come by."

"You came along at the right time," Phyllis said. "They needed someone to fill Benny Cagle's position."

"What happened to Benny Cagle?" Jace took a bite of the ham sandwich. It wasn't bad, but it would have been better with mayo.

"He got fired." Ed crunched down on a grape.

"Why'd he get fired?" Jace asked.

"He had a problem with drugs," Phyllis said. "Heroin."

"I heard it was meth," said a woman down the table.

"No, it was heroin," Phyllis said.

"When was he fired?" Jace asked.

"Oh, I guess it was a couple weeks ago now," Ed said.

"He kept showing up late for work—or not showing up at all," Phyllis said. "Everybody saw it coming, but you can't really talk to someone under the influence, can you?" She shrugged.

"Is he still here in town?" Jace asked.

"I heard he went to live with his sister in Vicksburg," Phyllis said.

"You play softball?" Ed asked Jace.

"Not in a long time," Jace said. "Why?"

"We got a coed team through the local rec league," Ed said. "You look like you could handle a bat."

"I'll think about it. Thanks." Though, with any luck, he'd be long gone by the time the season was in full swing.

Laura was waiting by the truck when Jace emerged into the parking lot later that afternoon. A soft breeze stirred her hair and fluttered the ruffles along the neck of her blouse. Jace faltered a little, struck by how pretty she looked. Not like the no-nonsense fed he'd come to know.

She spotted him and sent him an annoyed look. He started walking again, not hurrying. She never liked to wait. "How was your day?" he asked as he clicked the key fob to unlock the truck.

She opened the door and swung inside. "I got the name of an employee who was fired just a week ago," she said.

"Yeah. Benny Cagle." He started the truck and turned the air-conditioning up to full.

"Oh. You knew?" There was no hiding her disappointment.

"Some of my coworkers were talking about him at lunch today," Jace said. "They said he got canned for drugs—heroin or meth."

"The official file says he was fired for failing to show up for work and chronic tardiness," she said.

"Easier to prove than drugs," Jace said. "Probably looks better to insurance companies, too." He glanced at her. "Somebody said he's in Vicksburg, living with his sister."

"We need to make sure he didn't come back to town and plant a bomb," she said.

They spent the rest of the drive to their trailer debating the best way to investigate Cagle. As Jace turned into the driveway, Laura fell silent. Two big cardboard boxes leaned against the steps of the trailer. "What is that?" she asked, tense with wariness.

"That's your new bed." He climbed out of the truck and she followed.

"You ordered a bed delivered?" she asked, eyeing the boxes.

"Sure. Why not?" He examined the boxes then tapped the larger one. "This is the frame." He tapped the other box. "And this is the mattress." She was still frowning, so he added, "You needed a bed. We don't have time to shop."

She met his gaze, her expression softer. "Thank you," she said. "That was very thoughtful of you."

He looked away. She didn't have to act like he'd donated a kidney. "If you'll make dinner, I'll put all this together," he said, gesturing toward the boxes.

Dinner was pasta and chicken in some kind of sauce, which was good, and steamed broccoli—not his favorite, but he ate it because he was hungry. "The pasta is good," he said when they were done.

"It's lemon pepper chicken. I don't cook often," she said. "But I can cook."

"I never said you couldn't." He stood and helped clear the table, then touched her shoulder and turned her toward the door to the rest of the house. "Come see your new bed."

He'd chosen a simple metal frame, antique-looking, and one of those foam mattresses that expanded as soon as you unboxed it. Laura walked around it, surveying it from every angle, then sat on the edge of the mattress.

"How is it?" he asked, immediately annoyed that he cared what she thought.

"Better than the couch."

"That's all you can say?" He sat beside her and gave a little bounce. "Feels pretty good to me. Better than what I've got."

Then he saw the smile tugging at the corner of her

mouth. She'd been playing him for sure. She burst out laughing. "It's great, Jace. Thanks."

She looked so pretty when she smiled. Approachable. He leaned toward her, the flowers-and-vanilla scent of her swirling around him. Their eyes met and her lips parted. So inviting…

His phone rang, and they both jumped to their feet. Heart pounding, he fumbled for the phone, avoiding her eyes. What had almost happened there? Whatever it was, it wasn't going to happen again. "Hello," he barked into the phone.

"I'm sending you a report on Leo Elgin," Rogers said. "He's somebody we definitely want to take a closer look at."

"Why?" Jace asked.

"You'll see." Rogers ended the call.

Jace stuffed the phone back in his coveralls. "That was Rogers. He said…"

"I heard." Laura headed for the living room and Jace followed. By the time he reached her, she had her laptop up and running and was accessing the report. "This says Leo Elgin is employed by a firm in Nashville that makes sophisticated security systems for businesses and high-end homes," she said.

"That might give him the skill to create a bomb like the one that went off at the factory. The bomb itself was simple, but the trigger required a little sophistication," Jace said.

"Oh."

The single syllable was freighted with meaning—awe, dismay, interest. "What is it?" he asked and moved in beside her, shoulders brushing.

"Leo Elgin had some trouble in high school," she said. Her eyes met his, reflecting both fear and anger. "He was jailed briefly for giving a bomb to a teacher."

Chapter Five

Six for six.

The three words, bold print in a twenty-point font, stood out on the torn piece of printer paper. "It was in a plain envelope, addressed to me, in this morning's mail." Donna Stroud spoke calmly, only her tightly clenched hands betraying her agitation.

Ana examined the envelope, which she had already placed in a clear evidence pouch. It bore a local postmark, no return address, and had been mailed the day before. The paper that accompanied it looked like plain copy paper, torn in half. "What do you think it means?" Ana asked.

The vertical line between Donna's eyebrows deepened. "Six people died from the tainted Stomach Soothers," she said. "But I don't know what 'six for six' means."

"We'll see if we can get any fingerprints or other evidence from this." Ana slipped the evidence envelopes into her jacket. "Did anyone else in the office see this?"

"Merry Winger puts the mail on my desk, so she probably saw it. She collects it from the mailroom about nine thirty each morning. Someone in the mailroom would have seen it when they sorted it."

"Where can I find Merry?"

"Her desk is just to the left of the door to the outer office. She's the pretty blonde."

Merry was indeed a pretty blonde, all bouncy curls and

dramatic eye makeup, including spider-like fake eyelashes. "May I help you?" she asked when Ana approached her desk.

Ana showed her identification. "Do you remember putting this on Mrs. Stroud's desk this morning?" she asked.

Merry leaned forward and studied the envelope in its clear evidence pouch. She wrinkled her nose. "It might have been in with the other mail, but I don't really notice." She sat back and shrugged.

"What's your routine for handling the mail?" Ana asked.

"I go down the hall to the mailroom about nine thirty and collect whatever is in the boxes for this office. Dennis, the mail clerk, sorts everything after the carrier delivers it. I distribute everything for this office. Mrs. Stroud usually has the biggest stack. It used to be Mr. Stroud, but now that he's retired, Mrs. S gets everything that isn't addressed to accounting or personnel or a specific person."

"So you would have sorted this letter into the stack to go to Mrs. Stroud?"

"Well, yeah, but I just toss anything that isn't for anyone else into her pile. I don't stop and read anything or pay much attention." She leaned forward again, eyes bright with interest. "Why? Is that letter from the bomber?"

"Why do you think it might be from the bomber?" Ana asked.

"Well, duh! You're from the FBI, and you've got that envelope all sealed up in that pouch. If it was junk mail you wouldn't treat it that way."

"We don't know who the letter is from," Ana said. "I'm trying to find out."

"Sorry, I can't help you," Merry said.

"If you think of anything, let me know." Ana handed her card to the young woman and headed to the mail room, where Dennis told her he hadn't noticed anything unusual about the letter either.

Back at the situation room at the local police department that she and Rogers were using as their workspace, Rogers examined the letter and envelope. "'Six for six,'" he said. "A reference to the six people who were killed by the poisoned Stomach Soothers?"

"Donna Stroud thinks so." Ana studied the three words. "Maybe the bomber is saying he—or she—plans to kill six people in retaliation for the six who died."

"Kill as in set more bombs?"

"We don't know, do we?" She sank into one of the rolling desk chairs the local police had provided them. "People are poisoned and someone responds by planting a bomb. Where's the logic in that?"

"It makes sense to the bomber—our job is to get into his head and figure out how."

"Leo Elgin made it clear he blamed the Strouds for killing his mother," Ana said. "He has the skills to build a bomb and a history of making a bomb threat. It shows us he thinks of a bomb as a weapon."

Rogers nodded. "It's past time we talked to Leo."

"The bomb I gave Mrs. Pepper wasn't real," Leo said. "It was just a bunch of highway flares taped together and wired to a clock. Anyone with sense would have seen right away it was a fake. Which was the whole point, because Mrs. Pepper didn't have any sense."

Leo Elgin stared across the table at Ana, deep shadows beneath his eyes like smudges of soot, his hair falling listlessly across his pale forehead. He wore the same T-shirt and jeans he had had on when she had seen him at the memorial Sunday outside the Stroud plant, and the sour smell of his body odor hung in the air around him.

"Why did you give your teacher a fake bomb?" Ana asked.

"Because she was an idiot and I wanted to prove it. She

freaked out about a bomb that looked like something out of a cartoon."

"But you were the one who got into trouble." Rogers moved from where he had been leaning against the wall to loom over Elgin, his muscular bulk making the young man look even smaller. "You were expelled from school." The school district had eventually dropped the charges and Leo had been released from jail. It had taken some serious digging to uncover the incident.

Leo jutted out his lower lip like a pouting adolescent. "I hated the place anyway. It was full of idiots."

"Was Parker Stroud an idiot?" Rogers asked.

Something flickered across Leo's face—confusion? Fear? "Parker was okay," he said.

Ana leaned toward him. "Were you and Parker friends?" she asked.

"No, we weren't friends."

"But you knew him."

His nostrils flared as he blew out a breath. "We had, like, thirty people in our whole class. Everybody knew everybody. But it's not like we hung out or anything."

"Why didn't the school press charges against you?" Ana asked.

"Haven't you been listening? It wasn't a real bomb."

"You can be charged for threatening someone, even if your threat isn't real," Rogers said. "With all the incidents of school violence, how did you ever think you'd get away with such a stupid stunt?"

Leo flinched at the word "stupid," as if Rogers had slapped him. "People around here knew me. They knew I wasn't dangerous."

"Your mother worked for the Strouds," Ana said. "Maybe the Strouds put in a good word for you. After all, their business is the biggest employer in town. They probably had a lot of influence."

Leo's scowl turned ugly. "I didn't need the Strouds to pull any strings for me."

"Do you blame the Strouds for your mother's death?" Rogers asked.

A flash of anger this time. Leo sat up straighter. "They're responsible. The medication they make killed her. If they had any kind of quality control this wouldn't have happened."

"Your mother died." Rogers's voice was flat. Cold. "You held the Strouds responsible. So you decided to make them pay."

A sharp jerk of his head, left to right. "They'll pay," he said. "I've already talked to a lawyer. She thinks I have a good case."

"A bomb is quicker," Rogers said.

Leo's face twisted. "Look, I wouldn't do that. I knew Lydia. She was a nice person." His voice broke. "She and my mom were friends." He covered his eyes with one hand.

Rogers braced his hands on the table next to Leo. "We're going to search your mother's house, your car, and your apartment and office in Nashville," he said. "If you made that bomb, we're going to find out."

"Go ahead and look." Leo lowered his hand. "You won't find anything."

"How long do you plan to stay in Mayville?" Ana asked.

"Why? Are you going to tell me not to leave town?"

"Answer the question," Rogers said. "How long do you plan to be in town?"

Leo slumped in the chair. "I don't know. The…the service for my mother is Saturday, but then I need to decide what to do with the house and… I don't know. I can't really think of anything right now."

"When do you have to be back at work at Integrated Security?" Ana asked.

"I took a leave of absence. My boss said I could come

back when I'm ready." His eyes met hers. The anguish in them was like a raw wound. "She was all I had—my mother. It was just her and me, all those years. I don't know what I'm going to do without her."

Rogers moved away, toward the door. "You can go now, but we'll be in touch," he said.

When he was gone, Ana and Rogers moved to the room next door, where Smitty and Cantrell had been observing through the one-way glass. "Good call on asking about Parker Stroud," Cantrell said. "That got a reaction from him."

"It was a reaction," Rogers agreed. "I just don't know what it means."

"His grief was real," Ana said. "I think he's seriously depressed."

"I agree," Rogers said. "But that just gives him more of a motivation for wanting to harm the Strouds."

"Do you think the Strouds really persuaded the school not to press charges over that fake bomb?" Smitty asked.

Rogers shrugged. "It makes sense. His mother was a key employee, close to the same age as the Strouds. She probably went to them for help and they leaned on the school to get them to agree to not press charges, provided Leo transferred to another school."

"His mom sent him to a military academy for a year," Ana said, referring to her notes.

"That didn't come cheap," Cantrell said. "I wouldn't be surprised if the Strouds paid for that, too."

"If he owes the Strouds so much, why blame them for his mother's death?" Smitty asked.

"Maybe because he owes them so much," Cantrell said. "Obligation carries its own weight."

"You heard him," Rogers said. "Everyone at school was an idiot. His teacher was an idiot. Elgin thinks he's the smartest man in the room, whatever the room."

"Maybe he thinks he's smart enough to get away with planting a real bomb at the Stroud factory," Cantrell said.

"That bomb wasn't planted at a factory entrance," Smitty said. "It was wired to a door only office personnel used. Only a few people had a key that would trigger the detonation."

"Which brings us back to the Strouds," Ana said. "Donna, Steve and Parker all have keys."

"And Leo probably has Gini Elgin's key," Smitty said.

"The local police already searched her house," Rogers said. "They didn't find the key, or any bomb-making materials."

"We need to monitor his phone and computer usage," Cantrell said. "If he built that bomb, he had to get the materials from somewhere."

"Did his mother have a storage unit anywhere near here?" Smitty asked. "Maybe he's keeping the materials there."

"We haven't found anything yet," Rogers said. He pointed to Cantrell. "I'll see about getting permission to bug his place and monitor his computer."

"Let me know when you're ready," Cantrell said. He was the team's specialist in electronic surveillance.

"Have you two come up with anything yet?" Rogers asked.

Smitty shook her head. "Not yet."

"We checked out the fired employee, Benny Cagle," Ana said. "He was in jail in Vicksburg, Mississippi, where he had been living with his sister, when the bombing occurred."

"Had been since before the Stomach Soother tablets were poisoned," Rogers said.

"Do we think the crimes are related?" Smitty asked. "Are we looking for one person or two?"

"Seems a big coincidence to have two crimes like this

centered around one small-town business, so close together," Cantrell said.

"But two very different crimes," Smitty said. "So maybe two different people with similar motivations."

"What's the motivation?" Rogers asked.

"I don't know yet." She shook her head. "We need to dig deeper with the Strouds. Maybe they're hiding something."

"Everybody is hiding something," Cantrell said. "The question is whether their secrets are relevant to our investigation."

They tossed around more theories for a few minutes, then the meeting broke up. Ana and Smitty headed for the ladies' room. "How are things going with you and Jace?" Ana asked when she and Smitty were washing their hands at the row of sinks.

Smitty grimaced. "It's okay. At least I'm not sleeping on the couch anymore."

"Oh?" Ana didn't even try to hide her surprise.

Smitty flushed. "I mean, I have a bed now. There was only one when we moved in, and Jace took it."

"How gentlemanly of him."

Smitty waved aside the comment. "He's a lot taller than I am, so it made sense to stick me with the couch. I got the best revenge, though. My new bed is supposedly a lot more comfortable than the old one he's sleeping on."

Ana dug a tube of lipstick from her bag. "Things are going okay, then. Better than you expected?"

"Yeah. I guess so." Smitty combed her fingers through her long hair.

"For what it's worth, you two look good together." Ana studied her fellow agent in the mirror. "Like a real couple."

"Who would have guessed we were such good actors?" But Smitty's cheeks were still pink, and there was a brightness in her eyes Ana hadn't seen before. Ana smiled. She liked Smitty. She was a good agent, but maybe a little too tightly wound sometimes. Cantrell might change that.

"What are you smiling about?" Rogers asked when Ana rejoined him.

"I was thinking Smitty and Cantrell might make a good couple."

"No way! Those two are like oil and water. I'm surprised they've been able to live in that trailer for more than one night without coming to blows."

"They're professionals." But they were human, too. The job was only one aspect of their lives. She thought of her fiancé, Benning Reeves, and his two children. The four of them would soon be a family. Knowing that added meaning to her work.

"Cantrell and Smitty will both be glad when this case is over," Rogers said.

Maybe, Ana thought. And maybe she was being overly romantic, seeing a match for those two. But stranger things had happened in this line of work.

JACE PUT A hand at Laura's back as they walked across the parking lot from the police station. She forced herself not to shrug it off. It was the kind of gesture a husband might make to his wife and fit their cover. Truth be told, she didn't really want to shrug him off. The weight of his hand was warm and pleasant—almost comforting. "Some of the guys at the plant were telling me about a lake south of town," he said. "We should check it out."

"Why? Does it have something to do with the case?"

"I just thought it would be someplace nice to see. You know, to relax."

They reached the truck, he unlocked it, and they climbed in.

"All right." Though she felt anything but relaxed around this man. She was so hyperaware of him—of his bulk filling the driver's seat of the truck, the muscles in his forearm tensing as he shifted gears, the sweet scent of the cinnamon gum he chewed.

"Why do you always chew gum?" she asked.

He glanced at her. "Does it bother you?"

She shrugged. "I just wondered."

"I quit smoking six months ago. I guess you could say I traded a nicotine habit for a gum habit."

"Good for you."

"Yeah, well, I still miss it. It's just damned inconvenient when I'm working. Did you ever smoke?"

She shook her head.

"Yeah, I should have guessed."

"What is that supposed to mean?"

"You're like those girls I knew in high school—the ones who didn't drink or smoke or swear or skip school or so much as jaywalk. They always looked perfect and spoke perfect and acted perfect."

"And you didn't want anything to do with them," she said.

"Oh no. You've got it all wrong." He shook his head. "Those girls were untouchable. And I wanted so bad to touch them, to make them feel. To help them discover the bad girl I knew had to be hiding inside that pristine shell."

The rich velvet of his voice and the teasing words sent a quiver through her, low in the belly. She had been one of those girls, the ones too afraid to ever break the rules. He was the kind of boy she would have shunned, too terrified of the things he might make her feel.

She was a woman now, one with enough experience that men like him no longer frightened her. Or so she told herself.

Neither of them spoke on the rest of the drive to the lake. Laura leaned back in the seat and closed her eyes, reviewing the interview with Leo Elgin, trying to sort out where his evidence fit with everything else they knew about this case.

The silver-blue expanse of the lake reflected the pines that crowded the shore on three sides, with a rough sand beach bordered by picnic tables nearest the lot where they parked. Only half a dozen other vehicles shared space in the big lot. "They must get crowds here on the weekends, with a parking lot this size," Laura observed as she and Jace climbed out of the pickup truck.

"I'll bet a lot of high school kids come here at night to make out and party," Jace said. "At least, that's what I would have done."

Yes, Jace had probably been many a father's worst nightmare in high school. "Did you ever do that?" he asked. "Sneak out to the park and party with your friends—or make out with your boyfriend, music playing low on the radio, the moon shining down?"

He made it sound so carefree and romantic. "My father was a lieutenant colonel," she said. "And we usually lived on base."

"So no guy had the guts to risk sneaking around with you," Jace said.

"I guess." She wouldn't admit to Jace that she was the one who hadn't had the courage to defy her father.

They took a path that circled the lake. The earthy smell of sun-warmed weeds and lake water mingled with the heavier perfume of honeysuckle. Laura breathed in deeply, feeling some of the tension of the day easing from her shoulders. "This was a good idea," she said. "It's relaxing."

"It's the water," he said. "I read a study that says water relaxes us because it syncs up with our brain waves or something."

She laughed. "That's your scientific explanation—or something?"

He shrugged. "I don't have to understand why being

around water eases stress. I'm just glad it does." He scooped a rock from the shore and sent it skipping across the glassy surface of the water—one, two, three, four times, concentric circles spreading out and colliding to form mesmerizing patterns. He moved with the grace of a boy—and the bunching muscles and sinewy strength of a man. Being with him made Laura so much more aware of herself not only as a fellow agent, but also as a woman.

What was wrong with her? she wondered. She had worked with other men before, and she had never been attracted to any of them. Maybe that was because she always put the job first and didn't allow herself to focus on anything else.

Why was being with Jace so different?

"When I was a kid, for four or five years in a row, we went to a lake house on vacation," Jace said, as they continued on the path. "The place was just a little cabin, nothing fancy at all, but we loved it. We fished and paddled around in a canoe or swam off the dock. In the evenings, my dad would build a fire and we'd roast hot dogs or cook burgers in packets of foil, or even fish we'd caught. Looking back, I realize that for my folks, it was probably a really cheap vacation, but my sister and I loved it so much. I think we would have chosen that little lake house over a big amusement park. At least I know I would have."

"My parents sent me to a girl's camp in upstate New York one summer," Laura said. "Two weeks in a cabin with six other girls and six hundred spiders. I got poison ivy the third day, made a lanyard that was all knots, and almost shot my bunkmate in the head during archery practice."

"Good times," Jace said, and she laughed—a full belly laugh she couldn't keep back.

"Let's just say my first experience camping didn't make me want to try again," she said.

"I bet you'd be good at it now," he said.

"What makes you think that?" She genuinely wanted to know.

"Because you're not a whiner. And you're practical. You assess what needs to be done and you do it. Those are great strengths for camping."

"Who knew camping was so much like an investigation?" Their eyes met and her heart stuttered in its rhythm. When Jace looked at her, she felt as if he was really seeing her—all of her. She didn't like feeling so exposed, even if the heat behind his look told her he liked what he saw.

He was the first to look away, however. He frowned over her shoulder. "Isn't that Parker Stroud?" he asked.

She turned, moving slowly, as if she was merely brushing something from her shoulder, and glanced across the parking lot. Parker Stroud, dressed casually in jeans and a blue polo shirt, a West Virginia Mountaineers ball cap tugged down on his forehead, was striding away from a sleek black pickup truck. "That's him," she said.

"Let's go see what he's up to."

Keeping a line of trees between themselves and Parker, they trailed him to a fishing pier that jutted thirty feet out into the lake. He stood, looking out over the water, hands clasped behind his back. "He's waiting for someone," Laura said.

"Maybe he comes out here to look at the water because it's relaxing," Jace said.

"Then why doesn't he look more relaxed?"

Parker turned to glance toward the parking lot. Jace and Laura shrank further into the shadows as a slight figure in jeans and a gray hoodie slouched across the lot toward the pier. Laura studied the new arrival. Something about him was very familiar. "I think that's Leo Elgin," she whispered.

"Maybe," Jace said. "He changed clothes."

"He had time to do that."

The two men stood a couple of feet apart, Parker with his arms crossed tightly over his chest, Leo with his hands on his hips. Jace and Laura were too far away to hear the conversation, but the men's postures and expressions didn't appear friendly. Parker started shaking his head emphatically, and then Leo abruptly turned and fled.

Laura moved back through the trees toward the parking lot, following Leo, while Jace stayed to watch Parker. But by the time she reached the parking lot, all she could see was a pair of taillights receding into the distance.

Her cell phone buzzed and she read the text from Jace letting her know Parker was headed her way. She took cover behind a van and watched while Parker stalked to his truck, got in and drove off.

Jace jogged up to Laura. "Anything else happen?" he asked.

"Leo drove out of here before I could even get his plate number," she said. "The way he raced out of here, I'd say he was pretty upset."

"Leo blames the Strouds for killing his mother," Jace said. "Maybe he followed Parker here to have it out with him about that."

"Parker manages the manufacturing facilities at Stroud," Laura said. "So Leo may see him as being most responsible for the poisoned Stomach Soother tablets."

"It's not illegal to have a conversation," Jace said. "And they've never denied knowing each other."

"No." She turned back toward their truck. "But I think this wasn't a chance meeting. I think Parker was waiting for Leo."

"We need to find out what they were talking about," Jace said. "But we need to do it without blowing our cover."

"I'll see what I can get out of Parker," she said. Though, considering Stroud's generally surly attitude, that wouldn't be an easy task.

Chapter Six

Parker Stroud didn't appear in his office until almost noon the next day. He strode past Laura's desk without a glance in her direction and shut his door firmly behind him. Laura decided to wait to pass on the half-dozen messages that had come in his absence—two of them from his mother, who hadn't sounded too happy that her son hadn't shown up for work yet.

Ten minutes later, Laura's phone lit up. "I need hard copies of all the quality control reports for the first quarter," he said, and hung up before she could reply.

Since she had spent the morning continuing her search through the files, both online and off, Laura had no trouble locating the reports, though she wondered why Parker didn't pull them up on his computer. She spent the next half hour printing and collating the reports, which were submitted twice a week. Scanning the documents as she worked, she saw nothing that raised alarms. Stroud Pharmaceuticals had apparently been meticulous about maintaining quality control. So how had the ricin gotten into those tablets?

She knocked on Parker's door and, when he barked "Come in," slipped inside.

"Here are the reports," she said, laying the papers on his blotter. "And your messages." She added the stack of While You Were Out slips.

He grunted, focused on the screen of his desktop computer. After a moment, he finally looked at her. "What do you want?" he asked.

I want to know what you and Leo Elgin were talking about last night, she thought, but said, "Do you need anything else?"

"When I need something from you, I'll ask."

Yeah, getting anything out of this guy was going to be tough. She turned to go. "Laura?"

She stopped and faced him. "Yes?"

"What did the FBI ask you yesterday?"

"If we knew anything about the explosion. We didn't."

"You can't blame them for being suspicious. You and your husband are the only new people around here."

"I guess you knew the woman who was killed?"

The lines around his eyes tightened. "Yes."

"I always thought it would be nice, growing up in a small town where you knew everyone," she said. "But when something like this happens, I guess it makes it harder."

"Yes."

"Do you have any idea who planted that bomb?" she asked. "Who would want to do something so horrible?"

"No. Why are you so interested, anyway?"

"It's such a horrible thing. Especially after the poisonings."

"Maybe you don't want to work at such a horrible place. If you keep asking so many nosy questions, I think that could be arranged."

She backed out of the room, biting her lip to keep from making an angry retort. The phone rang as she was crossing to her desk. "Hello again, Laura." Donna Stroud had a pleasant voice, though Laura didn't miss the weariness underlying her words. "Has Parker made it in yet?"

"Yes ma'am. He came in a little while ago."

"Put me through to him, please."

Laura transferred the call. She debated listening in on the conversation, but before she could pick up the receiver again, Parker's voice sounded through the door, loud and clear. "I'm taking care of it, Mother. I'm not some idiot you have to micromanage... I put in plenty of hours for this company. If I want to come in late one morning, I can."

The receiver slammed down and seconds later Laura's intercom sounded. "Get me hard copies of the first quarter production reports."

"For which factory?"

"All of them!"

She hung up the phone and frowned at Parker's closed door. Was he trying to inundate her with busywork? Why would he need all these reports?

Unless, maybe, he wanted to share them with someone else—someone he couldn't merely forward computer links to.

JACE WAS WORKING the filling line today, monitoring the machinery that was calibrated to inject exactly .70 milliliters of solution into each bottle of Stroud's Soothing Eye Drops. No one spoke to him as he worked, or even looked at him directly, though he could feel the furtive glances of his coworkers. Word had probably gotten around that the FBI had questioned the new guy, and they were all wondering if he was responsible for the bomb that had killed Lydia Green.

Jace pretended not to notice the cold shoulder and concentrated on studying the manufacturing process, trying to spot the weak points in the system, where the poisoner might have introduced the ricin without being seen.

Even with the investigation to occupy his mind, the work was beyond boring. How did his coworkers stand it? He was all too aware that if he had stayed in his hometown, this would have been his lot. It was either that or the coal mines. Or the military. The army had been his ticket out—that and the education the army had paid for. Most of the people he had graduated high school with had opted to stay close to home and take what had looked like good jobs to them. Now the mines were shutting down and half the factories were shipping jobs overseas.

His sister's husband had been laid off so many times he had stopped looking for work.

Jobs like the one Jace was doing now were coveted in a place like Mayville. He had a hard time believing an employee would do anything to jeopardize them, but experience had taught him that people's motives for wrongdoing weren't always logical.

The time arrived for his mandatory break and he headed for the coffee machine. The quartet of fellow workers already in the break room ignored him as he entered, continuing their conversation. "I saw Leo at Bundy's Place night before last," an older man with a pockmarked face said.

"What were you doing at Bundy's Place?" a redhead with pink glasses asked.

"Hey, they have a great happy hour," the man said.

"Tonight is catfish night," a second man said. "There'll be a full house."

"Do you think Leo will be there?" a woman with her hair in braids asked. "I'd like to see him, and tell him how sorry I was about his mom."

"The bartender is a friend of mine," the first man said. "He told me Leo has been there every night. Drowning his sorrows, I guess."

"Miss Gini wouldn't be happy about that," Pink Glasses said.

"She wouldn't be happy about a lot of things that are happening around here lately."

The conversation ended as Barb entered the room.

Her gaze slid over the group, then fixed on Jace. "Well?" she asked.

Jace tossed his half-drunk coffee into the trash. "Well, what?"

"Well, did you have anything to do with that bomb?"

The others stared at him, mixed fear and anger on their grim faces.

"No," Jace said. "My wife and I came here to work, not to cause trouble."

"The FBI didn't arrest you," Pink Glasses said. "I guess if they thought you were guilty, you wouldn't be here now."

"Maybe the feds are watching, gathering evidence," Pockmarked Face said.

"They won't find any evidence against me," Jace said. "And why would I want to bomb the place where I'd only worked a day? I didn't even know the poor woman who died."

"Some people are just mean," the woman with the braids said.

Jace couldn't argue with that statement. He had met plenty of mean people in his life. But even mean people usually had a motive behind their meanness. It might be a misguided or completely unfounded motive, but in their minds it justified their meanness. Figuring out the motives behind the sabotage of Stroud Pharmaceuticals would go a long way toward finding the person responsible.

By the end of his shift, a few people had loosened up around Jace. But he was no closer to figuring out how the ricin had gotten into those tablets.

He was waiting for Laura at the truck when she emerged from the front offices. "How did it go?" he asked.

"Parker was in a foul mood," she said. "He didn't come in until noon, and then he spent the rest of the day keeping me running with busywork. I couldn't find any way to bring up Leo's name, much less the meeting at the park. What about you?"

"At least some of my coworkers no longer think I'm the mad bomber." He started the truck, the old engine rumbling roughly to life. "Let's go out tonight."

She blinked. "What? Why?"

"We're going out. To a place called Bundy's. I hear they have good catfish."

She wrinkled her nose. "Let me guess—it's fried."

"Of course."

She turned her head to gaze out the window. "I don't know if I want to go."

Did that translate to *I don't want to eat fried fish*, or *I don't want to go anywhere with you*? Probably both. Too bad. She was stuck with him for the duration. "You do want to go," he said. "It's where Leo Elgin has been drowning his sorrows every night this week."

She whipped her head back around. "Catfish it is, then."

BUNDY'S PLACE WAS a tin-roofed, windowless barn of a building at the intersection of two county roads five miles out of Mayville. Ancient oaks shaded the building, and the bass thump from a three-piece band reverberated across the parking lot which, by the time Laura and Jace arrived, was packed with cars and pickup trucks.

The smell of beer and frying fish perfumed the air as they stepped inside. They found a table with a view of the bar and Jace went to get drinks. He came back with two beers.

The beer was so cold it made her teeth hurt, but it tasted refreshing. She scanned the crowd, spotting several familiar faces from the plant. "I don't see Leo," she said.

"It's early yet." A waitress arrived to take their order and the tables around them began to fill. A few minutes later, their server returned, bearing two baskets full of catfish, fries and coleslaw. Laura stared at the food, suddenly ravenous. "Go ahead," Jace said. "It won't bite back."

The fish was tender and meaty, the cornmeal coating crispy and spicy, and not at all greasy. She didn't know when she had eaten something so delicious.

The band, which had taken a break, began playing again, an upbeat country song she recognized from the radio. Jace shoved back his chair and stood. "Let's dance," he said.

"We're supposed to be here spying on Leo Elgin," she reminded him.

"He hasn't shown up yet." He leaned over and tugged on her hand. "Shame to waste the evening."

She let him lead her onto the already crowded dance floor. She couldn't remember the last time she had danced, but Jace made it easy, guiding her through steps she thought she had forgotten, and even leading her through a few new moves. It was a heady feeling, being twirled around the dance floor by a capable partner.

The music changed to a slow ballad. Laura turned to leave the dance floor, but Jace pulled her close. He looked into her eyes, one brow quirked in silent question. *Why not?*

She settled against him. Being so close to him felt dangerous—and thrilling. She let herself enjoy the feel of his arm encircling her lightly, his hand clasping hers. The music was slow and dreamy. Sexy. She closed her eyes, feeling the music wash over her, breathing in the hint of cinnamon that always clung to him and leaning into his embrace. When she opened her eyes, he was looking at her, a raw longing in his gaze that made her breath catch and her heart beast faster. She tried to look away, only to shift her gaze to his lips, the pull of them impossible to resist. The song ended and she let the kiss come, his mouth firm and insistent, her body pressed against his.

A loud whistle, followed by laughter, broke the spell.

She stared up at Jace, who looked amused now, and heat flooded her cheeks. Backing away, she hurried off the dance floor to the ladies' room, where she sat in a stall, trying to catch her breath and pull herself together. She and Jace were supposed to be working together. They were professionals, yet they had just behaved very unprofessionally.

You're human, a small voice inside of her whispered—one she didn't listen to very often. She wasn't going to listen to it now.

When she was feeling more composed, she emerged from the stall, washed her hands and studied her face in the scratched mirror. She looked the same as always—a little pale, maybe, but calm. Competent. Not the type of woman who would get involved with a coworker on an assignment.

But what did that kind of woman look like, anyway?

She left the ladies' room, almost colliding with a man in the hallway. He mumbled an apology and brushed past, head down, but not before she had gotten a good look at him. She hurried back to their table, where Jace was accepting an order of two fresh beers from their waitress.

"You didn't have to run off," he said as she settled into the chair beside him. "But hey, I'm sorry if—"

She waved away the apology and leaned toward him, keeping her voice low. "I just saw Leo Elgin," she said.

"Where?"

"He was headed into the men's room." She swiveled in her chair to get a view of the hallway that led to the restrooms.

"There he is," Jace said as Leo merged with the crowd, moving toward the bar. Jace tapped her shoulder. "You go talk to him."

Laura made her way to the bar, hanging back until the chair next to Leo was vacated. She slipped up beside him and when he glanced her way, she stuck out her hand. "Hi,

I'm Laura," she said. "I'm new in town. Are you from around here?"

He looked down at his drink. "I'm not exactly good company right now. Maybe you should find someone else to talk to."

"Oh, what's wrong?" She leaned toward him. "If you want to talk about it, people tell me I'm a good listener. Sometimes it helps to get things off your chest, you know?"

"Talking won't help this." He took a long pull of his beer. "My mother died a week ago. She was murdered."

Laura gasped. "That's horrible! Who killed her? Do they know?"

He studied her, eyes narrowed. "She was one of the people who died after taking poisoned Stroud's Stomach Soother tablets."

"I'm so sorry." Laura lightly touched his shoulder. "That is just horrible. I heard about that on TV. Actually, I just went to work at Stroud. I wasn't so sure about the job, after what happened with those Stomach Soothers and everything, but I really needed the money, you know?"

"You work in the plant?" Leo asked.

"No, I'm in the office. I'm Parker Stroud's secretary."

Leo's eyes widened and he set his beer down with a thump. "Do you know Mr. Stroud?" Laura asked.

He looked away. "I know him a little."

"I'll admit, as a boss he's a little intimidating."

"Parker is all right. He's pretty torn up about what happened."

"Oh? You've spoken to him recently?"

"No. I just… I just know he's that kind of guy."

"I think if I was in your place, the Strouds wouldn't be my favorite people right now," she said. "I mean, aren't they supposed to have safety rules and stuff to keep that kind of thing from happening?"

"Yeah, but Parker's mom and dad really run the place.

They won't let him modernize the way he wants. He thinks he could have prevented this."

That was interesting. Were things really more lax than she and Jace suspected? Was Parker asking for all the safety and production reports in order to make a case for changes?

"Fight!" A roar rose up from the crowd behind them and she and Leo turned in time to see a chair sail through the air and crash against a pillar. Two men were grappling, rolling on the floor, fists flying.

"Jace!" Laura screamed the name as she recognized one of the men on the floor—who currently had blood streaming down his face.

Chapter Eleven

Chapter Seven

Jace knew trouble was headed his way the minute he saw the look in the man's eye. He just didn't have enough time to get out of the way. "Are you Jace Lovejoy?" the man—six-foot-four with eighteen-inch biceps—asked.

"Who's asking?" Jace stood, hands on the table, out where the man could see them.

"My name is Shay Green and my aunt was Lydia Green. Somebody told me the cops think you planted that bomb that killed her."

"I had nothing to do with that bomb," Jace said. "And I'm sorry about your—"

But he never finished the sentence. Green's fist was already headed his way. Jace ducked, and flipped the table at Green, throwing him off balance long enough for Jace to step up and land a blow that should have ended the fight before it started.

But Green—hyped-up on grief and adrenaline and the alcohol that came off of him in fumes—hadn't gotten the memo. He momentarily staggered under the force of the blow, then charged at Jace like an enraged bull.

The next thing Jace knew, he was on the floor with blood streaming from his nose and Green straddling his chest. Someone else tried to pull Green off of him and Jace took advantage of the distraction to squirm out from under him and knee him in the chin. Green's howl hurt his ears and he dove at Jace again.

They rolled across the floor, into tables, dodging people's feet. Jace would be on top, then Green. A circle of spectators had formed around them by the time they got to their feet again, grappling in the clumsy way of two evenly matched fighters, neither of whom would give an inch.

"The cops are on their way!" someone shouted, and Jace swore under his breath. He didn't want to have to explain this to the local police and risk blowing his cover. He shoved Green back. "You got the wrong guy!" he yelled. "Leave me alone."

In answer, Green punched him in the gut. Jace doubled over, fighting for breath, vision going gray. Two men dragged Green back, and Jace felt a hand on his back. He whirled, fist raised, to face Laura. She wrapped both hands around his arm and dragged him toward the edge of the crowd. "Come on," she said. "We've got to get out of here."

He didn't try to resist, but let her lead him through the crowd and out a side door to the parking lot. He was dazed and bleeding, and only when he felt her hand digging in his pants pocket did he wake up. "What are you doing?" he asked.

"I need the keys to the truck."

He pushed her hand away and fished out the keys. "Come on," she said, taking the keys and grabbing hold of his arm again.

They turned out of the parking lot just as the first patrol car turned in. Jace leaned back in the seat, eyes closed, trying not to think about how much his face hurt. "What was that all about?" Laura asked.

"He said he was Lydia Green's nephew." Jace's voice sounded thick and unfamiliar. "He was drunk and had it in his head that I was responsible for the bomb that killed his aunt."

"But a fight? What were you thinking? What if you had had to draw your weapon?"

Jace was very aware of the gun holstered out of sight at his ankle. "I wouldn't have shot the guy."

"What if he had threatened you with a gun?" she asked.

"That didn't happen. He used his fists." He gingerly touched his nose and winced. "He could have broken my nose."

She braked hard, throwing him forward against the seat belt. "Do we need to go to the doctor? The hospital?"

"I don't think my nose is broken. I just need to get back to the trailer and clean up." He shifted to dig a handkerchief from his pocket and pressed it to his still-bleeding nose. "What did you find out from Elgin?"

"He says Parker's parents are preventing Parker from modernizing the factory. I got the impression he blames Donna and Steve, but not Parker, for what happened to his mother."

"The two of them didn't look all that friendly when we saw them at the lake yesterday."

"No, and Leo didn't really talk about Parker as if they were best buddies. But he did talk as if he knew him well—as if maybe they had been closer once." She had detected a note of regret in Leo's voice when he spoke about Parker.

"Maybe Leo was confronting Parker about Leo's mother's death and he was angry Parker wasn't pressing his parents to do more," Jace said.

"Or maybe there's no way we'll ever know what they talked about unless they tell us." Laura turned the truck into the rutted drive to the trailer. She parked and climbed out, but Jace was slower to join her. He moved stiffly, as if in pain. "What's wrong?" she asked. "Did he hurt more than your nose?"

"I'm still feeling a couple of those punches." Jace tried to straighten, but grimaced and remained bent over.

Laura took his arm. "Come on. I think there's a first aid kit in the closet."

"Nothing a stiff whiskey and a good night's sleep won't cure."

She wanted to lecture him on the stupidity of fighting. If things had turned ugly and he'd had to pull his weapon to defend himself, their cover would have been blown and the operation aborted. Not to mention, he could have been seriously injured, and she'd have been without a partner. While Jace went into the bathroom to wash off as much blood as possible, she rummaged through shelves until she found the first aid kit. When he emerged, water still dripping from the ends of his hair, purpling bruises already forming beneath both eyes, she had an assortment of bandages and ointments laid out on the kitchen table.

"Are you sure your nose isn't broken?" she asked, eyeing him critically.

"I'm sure." He squeezed the tip between his thumb and forefinger, wincing as he did so. "I couldn't stand that if it was. But he did bang it up pretty good."

"At least put some antibiotic ointment on that cut on your lip and the one on your chin," she said. "He must have been wearing a big ring or something."

"Everything about the dude was big."

"I hope he doesn't decide to come after you again."

"I'm touched that you're so concerned for me," he said as he dabbed ointment onto his chin.

"I'm concerned for me. We live together."

His eyes met hers, and she felt that flare of heat again, the spark that seemed to ignite every time they were alone together. "About that kiss on the dance floor," he began.

"I don't want to talk about that kiss."

"We need to talk about the kiss." He reached out and captured her hand in his.

"It shouldn't have happened," she said, trying, and failing, to pull away from him. "It was a momentary lapse of judgment."

"I think it was the natural reaction of a man and a woman who are attracted to each other."

"We are work partners. Gender shouldn't figure into it."

"We're human beings, not robots. Gender is part of what makes us who we are." He rubbed his thumb across her knuckles, sending a current of sensation through her, like an electrical charge. "I'm pretty happy about that right now."

She jerked her hand away from him. "We have a job to do," she said. "We can't make this about us."

He straightened in his chair. "I respect your feelings, even though I think you're wrong. If you really believe the only way to handle this is to keep things strictly business between us, then I'll do that."

She forced herself to look him in the eye again. "I have to know that I can trust you," she said.

His expression hardened. "I never have and I never will force myself on a woman. You don't have to worry about anything like that."

"I didn't mean…" But what had she meant? Maybe it wasn't Jace she couldn't trust but herself when she was around him. He made her forget the woman she needed to be in favor of a wilder, more out-of-control version of herself. Losing herself that way felt more dangerous than any criminal she had ever faced.

Laura drove to work the next morning while Jace, his face an ugly mass of bruises, sat hunched over in the passenger seat. "Maybe you should have called in sick," she said.

"Everyone will have heard about the fight by now. If I don't show up for work, they'll think Green got the best of me."

"It looks to me like he did," she said.

He glared at her, which only made her grin. Grumpy Jace was certainly easier to handle than easygoing Jace, who always seemed to find a way to glide past her doubts and hesitations.

That wasn't quite a fair assessment, of course. True to his word, he hadn't so much as brushed up against her this morning, keeping a very respectful and businesslike distance between them and coming to the breakfast table this morning fully and properly dressed.

What did it say about her that she had spent half the meal picturing him without his shirt anyway?

She was on her way to her office when Donna Stroud intercepted her. "Laura, I was hoping I'd catch you," she said. "Could I speak with you in my office for a minute?"

Laura followed the older woman into her office. Donna settled heavily into the chair behind her desk. She looked as if she had aged in the last week, the lines around her eyes and on either side of her mouth deepened. "Is something wrong?" Laura asked.

"I'm hoping you can tell me if you've made any progress in this case," Donna said.

"I don't have anything I can share with you at this time," Laura said. They had one suspect for the bombing and nothing for the poisoning, and things were moving agonizingly slow. "Investigations like this take time," she continued. "There's a lot of evidence to sift through and people to question." Even then, sometimes a lucky break was as critical as good detective work. She was sure they had the latter in this case, but they needed the former.

"I feel as if my life is on hold, waiting for the other shoe to drop," Donna said. "First the poisoned Stomach Soothers, then the bombing—what next? Why is someone out to destroy me and my family?"

"Right now, we don't have anything to show that the same person committed both crimes," Laura said. "It could be that the bombing was done to retaliate for the poisoned stomach medication."

"Who would do something like that?"

"People who are grieving sometimes react drastically," Laura said, thinking of Lydia Green's nephew and Jace's bruised face. "That doesn't at all excuse what was done, but it does give us motivation and an idea of where to look."

"You're thinking of Leo Elgin, aren't you?" Donna shook her head. "I've known Leo since he was a little boy. A smart, quiet boy. I can't imagine him killing someone—a wonderful woman like Lydia Green. Especially not when he's grieving his mother's death."

"We're looking at a lot of different people and motives," Laura said. "That was just one example."

The door to Donna's office opened and an attractive man with thick silver hair entered. He smiled at Laura. "I'm sorry, dear. I didn't mean to interrupt."

Donna half rose from her chair. "I didn't know you were coming in today."

"Oh, I thought I should come in and check on things." He moved into the room, then looked at Laura again. "It's good to see you. It's been a while, hasn't it?"

"Steve, this is—" Donna began.

"Oh, I know who it is." The man—Laura realized it must be Steve Stroud—waved away the interruption. "I'm not likely to forget our future daughter-in-law, am I?"

"Steve, this is Laura Lovejoy. She's Parker's new administrative assistant, not his fiancée." Donna's voice was firm. "Parker and Kathleen split up almost two years ago."

Steve's face clouded. "They did? I guess… I guess it just slipped my mind." He offered Laura a sheepish smile. "You do look a lot like her. A very pretty young woman." He turned back to his wife. "Is Parker here?"

"I don't know," Donna said. "He's been coming in late some mornings."

"That's all right." Steve's expression remained benign. "The boy works too hard. Always burning the midnight oil, working late."

Donna and Laura exchanged glances. Certainly since Laura had been here, Parker had not worked late. "Why don't you go into your office?" Donna suggested. "I'll send some reports in that I need you to review."

He looked relieved. "Of course I'll review them for you," he said. "I did always have more patience for that sort of thing than you do."

"Go on and I'll send them over in a minute," Donna said.

She waited until her husband had entered his office and shut the door behind him before she dropped into her chair once more. "I'm sorry about that," she said. "He's not supposed to drive, but sometimes he gets away from the caretaker I've hired and heads down here. I'll have to call the caretaker and find out what happened." She glanced toward the office door. "And as you can see, he's not always well-oriented to time and place. He mixes up the past and present and simply doesn't remember other things."

"Who was Kathleen?" Laura asked.

"A young woman Parker dated for a time. They were engaged for a little over six months. Then she broke off the relationship and moved away."

"Where is she now? Do you know?"

"The last I heard, she was living in Washington, DC."

"I'll need her full name and address so we can check." At Donna's astonished look, she added, "She probably had nothing to do with any of this, but we need to check out anyone who has had a relationship with the family." Maybe things between Parker and Kathleen hadn't been so amicable.

"All right," Donna said. "I'll get that information for you."

"All this must be very stressful for you," Laura said.

"It is. But there's nothing to do but carry on."

"Parker mentioned that he had tried to persuade you to let him take on more of the day-to-day operation of the business," Laura said.

"He has." Her expression hardened. "I know that my son is not really your boss, at least not for the long term, but I still don't feel right discussing him with you this way."

"I'm only interested if it pertains to the case," Laura said. Not precisely true. She had a human curiosity to know more about the man she worked with every day. But she was professional enough not to give in to that curiosity.

"Then let's just say that I don't think Parker is ready for the responsibility of running this business," Donna said. "Especially not in this time of crisis." She stood again. "If you'll excuse me, I need to get some sort of paperwork to keep Steve occupied, before he decides to wander into the factory and cause trouble."

Laura left the office, pondering the dynamic between husband and wife. What would that be like, to watch the person you had vowed to love for better or worse slipping away right before your eyes?

When she reached her office, Laura was surprised to find Merry seated behind her desk. "Can I help you?" Laura asked, moving past the woman to stow her purse in the filing cabinet.

"I'm just waiting for Parker to come in." Merry swiveled back and forth in Laura's chair. "You're late."

"I stopped to talk with Mrs. Stroud."

"What would she want with you?"

Laura didn't bother answering the question. "I'll tell Parker you stopped by when he gets in," she said. "Right now, I have work I need to do."

Merry made no move to leave, swiveling back and forth

in the chair, a smirk on her face. "I think I'll wait here for Parker to get in."

"I don't care what you do, but you need to get out of my chair." Laura glared at the woman. She wasn't above yanking Merry out of the chair by her ponytail, but she hoped they could resolve this in a more adult fashion.

"I like this chair," Merry said. "It's more comfortable than mine."

Laura was debating her next move when the door behind them opened and Parker came in. "Good morning, Parker!" Merry called.

Parker looked from Laura to Merry. "What are you doing here?" he asked.

Merry vacated the chair at last and hurried around the desk. "I stopped by to say good morning," she said.

"Good morning," he said, then disappeared into his office and shut the door.

Merry stared at the closed door, looking close to tears. Laura settled into the chair behind her desk and booted up her computer.

"He doesn't like you," Merry said.

Laura looked up and Merry stalked over to the desk. "Parker was never like this when Cheryl worked for him. Having to work with you has put him in a bad mood."

Laura shrugged. "If you say so."

Merry leaned over the desk, both hands planted on its surface. "What are you doing here, anyway?"

"I'm trying to work." Laura turned back to her computer.

"Everyone thinks it's strange that you and your husband showed up here out of nowhere and the next day that bomb goes off. You're not even from here and you move into one of the top jobs at the company. We all think you're up to something."

"I'm not up to anything," Laura said.

"I think you are," Merry said. "And I'm going to find out what it is." She whirled and hurried away, reminding Laura of a defiant child. Her last words might as well have been, *I'm telling!*

"THE WARRANT CAME through to allow us to bug Leo Elgin's house," Jace said after dinner that evening. Laura had made tacos, so he was supposed to be cleaning up, though he lingered at the table over a glass of iced tea. His bruises looked worse than ever, though she had to admit the rugged look added an air of danger that suited him. "We'll go in tomorrow, during his mom's memorial service."

"What's your plan?" she asked. Jace always had a plan for these things. His aptitude for legal breaking and entering was one of the reasons he had been recruited for the tactical crime division.

"We're going in as caterers for the reception after the service."

"Leo is paying caterers for a reception?" He hadn't struck Laura as someone who would go to that much trouble.

"Stroud Pharmaceuticals arranged it all," he said. "Donna Stroud insisted."

"Ah." Laura nodded. "And we insisted that Donna Stroud insist."

"Ramirez might have encouraged her a little, but she doesn't know that we're going in or what we'll be doing."

"Of course not." She sighed. "What do you need me to do?"

He studied her across the table. "You need to get a wig," he said. "Something mousy. And a maid's uniform."

"I hope this isn't going where I think it's going," she said.

"Get your mind out of the gutter, Smitty," he said. "I'm

not talking about a *French* maid. Frankly, we need to drab you down so you're less noticeable."

"Since when am I noticeable?" She stared at him. "I'm a federal agent. I know how to blend in."

"You know how to blend in when you're wearing your black suit with your hair in a bun. But here in Mayville—trust me, you stand out."

"What do you mean, I stand out?"

He grinned. "Do you know how many men have come up to me and said something about the hot new blonde in Parker's office?"

She flushed. "What did you say?"

"I told them, yeah, that's my wife, so hands off."

Her expression must have conveyed her annoyance. "Hey, it's what they expect," he said. "Don't take it personally."

How could she not take it personally? On one hand, it bothered her to know men at the plant had been talking about her. On the other hand, she melted a little at the thought of Jace warning them off—as if he really did care.

"Headquarters is sending over a package tomorrow morning," he said. "It should have everything we need, including the disguises I asked for."

"Good. Because I think if I go shopping for a wig in Mayville, it's going to spark rumors."

His grin was positively wicked. "Then you could tell them you were just trying to liven things up in the bedroom."

She threw her spoon at him, but he caught it in the air and laughed. "What's your disguise?" she asked.

"Glasses, earring and fake tattoos."

She frowned. "Someone could recognize you."

"Trust me, they won't."

She slept fitfully that night, anxiety over the next day's job mingling with wild dreams of Jace—Jace kissing her, touching her, then leaving her, guaranteeing she awoke tired and out of sorts.

The promised box from headquarters arrived at nine thirty. The memorial service for Gini Elgin was due to begin at eleven. Jace figured they would have about an hour to get in and out before the real caterers showed up, followed by Leo and the other mourners. They each retired to their rooms to get ready.

The black pants, white shirt and gray apron were definitely on the drab side, Laura decided as she studied what she could see of herself in the dresser mirror. The wig—a mousy brown bob with thick bangs—also did little to draw attention to herself. She added the white Keds that had also been in the box, secured her weapon in its harness beneath the apron, and called it good.

She met up with Jace in the kitchen, where he was examining the electronics that had also been packed in their box. Laura stared at his transformation. He wore black pants and a tight black T-shirt that clung to his biceps and abs, showing off details she hadn't noticed before—mainly, that Jace Cantrell had put in his share of time in the gym. Below the short sleeves of the tee he'd added full-sleeve tattoos—a vividly colored tapestry of birds, fish, serpents and at least one skull. A gold hoop glinted at one ear, and he'd shaved his scruff into a soul patch.

"Is this your idea of drabbing down and not standing out?" she asked, trying—and failing—to tear her eyes away from him.

"I'm going for the opposite effect," he said. "If anyone does see me, they'll remember the body art. Once we're done with the job, I'll remove the sleeves and the earring, shave off the soul patch and essentially, vanish."

At ten forty-five, they left the trailer. At a warehouse on the other end of town they traded the pickup for a panel van, Bread and Butter Caterers stenciled on the side. Jace drove past the church where Gini's service was being held. The parking lot was full and more parked cars lined either side of the street. From there, it was only five blocks to Gini's house, where Leo was staying. The cottage sat well back from the road in a grove of mature trees. Roses climbed trellises on either side of the front door, their scent heavy in the humid air.

They headed for the front door, carrying two plastic totes that to any passerby would look like supplies for the catered reception. Laura blocked the view from the road while Jace made quick work of the front door lock, which didn't even have a dead bolt. Then they were in.

Gini Elgin had favored hominess over haute couture in her furnishings, a sagging sofa with faded floral cushions sharing space in the living room with a scuffed maple coffee table, an armchair upholstered in gold velvet, and a braided rug in shades of brown and gold. Dust filmed every flat surface, and Laura wondered if Leo had even been in here since his return.

The dining room and a small home office had the same air of disuse and abandonment. Only the kitchen looked lived-in, with a stained coffee cup in the sink and an open box of cereal on the counter. Jace went to the brick-like cordless phone in its charging station on one end of the counter. "I'll start here," he said. "Set out the food, and then see if you can find his bedroom."

Laura unpacked a tray of finger sandwiches and another of cookies and set them on the kitchen island. The real caterers would bring more food later. She and Jace had carried these two trays as part of their cover.

She turned her attention to the search for Leo's bedroom. Though she knew the house was empty, she moved cautiously down the hall, as wary of leaving evidence behind as of surprising an unforeseen occupant of the house. The first door she reached led to a bathroom with avocado-green tiles and an old-fashioned claw-foot tub. A blue bath towel hung crookedly on the towel bar by the tub, and a man's shaving kit balanced on the edge of the sink.

Leo's bedroom was next door—a child's room with a single unmade bed draped in a blue corduroy spread, posters for decades-old baseball players on the walls. Old athletic trophies shared space on a bookshelf with paperback thrillers and computer software manuals. A small desk in the corner held a laptop computer and a phone charger, minus the phone. Dirty dishes and fast food wrappers crowded the nightstand.

"This his room?" Jace looked in the doorway.

"Yeah." Laura stepped aside to let him get to the desk. "Pretty depressing. I think he's probably been spending most of his time in here."

"Makes our job easier." Jace assessed the room, then picked up the bedside lamp and examined it. "I'll put one bug here, another on the desk," he said. "It's overkill, but we've got the hardware, so why not use it?"

While he worked, Laura searched the bookcase, closet and dresser drawers. She felt under the mattress, looked behind the curtains and shone a flashlight into the heating vents, looking for any secret stash. The local police had already searched the house once and hadn't found anything linking Leo to the explosion at Stroud Pharmaceuticals, but it never hurt to give everything a second going-over.

"If he did plant that bomb, I think he made the device somewhere else," Jace said.

"Where else?" Laura asked. "This place doesn't even have a garage, just that little shed out back, and the report from the search team says it's full of gardening tools."

"A storage unit, maybe. An abandoned barn? There are probably a few of those around here."

"Maybe we'll hear something that will give us a better idea." She watched him fit the tiny listening device into the base of a stapler that sat on one corner of the desk, then snap the bottom of the stapler back in place.

She hugged her arms across her chest. "Let's get out of here," she said. "This place gives me the creeps."

He stowed his tools and they headed toward the door. One step into the hallway, Jace froze.

"What's wrong? Why did you stop?" She shoved at his back, then went cold all over as she recognized the sound of the front door opening, and someone coming inside.

Chapter Eight

Laura's anxiety radiated around her and through Jace. He reached back, grabbed her hand and squeezed.

"I'm okay," she whispered.

He released her hand and moved forward, stopping at the end of the hallway as Leo rounded the corner toward them. The younger man, face pale and eyes reddened, stared at them. "Who are you?" he demanded, his voice shaky.

"We're from the caterer." Jace extended a hand and Leo automatically took it. "We weren't expecting anyone so soon."

Leo dropped Jace's hand, and his gaze shifted away. "I... I needed to get out of there," he said.

"We're very sorry for your loss." Laura adopted a Southern accent and prayed Leo wouldn't see past her disguise to the woman who had chatted him up at the bar last night.

"What were you doing back there?" Leo looked past them, toward the back of the house.

"We like to check that the bathroom is ready for guests," Laura said.

Leo scowled. "It took two of you to do that?"

She didn't miss a beat. "There was a spider in the sink. I asked Jeff to kill it for me."

Great improvisation, Jace thought, though Laura didn't strike him as the type to freak out over a spider. In fact, the only time he'd ever seen her lose her cool was when he kissed her. She'd all but melted in his arms, making him believe that even if she resisted the idea of getting involved with him, she wanted him.

Now was not the time to be thinking about that, he reminded himself.

"You need to leave," Leo said.

"We won't be much longer," Jace said. "We just need to arrange a few things."

"No! I don't want you here." Leo's voice rose, his eyes wild. "It's bad enough I have to put up with all these people coming over after the funeral. You can at least leave me alone for now."

"All right." Laura took Jace's arm. "We can finish later."

They moved past him toward the kitchen, but paused in the hallway to listen as he made his way down the hall and shut the door to his room behind him. "Let's go," Laura said.

They left the food, grabbed up both totes and headed out the front door. Jace started the van, drove around the corner and parked behind a deserted office complex.

He texted Rogers that they were out, then leaned his head back against the seat and let out a breath, waiting for his racing heart to slow. As operations went, he had been in tighter spots. Still, it was unnerving when the surveillance subject found you in his house.

"Why did he leave his own mother's funeral scarcely twenty minutes into the service?" Laura asked.

"Funerals are hard for a lot of people," Jace said. "Maybe it got to him and he just wanted to be alone."

"Maybe." She swiveled toward him. "Drive back around to where we can get a good look at the house."

"All right." He started the engine again and drove around the block, parking at the end of the street, where they had a clear view of Leo's driveway and front door.

They had scarcely parked when a white Chevy sedan turned onto the street.

Laura gasped as the sedan passed, the driver never even glancing in their direction. "That's Merry Winger," she said.

"Remind me who she is."

"She's Parker Stroud's girlfriend."

Merry turned into the Elgins' driveway, got out and walked up to the door. She was a pretty blonde in a neat navy-blue miniskirt and a sleeveless white blouse, and very tall white heels. She rang the bell and a moment later, Leo answered the door.

"He doesn't look happy to see her," Laura said. She had pulled a pair of binoculars from the backpack at her feet and was studying the couple. As she said this, Leo stepped aside to let Merry in, and shut the door behind her.

Laura lowered the glasses. "How did you know he was going to meet someone?" Jace asked.

"It was just a hunch." She continued to stare toward the door. "But what is Parker's girlfriend doing meeting Leo Elgin in secret?"

"We don't know that it's secret."

"He left his mother's funeral to meet up with her. That's pretty secretive, if you ask me." She leaned forward, as if that would help her see through the closed door. "And where is Parker?"

"Maybe Leo and Merry have a thing on the side?" Jace speculated. "Or they were a couple before and now that he's back in town she's trying to renew the acquaintance?"

The door opened and Merry emerged. Head down, she hurried to her car, then drove away. Laura sat back in her seat. "She wasn't in there long enough to do anything," she said.

"He didn't even walk her to the door," Jace said. "So maybe they're not having an affair. Or maybe she came on to him and he turned her down."

Laura stowed the binoculars again. "Let's head back to the trailer. Maybe your recording devices will pick up something useful."

"He hasn't had a single phone call in the last twenty-four hours," Rogers said when Jace checked in with him Sunday afternoon. "No visitors since the reception after the funeral, and all of those conversations are variations of either condolences over the loss of his mother, or questions about what he plans to do next."

"What does he plan to do next?" Jace asked.

"He doesn't know. That's the answer he gave everyone, and if they tried to press, he either changed the subject or clammed up entirely."

"What about Merry Winger—the woman who showed up right after Laura and I left? What did they talk about?"

"She delivered something," Rogers said. "Here. Let me play you the recording."

Sound of door opening.
Leo: What do you want?
Merry: I brought you this.
Leo: You'd better go.
Merry: Not until you tell me what's going on.
Leo: Unintelligible mumble.
Merry: No. You men are all alike. You think I'm stupid and I'm not.
Leo: You need to go now.
Long pause. High heels clicking on hardwood. Slamming door.

"Any idea what she brought him?" Jace asked.

"It could have been a sympathy card or a cake or plastic explosives," Rogers said. "We can't tell from his reaction."

"Merry works in the Stroud offices with Laura. Let's

see what she can find out. In the meantime, we need eyes on Leo."

"We don't have enough people to babysit him full time," Rogers said. "At this point we don't have any proof he's even worth watching. It was a stretch getting the okay to bug his place."

"I'll watch him after my shift at the factory," Jace said.

"When will you sleep?"

"When he does. You can keep an eye on him while I'm at the factory."

"I have other work to do," Rogers said.

"When you have a free moment," Jace said. "Just for a few days."

Rogers grunted, which Jace chose to take as agreement. "What do you think we're going to find out?" Rogers asked.

"Who he's seeing, where he's going. If he assembled that explosive, he did it somewhere other than his mother's house."

"I'm willing to try for a few days," Rogers said. "But I'm not convinced we're not wasting our time."

Jace ended the call and looked up to find Laura studying him. "You're going to surveil Leo?" she asked.

"Merry brought him something yesterday. From the tone of their conversation, I don't think she was the person he was expecting to see, and he got rid of her as fast as he could."

"What did she bring him?"

"We don't know. The bugs haven't picked up any other suspicious conversations."

"So, if he left the funeral to meet someone, they either didn't show, or they sent Merry instead," Laura said.

"That's what I'm thinking."

"Maybe Parker sent her." The frown lines on Laura's

forehead deepened. "I got the impression if he said jump, she'd ask, how high?"

"Talk to her. See what you can find out."

"I'll try, but I'm not her favorite person. Apparently, she applied to be Parker's admin before I stepped in and took the job."

"Yeah, but it sounds to me like she wants to keep an eye on Parker. Maybe you can offer to be her spy."

Laura stared at him. "You really think she wants to keep tabs on him? I thought she wanted to be closer to him."

He shrugged. "Hey, I never claimed to be an expert on relationships. But I'm betting Parker wouldn't have picked her for the job. Most men don't like the woman they're involved with always looking over their shoulder."

He couldn't begin to decipher the look she shot him, though he would describe it as somewhere between disgust and incredulity. He started to reassure her that he knew she wasn't the type to get all up in his business, but bit back the words. He and Laura weren't "involved." Never mind that he couldn't be in the same room with her without being hyperaware of her: of her soft scent, her softer skin, and the hard shell around her emotions that he ached to break through.

"I'll see what I can do," she said. "What's your next move?"

He grabbed a backpack with binoculars, camera, water and snacks off the floor beside his chair. "I'm going to keep an eye on Leo. Don't wait up."

THE FIRST THING Laura noticed when she arrived at Stroud Pharmaceuticals on Monday was that the damage to the side door to the executive offices had been repaired, the police tape removed, and the sidewalk replaced, and everything sported a new coat of paint. A crew must have worked all weekend to effect the transformation.

Once inside, however, she noted people still avoided the area. Whether out of superstition or real fear, she couldn't tell. Her coworkers' reactions to her were still subdued, but she pretended not to notice. Maybe in their shoes, she'd be suspicious of the new couple, too. She didn't need to be best friends with any of these people in order to do her job.

She detoured to the break room and fetched two cups of coffee and two doughnuts from the open box on the table, then headed for Merry's desk. The younger woman looked up as Laura approached, eyes narrowed. "What do you want?" she asked.

"I need your advice." Laura set a cup of coffee and a doughnut in front of Merry, then slid a chair close to her desk.

Merry clearly hadn't expected this. "What kind of advice?" she asked, still wary.

"I want to do a good job," Laura said. "But Mr. Stroud—Parker—doesn't seem very happy with my performance. I figure you're the person who knows him best, so I thought maybe you could give me some tips on how to get on his good side."

"Why should I help you do the job I wanted?" Merry asked. "The job I still want?"

"I thought maybe I could do you a favor, too." Laura focused on stirring a packet of sugar into her coffee. "I know you and Parker have to be discreet about your relationship, what with working together and everything. I can make it easier for you to get in to see him, and I can make sure you have all the access you want."

"I can see Parker anytime." Merry tossed her head. "I don't need your help."

"I can run interference if anyone tries to interrupt you," Laura said. "And I can give you his schedule so you know when he's free."

"Why would you want to help me?" Merry asked.

"Because I need your help to do my job," Laura said. "And because Parker is always in a better mood after he's talked to you." The last part was a blatant lie, but she was counting on Merry wanting to believe it.

Merry relaxed a little. "I can give you a few pointers for dealing with him," she said. "But I can't promise they'll help. It could be he just doesn't like you." Her smirk said clearly that she didn't blame Parker.

"I'm grateful for any advice you can give me," Laura said, keeping her face straight.

Merry took a bite of doughnut and chewed, looking thoughtful. "I can't believe I'm even suggesting this to you, of all people," she said after she had swallowed. "But Parker likes women who keep themselves up. He'd probably like it if you dressed a little sexier—you know, shorter skirts and lower necklines."

Fat chance of that happening, but Laura nodded, her expression neutral. "Anything else?"

"He likes it when I compliment him. You know, some men need women to build up their egos."

Did she really believe that? "But you're his girlfriend," Laura said. "I'm just his assistant."

"Well, yeah." Merry shrugged. "I don't know what to tell you. Maybe smile more or have a better attitude. If he's grumpy around you, you must be doing something wrong."

Or maybe he's just a jerk, Laura thought. "I'll keep that in mind." She stood. "Thanks."

"Just remember—you owe me."

"I'll remember." She started to turn away, but hesitated. "Hey, did you go to Gini Elgin's services Saturday?" she asked.

"Yes. Why do you care?"

"I just wondered. I drove by the church and it looked like there were a lot of people there."

"Yeah, there was a big crowd."

"I guess you went with Parker, huh?"

"Well, yeah, though we had to pretend we weren't together when his parents were around." Merry rolled her eyes. "It's so silly, but Parker says I just have to be patient. All this fuss about the poisoned medication and the bomb is slowing everything down."

"I'm sure your patience will pay off," Laura said. "How was Gini's son—Leo?"

Confusion clouded Merry's eyes. "How do you know Leo?"

"I met him in town. He seemed really torn up about his mom's death."

"Yeah. They were close."

"Do you know him well?" Laura asked.

Merry wrinkled her nose. "No."

"I thought somebody told me the two of you used to date."

Merry laughed. "Me and Leo? Get out of here! Somebody was pulling your leg. He's definitely not my type." She shook her head, emphatic.

"I guess I misheard." Laura stepped away. "I'd better get to work. I'll talk to you later." She headed to her office, reviewing the conversation with Merry. She didn't think Merry was lying about her relationship with Leo. Gini's son wasn't handsome, wealthy, powerful or charming—all things Merry appeared to value. If she wasn't in a relationship with him, she must have gone to see him on Parker's behalf.

Parker was already in the office when Laura arrived. He turned from her desk. "Where have you been?" he demanded.

Laura moved around the desk and slid into her chair. "I was talking to Merry."

"About what?"

"About you." She looked him in the eye. One of her

early trainers had stressed the importance of sticking to the truth whenever possible. "I was asking her how I could do a better job for you."

"As if Merry would know anything about that," he scoffed.

"She's your girlfriend, isn't she?"

He frowned. "I guess she told you that."

"Yes. Why? Is it a big secret?"

"It isn't appropriate for me to be dating an employee of the company." He tapped his index finger on the papers in her in-box. "So don't mention it to anyone."

"Your secret is safe with me." She smiled and he took a step back. Before he could escape to his office, she asked, "How was the service for Gini Elgin? I drove by there Saturday and it looked like a big crowd."

"Gini had a lot of friends," Parker said. "She'll be missed."

"How's your friend Leo?"

"I don't imagine he's doing very well, considering his mother was killed."

"Do the police have any suspects yet?" she asked.

"I don't think so. We'll probably never know who did something so horrible." He turned away. "Block off the rest of my morning. I have a meeting with my mother." Not waiting for an answer, he left the office.

She settled behind her desk. She hadn't learned anything new from her questioning of Merry and Parker. Not that she had expected them to spill their secrets to the nosy new employee, but the lack of progress in the case frustrated her.

The door opened and Merry sauntered in. "I want to see Parker," she said, and headed for his office.

"He's not here," Laura said. "He said he had a meeting with his mother."

Merry pouted. "He really ought to be in charge of this place, not her." She sank into the chair across from Laura's desk. "Honestly, she treats him like a child. When we're married, things are going to be different. I'm not going to let her run over him this way."

Laura opened her mouth to ask what Merry intended to say to Mrs. Stroud when the building shuddered, and a deafening roar surrounded them. Both women dropped to their knees on the floor as pictures, coffee cups and a vase of flowers slid to the floor and shattered. As the concussion subsided, screams rose to take its place. Laura was on her feet and running, Merry at her heels.

"What happened?" The younger woman screamed as people, some bleeding, others showered with debris, raced past them, out of the building.

Laura shoved her way through the crowd, toward the source of the commotion. "I think there was another bomb," she said, more to herself than to Merry. Why had she been too late to stop it?

Chapter Nine

The man and woman looked up when Ana tapped on the partially open door to the hospital room. "Mrs. Stroud? We need to ask you and your son some questions."

Donna Stroud, her face washed of color except for the purple half moons beneath her eyes, pressed her lips together tightly and nodded. Parker, on his back in the hospital bed, white bandaging swathing his forehead, said nothing, though his gaze bored into Ana and Rogers as they entered the small room, which smelled of antiseptic and dry-erase marker. "How are you feeling, Mr. Stroud?" Ana asked.

"About like I would expect a person to feel who's been blown up." He pressed a button by his side to raise the head of the bed. "They tell me I have a concussion and contusions, which is medical talk for being beaten half to death."

"Where were you when the blast occurred?" Rogers asked.

"I was standing just outside the door to my mother's office. I was about to go in."

"Did you know Ms. Dupree was in the office?" Rogers asked.

"No. I didn't know anyone was in there."

"This is so horrible." Donna spoke in a hoarse voice, just above a whisper. "Angela wasn't just an employee. She was a friend." She swallowed hard. "I can't believe she's gone."

"Do you know why Ms. Dupree was in your office yesterday morning?" Ana asked.

Donna shook her head. "I don't know. But it wouldn't have been unusual for her to stop by and say hello. We often chatted at work."

"Ms. Dupree's assistant, Shania Merritt, said her boss was bringing some pay raise authorizations for you to okay," Ana said.

Donna nodded. "That sounds right."

"Why weren't you in the office, Mrs. Stroud?" Rogers asked. "Wouldn't you usually be there at that time of morning?"

"Yes, but…" She glanced at Parker. "My husband isn't well."

"Is this to do with his dementia, or something else?" Ana asked.

Donna looked pained. "Steve is forgetful, although most days he manages fine. But sometimes, he's frustrated by his inability to remember and gets confused. Then he becomes angry and we argue. Yesterday morning he was especially combative and I stayed home to try to calm him down."

"What was he being combative about?" Ana asked.

"He had gotten it into his head that Parker was negotiating to sell the business to a competitor and he insisted we should fire Parker." She shook her head. "It's utter nonsense, of course, but once he gets an idea like this into his head, there's no reasoning with him."

"Where would he get such an idea?" Rogers asked.

"There's no basis in reality for these delusions," Parker said. "It's a symptom of his disease. He could see something on TV or dream something and believe it's real."

"What were you doing outside your mother's office, Mr. Stroud?" Rogers asked. "Wouldn't you normally be in your own office at that time?"

"I wanted to speak to my mother about the production

schedule for next month. As the factory manager, I often consult with her."

"Your assistant, Ms. Lovejoy, told us you told her you had a meeting scheduled with your mother," Ana said. "She was told to leave your calendar clear for the whole morning because of this meeting."

"Yes, that's right."

Ana turned to Donna. "We didn't see any notice on your calendar of such a meeting, Mrs. Stroud."

"My son doesn't have to make an appointment to consult with me."

"So this wasn't a prescheduled meeting?" Rogers asked.

"No," Parker said. "If Ms. Lovejoy thought that, she was mistaken."

Or perhaps Parker had wanted Laura to think the meeting had been scheduled earlier, for whatever reason. Ana turned her attention to Donna again. The woman seemed to have aged five years since their first meeting a week ago. "I know you've answered this question before, but we need to ask again," she said. "Can you think of anyone who might wish to harm you?"

"Are you suggesting my mother was the target for this madman?" Parker asked.

"The bomb was in her office, we think under her desk," Rogers said. "It was designed to trigger when she opened her bottom desk drawer." He looked to Donna, who had blanched even paler. "We were told that drawer is where you keep a box of tissues and some other personal items."

She nodded. "I don't know of anyone who would…" She wet her lips. "Who would want to kill me?"

Parker struggled to sit up in bed. "You're upsetting my mother. Don't you think she's been through enough?"

"Why would Angela open that drawer?" Ana asked. "Do you know?"

"I… I can guess."

They waited as Donna stared at her fingers laced together in her lap. When she looked up, her eyes were desolate. "Angela was recently diagnosed with breast cancer. She was due to have surgery, then chemotherapy the week after. I was the only person she told. We had cried together over the news. I can guess that if she came to talk to me yesterday, she was going to let me know her treatment schedule. We would have cried again. When she didn't find me there, maybe she got teary-eyed. She knew I kept tissues in that drawer, so she might have opened it, intending to pull herself together before she went back into the outer office."

"Did you see anyone suspicious in or around the office that day or the day before?" Rogers asked Parker.

"No."

"Mrs. Stroud? Did you see anything or anyone suspicious?"

Donna shook her head. "No."

"Have you received any threatening letters or phone calls?" Ana asked.

"Only the one letter I gave you—the 'six for six' message. Nothing else."

"Are you going to find the person who did this?" Parker asked. "Because you're not doing a very good job so far."

Ana ignored the dig. In his place, she would probably have been frustrated by the lack of progress in the case, too. Civilians expected law enforcement to solve crimes quickly, in the space of a few days. Building a case and finding the guilty party usually took much longer. "Have you considered closing the plant temporarily?" she asked Donna.

"Out of the question," Parker said.

Donna's answer was less strident. "We have a hundred employees and their families who depend on us," she said. "We can't shut them out. As it is, we had to temporarily lay off fifty people when we shut down the plant that made the Stomach Soothers."

"We need you to find whoever is doing this so we can put this tragedy behind us," Parker said.

"This case is our top priority," Rogers said. A nurse entered the room and he moved toward the door. "We may need to talk to you again."

He and Ana moved into the hallway. He waited until they had reached their rental car before he spoke. "What do you think?"

"I think someone has targeted these people," she said.

"Leo Elgin?"

"Maybe. Has your surveillance turned up anything on him?" He and Jace had been trading off watching Leo during daylight hours.

"No. The plant is closed today, so Jace is watching Elgin. If he doesn't turn up anything, we need to focus on someone else."

"Who?"

"We're going to look at everyone who had access to that office," Rogers said.

"Donna Stroud had access," Ana said. "And she was conveniently not there this morning."

"Do you think she killed two of her employees and sabotaged her own product?"

"I think we both know criminals who have done stranger things."

He nodded. "Let's look closer at her and see if we can find out."

"And let's talk to that competitor Steve Stroud accused Parker of negotiating with. Maybe someone is angling to get Stroud Pharmaceuticals at a bargain price."

"Good idea." One more item on the long list of threads to pull in this case. This was the tedious part of working a case—following leads that went nowhere, talking to people who might or might not have something to hide and trying to put all the information together to form a picture that led to the guilty party. It took hours of effort and focus, but that, more than bravery or cunning, was what solved most cases. It was one reason the bureau hired as many accountants as military types. Brains counted more than brawn more often than not.

FOUR TO GO.

Merry had placed the envelope on the top of the pile of mail Tuesday morning, and pointed it out to Donna when she delivered it. "It looks like the other letter, doesn't it?" she asked, leaning in close, so that Donna caught the scent of her perfume—floral and delicate, if applied with a heavy hand. "The one the FBI was so concerned about."

Donna stared at the plain white envelope, with her name in dark block letters, no title, and the address for Stroud Pharmaceuticals. "Aren't you going to open it?" Merry asked.

"I think I should call the police," Donna said. "Or maybe Agent Ramirez. I have her card in my desk somewhere." But she made no move to search for it, fixated on the envelope.

"What if it's a solicitation from the local funeral home or something?" Merry asked. "I mean, really?" She plucked the envelope from the stack of mail and slid one pink-polished nail beneath the flap.

"You'll destroy fingerprints," Donna protested.

Merry shook her head. "Every criminal knows to wear gloves." She flicked open the envelope flap and dumped the contents onto the desk. The half sheet of copy paper lay crookedly on the blotter, twenty-point type exclaiming, *Four to go!*

Donna gasped and swayed.

"Mrs. Stroud, you've gone all pale." Merry took her

arm and eased her back in her chair. "You sit there and take deep breaths. You've had a shock." She left, then returned with a cup of water from the cooler in the corner. "Drink this."

Donna drank and began to feel a little steadier. "Thank you." She glanced at the words on the paper and suppressed a shudder, then opened her desk drawer and took out Ana Ramirez's card. "I'd better telephone for someone to deal with this."

"What does that mean?" Merry asked. "'Four to go'?"

"I don't know," Donna lied. Though she knew very well what it meant. Six people had died from taking poisoned Stomach Soothers. Two people had perished in the two bombings at Stroud Pharmaceuticals. Four more deaths before the score would be even, in the bomber's twisted logic.

JACE WAS NUMB with boredom after three nights of tailing Leo Elgin, but he forced himself to stick with the surveillance. The man might be the dullest person Jace had ever met, but that didn't mean he wasn't up to no good.

Though, as far as Jace could tell from the bugs he'd placed in the house, Leo wasn't up to anything but sitting in front of his computer playing hundreds of rounds of solitaire. He received no visitors or phone calls, and the only person he attempted to call was Parker Stroud. The afternoon after the bomb exploded that killed Angela Dupree, Leo tried to call Parker, who was in the hospital, six times. Parker never answered, though that wasn't too surprising, given that he was injured. Leo left only one message. "This is Leo. What's going on over there?"

Jace slumped in a van with the logo of a fake pest control company, parked on the street with a clear view of Elgin's house. Times like these, he missed smoking the most, even though smoking while on surveillance was forbidden—the scent of smoke might attract attention. Still, he missed how smoking gave him something to do with his hands and something to focus on besides his own breathing.

Movement in the house, followed by the sound of a door opening and closing. Jace sat up straighter. It sounded as if Leo had left the house, but Jace saw no movement near the front door. Had Leo gone out the back? Jace got out of the van and, walking purposefully, he marched down the sidewalk. When he reached Leo's house, he ducked down the side, into a screen of shrubbery between Leo's house and the neighbor's. He reached the backyard in time to see Leo unlock the door to a wooden shed in the back corner. With a sagging roof and sides almost devoid of paint, the shed looked on the verge of collapse.

Jace shoved further into the screen of bushes, gritting his teeth as thorns raked his arms and face. He could hear movement from inside the shed—something heavy being shoved around. He headed toward the back of the little building, hoping for a window or a missing board that would allow him to see inside. But instead of an opening, he discovered the back of the shed was all but covered by a five-foot mound of dirt and sod, as if the shed had been built into the side of a hill.

But this was no hill. Jace had seen a similar structure at his grandparents' farm. At some point the Elgins, or whoever had owned the property before them, had built an old-fashioned root cellar. Rather than digging out a space underground, they had built up the earth around the shed. Somewhere inside there was probably a door leading into the storage area within the mound of dirt.

The FBI had searched the Elgin property, but would they have recognized the root cellar?

Jace retreated the way he had come, and walked back to his van. He called Rogers. "The people who searched the Elgin home. Did they look in the root cellar?" he asked.

"Let me check." A moment later Rogers was on the line again. "There's no mention of a root cellar."

"It's at the back of that old shed, built into a mound of earth," Jace said. "They need to check it."

"We're not going to get another warrant," Rogers said. "We've already had complaints that we're harassing the locals and not finding anything."

"There's something going on in that shed," Jace said. "Leo is in there now. I could hear him moving stuff around."

"Maybe he's finally clearing out his mother's property."

"He's been calling Parker Stroud, leaving cryptic messages. Something is going on."

"Find proof then. You haven't got enough to go on."

Jace ended the call and sat back. He'd find the proof. He punched in another number.

Laura answered on the second ring. "Hello?"

"Don't wait up. I'll be working all night."

"What is it? Have you found something?"

"Maybe."

"What is it?"

"I don't know yet, but I need to hang around here tonight. I'll talk to you later."

He started to hang up, but her voice stopped him. "Jace?"

"Yeah?"

"Be careful."

She ended the call. He sat with the phone in his hand, an unsettling tremor in his chest. It was the kind of thing anyone might say to another person. But Laura wasn't just any other person, and when she had told him to be careful, she had sounded as if she really cared.

LAURA TUCKED HER phone back into her pocket. Why had she said that to Jace—"be careful"—as if she were his mother or his wife or something? She should have been demanding he tell her what he was up to. After all, they were partners in this investigation.

She pulled out her phone and hit Redial. "Yeah?" Jace answered.

"What is going on?" she asked. "What are you doing?"

"You don't want to know."

She gripped the phone harder. "Tell me."

"I think Leo is up to something in the old garden shed behind his house—or rather, in the attached root cellar."

"And?" There had to be an *and*.

"I'm going to wait until after dark and sneak in there and look around."

"You don't have a warrant." If he had a warrant, he wouldn't have hesitated to tell her. "Not only is what you're proposing illegal, nothing you find could be used in evidence. You'll compromise the whole case." This was just like him, wanting to take shortcuts, thinking the rules didn't apply to him. He'd gotten away with this kind of thing before now because he had good results, but this time he was going too far.

"I'm not compromising the case." His voice was calm, as if they'd been discussing what to eat for dinner. "I know how to get in and out without leaving a trace, and I won't touch anything. I just want to see if my hunch is right. Then I'll be able to get a warrant."

"How will you get a warrant if you don't reveal what you find in there?" she asked.

"I'll say I saw Leo do something suspicious, or carrying a suspicious object." She swore she could almost *hear* his sly grin. "It won't take much. I can be very persuasive."

"But you'd be lying!" She didn't even try to keep the horror from her voice. "You'd be manufacturing evidence."

"I wouldn't be manufacturing anything. I'll only speak to what I will know is in that root cellar."

"It's still a lie."

"A very small one, and for a good cause."

That's probably what every corrupt agent or politician or businessperson said when they started. But little lies led to big ones. And big lies led to the corruption of the whole situation. "Jace, don't do this," she said, unable to keep the pleading from her voice.

"Why not?" he asked.

"Because you're better than this."

He was silent so long she thought he had hung up. "Jace?" she asked.

"I'm here." He blew out a breath. "I need to get in there and look around," he said. "If Leo is responsible for those bombs, he's killed two people already. We can't let him kill anyone else."

"No." She felt her convictions wavering. Was Jace right, that the ends—stopping a murderer—justified the means? But then, where did she draw the line? "You can't lie to get the warrant," she said.

"Let me go in and see what I find," he said. "Maybe I'm wrong and I'm wasting our time. At least then we'll know we need to focus on someone beside Leo."

"All right."

"Right. Gotta go."

"Jace?"

"What?"

"Be careful."

THE ELGIN HOUSE was located in an older neighborhood on the edge of town. Most of the houses looked to have been built in the seventies or eighties and were occupied by older couples. By midnight, every house on the block was silent and dark. Leo had turned off the last light in his place an hour before and hadn't moved since.

Jace, dressed in jeans and a black hoodie, slipped out of the van and made his way along the side of the yard to the back, not in the bushes this time, but alongside them, concealed by deepest shadow. The night air was still and humid, like furnace exhaust, without a hint of coolness. Within five minutes, he was sweating in the heavy sweat-shirt.

The shed and root cellar hunched in the back corner of the yard, looking even more decrepit in the washed-out light of a quarter moon. Jace checked the windows on that side of the house for any sign of movement, but found none. Heart pounding, he stepped into the moonlight and walked over to the door.

Using his body as a shield, he trained the beam of a small penlight on the lock, a hefty padlock, so shiny it couldn't have been on here long. The lock was threaded through a rusty hasp—but the hasp was fashioned with new screws. *What are you so concerned about locking up in here, Leo?* Jace wondered. He'd have to check the records to see if this lock had been here when the FBI conducted their warranted search.

He studied the lock a moment, then took out a set of picks and went to work. The standard commercial lock popped open in less than two minutes. Jace lifted the hasp, opened the door, then hung the lock in place and slipped inside.

The shed smelled of mildew and weed killer. The pen-light revealed a shovel, rake and hoe on nails along the far wall. Bags of potting soil and several five-gallon buckets crammed with wood scraps and bits of rusty metal crowded the floor. A leaning metal shelf against the side wall held flower pots, bags of fertilizer and enough weed killing concoctions to poison half the town. If one of them had been found in the Stomach Soothers, Jace would have been suspicious Leo had decided to take out his own mother.

The root cellar was on the other side of the back wall. Jace played his light over the rough wood siding, looking for any kind of opening. It couldn't be obvious or the previous searchers would have found it right away. They would have found most hidden doors as well, so this had to be something especially clever.

A big copper pot, the kind once used for boiling clothing over an outside fire, took up most of the back corner of the shed, filled with tangled fishing gear and an old tarp. Recalling the noises he had heard when Leo first entered the shed, of something heavy being moved, Jace dragged the pot out of the way and shone his light into the corner.

Nothing looked out of the ordinary. The weathered boards of the shed appeared firmly nailed in place. One rusting nail stuck out of the wood a scant quarter inch. When Jace tugged at the nail, it didn't move. But when he grasped the nail like a handle and attempted to pull it, the whole section of siding slid toward him, and a wave of cooler air washed over him, smelling of machine oil and damp.

He stilled, ears straining for any sound, but all remained silent. He stepped around the pot and ducked into the opening. The root cellar was not large, perhaps five feet deep and seven feet wide, like a large closet, the ceiling so low he had to hunch to keep from brushing the top of his head against the chicken wire that had been used as a frame to support the sod laid over it. A wooden work bench took up most of the space, with a small drill press, scales, and various hand tools littering its top. Cardboard apple boxes filled the space beneath the bench. Jace nudged the lid off one box and let out a soft whistle as he played his light across the collection of wire, fuses, blasting caps, and a hefty bundle of dynamite.

The other boxes contained metal pipes, and some electronics he thought must be part of timing mechanisms. If the bomb-making materials matched those used in the Stroud explosions, there was enough evidence here to put

Leo away for a very long time. He switched off the light and backed out of the root cellar. He had just shoved the copper pot back into place and was moving toward the door when the clank of the padlock against the hasp and a soft curse made his heart stop beating.

He had just enough time to dive into the front corner and pull a tarp over his head before the door opened and Leo stepped inside.

Chapter Ten

Jace couldn't see through the tarp, which smelled of mud and decay. He crouched beneath it, one hand on the gun at his hip, his body tensed to spring if Leo discovered his hiding place. But Leo's footsteps moved away, toward the back corner. The copper pot scraped across the floor, a faint sliding sound announced the opening of the secret door, and something rattled on or beneath the workbench.

Jace risked rearranging the tarp so that he could peer from beneath it. Leo had switched on a light—maybe a battery-operated lantern—inside the root cellar, and its yellow glow illuminated the back of the shed as well. Jace had a limited view of a space just to the right of the secret door. He could hear Leo moving around in there, jostling boxes, rearranging tools. Unable to sleep, had he decided to build another bomb?

Seconds later, Leo emerged from the root cellar, carrying one of the apple boxes. He exited the shed, footsteps retreating across the yard. Jace's ears rang in the silence that followed. He remained still, counting to one hundred, giving Leo time to return to the house. He waited for the sound of the door opening and closing, but it didn't come. Instead, just as he was debating throwing off the tarp and making his way back to his van, a car started somewhere very nearby. Was Leo leaving the house, taking the apple box somewhere?

But instead of growing fainter as Leo drove away, the roar of the car's engine grew louder, until the vehicle was idling right outside the shed door. Then the engine died, the car door slammed, and Leo was inside the shed once more. He retrieved a second box from the root cellar, carried it to the car, then returned a third time.

Jace shifted beneath the tarp. He couldn't risk leaving his hiding place. But he couldn't let Leo move his bomb-making operation out of the shed without trying to stop him. He eased his phone from his pocket and tapped out a text to Laura: SOS I NEED YOU HERE ASAP.

ADRENALINE SURGED THROUGH Laura as she read Jace's text. She traded the shorts she was wearing for jeans, pulled on her weapon harness and boots, and grabbed a big flashlight that could double as a truncheon. In the truck, she called Ramirez. Though she had probably been asleep at this late hour, Ana sounded alert. "What's going on?" she asked.

"I just got a text from Jace," Laura said. "He's at Leo's place and it sounds like he's in trouble."

"What was he doing at Leo's at this hour?"

"He said something about a shed in the backyard. He'd seen suspicious activity around it." She didn't want to get Jace in trouble with the complete truth, and she didn't want to jeopardize their case.

"We'll be right there," Ramirez said.

Laura pushed the truck hard across town through the darkened streets, mind racing. Jace had planned to search the shed behind Leo's house. Had Leo surprised him? Had Leo shot him? Pain squeezed her chest at the thought, and she pressed harder on the gas, hands white-knuckled on the steering wheel.

She turned onto Leo's street and spotted Jace's van right away. She parked behind it, then ran to Leo's house. She drew her weapon and, keeping to the darkest shadows, she headed for the backyard, where Jace had said the shed was located.

She spotted the car first, the driver's door and the trunk open, spilling light onto the weedy space in front of a leaning wooden shed. She froze as someone emerged from the shed. Leo, carrying a cardboard box.

A car passed in front of the house. Leo didn't even look up. He stowed the box in the trunk of the car and returned to the shed. Her phone vibrated and she pulled it from her pocket and glanced at the screen. Where are you? From Ramirez.

North side of the property, toward the back. Leo is at the shed.

Moments later, two dark shapes moved toward her. She waited until they were almost on her before she whispered, "Over here."

Ramirez moved in close behind her, followed by Rogers. "What's going on?" Ramirez asked.

"Leo's moving something out of that shed."

"Any sign of Jace?"

Laura shook her head. She could try to text him, but what if he wasn't in a position to answer her?

Leo emerged from the shed again with another box. "What's he got?" Rogers asked.

"I think we should find out," Laura said. She pulled the big Maglite from her belt, aimed it toward Leo and pressed the on switch.

"FBI!" Rogers shouted. "Drop the box and put your hands in the air."

Leo dropped the box and looked around wildly. "Put your hands up!" Rogers ordered, his voice booming.

Leo tentatively stretched his hands up. Ramirez and Rogers raced forward. Laura hung back, keeping the light trained on Leo and her face in the shadows. If possible, she and Jace needed to protect their cover.

While Ramirez and Rogers dealt with Leo, she slipped past them into the shed. "Jace?" she called.

"I'm over here."

She turned toward the sound of his voice as he emerged from beneath a brown tarp. Something loosened in her chest as he moved toward her, no sign of blood or injury, only a smear of dirt across one cheek. "Where's Leo?" he asked, looking toward the open shed door.

"Rogers and Ramirez have him. What's going on?"

He switched on a penlight and shone the beam on an opening in the far wall. "There's a workshop in there full of bomb-making materials," he said. "Or there was, until Leo started moving them out."

"Leo is the bomber?" The knowledge didn't surprise her, but it did disappoint her. Leo had seemed more pathetic than evil to her. Yet he had murdered two people.

Ramirez joined them in the shed. "Rogers has Leo cuffed in our vehicle and the local police are on their way," she said.

"What was in those boxes?" Laura asked.

"Electronics, wiring, fuses and explosives," Jace said. "Everything you'd need to make a bomb. Lots of bombs, I'd guess."

"Has Leo said anything?" Jace asked.

"Only that he didn't kill anyone. Then he asked for his lawyer and shut up." Ramirez shrugged. "We'll get the whole story, eventually." She looked Jace up and down. "You okay?"

"Yeah." He gestured toward the shed. "I saw Leo in here moving around and got curious. I came to get a closer look, then got trapped when he started moving in and out. I texted Laura for help."

"He didn't resist," Ramirez said. "I don't even think he

was armed. We'll wrap things up here. You two should go before your cover is blown."

They headed back toward the truck and the van. "You could have arrested him yourself," Laura said. "Why did you call me? To preserve your cover?"

"That, and to make sure there were plenty of witnesses to catch him red-handed with those bomb-making supplies." He grinned. "I wouldn't want anyone to accuse me of taking short cuts and jeopardizing the case."

She wanted to give him a good shove. She also wanted to throw her arms around him and tell him how glad she was that he was safe. Instead, she moved away from him, toward her truck, before she let emotion get the better of her.

"I DIDN'T KILL ANYONE." Leo Elgin, in an orange jumpsuit with PRISONER in large white letters stenciled across the front and back, sat across the table from Ana and Rogers at the Mayville Police Department, his wrists and ankles shackled, his court-appointed attorney on one side of him, a police officer on the other.

"Leo, we can match materials we found in your workshop to both the bombs that exploded at Stroud Pharmaceuticals," Ana said. "The bombs that killed Lydia Green and Angela Dupree."

"Did Angela or Lydia put that poison in the Stomach Soothers?" Leo asked, more desperate than defiant. "The poison that killed my mother?"

"Is that what you think?" Ana leaned across the table toward him. "That Lydia and Angela killed your mother, so you planted the bombs to kill them?"

"Did they?"

"We haven't found anything to link either of them to the poisoned medication," Rogers said.

Leo buried his face in his hands and began to sob.

"My client is clearly distraught," said the attorney, a motherly woman in her midfifties, with silver curls and tortoise-shell bifocals. "He has nothing else to say to you at this time."

Ana and Rogers rose. "We have more questions for you, Leo," Ana said. "We know you made those bombs. That makes you guilty of murder, whether you put them at the plant or not. If you didn't, as you say, kill Lydia and Angela, then who did?"

She followed Rogers from the room. The chief of police, Gary Simonson, met them at the end of the hall. "Did you get anything out of him?" he asked.

Rogers shook his head. "But Leo made those bombs. I don't have any doubt about that."

"But did he plant them at the factory?" Ana asked.

"Maybe." Rogers rubbed his jaw, stubble rasping against his palm. Like Ana, he had had only a couple of hours of sleep in the past two days, and his eyes looked sunken in his handsome face. "Probably. He had his mother's key and pass to get in. She had worked there for years, so he probably knew his way around."

"But who poisoned the medication?" Ana asked. "Was it really Lydia and Angela?"

"Is that what he's saying?" Simonson asked. "That he killed those women because they poisoned his mother?"

"We'll take a closer look at them, but nothing in the backgrounds of any of the Stroud employees points to a motive for the poisonings," Rogers said. "Both Angela and Lydia had worked for Stroud for years, with good reports. They didn't have so much as a traffic ticket on their records."

"He asked us if they put the poison in the Stomach Soothers," Ana said. "As if he wanted us to confirm what he thought." She frowned. "Though really, he sounded unsure. And he kept insisting he didn't kill anyone."

"The bombs he made killed them," Rogers said. "That makes him a murderer."

"You and I know that, but maybe Leo wasn't clear on that," she said. "Maybe he made the bombs for someone else to use. Or he thought they would be used for some other purpose." The more she considered Leo's words and reactions, the more this idea fit.

Her phone rang. She checked the display. "It's Maynard," she said. "I'd better take it."

She moved down the hall, leaving Rogers with the police chief. "Hey Hendrick," she answered the call from the team's technology expert. "What have you got for me?"

"I've been through all the video you sent from Stroud Pharmaceuticals' security cameras. All of it," he emphasized. "Three weeks' worth of footage, inside and out."

"And?" She pressed the phone more tightly to her ear.

"There were hundreds of people going in and out of that place, but all of them were either employees, vendors, or family members of employees. My team was able to identify every single person on those feeds."

"Great job." She tried to put more enthusiasm into her voice than she felt. "Anything significant?"

"The only thing significant is who *isn't* there," Hendrick said.

Her stomach churned. "Who isn't there?"

"Leo Elgin isn't there. Not inside the buildings. Not outside the buildings. We've got good footage of the areas around both bombing sites and Leo was never there."

Rogers joined her. She met his questioning gaze and shook her head. "Thanks, Hendrick," she said, and ended the call.

"Leo Elgin isn't in any of the security footage from Stroud," she said. "He may have made those two bombs, but he didn't plant them."

"So he has an accomplice who works for Stroud?" Rogers asked.

"He must have. But who?"

"There's only a couple of people we know he's met with since he got back in town," Rogers said. "Let's get Parker Stroud in here and talk to him."

Chapter Eleven

At work Wednesday, Parker, still sporting a few bruises but otherwise seemingly unhurt, asked Laura for more reports. "Why are you looking at everything from the first quarter?" she asked when she delivered the first batch to his desk.

"Not that it's any of your business, but I'm working on a new design that will make us even more efficient and productive."

"I heard there might be another bomb," she said. "Do you think that's true?"

His eyes narrowed. "Who told you that?"

She shrugged. "I just heard some people talk."

"Haven't you heard talk is cheap?"

"But do you think there could be another bomb?"

"I don't know. Maybe."

"But why?"

"Because someone is out to destroy this business and my family." She heard no anger behind his words, only bleak resignation. "Now get out of here and leave me to work in peace."

She left and remained at her desk the rest of the morning, having finally hacked into Stroud Pharmaceuticals' financial records for the past two quarters. On the surface the reports were competent, but the deeper she dug, the messier things got. Was Virginia Elgin that incompetent, or had someone conveniently deleted chunks of data from the files?

Parker wasn't at his desk when Ramirez and Rogers arrived after lunch and asked to speak to him. "He stepped away half an hour ago," Laura said. "He didn't tell me where he was going."

"Any idea where we should look?" Rogers asked.

"Let me see if I can find him," she said, and hurried away. Better she should go roaming through the plant than two known federal agents, who would raise alarms and have everyone competing to come up with ever-wilder explanations for their presence.

When the coffee room and his mother's office showed no signs of Parker, she headed for the factory floor and found him with Jace, of all people, discussing a malfunction with the fill machine. Jace gave her a warm smile. "Hey, sweetheart," he said.

She ignored him and focused on Parker. "There are two FBI agents here who want to talk to you," she said.

He masked his alarm so quickly she might not have noticed if she hadn't been watching for it. "Tell them I'm unavailable," he said.

"I can't do that," she protested. "They're the FBI."

"And I don't have time to talk to them. Tell them you couldn't find me. You don't know where I am." He turned to Jace. "That goes for you, too," he said.

"Yes, sir." Jace met Laura's gaze, one eyebrow raised in question.

"Yes, sir," she said, and turned away.

Back at the office, she found Ramirez and Rogers still standing. "He's on the factory floor," she said. "Packaging. But my guess is he'll be headed for the parking lot soon. If you hurry, you can catch him."

Ten minutes later, Ramirez and Rogers followed Parker back into the office. He headed for his private sanctum without a glance in Laura's direction. Ramirez nodded at her and followed Parker and Rogers, but she left the door open a scant half inch.

Laura moved to the door. "Why were you running away from us?" Rogers asked.

"I wasn't running," Parker said. "I had an appointment to meet our regional sales manager. If you want to speak with me, you can schedule a meeting with my secretary."

"This can't wait," Rogers said. "We want to talk to you about your relationship with Leo Elgin."

"I don't know what you're talking about." Parker's voice was forceful and sure. He was a good bluffer. But not good enough.

"You know Leo Elgin," Ramirez said.

"Yes." Parker's chair creaked. "His mother worked for us before her tragic death. And Leo and I went to the same high school."

"The two of you are friends," Ramirez said.

"We're acquaintances. And what difference does that make, anyway? I know a lot of people."

"Leo Elgin was arrested early this morning, and charged with manufacturing the explosive devices that killed Lydia Green and Angela Dupree," Rogers said.

Silence, then Ramirez's voice. "Mr. Stroud? Are you all right?"

When Parker finally spoke, his voice had lost all its energy and defiance. "Leo planted those bombs here? But why?"

"Why don't you take a moment to pull yourself together," Ramirez said. She moved to the doorway. "Mr. Stroud needs some water," she said.

Laura filled a paper cup from a dispenser across the room and brought it to her. "What happened?" she asked, her voice low.

"The news of Leo's arrest clearly shocked him," Ramirez said. "I thought he was going to pass out."

She moved into Parker's office once more, still leaving the door ajar. "Mr. Stroud, how well did you know Ms. Green and Ms. Dupree?" Rogers asked.

"They were family friends as well as employees, but my mother knows—knew—both of them better than I did." Parker paused, perhaps to sip water, then added, "I'm still upset about their deaths. Such a waste."

"Do you know of any reason either woman might have wanted to sabotage the Stomach Soothers?" Rogers asked. "Could they have put the poison in the tablets?"

"Angela and Lydia?"

"One or both of them," Ramirez said.

"No! Why would they? They were good women. Lydia taught Sunday school. Angela and my mother were best friends. Besides all that, neither of them came near the factory operations. I don't see when or how they could have introduced the poison into the tablets." Another pause. "Are you suggesting Leo planted the bombs to kill those women because he believed they were responsible for Gini's death?"

"We're exploring a number of possible motives," Rogers said. "Right now, we want to know more about your dealings with Leo Elgin."

"I didn't have any dealings with Leo."

"We have witnesses who have seen you together on at least two occasions recently," Rogers said.

Parker's voice remained calm. Reasonable. "We've run into each other a couple of times since he returned to town and I've offered my condolences, that's all."

"What about the money you gave him?" Rogers asked.

"What money?" Parker's voice was sharp, with a hint of outrage.

"The money you had your girlfriend, Merry Winger, deliver to Leo last Saturday," Rogers said. "The day of Gini Elgin's memorial service. Ms. Winger says you asked her to leave the service, drive to the Elgin home, and give an envelope of money to Leo Elgin."

"My family wanted to contribute to the funeral costs. Leo was too proud to take the money when I originally offered it, but I thought if Merry delivered it he would accept it, and I was right."

"You were already paying for the catering for the reception after the service," Ramirez said.

"Yes, but we wanted to do more," Parker said. "Gini was a beloved, long-time employee of Stroud Pharmaceuticals and while we didn't cause her death, we feel terrible that one of our products was the instrument of her demise."

The instrument of her demise? Really? Laura wondered if he had practiced delivering that line.

"What do you think you're doing?"

She turned to find Merry in the doorway. "Two FBI agents are in there questioning Parker," Laura said, keeping her voice low.

Merry's eyes widened and she hurried to join Laura by Parker's door. "What does the FBI want with Parker?" she whispered.

Laura led her back to the desk. "They asked about the money you delivered to Leo Elgin the day of the funeral," she said.

Merry scowled. "What does that have to do with anything?"

"Why did you leave Gini's funeral to deliver that money to Leo?" Laura asked.

"Parker asked me to do it." She dropped into the chair in front of the desk. "He begged me to do it, really. Finally, he agreed to buy me a pair of diamond earrings if I would do it for him." She fingered the glittering earrings at her lobes.

Laura leaned back against the front of the desk. "But

why did he want you to go to Leo's during the funeral?" she asked.

"He said he didn't want to embarrass Leo." She looked toward the office door. "What did Parker say when the feds asked him about the envelope?"

"He said the money was to help pay for Gini's funeral."

Merry raised her hands, clearly exasperated. "Why couldn't Parker tell me that? He just said to give the envelope to Leo and not to ask more questions. He didn't even tell me it was full of money—to find that out, I had to peek."

"What did you think when you saw the money?" Laura asked.

"I was worried Parker was buying drugs off Leo or something."

"How much money was it?"

"A lot. There was a thick stack of hundred-dollar bills."

Laura crossed her arms over her chest. "Would a funeral cost that much?"

"I don't know. I never had to pay for one. But I've always heard how expensive they are."

"Do you think Parker is doing drugs?" Laura asked.

"Well, no," Merry said. "I mean, when we go out he hardly ever has more than one beer. He doesn't smoke, either." She smiled. "It's one of the things I like about him. He doesn't really have any bad habits. If you ask him, he'll say his only vice is that he works too hard."

Laura hadn't seen much evidence of that, considering how often her boss came in late or left early. "Why would Parker give Leo money for his mother's funeral?" she asked.

"Because he felt terrible about Gini's death. He really did. I was with him when he got the news that she died. He went paper white and I thought he might pass out. He kept saying 'no, no, no.' I didn't know he was that close to

Gini, but she had worked here a long time, so I guess he thought of her like an aunt."

Or maybe Parker had paid Leo to keep quiet about something. Or to stop publicly blaming Stroud Pharmaceuticals for his mother's death. The bad publicity surrounding the poisonings had hurt the business and though there were signs of things improving, it would take a long time to fully recover from this. Paying for the funeral might be an acceptable way to buy Leo's silence and cooperation.

The door to Parker's office opened and Parker, Ramirez and Rogers emerged. "If you think of anything else that might help us in our investigation, please call," Ramirez said.

Parker said nothing, and when Rogers and Ramirez were gone, Merry rushed to his side. "What did they want?" she asked.

"They've arrested Leo in connection with the two bombings here at the plant," Parker said. He looked older, the lines around his eyes and mouth deeper, his skin tinged with an unhealthy pallor.

"Leo planted those bombs!" Merry's voice rose. "Leo, who wouldn't say boo to a fly?"

"They think he was working with someone here at the plant," Parker said. "Someone who helped him gain access."

"But why?" Merry asked. "I mean, his mother dies, so he's going to take out two more random people? That doesn't even make sense."

"Grief can do strange things to people." Parker fixed Merry with a chilly gaze. "Can you think of anyone here who might be helping Leo?"

"No! Why are you looking at me that way?" She put a hand to her chest. "I certainly didn't help him. I think he's creepy."

"You just said he was harmless," Laura said.

"Well, yeah. Harmless, but creepy. As far as I know, he doesn't even have friends. At least, not here."

"They asked a lot of questions about the money I gave Leo." Parker's expression grew more frigid. "What were you doing, talking to the FBI about me?"

Merry took a step back. "They questioned me. I couldn't not answer their questions, could I? I mean, they're the FBI!"

"You should have kept your mouth shut."

"Parker, I—"

He put a hand on her shoulder and steered her to the door. "You need to go now." He opened the door, pushed her into the hallway, then shut the door in her face.

She left and Laura moved back to her desk. "I know you were listening at the door," Parker said.

"I was curious what they wanted with you."

"Are those the two who interviewed you and your husband?"

"Yes."

"Did they ask you if you knew Leo?"

"No."

"Don't worry, they probably will. They're not making any progress in the case, so they're grasping at straws." He started out of the office.

"Where are you going?" she asked. When he glared at her, she added, "In case anyone is looking for you."

"I'm going back to work. You should do the same."

He had been gone less than a minute when the phone on Laura's desk rang. "Hello?" she answered.

"I just saw Ramirez and Rogers leave," Jace said. "What happened up there?"

"They questioned Parker."

"And?"

She glanced toward the open door and lowered her voice. "Apparently, the envelope Merry delivered to Leo the day of his mother's funeral was full of hundred-dollar bills, from Parker."

Jace whistled. "What was the money for?"

"Parker says it was to pay for Gini's funeral. He had Merry deliver it during the service to avoid embarrassing Leo."

"Do you believe him?"

"I don't know. What does Leo say about what happened?"

"Leo isn't talking."

"Maybe we should make a deal with him—the name of his partner for a lighter sentence or reduction of charges."

"He's responsible for the deaths of two people." Jace sounded outraged. "And we caught him red-handed with the bomb-making materials. We're not going to make any deals with him."

"Maybe we should. In case there's another bomb."

"He's not going to be making any more bombs in prison," Jace said.

"There was a lot of material in that root cellar," Laura said. "Enough for a dozen more bombs. What if he made more than two to begin with? What if there's another one out there, ready to go off any minute now?"

Chapter Twelve

"We're not getting anywhere with Elgin." Rogers's frustration threaded his voice. "He's scared, and we're trying to use that to get him to cooperate, but so far he hasn't given us anything."

Jace tucked the phone under his chin and began turning the burgers that sizzled on the grill in the shade of the catalpa tree behind the trailer. "Did you get anything out of Parker Stroud this morning?"

"He's hiding something, but a lot of people are," Rogers said. "Maybe the money he gave Elgin really was for Gini's funeral. Right now we can't prove it wasn't."

"Laura thinks Elgin might have built more than the two bombs. There was enough material in that root cellar for that."

"Maybe. We're working on tracking all his movements for the last month. You know this isn't a fast process."

Right. But sometimes the Bureau was too methodical for Jace's taste. While they dotted all the *i*'s and crossed all the *t*'s, someone else could get hurt—or killed.

He ended the call and thought about going into the house to find Laura. But that would mean leaving the burgers to possibly burn. Instead, he took his phone out again and texted her. Heard from D. Come out here for update and dinner.

Five long minutes passed before the back door opened

and Laura stepped out, balancing a stack of plates and silverware and a tray of condiments. She wore shorts that showed off smooth, toned legs and he had to force himself not to stare. Fortunately, she was too focused on her task to notice his reaction. "What did Rogers say?" she asked and set her burden on the picnic table near the grill.

"They're not getting anything out of Elgin."

She settled at the picnic table. "If a suspect won't talk to us, it's usually because they're more afraid of someone else than they are of us," she said.

They had changed out of their work clothes into shorts and T-shirts, and it was surprisingly pleasant in the shaded backyard, almost relaxing, except for the case that nagged at them. Jace topped the burgers with cheese and waited for it to melt. "Who's he afraid of? His partner?"

"That would be my guess," she said.

He slid the burgers onto a plate and joined her at the table. Guesses were fine for steering the investigation in a likely direction, but what they needed now was proof. He didn't have to point that out to Laura. She had been with the Bureau longer than he had, and she seemed much more comfortable with the way they worked. He admired her smarts and dedication, if not her play-by-the-rules attitude.

"I've found something worth looking into," she said.

The way she delivered this news—oh so casual—had him on high alert. "What did you find?"

"I've been digging through Parker Stroud's financial records." She spread mustard on her burger and arranged lettuce and tomato.

Jace sat across from her and focused on his own burger. "What did you find?"

"I found a secret bank account, under the name Steven Parker. With a balance of $10 million."

Jace whistled. "Where did Parker get $10 million to stash away?"

"I wondered that, too," she said. "The money began showing up about two years ago—a few thousand here, ten thousand there. But the pace of deposits has really accelerated in the past six months."

"That doesn't sound like an inheritance or a lucky investment," Jace said.

"No. And here's something else even more interesting." She picked up her burger. "The money isn't just going in. It's going out, to the tune of two payments of $50,000 each over the past two weeks."

"Is he buying up property or other investments?" Jace asked.

"Let me give you another clue. The first payment was made three days after the first victim was poisoned by Stomach Soothers. Two days after Gini Elgin died."

Their eyes met, a look of triumph lighting hers. "You think someone is blackmailing Parker because he poisoned the Stomach Soothers," Jace said.

"I think it would be a good idea to ask him, don't you?"

Jace glanced at his plate. "Can I finish my burger first? I mean, he's not likely to run, is he?"

"He's at a Rotary Club meeting, of all things, tonight. And he's supposed to be at work in the morning. I haven't seen any sign of him wanting to run. So I think we're good. I'll pass this info on to Ramirez and Rogers and let them handle it."

"That's great work," Jace said.

Her cheeks went a shade pinker, until she took a big bite and chewed, looking thoughtful. With her hair down around her shoulders and no makeup, she looked young and soft. Not weak, but...touchable.

She took a long sip from a bottle of a local microbrew and sighed. "It would fit so neatly if we found out Parker had planted the poison in those tablets and was setting off these bombs," she said. "But he's given every indication that he's desperate to keep the business going—so why do something like planting poison in the company's top product? It's going to take years to recover from the bad press. And from what I can tell from looking at the company financials, there's a very real risk they won't pull out."

"See anything alarming in the company books?" Jace asked.

"Only that they're a mess. Gini Elgin may have been a wonderful person, but she kept terrible records. It would require months of close work to straighten out completely. I've only been able to look at them in my spare time."

"I agree that Parker doesn't have a good motive for the poisoning," Jace said. "So where does that leave us?"

"I don't think Angela or Lydia did it," she said. "There's no motive and even less opportunity. They both worked in the offices, not on the factory floor. And I don't think Leo did it."

"Maybe he didn't do it intending to kill his mother," Jace said. "Her death was an accident."

Laura shook her head. "Leo was in Nashville when the poisonings began. He hadn't been back to Mayville in four months."

"That we know of. It's only a six-hour drive, and only a couple hours on a plane. He could be here and back in well under a day."

"I still don't think he did it."

"Then who did?"

She set aside her partially eaten burger. "Maybe we've been looking at this all wrong," she said. "Maybe the poisoning didn't have anything to do with Stroud. Maybe some nutso contaminated the pills after they were placed on store shelves—like the Tylenol case."

In Chicago in 1982, someone had removed bottles of Tylenol from store shelves and contaminated the pills with potassium cyanide. Seven people had died, and requirements for tamper-resistant packaging had been instituted as a result.

"We haven't found any evidence of tampering with the safety seals on the bottles of Stomach Soothers or the boxes containing the bottles," Jace said. "The forensic people examined every container they could get their hands on with X-rays. And how do we account for the missing bottles? They never made it from the factory to a store."

"Which brings us back to the idea that someone working in the factory slipped the ricin into the bottles during the packaging process?" She picked up her burger and took another bite.

"That person might be Elgin's partner," Jace said. "The one who planted the bomb. But what's the motive?"

"To destroy the company? Or maybe the Stroud family?"

"It seems like if you had an enemy who hated you that much, you'd know about it," Jace said. "And the Strouds insist they have no idea who is doing this."

"People lie," Laura said.

"They do, but we ought to be able to spot the lies."

They fell into silence, finishing their burgers and beer, letting the late afternoon stillness wash over them, a hot breeze fluttering their paper napkins and stirring the ends of Laura's hair. They were seated across from each other, not touching, yet the moment felt intimate. She pushed her empty plate away and sat back. "I like it here a lot more than I thought I would," she said, glancing around the weedy backyard, with its scraggly line of bright yellow daylilies along the fence and the arching branches of oak and catalpa providing shade.

"It has a way of getting to you," he said. "Life here moves at a slower pace, the people are a little less guarded, the landscape is so lush." He felt the pull of settling into old routines, and he couldn't say he liked it.

"How is your family?"

The question caught him off guard. He shrugged. "They're my family." He kept in touch by phone, but he hadn't let anyone know he was working so nearby. "Like all families, they do things that I love and things that drive me crazy."

She leaned toward him, elbows on the picnic table. "Like what?"

He shook his head. "They don't understand why I ever left home. Ambition isn't something they admire. It's just another word for 'getting above yourself.' They judge me for my choices, but if I do the same to them I must think I'm better than them." He shrugged. "I can't change them. I don't try anymore, and maybe that's a good thing. What about your family?"

"There's just my dad. My mom died when I was ten."

"That's rough. Do you have any brothers and sisters?"

She shook her head. "And no close family. We moved a lot, so my dad and I relied on each other."

"Still, it must have been hard, always being the new kid."

She sat up straighter. "It taught me to adapt, to learn how to fit in."

He studied her a moment. Maybe it was that second beer loosening his tongue—or maybe he just wanted to risk being honest with her. "I think it taught you to keep your distance, to not get too involved."

She frowned. He held up a hand and said, "Don't look at me that way. I didn't say there was necessarily anything wrong with that."

"You think I'm cold." Pain clouded her blue eyes. "It's all right. You wouldn't be the first to say so."

"Oh, you ought to know by now that I don't think you're cold." He moved around the table and slid onto the bench beside her. She watched him, wary, but didn't resist when he pulled her into his arms and kissed her.

YOU SHOULDN'T BE kissing him. It isn't professional. It isn't part of your mission.

Shut up. I'm not a robot. I have a life outside the mission. Laura shut her eyes, shutting out the nagging voice inside of herself—a voice that too often sounded like her father—and surrendered to the pure pleasure of kissing Jace. The pressure of his lips on hers sent sparks of awareness dancing along her nerves, awakening desires that had lain dormant too long. She leaned into his embrace, done with fighting her attraction to him.

When she finally pulled away, the heated longing in his eyes made her toes curl. "What are you thinking?" he asked.

"That we should take this inside." She stood and tugged him to his feet. Grinning now, he let her lead him into the house. When the door was closed behind them, she kissed him again, his back against the wall, his hunger matching her own.

His skin smelled of pine and soap, and the faint whiff of the barbecue smoke. He tasted of salt and cinnamon as she traced her tongue along his jaw. He groaned when she nipped at his throat, and slid his hands around to cup her bottom and snug her more firmly against him. Oh, yes— those shorts of his didn't leave any doubt how he felt about her. She smiled up at him. "Want to try out my new bed?"

"I thought you'd never ask."

She hurried through the awkwardness of shedding her clothes, sneaking looks as he took off his shorts, shirt and underwear, her heart speeding up in appreciation for his naked body. She had seen him a few times in the gym at headquarters, but she'd never admired him with the same interest before. He had plenty of sexy muscles to go with the brains and bravery that had attracted her in the first place.

They crawled into bed and moved into each other's arms, a sigh escaping her as she pressed her body to his. His hands slid up her thighs, calluses dragging on her smooth skin. The heat of his fingers pressed into her soft flesh and delved into the wetness between her legs.

She moaned, the sound muffled by the liquid heat of his tongue tangling with her own. He dipped his head to kiss her naked breasts—butterfly touches of his lips over and around the swelling flesh, then latching on to her sensitive, distended nipple, sucking hard, the pulling sensation reaching all the way to her groin, where she tightened around his plunging finger.

He stretched out beside her, kissing her deeply while his hands caressed, stroking her breasts and tracing the curve of her hips and stomach, never lingering too long at any one place. She arched toward him, anxious with need. "Shh," he soothed. "We don't have to hurry." He patted her stomach. "I'll be right back," he said, then rose and padded out of the room.

Curious, she propped herself on her elbow and enjoyed the view of him leaving the room. When he returned holding a condom packet aloft, she laughed and opened her arms to welcome him back.

The sight of him sheathing himself left her breathless. He levered himself over her, and she raised her knees and spread her legs to allow him access, but he only smiled and slid down her body, his tongue tracing the curve of her breasts, the ridges of her ribs and the hollow of her navel. By the time he plunged his tongue into her wet channel, she was quivering with need, half-mad with lust. She buried her fingers in his hair as he stroked her clit with his tongue.

"What do you want?" he whispered, his voice rough, as if he was fighting for control.

"I want you." Her voice rose at the last word, as he levered himself over her and entered her, his fingers digging into her bottom. The sensation of him filling her, stretching her, moving inside her, made her dizzy. "Don't stop," she gasped. "Please don't stop."

"I won't stop. I promise I won't stop."

He drove hard, but held her so gently, his fingers stroking, caressing, even as his hips pumped. She slid her hands around to cup his ass, marveling at the feel of his muscles contracting and relaxing with each powerful thrust.

He slipped his hand between them and began to fondle her clit, each deft move sending the tension within her coiling tighter. He kissed the soft flesh at the base of her throat. "I want to make it good for you," he murmured. "So good."

She sensed him holding back, waiting for her. When her climax overtook her, he swallowed her cries, then mingled them with his own as his release shuddered through them both.

MUCH LATER, THE dull buzz of Jace's phone vibrating across the bedside table pulled him from sleep. Eyes half-open, he groped for the device and swiped to answer it. "Hello?"

"Jace, it's Ramirez." The tension in Ramirez's voice snapped him awake. He swung his legs up to sit on the side of the bed as Laura propped herself up beside him.

"What's happened?" he asked.

"There's been another explosion at Stroud Pharmaceuticals," she said. "It's bad. That's all I know. Just…bad."

Chapter Thirteen

The chaos at Stroud Pharmaceuticals overflowed into the streets, so that blocks away, Jace maneuvered the truck through crowds of people, some openly weeping, others agitated or merely excited to know what was happening. The strobe of the light bars atop police cruisers looked garish against the soft pink and orange of sunrise.

He parked three blocks from the Stroud compound, unable to go farther, and he and Laura walked the rest of the way, joining a parade of Stroud employees headed in that direction. "I swear I heard the bomb go off," said a woman named Janice, who worked in packaging. "I had just let the dog out and I heard it. I thought it was someone hunting."

Police and county sheriff's vehicles formed a barricade at the entrance to the factory and offices. Media trucks ringed the area, satellite dishes pointed to the sky. Jace thought he spotted Rogers talking to one of the cops, and then he was swallowed up in the confusion. "I heard Mr. Stroud—Mr. Steve—is dead," Barb Falk said.

"Mr. Parker is in the hospital," Phyllis Neighbors added, blotting tears from her eyes with her index fingers.

"This is so awful," a woman Jace didn't know said. "It just keeps happening. I'm too afraid to go back in there again. Not with some nut job trying to blow up everybody."

"There's Donna." Laura tugged at Jace's sleeve and he followed her gaze to where Donna Stroud, dressed in a navy pantsuit, stood surrounded by reporters, microphones and recorders all but obscuring her face.

Jace and Laura shoved forward, ignoring the grumbling of those they displaced, until they reached the ring of reporters.

Donna Stroud's face looked drained of blood, and her voice was strained. "We will stop production for the next few days out of respect for my husband, and to protect the safety of our employees," she said.

"Do you have any idea who did this?"

"What about the suspect the police have in custody? Do they have the wrong man?"

"Why hasn't the FBI stopped this?" The reporters fired questions at the dazed woman.

"Why haven't we stopped this?" Laura muttered. Anguish haunted her gaze and anger weighted her words. "I knew there were more bombs out there. We should have insisted they close the factory."

She kept her voice low, barely audible even to Jace, but still he put his arm around her and turned her away from the reporters. "We could have insisted the Strouds close the plant, but everyone from the state legislator to local officials to the Strouds themselves would have refused," he said.

"They don't have any choice now," she said. She scanned the crowd. "Most of the employees are probably too frightened to return to work."

"Let me through. I have to talk to Donna. I have to find out about Parker."

The crowd parted and Merry, wet hair straggling around her shoulders, eyes swollen from crying, staggered forward. She clutched at Laura's shoulder. "I was in the shower when a friend called to tell me what had happened," she half sobbed. "Parker's in the hospital, but when I went down there, they wouldn't let me see him!"

Her voice rose in a wail that attracted the attention of the reporters and Donna.

Laura took the distraught young woman's arm and led her away. Jace followed, shielding them from the curious stares of those around them. "When was the last time you saw Parker?" Laura asked.

Merry sniffed. "He spent the night at my place," she said. "But he left really early this morning. His mom called about some problem with Parker's dad. He had to leave to deal with that."

"What was the problem?" Jace asked.

"I don't know. He just said he had to go deal with his dad."

"What time was this?" Laura asked.

"Early. About five o'clock." She yawned. "I went back to bed. That was the last I heard until my friend Margo called me about seven." Her face crumpled again. "She said Parker was hurt in the explosion, but no one at the hospital will tell me anything."

"Merry, pull yourself together. Parker is going to be all right." Donna Stroud moved in and put her arm around the weeping woman. "He had surgery to remove some shrapnel from his legs, but he's going to be okay."

"What happened?" Laura asked. "Merry said Parker left early this morning to help his dad?"

The lines around Donna's eyes deepened. "I woke up early this morning and Steve wasn't in bed. I realized what had woken me was the garage door opening and closing. He does that sometimes, gets restless and goes for a drive. No matter how well I think I hide the car keys, he always seems to find them."

"Where does he go?" Jace asked.

Guilt pinched her features. "Often, he comes here, to his office. That's why I called Parker. He's better at reasoning with his dad, persuading him to return home. But apparently when they got here..." She covered her mouth with one hand, choking back a sob.

"Is there anything I can do to help?" Laura asked. Something in her voice made Jace think she wasn't asking merely as a way of finding out more information, but out of genuine concern for Mrs. Stroud.

"I may need you to retrieve some reports and things from Parker's office later," Donna said. "Though I know that isn't really your job."

"For now, it is my job," Laura said, with a warning glance at Merry.

Merry seemed not to have even heard. She clutched Donna's arm. "Mrs. Stroud, was there a note?" she asked.

"I don't think now is the time to talk about that," Donna said.

Merry frowned at Jace and Laura. "Don't tell me you haven't heard about the notes from the bomber. I thought everyone knew about them by now."

"We have heard some rumors," Laura said.

Donna sighed, then reached into her pocket and took out a crumpled envelope. "This was on my desk when I got in this morning."

Jace took the envelope, handling it carefully. It was different from the others in that this one had no stamp or postmark. "What does the note inside say?" Jace asked.

"It says 'three down, three more soon.'" Donna took the note from him and returned it to her pocket. "I'll give this to Agent Ramirez or Agent Rogers when I see them," she said. "But for now, I need to focus on handling the plant closure and taking care of my family. And I need to deal with these reporters." She turned away, head up, shoulders back, a woman prepared to do battle.

"How long is the plant going to be closed?" Merry asked.

Jace had almost forgotten Merry. Now she inserted herself between him and Laura, tears and hair both drying in the early morning heat. The crowd around them had thinned somewhat, many employees drifting back to their homes or vehicles, or gathering at the far end of the parking lot to watch from a distance.

"I guess they'll keep the plant closed until they figure out who's responsible for the bombs," he said.

"They arrested Leo," Merry said. "I thought he's the one who did this. It's no secret he blames the Strouds for killing his mother."

"Leo was in jail when this bomb exploded," Jace said.

"Maybe he planted it before he was arrested."

"Maybe." None of the other explosives had been equipped with a timing mechanism, but maybe this one was different.

"I'm going to tell Donna she needs to call the hospital and let me in to see Parker," Merry said, and started after the older woman.

Laura moved in close to Jace once more. "We need to get to the hospital and talk to Parker," she said.

"How are we going to do that without blowing our cover?" he asked.

"I'm his admin. I'll say how concerned I am for him and is there anything I can do to help his mother at this difficult time."

He put his arm around her. "Has anyone ever told you you'd make a good secret agent?"

She made a face, but didn't move away. The public display of affection fit with their cover, but Jace hoped there was more than that to her desire to be close to him.

THEY HEARD PARKER long before they reached his room, his voice reverberating down the hospital corridor. "I told you I need something stronger for this pain. You need to get hold of that doctor now. I don't want to hear any more of your lame excuses."

"I see the explosion didn't do anything to dampen his charm," Jace said.

"At least he's awake and lucid enough," Laura said. They halted outside Parker's door as a young black man in blue scrubs hurried into the hallway. He scarcely glanced at them as he headed toward the nurse's station. Laura tapped on the door.

"Come in!" Parker barked.

Laura pushed open the door. "Mr. Stroud, it's me, Laura. My husband is with me."

Parker, his hair uncombed and day-old stubble softening the line of his jaw, looked younger and slightly vulnerable. Or maybe it was the faded hospital gown and network of tubes and monitors that added to his air of helplessness. "How did you get in here?" he asked. "I told them no visitors."

"No one said anything to us," Laura said. Security clearly wasn't a priority at this small hospital. Jace had popped the lock on the outside door leading to the stairway at the end of this hall and they had been able to stroll in, bypassing the nurse's station and any other authority figures. "Is there anything I can do for you?" Laura asked, approaching the bed.

"You can find my doctor and tell him I need something stronger for pain than aspirin."

"What happened?" Laura asked. "Your mother said she sent you to look for your father."

"So you've been talking to her." His expression softened. "How is she?"

"She's staying tough," Jace said. "In shock, I think, but handling the press."

"She announced she's shutting down the factory until

the police catch who did this," Laura said. "I was sorry to hear about your father."

"The stupid old fool." There was no heat behind the words. Parker slumped against the pillows. "He likes to sneak away and come to the office. It doesn't hurt anything. He types up memos or prints out reports. He doesn't even know what day it is much of the time, but he's harmless. But Mom worries, so I agreed to go get him and bring him home."

He fell silent and they waited, the silence punctuated by the beep of monitors and the whirring of the automatic blood pressure cuff.

"What happened?" Laura prompted.

"I saw his car in the parking lot, and then I spotted him going into the building," Parker said. "I followed him and he was just unlocking the door to his office when I reached him. I called out his name and he turned to me. Then everything just disintegrated." His face crumpled. "He was smiling, like he was so happy to see me."

Laura plucked a tissue from the box by the bed and passed it to him. They waited while he wept. When he had pulled himself together, Jace asked, "Did you see anything else when you got to the plant this morning? Any other cars in the lot, or anyone hanging around?"

Parker grimaced. "You sound like a cop."

"I'm curious. Who wouldn't be?"

"I didn't see anyone," Parker said. "It was early and most people were still in bed. I only passed one car on the way to the plant, and that was Phil Dorsey, on his way to open the café for breakfast."

"Merry said you were with her last night," Laura said.

"So you talked to her already," Parker said.

"She was at the plant," Laura said. "She was upset that hospital personnel wouldn't let her see you."

"I couldn't deal with her distress right now."

"But you were with her last night?" Jace asked.

"I was." He laughed, a bitter sound. "Don't ever play poker, Laura dear. Your opinion of me shows all too clearly."

Only because I wasn't trying to hide it, she thought.

"You think I'm taking advantage of the poor girl, stringing her along and taking what I want. Believe me, she's getting what she wants, too."

"What does she want?" Laura asked.

"Money. The status of being associated with my name. It may not mean much to you, but in this town, the Strouds are about as big as they get."

"Merry believes you're going to marry her," Laura said.

"I've never proposed. She doesn't have a ring."

But you haven't told her it will never happen. "Were you with Merry all night?" Jace asked.

"Yes. Though that's none of your business."

The door opened and an older woman in a skirt and blouse, a stethoscope around her neck, entered. "Mr. Stroud, I understand you're experiencing some pain."

"It's about time you got here. And yes, I'm experiencing pain. A lot of it."

Laura and Jace took that as their cue to leave. She waited until they were in the truck before she spoke. "He's terrified," she said. "That's what's behind his bluster."

"He was lucky he wasn't killed," Jace said. "His father was. That's enough to terrify anyone."

"I was almost sure he was Leo's partner," she said. The two of them had been seen together several times, and Parker was so circumspect about their relationship."

"But now you're not so sure?" Jace prompted.

"No. Why would he kill his father and risk his own life?"

"If he killed his father, he'd be more likely to inherit the business sooner," Jace said. "He hasn't made a secret of wanting his mother to turn everything over to him. And there are those rumors that he's been talking about selling to a competitor."

"But poisoning the best-selling product you make and blowing up people aren't going to get you a good price for the business," Laura said. She shifted to angle toward Jace. "And Parker couldn't count on his father going to the office this morning."

"Maybe he had the explosive with him and saw his chance," Jace said.

She took out her phone and pulled up Ramirez's number. "We stopped by the hospital and spoke to Parker," she said after her colleague had answered. "He says the bomb exploded when his dad started to open his office door."

"That sounds right," Ramirez said. "The explosives expert says this was like the others, wired to go off when a door opened."

"So no timer?" Laura asked.

"No timer," Ramirez said. "And nothing to say when the bomb was put there. Donna Stroud says no one has been in her husband's office all week. After he was diagnosed with dementia and stopped working, she moved out anything that pertained to active business. She left a computer and some older files to keep him calm on the days when he did venture into the office."

"Did she say how often Steve came in to work?" Laura asked.

"Every week to ten days he would slip away from her or his minder and come down there."

"So Steve Stroud was the intended target?" Laura asked.

"It looks that way."

"What does Leo say?"

"We haven't talked to him, but we will soon."

"I've been looking into Parker's financials and I found

some things you need to know," Laura said. She filled Ramirez in on the secret bank account and the possible blackmail.

"When did you find this out?" Ramirez asked.

"Last night." She felt a stab of guilt as she remembered her initial resolve to contact her fellow agent right away, a resolve that had faded as soon as she was in Jace's arms.

"Steve Stroud's death tells us this was definitely aimed at the Stroud family, not just the factory," Ramirez said. "That's the angle we'll be hitting hard going forward."

"Anything else we should know?" Laura asked.

"The girlfriend, Ms. Winger, was here causing a scene. She corralled a bunch of reporters and told them it was the FBI's fault that her fiancé was at death's door."

"She won't be the last person to say that," Laura said.

"I didn't join the Bureau because I wanted to be popular, did you?" Ramirez asked.

"No," Laura said, and ended the call.

"I caught most of that," Jace said. "Sounds like Merry was grabbing the spotlight while she could."

"If she keeps this up, everyone except Parker is going to think of her as his fiancé." Laura tucked her phone into the pocket of her jeans.

"That may be what she's hoping for," Jace said. "Where to now?"

"Let's go back to the trailer and I'll make breakfast," she said. "Let's review what we know and brainstorm." Maybe together they could figure out the right angle of approach.

"All right." He took the next left turn and headed back toward the trailer. Away from the Stroud factory, the town looked almost normal, only the occasional media van out of place in the everyday bustle downtown. This was the atmosphere Jace had grown up in, a small town where everyone knew everyone else, so different from the string of army bases, all different yet all the same, that had made up Laura's world back then.

"Why did you join the FBI?" she asked after a moment.

"I needed a job after I came out of the military and hunting down bad guys sounded interesting. Why did you join?"

"My father suggested it." She cleared her throat. "He knew someone who knew someone—next thing I knew, I had an interview."

"Was there something else you wanted to do instead?"

"I thought about going to vet school." At his look of surprise, she added, "I like animals."

"But you don't have a pet. Do you?"

"No. This job makes it tough. But I'd like to, one day." A dog would be great, though a cat might be easier, at least at first.

"If you could go back and do things over, would you become a veterinarian?" he asked.

"No. I like this work. And I'm good at it. I'm probably a better agent than I would have been a vet."

"I was intimidated about working with you, you know?"

She stared at him. "You're kidding."

"It's the truth. I checked your record. Commendation after commendation. You have future Special Agent in Charge written all over you. Next to you, I'm a total slacker."

She cleared her throat. "I wouldn't call you a slacker." She'd checked up on him, too. He'd been a key figure in a number of high-profile investigations, but he had also been reprimanded a handful of times for crossing the line and breaking the rules. At the time, she had resented him for taking short cuts. Now, part of her envied his willingness to take risks.

"You're not as uptight as I feared," he said.

There hadn't been anything uptight about her last night.

She squirmed at the memory. "I believe in playing by the rules," she said. "They're there to protect everyone. But I can see there are times when intent is as important as the letter of the law." Her father would groan if he heard such rationalization. He had raised her to walk a straight line and never question authority. But she wasn't a soldier on a battlefield. She was a civilian, involved in a different kind of battle, where the enemy was rarely obvious or even visible.

Chapter Fourteen

Merry kept an eye on Laura and Jace until they had gotten into their truck and driven away. Something wasn't right about those two, the way they had just showed up in town, not knowing anybody, and now they were up in everybody's business, asking all those questions like they had a right to know the answers. She hadn't missed the way they had cozied up to Donna Stroud, either, all sympathetic and helpful. They might have fooled the old woman into trusting them, but Merry was going to be keeping an eye on them.

Most of the reporters were drifting away now. Getting their attention had been a smart move. Now everyone would know how concerned she was for Parker and his family. How close she was to them. She spotted Donna trying to slip away and picked up her pace to intercept her. "Donna, wait!" she called.

Donna turned, the blank expression in her eyes like a slap to Merry. Parker's mother didn't even recognize her. "Have you heard how Parker is doing?" she asked. "I've been so worried." Maybe she should have said something about Steve first, but no, Parker needed their concern now. She stopped beside Donna. Merry couldn't believe the woman had gone to the trouble to put on a suit before coming down to face everyone. As if her image as a businesswoman was more important than this tragedy. "I wanted to visit Parker in the hospital, but they wouldn't let me in to see him," Merry said. "Maybe you could talk to them about that."

Donna was frowning now. "Merry, isn't it?" She didn't wait for confirmation. "Parker had surgery and is going to be all right but he needs his rest. I appreciate your concern, except it would be better if you didn't visit."

"Well, of course we don't want just anyone bothering him," Merry said. "But I'm a little different, don't you think? I mean, Parker and I are practically engaged."

"But since you aren't engaged yet, we're limiting visitation to immediate family."

Who was this "we"? And who was this witch to say who her son—a grown man—could see or not see? "Parker was with me last night," she said. "I think he'd want to see me."

Donna didn't say anything, merely looked right through her. Merry glared at her. "Parker hates you," she said. "Did you know that? He's a grown man, but you treat him like he's a fourteen-year-old. He'd do a great job of managing this business, but you'd rather leave a loony old man in charge than trust your own son."

Two spots of bright pink bloomed on Donna's cheeks, against her otherwise paper-white skin. "You have no right to talk to me that way," she said. "You need to leave now."

"I'll leave," Merry said. "But you won't get rid of me that easily. When Parker and I are married, just remember—I'm the one who'll be picking out your nursing home."

She felt Donna's stare like daggers in her back as she headed across the parking lot. That woman had better watch her step. Merry could make a lot more trouble for her than she could begin to imagine.

"How is a man supposed to get some rest if people keep interrupting me?" Parker Stroud raged from his hospital bed. "I told the nurse no visitors!"

"We need to talk to you now," Ana said.

Rogers followed and shut the door behind them. "What is this about?" Jace asked.

"We know about the blackmail." Ana kept her voice low. Conversational.

Parker visibly flinched. "What did you say?"

"We know about the money you paid out to your blackmailer—$100,000 so far." She shifted on the bed to face him more directly. "Of course, that's just a drop in the bucket compared to the balance in your Steven Parker account, but at this pace, it won't be long before you're all but bankrupt."

"I... I don't know what you're talking about." But all color had drained from his face and his heart monitor beat a rapid tattoo. As good as a lie detector, Ana thought.

"You do," Rogers said. "Someone is extorting money from you. Why is that? Is it because you put that poison in the Stomach Soothers?"

Parker swallowed and regained some of his composure. "You're just making wild accusations," he said. "You can't prove anything."

"But we will," Ana said. "We'll find out who those payments were to, and we'll trace the poison, too."

"Get out of here," he ordered. "This is harassment."

Ana stood. "We'll leave. But we're going to be watching you closely. Don't do anything foolish."

BACK AT THE TRAILER, Jace made a fresh pot of coffee while Laura tore off a big piece of parchment paper from the roll in the pantry and pinned it to the pantry door, across from the kitchen table. She unearthed a couple of markers. She welcomed the opportunity to focus on the case, to prove, if only to herself, that she and Jace could still work well together even after they had become intimate. She had always been very disciplined about keeping her personal and business lives separate. The line was fuzzier with Jace, but she intended to try to keep it clear. "Sit down and let's review what we know about this case," she said.

Chuckling, Jace pulled out a chair and dropped into it. He sipped his coffee, a half smile teasing his lips.

"What's so amusing?" Laura asked.

"Like I said, you're a future Special Agent in Charge."

He probably meant that as an insult, but she refused to take it that way. "Do you want to stand up here and write?" she asked. "Because you can."

"Oh, no. You're much better at this than I am." He sipped his coffee. "It's a good idea," he added. "Let's get to it."

She uncapped the marker and turned to the paper. "Let's start with the timeline." She wrote "May 1. First victims of poisoned Stomach Soothers."

"Go back further," Jace said. "To April 29. That's when that particular lot of medication was manufactured. It was shipped the next day."

"That's good to know." She added in this information, then listed the other known deaths. "Gini Elgin died May 2," she said. "As far as we know, that's what brings Leo into the case."

"As far as we know," Jace said.

She wrote "May 6—first bombing at Stroud Pharmaceuticals," then added in the dates of the other bombings, along with the fatalities from each.

"All the bombs were in the executive offices," Jace said. "All places Donna Stroud was most likely to have been— the door she used when she arrived early at the office, the door to her office, and the door to her husband's office."

"She said she didn't use her husband's office," Laura said.

"But I'll bet she went in there sometimes. She was more likely to do so than anyone else."

"Donna Stroud was the most likely target," Laura said. "Why?"

"With her husband incapacitated, she's in charge of the business," Jace said.

"Who stands to gain with her out of the picture?" Laura asked. "A rival?"

"Her son would take over the business if she died or couldn't continue to manage it," Jace said.

"Anyone else?"

"We'll have to find out if anyone else inherits," Jace said.

"Merry would benefit if she married Parker," Laura said.

"I don't think Parker has any intention of marrying her," Jace said. "And unless she's a lot dimmer than she looks, she knows it."

Laura studied the paper a moment. "Let's talk about the poisoning for a minute. That's the first tragedy, and maybe it triggered everything else. Could it have been an accident? Something gone wrong in the manufacturing process? All the ingredients in the product are natural, right? Ricin is natural, too. It's from the castor bean plant. Maybe someone mistook it for something else."

"Ricin is deadly," Jace said. "It's not something people have just lying around. It certainly isn't used in anything Stroud makes. And only a few bottles of Stomach Soothers were found to be contaminated—less than a dozen. If the ricin was mistakenly used in a whole batch of product, we would have found hundreds of bottles that were contaminated."

"Which brings us back to who had the opportunity to insert the poison in those bottles, and why?"

"There were eight people on the manufacturing line the day those packages were processed." Jace ticked the names off on his fingers. "All of them are long-time employees who are still with the company. We've checked them and nothing stands out or suggests a motive for sabotage."

"Parker Stroud runs the plant and would have easy access to all parts of the manufacturing process," Laura said.

"So would his mother," Jace said. "And his father, too."

Laura frowned. "Would Steve Stroud have put ricin in those bottles of pills? Why?"

"Let's find out where he was, just to be sure," Jace said. "I looked up the report on the security footage for that day. It doesn't cover the whole line, but it does show that Donna and Parker Stroud were both on the production floor, along with Gini Elgin and Merry Winger."

"Merry was there? And Gini?"

"Merry brought lunch to Parker. Gini came down to talk to him."

Laura added this information to the paper, then backed up to stand beside Jace. "Parker still has the best motive and opportunity for all the crimes," she said. "Maybe he had set the bomb for his mother and his father getting there first was an accident. Trying to save his father, Parker was hurt, which tends to direct our suspicions away from him."

"I want to talk to Merry again," Jace said. "I think she knows something she isn't telling us."

"Something about Parker?" Laura asked.

"She's hiding something. I just haven't figured out what yet."

"PARKER IS HURT? Mr. Stroud dead?" Leo clutched his head and moaned. "That wasn't supposed to happen."

"What was supposed to happen, Leo?" Rogers slapped both palms on the table and leaned over the younger man. "We know you made those bombs. Another person is dead and one badly injured because of you. If you want this to stop, you have to tell us who has the other explosives, so we can stop them."

Leo moaned and rocked in his chair. Ana sat beside him. "I know you didn't mean for this to happen," she said, her voice soft.

He shook his head. "No."

"Maybe you just thought the bombs would frighten people," Ana said. "You wanted to make them listen."

His answering groan could have been a yes.

Ana put a hand on his arm. "How many bombs did you make?" she asked.

"Six." Another long moan.

Ana locked eyes with Rogers, her alarm evident. Three people had died in the first three explosions. How many more would die if three more bombs were let loose?

"Who did you give the bombs to?" Ana asked.

He shook his head. "I can't tell you."

Rogers leaned forward again, but Ana waved him away. "Why can't you tell us?" she asked.

"Because I promised." He raised his head, his face a mask of anguish. "I swore on my mother's grave."

"I think your mother would want you to help us and stop the killing," Ana said.

"Is Parker going to be all right?"

"He had to have surgery to remove some shrapnel," Rogers said. "He should recover, though he'll probably have scars the rest of his life."

Leo's lips trembled, and he struggled for control. "Parker tried to make things right after my mother died," he said. "I didn't want to listen to him, but he never stopped reaching out. We were friends in school. He never shut me out the way some people did. The way his mother did."

"How did Donna Stroud shut you out?" Ana asked.

Anger hardened his features, making him look older. "I went to see her and she refused to talk to me. She shut the door in my face."

"I'll bet that made you angry," Rogers said. "If I were

in your position, I might have wanted to do something to hurt her."

Leo didn't confirm or deny this.

"You made the bombs," Rogers continued. "Six of them. Why six?"

"I only made one to begin with. It wasn't supposed to kill anyone. Just frighten them."

"So you put the first bomb at Stroud Pharmaceuticals," Rogers said. "The one that killed Lydia Green?"

"No! I wouldn't do that. I told you, I liked Lydia."

"So you made the first bomb," Rogers said. "Then you made more?"

"Leo, you didn't put those bombs at the Stroud offices, did you?" Ana asked.

"No! I didn't. I didn't have anything to do with that."

"But you know who did put them there," Ana said. "We need to know who that person is so that we can stop them before they hurt someone else."

Leo shook his head.

Rogers leaned over Leo, his face very close, his eyes fierce. "Three bombs have exploded, Leo. Three people have died. How many more bombs are going to kill how many more people before you tell us the truth?"

"I can't tell you." He shoved back his chair and stood, Rogers and Ana rising to their feet also. "I don't want to talk anymore," Leo said. "I want to see my lawyer."

Ana and Rogers's eyes locked again. "We'll call your lawyer," Rogers said. "She'll tell you it's in your best interest to talk to us."

He led the way out of the room, as two officers entered to escort Leo back to his cell. "He's going to break," Rogers said.

"Yes," Ana agreed. "But will he tell us in time to prevent more people dying?"

MERRY LIVED IN a pale gray cottage in a neighborhood of older homes, many in the process of being renovated. Flowers crowded the beds alongside the front fence and either side of the walkway leading to the front door—ruffled hollyhocks in every shade of pink, orange daylilies like upturned bells, red and yellow and white zinnias and snapdragons filling every gap like dropped candies. "What do you two want?" Merry asked when she answered the door.

"We wanted to make sure you're okay," Laura said.

"Why wouldn't I be okay?"

"Your fiancé is in the hospital," Laura said. "Did you get to see him?"

"No." Merry stepped onto the porch and pulled the door shut behind her. "We can talk out here." She led the way into the garden. "I tried to see him and this sour-faced nurse told me only family was allowed to visit. Then I asked Donna to talk to her and she had the nerve to tell me that until Parker and I are officially engaged, I'm not family." She snapped a fading flower from one of the hollyhocks and crushed it in her hand.

"That was harsh," Jace said.

"Oh, I wasn't surprised." Merry snatched another wilting flower head and flung it into the grass. "She's as cold as they come. She's made Parker's life miserable. He's an intelligent man with lots of great ideas for the business, yet she treats him like a stupid boy."

"Merry, you're probably closer to Parker than anyone," Jace said. "Do you have any idea who might want to hurt him or his family?"

Merry stopped and looked him in the eye. "Why are you so interested?" she demanded.

"With the factory closed, we don't have jobs," Laura said. "The police and FBI aren't getting anywhere finding the person who planted those bombs, so we figure we might as well try to solve the case ourselves."

"We haven't got anything better to do," Jace said. "Maybe, being amateurs, we'll get lucky." He winked at Laura, who quickly looked away, biting the inside of her cheek to keep from laughing.

Merry returned to dead-heading spent flowers. "If you ask me, the cops ought to be taking a closer look at Donna."

"Donna Stroud?" Laura asked.

Merry nodded. "I already told you she's cold. She probably set those bombs herself to get rid of her loony husband. She had to be paying out a fortune to have people watch him while she's working."

"But what about Angela Dupree and Lydia Green?" Laura asked. "Why would she want to kill them?"

"I don't know. Maybe Angela was too needy. Maybe the cleaner found something incriminating in the trash can and was blackmailing her?"

"Do you think Parker could have set those bombs?" Laura asked. "Maybe because he resented the way his mother treated him? He wants to be in charge of the business."

"Parker?" Merry laughed. "Parker could never kill anyone. He doesn't have the nerve." She brushed her hands on the thighs of her denim shorts. "Parker likes to complain, but he doesn't have the guts to do something like that."

"Who would you say does have the guts?" Jace asked.

Merry smiled. "His mother, but you already know that. I can't think of anyone else." She faced them, hands on her hips. "Now let me ask you a question—what are you really up to?"

Laura kept her expression bland. "What do you mean? We're trying to solve this crime so we can get our jobs back."

"I mean, what are you doing in Mayville? You don't

have relatives here. You didn't know anyone here before you showed up out of the blue. This isn't some garden spot everyone wants to come to. You must have had a reason."

Laura searched for a plausible answer. She was usually good at thinking on her feet but right now she was struggling.

"My family is in Hatcher, just across the border in Tennessee," Jace said. "We wanted to be close to them, but not too close. Anyway, there aren't any jobs in Hatcher. There are here."

Merry looked disappointed. "That's the truth?"

"What were you expecting, Merry?" Laura asked. "We came for the jobs. As you pointed out, there's no other reason to be here."

"You get on so well with Donna Stroud, I thought maybe you had some connection to the family."

Jace laughed. "That's rich. So, what are we, the poor relations thrilled about living in a crappy trailer and working in their factory?"

Merry smiled. "I guess it is a little silly." The smile faded. "And I guess it shows how much Donna hates me. She'd rather hire a stranger to be her son's admin than give me the job."

"Some women are very protective of their sons," Laura said. Though she felt a pinch of sympathy for Merry. She had painted a not very attractive picture of Donna Stroud.

"Let us know if you hear anything interesting and we'll do the same," Jace said. He took Laura's arm. "We'll get out of your hair now."

Arm in arm, they left the yard. When Merry and her cottage were no longer visible, Laura relaxed a little. "Do you still think she's hiding something?"

"I don't know. But we'd better let Ramirez and Rogers know they should take a closer look at Donna Stroud."

"Yeah." They hadn't considered Donna as a suspect

before now because she seemed to be the person with the most to lose in all these crimes. But what if she had even more to gain?

"For what it's worth, my mom would be thrilled to know I'd taken up with you," Jace said.

The statement, or rather, the idea that he had been thinking of her in relation to his family, startled her. "Would she really? Why?"

"You're smart. Beautiful. Not afraid to get in my face when you think I screw up. My mom would appreciate all of that."

The idea was flattering, but when she considered her father's likely reaction to Jace, the fleeting satisfaction vanished. "My dad is harder to read."

"I'm betting I dealt with plenty like him in the army. Proud, strong and loyal. Also by the book and unbending. He'd hate my guts. At least until I won him over." He grinned, surprising a laugh from her. "What? You don't think I could win him over?"

She shook her head, unable to speak. Jace had won her over, and not that long ago she would have said that was impossible. "I'm not worried about my dad." She took his hand. "My dad taught me to make my own decisions, so my opinion is the only one that really counts."

"What is your opinion?" He tried to keep his voice light, but she heard the tension in his words.

"You're more complicated than I thought," she said. "I like complicated."

"We have that in common." He squeezed her hand, sending a thrill through her. She could get used to this, but she didn't trust the feeling. As an agent, she was confident in her ability to evaluate a situation and stay on top of a case. But when it came to romance, she was a rank amateur, and she didn't like her odds of succeeding.

THE FOURTH BOMB exploded at two o'clock the next morning, on Merry Winger's front porch. No one was injured, but the explosion sent a wave of terror through the town. Before, the Strouds had clearly been the target of the bomber. Now, it seemed, almost anyone could be a victim.

The poisonings had frightened people, but to avoid that danger, all you had to do was avoid taking Stomach Soothers—or all Stroud products if you were extra cautious.

But a bomb—how did you avoid a bomb? How did you live with that kind of fear?

Chapter Fifteen

"Where were you last night from approximately 8 p.m. until 6 a.m.?"

Donna Stroud, pale and disheveled, didn't look like herself without her suit and makeup. The local police had visited her home a little after seven that morning, and found her dressed in faded pink cotton trousers and a Smoky Mountains National Park T-shirt. To Ana, she scarcely resembled the competent professional she had met with her first day in town.

"Where was I last night?" Confusion clouded Donna's blue eyes. "Why is that important?"

"Please answer the question," Ana said. She and Rogers and Captain Simonson, of the Mayville Police Department, sat across the table from Donna and her lawyer, Adam Sepulveda, a local attorney who, after blustering a few feeble protests, had remained silent, occasionally fidgeting in his chair or tugging at his tie.

"I was at the hospital, visiting my son, until almost eight," Donna said. "Then I went home."

"Was anyone at home with you?" Ana asked.

"No."

"Did you talk to anyone on the phone, or speak to a neighbor? Is there anyone who can confirm that you were home last night?"

Donna sat up straighter, a little life coming back into

her face. "I told you I was there and I don't lie. There isn't any other proof, but I don't see why you need it."

"What's your relationship with Merry Winger?" Rogers asked.

Donna's eyebrows rose, disappearing beneath her fringe of short bangs. "Merry works in the administrative offices of Stroud Pharmaceuticals. She is also involved with my son."

"Involved?" Ana thought this was an interesting word choice.

"I know he sleeps with her and buys her gifts, but I've rarely seen them out together, and he's never brought her to our house, so I wouldn't call her his girlfriend."

"You don't like her," Rogers said.

"She wouldn't be my first choice for my son, but most people learn best by making their own mistakes."

"You think Merry is a mistake?" Ana asked.

"Time will tell." She spread her hands flat on the table in front of her. "What is this about? Has something happened to that girl?"

"Why do you think something happened to her?" Rogers asked. "What would have happened?"

"You asked me where I was last night. That tells me you're trying to establish my alibi. Then you ask me about Merry, a young woman I scarcely know. I don't have to be an amateur detective to put the two ideas together. Did something happen to her?"

"Merry is fine," Ana said. "But a bomb exploded on her front porch this morning."

Donna stared, mouth slack and eyes wide. She made a low sound in the back of her throat, and Ana was afraid for a moment that the older woman was having a heart attack or stroke. Ana touched her arm and Donna stared at her, then gradually came back to herself. She wet her lips. "Was it…was it like the others?" she asked.

"It was similar," Rogers said.

In fact, the bomb was identical to the other three, set to go off when the front door was opened, as Merry would have done when she went out to work in her flower garden or to get into her car, parked at the curb. Instead, the bomb had exploded when her neighbor had driven by on his way to work, in a custom pickup with oversized tires, rumbling exhaust and throbbing bass that shook the windows of every house as it passed.

"The bomb exploded accidentally," Ana said. "No one was hurt, but if Merry had opened her front door, she would have been killed, or very badly injured."

Donna covered her mouth with her hand and tears filled her eyes.

"Did you put that explosive device on Merry Winger's front porch?" Rogers asked.

"No! I would never do something like that. Not to anyone, ever!"

"My client is a law-abiding pillar of the community who has never had so much as a traffic ticket," the lawyer said. "I strongly object to this line of questioning."

"You're not in court," Rogers said. He turned his attention back to Donna. "Do you have any idea who might have put that bomb on Merry's front porch?"

"No. I swear if I did, I would tell you. I want this to stop."

"Mrs. Stroud, the first explosion at Stroud Pharmaceuticals, on May 6, was wired to a side door used only by personnel who had a key," Rogers said. "You yourself stated that you were usually the first person at the office each morning, and that you always entered via that door. Several people have confirmed this."

"Yes."

"Yet the morning the bomb exploded, you were not the

first to arrive at the building. Instead, Lydia Green opened that door and was killed."

"I was dealing with my husband. He was agitated and I had to calm him down before I came to work."

"The second explosive device was wired to the door of your office," Rogers continued. When it exploded, it killed Angela Dupree. Again, you were late for work that day, something several people have stated was highly unusual."

"My husband isn't at his best in the mornings."

"The third explosion, the one that killed your husband and injured your son, was wired to your husband's office door," Rogers said. "Everyone we spoke with said that you and your husband were the only people who entered that office since your husband's retirement, but he was there only occasionally. You were the mostly likely target of that explosive device and yet once again, you escaped injury."

"What are you implying?" Donna asked.

"We've reviewed the incorporation papers for Stroud Pharmaceuticals," Ana said. "As written, your husband has primary authority over the business until his death. No provision was made in the case of his disability by illness or injury. While you were acting administrator, you had no real authority to expand or sell the business. Your ability to borrow money for the business was also limited. Your husband's death frees you to make those kind of decisions."

"I did not kill my husband," Donna said, her voice trembling. She gripped the edge of the table. "I didn't kill anyone."

"Mrs. Stroud has lost her husband." The lawyer stood. "Her own life has been threatened several times. For you to suggest—"

"Someone connected with Stroud Pharmaceuticals is planting these bombs and killing people," Rogers said. "It's our job to take a hard look at everyone who had motive and opportunity. Mrs. Stroud had both."

"I didn't do it," Donna said. "I swear." She bent her head and began to weep, shoulders shaking.

Ana turned away. Though she wasn't convinced of Donna's innocence, she felt sorry for this woman who had lost so much.

"We can continue this interview later," Rogers said.

"I demand that you release my client at once," the lawyer said.

"She's free to go," Rogers said. "But we're continuing our investigation."

Ana walked with Rogers to the observation room where Smitty and Cantrell waited with Rowan, who had returned to Mayville last night. "How long do you think it's going to be before a story shows up in the local paper about how the FBI is bullying the newly widowed patron saint of Mayville?" Rowan asked.

Rogers dropped into the chair at the end of the table. "You tell me—how long?"

"I'd say about twenty-four hours. That lawyer had the look of someone who will hurry to get the press on his client's side."

"Then he's smarter than I gave him credit for," Rogers said. "You and I both know we're not here to win friends. And right now, Donna Stroud had the most to gain from getting rid of her husband, the chief financial officer who maybe had too tight a hold on the company purse strings, and her son's lover whom she didn't approve of."

"She also had the most to lose," Smitty said. "Her husband, her best friend, and the reputation of the business she devoted most of her adult life to."

"Do you think she's innocent?" Ana asked.

Smitty tucked her long hair behind one ear. "I'm not saying she's innocent or guilty," she said. "I just think it's good to keep all the evidence in mind, not just the parts that fit one theory."

That was vintage by-the-book Smitty. Rogers glared at her. He and Smitty had clashed more than once over her penchant for telling others how to do their jobs.

Ana shifted her gaze to Cantrell. Of all the team members, he and Smitty had locked horns the most, and she expected him to come to Rogers's defense. Instead, he leaned back in his chair, relaxed. "The trouble with this case is, every one of our suspects has just as good reasons he or she isn't responsible for these crimes as anyone else," he said.

"That just tells me we need more evidence," Rogers said. "We get the right information, we'll find the right person."

"Did the locals uncover anything useful at Merry's house?" Smitty asked.

"We gave it a good going over and didn't find anything," Chief Simonson said.

"Merry says she worked in her garden until about eight last night," Rogers said. "She went in, ate a sandwich and watched TV in her bedroom until ten thirty, then went to bed. She never heard anyone outside and she didn't see anything suspicious."

"Her bedroom is at the back of the house," Simonson said. "If she had the television on, she probably wouldn't hear anyone up front. She doesn't have a dog to alert her to a stranger's presence."

"All the other explosives have been at the Stroud plant," Ana said. "Why target Merry with this one?"

"Because someone—Donna Stroud, or maybe Parker Stroud—wants to get rid of her," Cantrell said.

"Or because the bomber thinks Merry knows something, and is afraid she'll tell," Smitty said.

"Parker was in the hospital last night," Simonson said. "He's supposed to be discharged this morning."

"What about Leo?" Rogers asked.

"He's still locked up tight. And he hasn't had any visitors or talked to anyone but his lawyer, who is still advising him not to talk to law enforcement."

"Has anyone told him about this latest bombing?" Smitty asked.

"I don't think so," the captain said.

"Tell him, and let us know his reaction," Rogers said.

The door to the conference room opened and a young woman stuck her head in. "I'm sorry to disturb you, Chief, but you're needed up front. We have a, um, situation."

"What kind of situation?" Simonson asked, already on his feet.

"Parker Stroud is up front, demanding to see you."

Ana and Rogers followed the captain down the hall to the police department lobby, where Parker Stroud looked as enraged as a man can when he's leaning on crutches and dressed in sweat pants, rubber sandals and an untucked dress shirt. When he spotted the captain, he lurched forward. "Are you out of your mind?" he shouted. "Arresting my mother? Hasn't the woman suffered enough without you digging your knife in?"

"Your mother is not under arrest," the captain said. "She agreed to answer some questions for us and you should find her at home now."

Parker spotted Ana and Rogers. "You're behind this," he said. "You can't find anyone else to pin this on, so you go after a helpless old woman."

Ana doubted Donna would thank her son for referring to her as either helpless or old. "Gathering evidence in a case like this requires asking lots of questions," she said. "We can't afford to omit anyone who might have the answers we need."

"My mother doesn't know anything." He leaned more heavily on his crutches, his face gray beneath the scruff of beard. "And she's the person someone is obviously trying to kill."

"And you have no idea who that person might be?" Rogers asked.

"No." Parker shook his head.

"What about Merry?" Ana asked.

He frowned. "What about her?"

"A bomb exploded on her front porch early this morning," Rogers said.

"Oh God." He wiped his face with his hand. "Is she—"

"She's fine," Ana said. "She was inside when it happened. No one was hurt. You hadn't heard?"

"I was just released from the hospital. No one there said anything. Where is she now?"

"I believe she's home," the captain said. "The damage was only to the porch and the front room."

"I should probably go see her," Parker said.

"You don't sound very enthusiastic," Rogers said.

"Yeah, well, I've been trying to find a way to break things off with her."

"You don't think she'll take it well?" Ana asked.

He grimaced. "Let's put it this way—if Merry gets her hand on one of those bombs, she'll probably gladly launch it at me."

Chapter Sixteen

"What are we missing?" Laura stared at the sheets of parchment she had taped to the pantry door, each filled with the notes she and Jace had made about the case. For the last hour, they had been going over everything on those pages, searching for a clue they had previously overlooked. Lists of victims, suspects, timelines, data, and other details that might or might not help solve the crimes crowded the paper, written in Laura's neat block printing.

She stabbed a finger at Steve Stroud's name. "We should have talked to him," she said. "He accused Parker of negotiating to sell the business to a competitor. What if that was true? And he kept insisting on sneaking off to his office—maybe because he knew something shady was going on there. Now we'll never have a chance to hear what he might have told us."

"He had dementia." Jace slouched in a kitchen chair, legs stretched out in front of him, hands shoved deep in the pockets of his jeans. "We didn't question him because he wasn't a reliable witness."

"We should have tried," she said. "A mistake like that could cost us this case. It may have already cost lives." The idea that Steve might still be alive if she had acted faster or done a better job nagged at her.

"Beating yourself up over this isn't going to help." Jace stood and walked to her. "Let's give it a rest." He put his arms around her and drew her close. "Tomorrow morning we'll be fresher. Maybe we'll see something new."

She leaned against him, drawing strength from the power of his arms around her. She had always resisted the idea of dating within the Bureau, believing it wise to keep her work life and the rest of her life strictly separate. But there was something to be said for being with someone who understood how consuming the job could be, and the emotional as well as the physical toll the work could take.

He brushed his lips across her temple, then her cheek, then he found her mouth and kissed her deeply, until she was breathless, her whole body humming with desire. He danced his fingers down her bare arms, sending tremors of pleasure through her. He grasped her hips and she arched toward him, weak-kneed with wanting.

"I think we should go to bed now," he said, his voice rough. "Though I'm tempted to take you right there on the table."

His impatience sent a fresh heat through her. She had a vision of plates and papers flying as he laid her back on the table. "Too messy," she said, breathless. "Too...hard."

"I thought you liked it hard." He rocked forward, letting her feel how ready he was for her.

She responded by cupping his fly, smiling as he hissed out a breath through his teeth. Still holding him, she started backing toward the bedroom, thrilling to the naked desire in his eyes as he followed her.

She was more sure of herself with him this time, a little more bold. After they undressed, when he took the condom from the box by the bed, she claimed the little packet, pushed him back on the mattress, and sheathed him while he watched, reaching for her when she straddled him.

They made love at a leisurely pace, watching each other as they moved, not saying much, but so intensely in the moment words hardly seemed necessary. He let her take the lead, responding to her guidance with a skill that kept her on edge for a long time before she came.

Afterward, she lay in his arms, spent and satisfied. "No more bombs tonight," he murmured, pulling the blankets over her shoulders. "I feel too good to move for at least the next eight hours."

She tried to think of a reply, but drifted to sleep before the words came to her.

Then she was in a house full of dark rooms, running from some unseen pursuer, barefoot and panicked, up steep flights of stairs and down long, narrow hallways. She stopped at the door at the end of the hallway, but it refused to open, no matter how hard she pulled on the knob or shoved at the swollen frame. Meanwhile, her pursuer came closer, his footsteps heavy on the bare wooden floors, his dark silhouette filling her with terror.

"Laura, wake up. It's all right. It's only a dream."

She came to with the sensation of landing hard on the floor, though she was safe in bed, Jace holding her to him. "It's okay." He smoothed her hair back from her face and kissed her forehead. "You're safe," he said.

"I dreamed someone was chasing me," she said. "And I couldn't get away. The door was locked and I couldn't escape."

"It doesn't take Freud to figure out that one," he said. "You're pursued by the case you can't solve." He pulled her closer. "Don't be so hard on yourself. You're doing all you can. We all are."

She nodded, but she didn't believe him. Yes, everyone on the team was working hard, but was it hard enough? Was she letting her personal life—her relationship with Jace—distract her from the job? Her father's voice echoed in her head: *Duty before self. Service to your country demands no less.* That was the life he had lived, reminding her whenever she whined about not seeing him enough that he had a whole company of soldiers who depended on him, and she was just one little girl.

"No more bad dreams," Jace said, rubbing her shoulder. "I'm here with you."

Her eyes stung, and she closed her eyes to hold back the tears, breathed in deeply his clean, masculine scent, and fell asleep in his arms, not dreaming, not afraid, not alone.

JACE WOKE AT first light and slipped out of bed without waking Laura. He went into the kitchen and started coffee, then stood at the back window and watched the sunrise filter through the trees. The world looked so peaceful this time of day. Even in the worst of the fighting in Afghanistan there had been a kind of peace at sunrise, as if everything was pausing, taking a deep breath before the next bad thing happened.

The rich aroma of coffee drifted to him and he turned to pull a mug from the cabinet. The sound of water running told him Laura was awake, and he took down a second mug for her, then smiled to himself. He had begun this assignment thinking it might be difficult to pretend to be married to her. Instead, he had fallen into the role so easily it frightened him sometimes. She was so fierce, and prickly, strong yet sensitive. He felt protective of her, though he was aware she didn't really need him at all. She wasn't his type—he liked simple women who didn't demand a lot from him. Laura was complicated, the type of woman with high standards he had no hope of meeting.

Yet here they were together, and it felt good. It felt right. He swallowed coffee, almost burning his tongue, glad of the pain to clear some of the sentimental fog from his head. Being with Laura right now was great, but he'd be a fool to think they had a future together. Sooner or later the lust would wear off and they'd go back to being two people with different ways of looking at the world.

Laura shuffled into the kitchen, damp hair curling around her face. "Good morning," he said, and filled a mug with coffee and handed it to her.

"Thanks." She closed her eyes and drank deeply, then sighed. "I've been thinking about the case," she said.

And here I was hoping you were thinking about me. But he didn't say it—the words were too close to the truth. "Did you come up with any new angles?" he asked instead.

"Whoever Leo made those bombs for, it's someone who knew he had the ability to make them," she said. "Someone he cares enough about to risk breaking the law for. Someone he won't give up, even to save himself."

Leo didn't have siblings or children of his own. "A lover?" Jace asked.

"I think so." Laura sipped more coffee.

"Man or woman?" Jace asked.

"It could be either," she said. "We need to dig deeper."

"He's not that old," Jace said. "I can't think he would have had that many serious relationships."

"We should start with high school," she said. "He went to school here in town and sometimes young relationships are extra intense. Maybe he reconnected when he came back here following his mother's death. His old flame saw the chance to even some scores with the Strouds."

"You're thinking someone who works at the plant?" Jace asked. "All the evidence points that way."

"Right. So we go to the school, ask questions, check the yearbook. He was the mad bomber, so he has that reputation to build on, even if the bomb he made back then wasn't real." She set her cup aside and straightened. "It's your turn to make breakfast while I get dressed. Then we can visit the high school."

And that was that. No good morning kiss. Nothing about

last night. The ardent lover of last night replaced by all-business Special Agent Smith.

Complicated.

MAYVILLE HIGH SCHOOL—Home of the Mayville Wild Cats!—had the institutional appearance shared by schools and prisons, the former usually with a large sports complex nearby, the latter encircled with razor wire. On this late-spring Saturday, the campus was nearly deserted, and their steps echoed as they crossed the empty parking lot to the front entrance.

"Were you a jock in high school?" Laura asked. "Quarterback of the football team, basketball star?"

"Tight end," he said. "And I played baseball, not basketball. Pitcher." In those days, he had dreamed of going pro, but he'd never had that kind of talent. "Let me guess, you were valedictorian."

She stared. "How did you know?"

"How could you not be?" He held open the door to the front office. Principal Mike Caldwell had agreed to meet them here.

The burly man with the gray crew cut who emerged from a back office to greet them reminded Jace of every drill sergeant he had ever met. Caldwell shook both their hands, examined their IDs, then ushered them into his office. "I'm guessing this has something to do with that mess over at Stroud," he said, settling his big frame behind a desk almost obscured by neat stacks of papers. "How can I help?"

"We're trying to find out more about a former student," Laura said. "Leo Elgin."

"I heard you'd arrested him. I suppose you heard about that whole mad bomber fiasco. It wasn't a real bomb, just a hotheaded kid being stupid."

"Did you know Leo?" Laura asked.

"Oh, I knew him. I coached football and track and taught civics. I had Leo in one of my classes."

"What was he like?" Jace asked. "Other than hot-headed."

"He was smart. Too smart for his own good. What I mean is kids like that get bored, then they get into trouble, like that fake bomb thing." He leaned forward, hands clasped on the desk. "Leo had a beef with the teacher he'd given the thing to. She'd marked him down on an exam for getting an answer wrong. Something to do with a higher mathematical theory. Turns out, Leo was right and she was wrong, but he never forgave her for the mistake."

"So he held grudges?" Laura asked.

"Yes, I'd say so."

"Was he popular?" Jace asked. "Who were his friends?"

"He was popular enough. Not in the most popular crowd, but most people seemed to like him. He had a reputation as a kind of a rebel and some kids admire that."

"Any girlfriends?" Jace asked.

Caldwell nodded. "He was surprisingly popular with the girls. I don't remember him being involved with anyone in particular, but he had quite a few female admirers, considering he wasn't athletic or all that good-looking."

"Can you think of anyone he dated who still lives in the area?" Jace asked. "Anyone who works at Stroud?"

Caldwell rubbed his chin. "I can't, really," he said.

"Do you have yearbooks from when Leo was a student here?" Laura asked. "We'd like to look at them."

"I do." He rolled his chair to the bookcase that filled most of the back wall, selected four thick volumes, then rolled over to the desk and slid them to Laura.

"The Beacon," Jace read the name on the cover of the top volume.

Caldwell stood. "I've got to attend a graduation rehearsal this afternoon, but you're welcome to use my office to look at those."

"Thanks," Jace said. "But we might want to take one or more of them with us."

"Just promise to return them, please. We have a complete set dating back to 1926 and I'd hate to break up the collection."

"Sure thing. We'll give you a receipt."

Laura was already engrossed in the first volume by the time Jace pulled the truck into the driveway of the trailer. "The index has a list of every student by class," she said. "Start there and see how many names ring a bell. Later, we can compare them with the employee list from Stroud."

In the next hour they found the names of a dozen former students who now worked at Stroud, including Parker Stroud. They looked at Leo's picture. He stared into the camera directly, an approximation of a sneer curling his lip. "Tell me the truth," Jace said. "Would he have done it for you when you were a high school girl?"

She shrugged. "Hard to say. I liked smart guys. And there's something about a bad boy." Laughter danced in her eyes and he fought the urge to lean over and kiss her.

Instead, he shut the book. "There are pictures in here of Leo with groups of kids, but nothing that says 'big romance' to me."

"To me, either." She studied the stack of books and shook her head. "I don't think there's anything here. We need to try college."

"He attended West Virginia University," Jace said. "That's about three hours from here."

Laura shoved back her chair and rose. "Then it's time for a road trip."

Chapter Seventeen

Merry logged on to her online bank account Saturday morning and smiled to herself when she saw the balance. Parker was so generous. Too bad things weren't going to work out the way she had hoped. But a smart woman knew when to cut her losses.

She signed out of the bank's website and clicked over to the travel page she had bookmarked. Where should she take her dream vacation?

Her phone rang. Annoyed at the interruption, she checked the display. Why was Donna Stroud calling her? Maybe all the bad press had guilted the Strouds into offering to pay the employees who'd been put out of work by the sudden plant closure. It wasn't like the family couldn't afford it. "Hello?" Merry injected an extra note of pleasantness into her voice.

"Merry, it's Donna Stroud."

Had the woman never heard of caller ID? "Hello, Mrs. Stroud. How are you doing?"

"I'm as well as can be expected. I called because I've decided to operate Stroud Pharmaceuticals out of my home office until the plant reopens. I'll need you to report there for work at nine Monday morning. You know where that is, don't you?"

Did she know where that was—really! The Strouds only owned the biggest house in town, a white-columned monstrosity straight out of *Gone with the Wind*. "I can't come in Monday," Merry said.

"Why not?" Donna asked.

"I have two weeks' time off due. While the plant is closed, I decided to take a vacation."

"I really need you to put that on hold until this situation is resolved," Donna said. "I know it's a sacrifice, but it's necessary for the future health of the company."

Merry didn't give a fig about the company. "I'm sorry, but I've already booked my tickets." She hit the Purchase Reservation button.

"How long will you be gone?" Donna asked.

"I'm not sure." She had purchased a one-way ticket.

"Merry, I can't allow this," Donna said. "You should have talked to me before you made your plans."

"Excuse me, but you're not my mother. I don't need your permission to take a vacation."

"There's no need to take that attitude. I'm simply saying I expect every team member to contribute one-hundred percent during this crisis."

"Then I guess I'm no longer a part of the team." Elation surged through her. She only wished she could see Donna's face.

"What did you say?" Donna asked.

"I said I quit. I'm going on vacation." She ended the call and tossed the phone on the desk. Then she hit Print and turned to collect the reservation confirmation from the printer behind her. A one-way ticket to Brazil.

She had always wanted to see Rio.

THE SECURITY FIRM Donna Stroud had hired to patrol the closed campus of Stroud Pharmaceuticals hesitated only a moment when Merry presented them with a letter on Donna Stroud's personal stationery, authorizing Merry Winger to access the executive offices for the purpose of retrieving some important documents. "This won't take long," Merry reassured the guard when he told her she could go on in. She already had all the papers she needed. This visit was merely so the guard would remember her and verify she had indeed been there.

She unlocked the door and went first to the executive offices. She rifled through all the desks, scoring about forty dollars in miscellaneous coins and bills and a hidden stash of pain pills—you never knew when those might come in handy.

In Donna Stroud's desk she found a file conveniently labeled FBI. Curious, she flipped through it, a thrill rushing through her as she found the employment paperwork for Laura Lovejoy—real name, Laura Smith. Or rather, Special Agent Laura Smith.

Parker's new admin was a spy! So, apparently, was her husband, whose name wasn't Lovejoy either, but Jason Cantrell. Now wasn't that interesting?

Merry returned the file to the drawer, spent a few more minutes in Donna's office, then hurried down the hall to Parker's office.

She felt under Parker's center desk drawer and found the little lever that released the catch on a second, thinner drawer. She already had a copy of the bank book inside the drawer, but why not retrieve the original, as long as she was here? She smiled at the small black book, and at Parker's fondness for paper trails. She slid the book into her purse, then left the office with only a small pang of regret. She would have enjoyed being Mrs. Parker Stroud. Parker wasn't bad-looking, was a decent lover, and his money and name would have eased any dissatisfaction she might have experienced down the road. But maybe she was destined for better things.

She waved to the guard and drove out of the lot, then picked up her phone and hit the button to dial the number she had already typed in. "Hello?" Laura Lovejoy sounded annoyed.

"I need to see you right away," Merry said. "It's really important."

"We're on our way out of town," Laura said. "Maybe later—"

"Not later. Now." Merry was the one calling the shots here. "I've found out something important about Parker that the FBI needs to know."

"Then why are you calling me?" Laura asked.

"Because I know who you are, Agent Smith. And we need to talk now."

"Fine." The word was clipped. Impatient. "Where do you want to meet?"

"I'll come to you. Don't worry, I know the address."

Ten minutes later, she turned onto the rutted dirt road that led to the single-wide trailer set back under the trees. Jace and Laura stood on the porch and watched Merry climb out of her car. "The feds couldn't find any better place to put you up than this dump?" Merry asked as she made her way up the graveled path that led to the bottom of the steps.

Jace opened the front door wider. "Come in, Merry."

"How did you find out our identities?" Laura asked as she followed Merry into the living room.

"Because I'm smart." She sat in the recliner and looked up at them. They took up positions on either end of the sofa. "Are you two really married, or is that part of the play-acting, too?" Merry asked.

"What did you want to talk to us about?" Jace asked.

She reached for her purse and both agents tensed. "Don't worry, I'm not pulling a gun," Merry said. She took out the bank book and tossed it to Laura. "Take a look at that."

Laura flipped through the book, then handed it to Jace. "Where did you get that?"

"I found it in Parker's desk," Merry said. "Just now, when I went to pick up some papers for Mrs. Stroud." If they bothered to check with Donna, the old woman would deny sending Merry on such an errand, but Merry was counting on the cops to be so anxious to get their hands on Parker, they wouldn't bother to check her story until she was long gone to Rio.

"Thank you for bringing this to us," Laura said. "We'll certainly look into it."

She didn't even act surprised. Which meant the FBI already knew about Parker's secret account. Disappointing. But all wasn't lost. "Don't you want to know what it means?"

"What do you think it means?" Jace asked.

Merry adopted a sad face. Sad, and a little terrified. "I think Parker is the one who poisoned the Stomach Soothers. Looking back, it all makes sense now."

Another exchange of looks between the two. "Tell us what you know," Jace said.

She bit her lip, as if reluctant to get Parker—the man she loved—into trouble. Then she nodded. She had to do the right thing, even if it cost her her future happiness. "I think Parker was embezzling money from his family's company," she said. "He put the proceeds into that secret account. But Gini Elgin, the chief financial officer, must have noticed something was off. I overheard her confronting him on the factory floor one day. I caught the words 'the money isn't right.' That night, Parker was so furious. He wouldn't tell me why, but he did say that Gini was poking her nose where it didn't belong. The next day, I caught him in the herb garden."

"The herb garden?" Laura was wearing her annoyed look again. Merry wanted to laugh.

"It's a garden in front of the Stroud plant, with examples of all the plants Evangeline Stroud, the company founder, used in her original herbal remedies. There are paths and a gazebo and little markers identifying everything. I helped with some of the plantings, since I have a green thumb."

"What was the significance of Parker being in the garden?" Jace asked.

"First of all, he never went there," Merry said. "He used to tease me about my interest in gardening. But he was there that day, so I paid closer attention, to see what he was doing. That's when I noticed he was standing right next to the castor plant. You know about castor plants, right?"

"Ricin is derived from castor beans," Laura said.

Merry nodded. "That didn't register with me until much later, but I think now he poisoned those tablets in order to kill Gini without anyone suspecting him. As plant manager, he had plenty of opportunity to slip the poison into the pills and substitute that bottle for the one she always kept in her desk. Everyone knew she took the Stomach Soothers all the time."

"This is really important," Jace said. "Do you know if Parker has any more ricin? Or more contaminated pills?"

Why hadn't she thought of this? The idea scared her a little. "I don't know," she said. "I haven't seen any in his home or office."

"When did you start blackmailing him?" Jace asked, just as smooth as if he'd been asking how she took her coffee.

But Merry didn't even blink. "Blackmail?" she asked.

"You went to Parker, told him what you knew, and he paid you $50,000 a week," Laura said.

Merry laughed. "I wish. But seriously, I didn't need to blackmail Parker. We were going to get married. He's so generous, buying me anything I want, and everything he had was going to be mine."

"You're using the past tense," Jace said. "Is the wedding off?"

Tears stung her eyes. She was really good at this acting stuff, wasn't she? "I can't marry a man who murdered six people," she said. "I love Parker, but he needs help. And what if my life is in danger because I told you?" She jumped up and turned as if to leave.

Jace took her arm. Not roughly, but there was muscle behind his grip. "Calm down," he said. "Sit down and tell us what you know about the bombs."

She sat, taking the opportunity to regroup. "I don't know anything about the bombs," she said.

"Do you think Parker set them?" Laura asked.

"I don't know what to think." She stared at her lap, then lifted her head to meet Laura's gaze. "I would have said Parker would never do something like that, but he and Leo have been friends for years, and then when that bomb exploded at my house…"

"You thought Parker was trying to kill you?" Jace asked.

"I thought maybe he saw me the day he was in the garden, and he was afraid I'd tell someone." She buried her face in her hands. "Now I'm terrified. You have to do something." This time when she stood, no one tried to stop her.

"We can take you into protective custody," Laura said. "Keep you safe."

"No. I don't want that!" She softened her voice. "I'll be okay. Just keep me posted, okay?" She paused at the door. "And I promise not to tell anybody you're agents," she said.

"We will be in touch." Laura put her hand over Merry's on the doorknob. "We'll be checking and if we find out you blackmailed Parker, we will arrest you."

Merry glared, then shoved past Laura and out the door. Let them look. Parker wasn't the only one with a secret account, and even if the feds found that bank, Merry had already moved the funds to an even more secure location. Tomorrow she'd be on her way to Brazil, out of their reach forever.

Chapter Eighteen

Sunday morning, Laura felt more like herself again, dressed in her own clothes. She patted her chignon, every hair in place, and buttoned the middle button of her suit jacket, then went to meet Jace in the living room of the trailer. With luck, by this time tomorrow they'd both be back in their own apartments in Knoxville.

Jace had donned a suit for this occasion as well, though he had yet to put on the jacket. His gaze swept over her as she entered the room, and she wondered if he was comparing her current look to the clothing she had worn while posing as a struggling newlywed.

Or maybe he was just remembering how she looked naked.

"Are you ready to do this?" he asked.

"I've been looking forward to it."

Driving to arrest someone in a beat-up mustard-colored pickup didn't have the same panache as arriving in a black sedan, but at least Parker Stroud wouldn't be overly alarmed when he saw them pull up to his house.

The two police cruisers and Ramirez and Rogers's sedan might set off a few alarm bells, of course, but, since they would have the house surrounded, Laura wasn't expecting Parker to give them much trouble.

As it was, they had to wait on the front steps of his house for several minutes and ring the bell three times before

Parker, hobbling on crutches, answered the door. "What are you doing here?" he demanded, scowling.

Laura opened the folder with her credentials and held them at eye level. "Parker Stroud, I'm arresting you for the murders of Virginia Elgin, Herbert Baker, Gail Benito..." She read off all the names of the people who had died after ingesting the tainted Stomach Soothers. She might have added the names of those who had died in the bombings—including Parker's own father—but the team was still building that case.

As she spoke, Parker's jaw went slack and all color drained from his face. When she had finished reciting the charges, Jace stepped forward. "Turn around and put your hands behind your back," he said, relieving Parker of his crutches and steadying him as he did so.

"There must be some mistake." Parker's voice was thin and reedy, more frightened boy than murderous man.

"Turn around, Mr. Stroud." Jace continued to steady him, alert for any attempt to fight back.

He turned, but looked back at Laura as Jace cuffed him. "I want my lawyer," he said.

"You can contact him when we get to the station." Local police would process and hold Parker until he could be transported to a federal facility. "You have the right to remain silent..."

She recited the Miranda warning, but she doubted if much was registering. Two police cars, along with Ramirez and Rogers, had arrived before Parker snapped out of his daze. "Hey!" he called as Laura was moving away, having handed him over to two officers for transport to the station. "What are you doing arresting me? You're my secretary."

"I have a lot of talents," she said, and walked back to the truck.

Jace fell into step beside her. "That's you," he said. "Multitalented." Somehow, he managed to imbue the words

with a sexy heat that melted a few synapses. She shot him
a stern look, which he met with a wicked grin that turned
up the heat another notch.

While the local cops processed Parker, Laura and
Ramirez joined Rogers in searching Parker's home. The
four-bedroom, five-bath home featured a media room, bil-
liard table, walk-in closets, and a pool and spa. One of the
bedrooms was being used as a home office and they started
the search there, donning gloves and methodically comb-
ing through every drawer, opening every book, and feeling behind every painting.

Laura found the flash drive, tucked in the toe of a pair
of dress shoes at the back of the master bedroom closet.
She connected it to the laptop from the office and smiled
as rows of figures populated the screen.

"What are we looking at?" Jace leaned over her shoulder and studied the images.

"I'm pretty sure these are the missing financials from
Stroud Pharmaceuticals," she said. She pointed to a column
of red figures. "These are all the places the income and
expenses don't match up. My guess is Gini Elgin spotted
these and connected the missing money to Parker. That's
probably what they were arguing about that day on the factory floor, and why he decided to kill her."

"Why keep these files?" he asked. "Why not destroy
them?"

"Sooner or later, the company would be due for an audit.
Missing data gets flagged and that would be a real problem. So I think he planned to use this file as a basis for re-
constructing the data to paint a more favorable financial
picture. Especially if he planned to partner with a competitor, or even sell the business outright."

"Steve Stroud was telling the truth," Jace said. "Even
if no one believed him."

"Maybe that's why Parker planted that bomb in his

dad's office," she said. "He couldn't risk someone—like the FBI—finally paying attention to Steve."

"He took a big risk, following his father into the building," Jace said.

"Maybe he thought doing so would remove suspicion from him." Laura removed the drive from the computer and slipped it into an evidence bag. "It almost worked."

Ramirez and Rogers joined them in the office. "We've been through the whole house," Rogers said. "No medication, though we found a container of castor beans in the back of the pantry."

"We'll get a team out here tomorrow to start looking in the walls and floors," Ramirez said. "Let's go talk to Parker and see what he has to say for himself."

PARKER REMINDED JACE of a life-sized balloon figure that had sprung a leak. Everything about him sagged, from his shoulders to his face. He didn't even look up when Jace and Laura entered the room. They had decided they would question him first, and depending on the progress they made, Ramirez and Rogers would follow up.

A handsome older man with a luxurious white moustache stood to greet the two agents and introduced himself as Gerald Kirkbaum. "I commend you on your dedication to finding the person responsible for these tragic deaths," he said. "But there's been some terrible mistake. Mr. Stroud had nothing to do with those deaths. He had no reason to do such a horrible thing."

Parker didn't look innocent to Jace. In fact, he had never seen anyone who looked guiltier. "We think he did have a reason," Laura said.

She pulled out a chair and sat. Parker still hadn't looked at her. Mr. Kirkbaum remained standing, as did Jace. "You have no evidence—" Kirkbaum began.

"We have evidence," Laura said, speaking to Parker.

"We have a witness who presented us with a bank book, showing the secret account where you've been stashing the money you embezzled from Stroud Pharmaceuticals." She leaned toward him, addressing the top of his bowed head. "This same witness saw you arguing with Gini Elgin when she confronted you about the missing money. And she will testify that she saw you in the garden with the castor bean plants. Castor beans are the source of ricin. But you know that, don't you? We found the castor beans in your pantry."

"Merry is a liar," he said, still not raising his head. "She's upset because I won't marry her, so she told these lies."

"I've seen the financials, and the bank account, and the castor beans," Laura said. "She isn't lying." She leaned toward him, lowering her voice. "How much did you pay Leo Elgin for those bombs? Did you think if you killed your mother and father you'd finally inherit the family business? You could run it the way you saw fit, even sell it if you liked? After all, you'd already killed six people. What were a few more? And hey, your dad was already half-gone, so what did it matter if you killed him?"

"I had nothing to do with that!" Parker's head came up and he straightened, like a puppet come to life.

Jace stepped forward. "Tell us where the other bombs are," he said. "How many did Leo make for you? Six? Or more?"

"No. I had nothing to do with that."

"I've met some heartless people in this job," Jace said. "But a man who would kill his own father, and try to kill his mother—that's lower than low."

"I didn't do it!" His shout echoed in the small room.

"We need to stop this questioning now," Kirkbaum said. "Parker, don't say another word."

But Parker was weeping, tears streaming down his face. He held out his cuffed hands to Laura, pleading. "I only meant to kill Gini. I didn't want to, but she'd found out about the money and threatened to tell my mother. I couldn't let them find out. My dad had already retired and I thought if I kept working on my mother, she'd eventually relent and turn everything over to me. Then no one would have to know."

"You're saying you put the ricin in the Stomach Soother tablets for the purpose of killing Virginia Elgin?" Jace said.

"Yes." The words were barely audible since Parker had buried his head in his hands.

"Parker, you need to shut up now." Kirkbaum leaned over his client. "You're not helping yourself."

"I didn't kill my father," Parker said, raising his head again. "And I didn't try to kill my mother. I never bought any bombs from Leo."

"Tell us more about the ricin," Laura said. "How did you know how to make it?"

"I looked on the internet," he said. "I knew about the castor bean plant because Merry had pointed it out to me. She was really into gardening and knew a lot about plants. I liked that I could make the poison myself, without having to buy anything that might be traced. I had to be careful, but it wasn't really that hard."

"How many bottles did you put the ricin in?" Jace asked.

"A whole tray. Twelve. It was the quickest way, slipping it in as they passed the filler mechanism. I went in one night after everything shut down and ran the machinery myself. I shut off all the security cameras. Then I took the whole lot out before it reached shipping." He frowned. "But I must have missed a few bottles that got slipped into the distribution stream. I put one of the bottles in Gini's desk, to replace the bottle she always kept there. But the next thing I know, all these other people were dying." He covered his face with his hands. "I never meant for that to happen."

Parker was probably hoping they would feel as sorry for him as he felt for himself, but all Jace's compassion was reserved for the six people the man had murdered. "What did you do with the rest of the bottles you pulled off the line?" he asked.

"I buried them."

"Where did you bury them?" Laura asked.

"In my mother's backyard. By the barbecue pit. I didn't know what else to do."

Jace glanced toward the observation window. Ramirez or Rogers would send someone to the Stroud home to collect that dangerous buried treasure pronto.

"When did Merry find out about what you'd done?" Laura asked.

"She saw me in the garden at the plant that day, and she saw me arguing with Gini before that. I guess after she heard how Gini died, she put everything together."

"She was blackmailing you," Laura said.

Parker nodded. "She came to me a couple of days after Gini died."

"She wanted $50,000?" Laura asked.

"That's the thing. She didn't ask for the money at first. She said if we got married right away, she wouldn't be able to testify against me."

No one bothered to point out that this wasn't how spousal privilege worked. "But you didn't marry her," Jace said.

"I couldn't. My parents would have stroked out at the idea. There was no way my mom would have turned over the business to me if I even got engaged to Merry. And I had to get control of the business. So I made a deal to pay her the $50,000 a week and I'd marry her as soon as my mom signed the paperwork to put me in charge."

"How did she react to that?" Laura asked.

"She didn't like it, but I persuaded her it was the only way. She really wanted to be Mrs. Parker Stroud."

"She loved you that much?" Jace tried to keep the doubt from his voice.

"She didn't love me as much as she loved the idea of living in a big house and having everyone in town and most of the state fall over themselves to be her best friend. Or at least, that's how she saw it. I tried to tell her it wouldn't be like that, but she wouldn't listen."

"So Merry knew what you had done, at least since two days after Gini Elgin died," Laura said. "But she told us she didn't figure it out until a few days ago."

"If you know about my bank account, then you saw the payments I made to her," Parker said. "I made the first one on the fourth."

That matched up with the entries in the bank register Merry had given them. "Why did Merry lie to us?" Laura asked. "Did the two of you have an argument?"

"She was getting impatient. She told me I needed to stand up to my mother and insist on taking over the business and marrying her. I tried to tell her that my father had just died—this wasn't the right time, but she wouldn't listen. She said she had waited long enough. But I never thought she'd turn me in."

Laura leaned toward him. "So your agreement with Merry was that when you got control of Stroud Pharmaceuticals, you'd marry her."

"Yes."

"If your parents died, you would inherit the business," Laura said.

"I don't care what kind of monster you think I am, but I wouldn't do that." Parker's voice rose. "What do I have to do to get you to believe me?"

"I believe you," Laura said. "But if Merry thought your parents' deaths would get her what she wanted, do you think she'd try to hurry things along?"

Jace recognized the fear that blossomed in Parker's eyes.

The handcuffed man opened his mouth as if to protest, but no words came out. "She asked me about Leo one day, not long after she figured out what I'd done with the Stomach Soothers," Parker said. "I told her the mad bomber story." He wet his lips. "I didn't think anything of it, but then later, Leo told me Merry had been to see him. He said she'd been really nice and asked about his job, and agreed with him that the Strouds—my mom and dad—were as good as murderers."

"When did he tell you that?" Jace asked.

"We met at the lake one evening, a few days before his mother's funeral. I'd heard what he was saying around town—that my family had killed his mother. I tried to talk some sense to him, but he wouldn't listen."

"What about the money you paid him?" Laura asked.

"It really was for the funeral." He looked pained. "But Merry volunteered to deliver it to him. She said Leo would take it better coming from her, that the two of them were friends now, because they both knew what it was like to get a raw deal from the Strouds."

"That's pretty harsh," Jace said.

"She could say anything she wanted to me now and I couldn't do anything about it."

Laura's chair scraped back and she stood. "That's all the questions we have for now."

She left the room, Jace on her heels. "We need to find Merry," she said as they hurried down the hall.

"You think she planted those bombs," Jace said.

"Yes, and you saw those notes she sent to Donna. She isn't finished yet."

Chapter Nineteen

Merry hefted the second of two large suitcases into the trunk of her car, then slammed the lid. She had spent too much time packing, but it had been hard to decide what to take. She would be gone a long time, and she wasn't sure what she'd need. In the end, she'd consoled herself with the knowledge that she had enough money to buy new things. And what she did have was bound to go farther in South America, right?

Besides, she had a lot more money now. The cops—and eventually Parker—would think she'd just stolen Parker's passbook to turn over to the police, but she'd also taken his passwords, and even the answers to his secret questions that were part of account security. With that information, she'd been able to transfer most of the $10 million balance into her own account. It had been so easy. And with that kind of money, who needed the Strouds? They were nobodies.

She slid into the driver's seat and drove toward town. She had one quick stop before she headed to the airport. In the oppressive afternoon heat, the trailer looked even shabbier than she remembered, the heart-shaped catalpa leaves drooping.

She parked in the shade of that tree and hurried up the walk. The cheap lock popped with one thrust of her credit card between the door and the jamb, and Merry was in and out in less than five minutes. Then again, she'd had a lot of practice delivering her little gifts.

Humming to herself, she pressed down on the gas, the speedometer climbing as she rushed toward the airport.

"SHE'S NOT HERE," Laura said as Jace pulled into Merry's driveway. "Her car isn't out front."

"Maybe she has parking in the back," Jace said. He doubted it, but it didn't pay to overlook any possibility.

"I hope you're right." Laura shoved open the door of the truck and raced up the drive, Jace at her heels. She pounded on the front door. "Merry! It's Laura. I need to talk to you. It's an emergency."

No answer. Jace pressed his ear to the door. No sounds of movement inside. He stepped back.

"You need to break the door down."

"Without a warrant?" He feigned shock.

She scowled at him. He stepped back, then aimed a powerful kick at the door, just above the knob. The wood splintered. Another hard kick and it sagged inward. He drew his weapon, and then they went in. "FBI!" he shouted.

The only answer was the low hum of the air conditioning.

"I'll take the bedroom. You search the rest of the house," Laura said.

"I love it when you're bossy," he called after her.

A search of the living room revealed no Merry, but in the dining room, a piece of white paper taped to the table caught his attention.

ALL THAT'S LEFT ARE TWO. GUESS WHO?

Laura appeared in the doorway to the dining room. "She's gone," she said. "There are too many empty hangers in her closet, and there's no makeup or shampoo in the bathroom."

"She left a note." Jace gestured to the table.

Laura glanced at the note, then headed for the door. "I'll call the team while you drive. The local police can put out an APB in case she's driving somewhere."

Jace finished the thought. "Meanwhile, we've got to drive to the airport."

MERRY PULLED INTO the valet lane for airport parking. No more economy lot for her. She handed the attendant her key, flagged down a red cap to take her luggage and gave him the name of her airline. She bypassed the waiting crowd and strolled to the first class desk. "Enjoy your flight, Ms. Winger," the agent said.

Yes! She could definitely get used to service like this.

She glanced around as she made her way to the security checkpoint. No one paid any attention to her. She'd taken a chance, leaving that note, but she figured Laura and her fellow feds would be busy with Parker for the next little while.

The dumb sap. He'd been stupid to think he could get away with poisoning people in the first place, and then he had made things worse by trying to play her. If he had only married her when she asked him to, she would have taken care of everything. Instead, he'd almost gotten himself blown up—twice—and now he was going to jail for the rest of his life.

She reached her gate just as the agent was calling for first class passengers. She handed over her boarding pass and walked down the Jetway to her comfortable seat. Moments later, she was sipping a glass of champagne and contemplating the future. She'd do some shopping tomorrow—buy a new bikini, or several, and clothes more suitable for the tropics. Then she'd visit a real estate agent and look into renting a nice villa. One in a good neighborhood, with security.

She only regretted she couldn't stay in Mayville to hear

about the last two bombs. Leo had balked at making six for her at first, but she had promised to find the person who had killed his mother and make them pay. That, and the promise of mind-blowing sex, had persuaded him. She had never intended to deliver on the sex, but he didn't know that.

Then she had sworn to find him and castrate him if he ever told a soul about her. She had made sure he believed her, too.

Men. They were so easy to manipulate.

The last few passengers filed on and the flight attendants began closing overhead bins and readying for take-off. Merry leaned back and closed her eyes, some of the tension that had been building these last few weeks easing away. This time tomorrow she'd be sipping a cool drink in the hot sun, planning the rest of a life of luxury.

"I'VE GOT A list of all the flights leaving from Yeager Airport in the next three hours," Laura said as Jace pulled into the valet lane for airport parking. "We're lucky this isn't a bigger airport."

"How many flights?" Jace asked as he handed the attendant his keys.

"Five."

Jace pulled up Merry's picture on his phone and showed it to the attendant. "Has this woman been through here in the last hour or so?" he asked.

The young man studied the photo, then shook his head. "I haven't seen her."

Jace turned as a second man approached. "Have you seen her?" he asked.

The second man's eyes widened. "Yeah, she was just here—maybe half an hour ago."

"What was she driving?" Laura asked.

"A white Chevy sedan."

"Thanks." Jace and Laura sprinted into the terminal.

"You take the desks on the right, I'll take the left," Laura said as they reached the check-in level.

Passengers grumbled as Jace cut to the front of the line at the first desk, but his badge silenced the agent's rebuke. "Merry Winger," he said. "Has she checked in here? She may have been using another name, but she looks like this." He showed the picture.

He struck out at the first two desks, but at the third, the agent verified that Merry Winger had checked in forty minutes before, using a one-way ticket with a final destination of Rio de Janeiro.

Jace texted Laura and headed to security. She met him there and they badged their way to the gate. An air marshal, alerted by TSA, met them. "The plane has already pulled away from the Jetway," the marshal said.

"Then they need to come back," Laura said.

"And don't let her know why the plane is returning," Jace said. "She's already killed at least three people. There's no telling what she'll do if she's cornered."

"Understood," the marshal said. "We'll do what we can to make this seem routine."

MERRY OPENED HER eyes as the speaker overhead crackled to life. "Folks, this is the captain speaking. We've got to return to the gate for a moment. No need for alarm, just a routine precaution. We promise to have you all on your way as quickly as possible."

Merry's stomach fluttered. She flagged down the flight attendant. "Why are we returning to the gate?" she asked. "I have a connection to make in Charlotte."

"You shouldn't have any trouble with your connection," she said. "The pilot is telling us this is only a quick stop."

"But why?" Merry asked, anxiety building. "We were already on the runway. They can't just make us go back."

"It happens." The flight attendant shrugged. "Try not to stress. Would you like another glass of champagne?"

Merry had just accepted the champagne when the flight reached the terminal. But instead of parking at a gate, the plane stopped away from the gates. "What's happening?" Merry asked, trying to see across the aisle and out the window that faced the terminal.

"They're bringing out one of those rolling stairs," a man across the aisle said.

"I bet they're boarding some bigwig who was late for the flight," another man said.

"Maybe it's a celebrity," a woman suggested.

"It's two people," the first man said, craning to see out the window. "Nobody I recognize, though."

Two people. Merry unbuckled her seat belt and scanned the aisle, searching for some avenue of escape. She didn't know for sure that the two people were FBI agents or police, but she wanted to be prepared, just in case.

She stood and the flight attendant hurried to her. "You need to remain in your seat, with your seat belt fastened," the attendant said.

Merry offered an apologetic smile. "I really need to use the ladies' room," she said. "All that champagne."

"I'm sorry, but you'll have to wait a few minutes more." The flight attendant blocked the aisle, refusing to let Merry move past.

Behind her, the exit door swung open. Laura entered first, followed by Jace. "Hello, Merry," Laura said.

Merry shoved the flight attendant aside. Someone screamed as Merry raced past, through the curtain separating first class from economy. "Stop that woman!" Jace shouted.

A man stood in the aisle, but Merry plowed past him, sending him staggering back into the lap of a woman seated beside the aisle.

Someone else grabbed her arm and refused to let go. She jammed her elbow into his jaw, but still he wouldn't release her. She turned to hit him again, then Laura tackled her, taking her to the floor. Strong arms dragged Merry's hands behind her back and cuffed her, and then stronger arms pulled her to her feet.

"Merry Winger, you're under arrest for three counts of murder," Laura said, as a plane full of passengers looked on, several filming the action with their phones.

Merry glared at her. "Only three?" she asked. "I guess you didn't find the other bombs yet."

"Where are the other bombs?" Jace asked.

"As if I'd tell you." She smiled. "It will be so much better if you find that out for yourself."

Chapter Twenty

"We don't know where Merry Winger planted those last two bombs, but her past behavior should give us some clues." Laura addressed the assembled team, consisting of FBI agents, local police and the county's bomb squad and SWAT. She indicated the list of previous bomb locations. "The first three were detonated at Stroud Pharmaceuticals' administrative offices. The fourth went off at Merry's home, deliberately set there by her to divert suspicion."

"So the most likely location for the fifth and sixth bombs is Stroud Pharmaceuticals," one of the SWAT members said.

"Except Stroud is shut down right now," Ramirez said. "There's no one there to be a target of the bomb."

"Yes, I think the key lies in considering the target," Laura said. "The first two bombs at Stroud killed people other than their intended target. We believe Merry set those bombs intending to kill Donna Stroud, who she saw as standing between her and her goal of marrying Parker Stroud. The third bomb, the one that killed Steve Stroud, may have been intended for Donna also."

"One of the two remaining bombs is probably intended to harm Donna," Jace said. "She's unfinished business for Merry."

"Exactly," Laura said. "We've already contacted Mrs.

Stroud and local police have escorted her from her home. We have a team searching there right now."

"What about Parker Stroud?" Rogers studied the white board, arms folded across his muscular chest. "Even though Merry claimed to be in love with him, she threw him under the bus, coming to you with that bank book and her story about seeing him with the castor plant."

Ramirez nodded. "Parker is with his mother at a safe location now, but we should have a team search his house, too."

Laura surveyed the faces of those before her, each tense with the knowledge that lives depended on them making the right guess and finding those bombs. "Any other ideas?"

"We should talk to Leo," Ramirez said. "Maybe Merry told him something about who she intended to target."

Laura mentally kicked herself for not thinking of this earlier. "Great idea," she said. "Let's do it."

Leo was still being held in the local jail, so twenty minutes later Laura, Ramirez, Jace and Rogers crowded into an interview room where Leo Elgin waited. Dressed in a baggy orange jumpsuit, his hair in need of a trim, he looked younger than his twenty-three years.

"We've arrested Parker Stroud for your mother's murder," Jace said. "He's admitted putting the ricin into the bottles of Stomach Soothers."

Leo stared at him. "Parker?" He wet his lips. "Why would he do something like that?"

"Apparently, he was embezzling money from Stroud Pharmaceuticals," Laura said. "Your mother noticed some discrepancies in the accounts and confronted him. He killed her to keep her from going public with the information. We believe the other deaths were to hide what he'd done and divert suspicion away from him."

Pale and clearly shaken, Leo shook his head. "I thought he was my friend. He was always trying to help me."

"Maybe he felt guilty," Rogers said. He sat in the chair across from Leo. "We've also arrested Merry Winger. She told us you sold her the bombs that killed Lydia Green, Angela Dupree and Steven Stroud."

"I sold her the bombs," he said. "She never told me what she was going to do with them."

"Weren't you a little curious?" Rogers asked.

Leo shook his head, emphatic. "I didn't want to know."

"So some woman comes up to you, says she wants you to make her six bombs and you're like, 'Sure. No problem'?" Rogers tilted his head to one side and squinted at Leo. "If this is a side business of yours, building bombs to order, who else have you sold explosives to?"

"Nobody else, I swear."

"So Merry was the first person you made bombs for?" Laura stood behind Rogers and addressed Leo.

"Yes."

"You didn't think it was strange she wanted you to make a bomb—much less six of them?" Laura asked.

"She promised to find the person who killed my mother!" He buried his head in his shackled hands and the room fell silent. Laura scarcely breathed.

At last, Leo raised his head and looked at her, his eyes filled with sadness. "Look, I know it was wrong, but I was so angry. My mother was dead and she died a horrible death. I wanted the people responsible to pay, and Merry convinced me she wanted to help."

"But why a bomb?" Rogers asked. "Why not more poison?"

"She said she had heard I was the mad bomber." He flushed. "I tried to tell her that was just a stupid kid stunt, but she went on and on about it. She…she flattered me. She was really pretty and I was lonely and…" His voice trailed away and he shrugged, his cheeks flushed.

"But how did you know how to build the bombs?" Rogers asked. "Had you done something like this before?"

"No, but I found a lot of information on the internet. And I work with trip alarms all the time, so setting the trigger wasn't all that different."

"What did you think when you heard Lydia Green and Angela Dupree died because of bombs you built?" Ramirez asked.

Leo bowed his head again. "I felt terrible. I panicked and called Merry and tried to get her to return the rest of the bombs. But she wouldn't. She said I didn't need to worry, that everything would work out and the two of us would go away together."

"Where were you going to go?" Laura asked.

"Australia. Or maybe New Zealand." He looked away again. "I guess you think I'm pretty dumb, but she made me believe her."

"There are two more bombs that haven't exploded," Jace slid into the chair next to Leo. "We need to find them before some other innocent person gets hurt. Do you have any idea where Merry put them?"

"No." He angled his body toward Jace. "I promise if I knew I'd tell you. I don't want anyone else to die."

Laura's phone signaled an incoming text. She checked the display.

#5 safely removed from D. Stroud's home. Nothing at P. Stroud's

She glanced up. Jace was checking his phone also. He looked up and held her gaze. *We're getting close*, he seemed to say.

"Leo, did Merry ever mention a name of any particular person she wanted to take out with the bombs?" Laura asked.

"No. We never talked about it. She knew it upset me and she said she would rather talk about me. About us." He had the same dumbfounded look as a kid who had just learned Santa Claus wasn't real. Part of him couldn't believe Merry had lied about wanting to be with him.

"We need to go," Laura said abruptly, and left the room.

Jace hurried after her. "Why the rush?" he asked, catching up to her at the end of the hall. "What set you off?"

"He's still in love with her. She used him to kill three people so far and if she walked in that door right now and said she was ready to run away with him, he'd leave right away, if he could."

"I agree it's twisted, but it's nothing we haven't seen before."

"It just struck me how often love has been used to manipulate people in this case," she said. "Not just Leo, but Parker, too. Merry professed to love him and want to be his wife, but really all she wanted was his money. And even Donna Stroud refused to let Parker have a bigger say in running the company when he could have been a real help to her. Instead, she tried to cover up the severity of her husband's dementia and run things on her own, probably out of love."

"So love—or the wrong kind of love, or the wrong idea of love, can lead people to do bad things," Jace said. "We know that. But we also know the right kind of love can lead to truly wonderful things." He slid one arm around her waist and pulled her close.

She turned to him, fighting against the anguish building inside her. "What are we going to do after this case is over?" she asked.

To his credit, he didn't flinch, or ask her to explain what she meant. "What do you want to do?" he asked.

"We won't be pretending anymore to be husband and wife," she said. "We won't be living together, but we'll still be working together."

"I was getting used to seeing you when I wake up in the morning and at dinner every night," he said. His voice had the low, seductive quality that usually made her weak at the knees, but right now it just made her want to cry. "I was even getting used to all the vegetables you keep feeding me."

She pulled away from him, needing space to think. "Office romances are a bad idea," she said.

"There's nothing against them in the regulations. The Bureau has a history of accommodating married couples."

"Who said anything about marriage?" Panic clawed at her throat. This was Jace she was talking to. Not Jace Lovejoy, her pretend husband, but wild man Jace, who was reckless and cocky and everything she was not.

"I'm not trying to rush you," he said. "I'm just pointing out that if our supervisors don't have a problem with relationships between agents, why should you?"

"I can't talk about this now."

Something flared in his eyes, and she readied herself for a verbal battle. Maybe that was what she had wanted all along, to pick a fight that would lead to them breaking up. At least then she would prove she couldn't depend on a man like him.

"All right," he said, his voice even. "We won't talk now, but we need to talk later."

She didn't have to come up with an answer to that, because Ramirez and Rogers joined them. "We need to go through the list of Stroud employees," Ramirez said. "We think one of them will be the most likely target of the last bomb. You have a list, don't you?"

"It's on my laptop at the trailer," Laura said. "I'll go get it."

"I'll come with you," Jace said.

"No, you stay here." She looked at the other two. If she glanced at him, she might give away all her mixed-up feelings. "You should talk to Merry. See what she has to say. Jace can help with that."

"All right," Ramirez said. "We were just on our way to interview her."

Laura left before Jace could weigh in with his opinion. All she wanted was a little time alone to pull herself together. She needed to bring her focus back to the case, away from the man who had turned her life upside down.

JACE STARED AFTER LAURA. Just when he thought he had torn down the protective wall she had built around herself, she was working hard to build it back up again.

"Come on," Ramirez said. "Let's see if we can get anything out of Merry."

He had expected Merry to be afraid. She had no criminal record and for most people, being handcuffed, fingerprinted and photographed, and locked in a cell was a terrifying experience.

But Merry held her head up and looked him in the eye when he and Ramirez entered the interview room. "Where's Laura?" she asked.

"She had something else to do," Jace said.

"She didn't want to face me, did she?" Merry said.

"Would you prefer that Laura be here for this interview?" Ramirez asked. "I can get her."

"No way." Merry waved her hand in front of her face as if shooing away a fly. "I never liked her. Why would I want her here now?"

Ana sat across from Merry while Jace stood by the door. "Tell us about the bombs," Ramirez said after she had completed the preliminaries for the recording. "Why did you decide to set them?"

"You can't ignore a bomb, or pretend it was an accident. A little mistake. Bombs make a statement."

"What statement do they make?"

"I'm here and you're not going to ignore me."

"Who was ignoring you?" Ramirez asked.

"The Strouds ignored me. They thought I wasn't good enough for their perfect son." She sniffed. "I wonder if Donna thinks he's so perfect now that she knows he's a murderer."

"We found the fifth bomb, in Donna Stroud's car," Ramirez said. "We safely removed it and Donna is fine."

Merry frowned and said nothing.

"Where is the sixth bomb?" Jace asked.

Merry shifted her gaze to him. "You really haven't figured that out?"

"No," he admitted.

She looked amused. "Don't worry, you will."

The look in her eyes froze Jace. Ramirez asked another question and Merry looked away, but the smugness in Merry's gaze was burned on his retinas. She thought she had gotten away with something.

Revenge on someone she didn't like.

He left the room, pulling out his phone as he walked. He texted Laura. Come back. Don't go into the trailer. DON'T.

He punched in her number and listened to the call going through, running now. Then he remembered Laura had the truck. He grabbed a passing officer. "I need your keys."

The cop stared at him. "My keys?"

Laura wasn't answering her phone. Why wasn't she answering her phone? "Your car keys. I need your car keys." He dug out his badge and flipped it open. "It's an emergency."

Something in Jace's expression persuaded the man. He dug a bunch of keys from his pocket. "It's a blue Nissan Rogue, in the employee lot."

Jace found the car and started it, then fastened his seat belt with one hand while he hit Redial for Laura's number. "Pick up the phone!" he ranted as he peeled rubber on the turn from the parking lot.

He drove like a man possessed, barreling down the road with his emergency flashers on, sounding the horn at anyone who got in his way. Laura's phone went to voice mail. He ended the call and hit Redial again.

He was still half a mile from the trailer when she answered. "Sorry, I was on another call. What do you need?"

"Where are you?" he demanded, the car careening wildly as he took a sharp curve at speed.

"I'm just at the trailer. Give me a second."

"Don't go in." His heart pounded as if it would burst from his chest. He could hardly control the car on the rough road. "The bomb. I think the bomb is in the trailer," he said.

"The bomb?"

But he was already racing up the driveway, the car fishtailing as he braked hard and slid to a stop behind the truck.

Laura stood, halfway up the walk, gaping at him. He burst from the car, ran to her and pulled her close.

"Jace, what is going on?" she asked, her voice muffled against his chest.

"I was almost too late." His voice broke, and he could feel the tears hot on his cheeks, but he didn't care. He looked down at her. "I almost lost you," he said.

"I'm right here." She cupped his face in both hands and kissed him. A tender, comforting kiss that he never wanted to end.

The cop whose car he had borrowed arrived first, with Rogers and Ramirez, followed by a bomb squad with a German shepherd that alerted on the front door. "There's a bomb here, all right," a heavily helmeted man called. "Clear the area."

Laura insisted on driving. Shaken as she was, Jace

looked worse. He said nothing as she drove, not to police headquarters, where the others were headed, but to the lake, where they had spied on Leo and Parker. Was that really only ten days ago?

She parked in the lot and turned off the engine. They sat in silence for a long moment, the distant sounds of laughter and muffled conversation drifting to them on a hot breeze through the open windows.

"I guess it's over now," Jace said.

"Everything but the paperwork," Laura said.

"We can go back to Knoxville and our normal lives," he said.

Except her life would never be the same again. She unfastened her seat belt and turned toward him. "What you said before, about us. Being a couple."

"Yes?"

"I want to try. When you came running up to me outside the trailer—no one has ever looked at me that way before—as if I was the most precious thing in the whole world."

"That's because to me, you are."

He pressed the button to release his own seat belt and slid over to her. She tilted her head up for his kiss, but he merely smoothed her hair back from her forehead. "I love you, Laura Smith," he said. "I love how you always play by the rules because you recognize how quickly things can fall apart without them. I love that you're brave but not reckless, and you have the courage to try new things, even when it makes you uncomfortable."

"You make me uncomfortable." She slid her hand around the back of his neck. "In a good way."

"I'll keep working on that." He started to kiss her, but she held him off. "What?" he asked.

"I love you, too. And I've never said that to a man before." She swallowed. "Not even my dad. Do you think that's strange?"

The lines around his eyes tightened. "It's not strange," he said, his voice rough with emotion. "And I'm honored to be the first."

Then he did kiss her, and she fell into the kiss, diving in deep into this crazy lake of emotion that frightened her and thrilled her and made her happier than she had ever thought she could be.

* * * * *

COMING SOON!

We really hope you enjoyed reading this book.
If you're looking for more romance, be sure to
head to the shops when new books are
available on

Thursday 9th July

To see which titles are coming soon, please visit

millsandboon.co.uk/nextmonth

MILLS & BOON

LET'S TALK
Romance

For exclusive extracts, competitions
and special offers, find us online:

- **f** facebook.com/millsandboon
- 🐦 @MillsandBoon
- 📷 @MillsandBoonUK

Get in touch on 01413 063232

For all the latest titles coming soon, visit
millsandboon.co.uk/nextmonth

MILLS & BOON
MEDICAL
Pulse-Racing Passion

Set your pulse racing with dedicated, delectable doctors in the high-pressure world of medicine, where emotions run high and passion, comfort and love are the best medicine.

ight Medical stories published every month, find them all at:

millsandboon.co.uk

MILLS & BOON
Desire

Indulge in secrets and scandal, intense drama and plenty of sizzling hot action with powerful and passionate heroes who have it all: wealth, status, good looks... everything but the right woman.